THE WORLD WE HAVE LOST

The World we have lost
by Peter Laslett

Methuen and Company Limited
11 New Fetter Lane, London EC4

First published by Methuen & Co Ltd 1965
Reprinted 1968
Second Edition 1971
© 1965 and 1971 by Peter Laslett

Printed and bound in Great Britain by
Butler & Tanner Ltd, Frome and London

SBN 416 08390 0 (*hardback edition*)
416 08400 1 (*paperback edition*)

*This book was designed
by Douglas Merritt MSIA*

Contents

Introduction to the First Edition, 1965

This essay has been six years in the making, and is on the way to being overtaken by events. It began as an attempt to write out in a straightforward way the introductory facts about the structure of English society as it was before the Industrial Revolution, and to make some comparison with its structure in the twentieth century. But the idea of an introduction to a subject of this kind turned out to be peculiarly elusive. Even the choice of the point at which to start is a problem, for it may determine the view of the whole which will be taken. Every descriptive remark after that may also mask the reality it aims to convey. Accordingly I have found that the task of working out an intelligible plan of a complete social structure is extraordinarily formidable; putting it down in clear, readable form has been even more so.

Hence a whole series of successive provisional drafts of the text over the six years, of which the one printed here is the last. The difficulties have not been entirely intellectual and literary. Since 1959, when a casual reference brought *The Rector's Book, Clayworth, Nottinghamshire* up out of the vaults of the Library of Congress, sources for this study have been coming to light so rapidly that it has been almost impossible to decide when the time had come to pause and write down a summary of knowledge acquired to date. In this situation resort was had to the Third Programme of the British Broadcasting Corporation, and some of the material of *The World we have lost*, as well as its title, appeared as talks and in *The Listener* in the years 1960, 1962, and 1963.

It became clear quite early that two much more important things were wanted in addition to an introductory essay to the subject as a whole. One was an arrangement to collaborative research, which would make it possible to undertake tasks no man could hope to carry out on his own. The second was the fund of information and the necessary time to write a large and something like a definitive study of the social structure of pre-industrial England, and perhaps of Europe generally.

The first of these objects has been happily attained, and the *Cambridge Group for the History of Population and Social Structure* began its official life in 1964, with the generous support of the Calouste Gulbenkian Foundation of Lisbon,

London branch. This should secure the second object as well. One of the titles in the series of works to be published by the Cambridge Group will be the full treatise of which the present essay is merely a foretaste. This wholly more academic treatise will print as much of the evidence as seems to be required, and others of the monographs which we are planning, together with various articles, will also contain instalments of the full facts and figures which have been used so sketchily here.

But though *The World we have lost* is in a sense a collaborative work, and could never have been written if only one man had been at work, it is emphatically not a publication of the *Cambridge Group for the History of Population and Social Structure* and does not appear under that imprint. The first of the series to be issued by the Group will in fact come out early in 1966, an *Introduction to English Historical Demography*, edited by E. A. Wrigley, with contributions from him, from the present author and others. That work, and other publications, will contain instalments of precisely those findings which are repeatedly mentioned in this book as being urgently needed and probably obtainable, since some of them have already been worked out in France, mainly statistics of population. In this sense that it is possible to say that *The World we have lost* is fortunately about to be overtaken, in respect at least of the research results which it presents.

The rougher facts and figures used here belong to an earlier and less regular period in the initial stages of this departure in historical and social research. The present essay has been dedicated to three of the volunteers who undertook the wearisome tasks of working through the newly-found documents to find out if the newly-worked-out hypothesis were of any value. Several other volunteers should also be thanked for their part in the investigations and in the consultations which took place in Cambridge: Mr Newman Brown, Mr John Montgomery, Mrs Bessie Maltby and Mr F. G. Emmison. Nearly all these historians are still working in correspondence with the Cambridge Group, but in the more advanced and regular way which has now become possible.

The list of those to whom I owe thanks and acknowledgements is so long that it could only be unreadable in full. There are first of all the French scholars, without whose achievements and example many of the activities reported here could never have gone forward. I hope Louis Henry and

Pierre Goubert will accept this tribute to their pre-eminence, and my thanks for their friendliness and forbearance with an awkward English visitor. M. Alfred Sauvy, the *doyen* (now in the English sense only) of the Institut National d'Études Demographiques and of demographic studies all over the world, has been very obliging, and I owe much to J.-N. Biraben and other members of the staff of the Institut.

The social scientists nearer home who have been good enough to guide me are also a large company, and I wish that I had been a better pupil. David Glass, Tom Marshall, Max Gluckman, Meyer Fortes, Jack Goody, Audrey Richards, David Lockwood, John Goldthorpe and Edmund Leach are some of them, and I owe a great deal to Edward Shils, my caustic mentor now for nearly twenty years. David Eversley has been an unfailing source of help and friendliness. Many people have given quite unlooked for assistance far in excess of what a researcher has a right to expect; there are Mr and Mrs Gooder of the Birmingham Extra-Mural Board as one instance, or the many clergy of the English Church who have responded to queries and given access to the documents in their care. A number of literary scholars have assisted too; there is Mrs Florence Trefethen, of Lexington, Massachusetts, and Professor Muriel Bradbrook.

Like every other writer with a case I have learnt a lot from those with whom I wish to disagree, at least to some extent; here Eric Hobsbawm and Christopher Hill are two names to mention, whilst Brough Macpherson has been a most friendly and useful collaborator and critic. E. H. Carr has encouraged me a great deal too and I should like to record my gratitude to him. Sir Charles Snow, Sir Anthony Wagner and Asa Briggs have been amongst the patrons of social structural research, and I can only hope that they may like this first instalment of its results.

Even this may seem an inordinate list of debts for so short a book, but I have still to reach my more personal acknowledgements. There is Anna Kallin, late and for so long acknowledged as the reigning princess of the Third Programme. There is Maurice Ashley, editor of *The Listener*, a longstanding, faithful friend to studies of this kind. There are those who took the trouble to write to me after hearing broadcast talks. There is Trevor Dannatt, the architect, whose friendship is so valuable to me and his opinion so important. He introduced me to Douglas Merritt, who designed this book, and has shown an extraordinary insight and sympathy with the work reported upon. My long-suffering wife, after all those rejected drafts, set to and made out the index in two weeks, amidst everything else.

Trinity College, Cambridge – *August 1965*

Introduction to the Second Edition, 1970

Revision and republication of this book have become necessary because the completion of the full treatise referred to in
the original introduction remains at the stage of research.
It seems that a brief, introductory work is still required, and
that what was written in the early 1960's has not, after all,
been wholly overtaken by events. The text of 1965 has accordingly been brought up to date and issued again.

Before the revisions and their purpose are described, I
should like to repeat an assertion made above about the composition of the book. It was insisted in 1965 that *The World
we have lost* was not a publication of the Cambridge Group
for the History of Population and Social Structure. The
statements made and the research reported belonged wholly
to the period before the Group was founded in 1964. Indeed
the importance of distinguishing the book from the produc-
tions of the Cambridge Group, which began to appear in 1966,
persuaded me that it was necessary to bring the book out at
at the earliest possible moment, and in great haste.

Nevertheless the somewhat premature date of publication
did not seem to have its intended effect of establishing an
independent identity for the volume and it has become
associated with the work going on at Cambridge after all.
The textual imperfections and factual errors of the first
printing have, I hope, been gradually worked out in the
course of successive impressions made in London, New York
and Paris (translated by Christophe Campos, Flammarion,
1969, as *Un Monde que nous avons perdu*).

The book was originally planned in two sections – an essay
in very general form addressed to the widest possible readership for a subject of this kind, followed by a distinct section
containing notes and references and intended for more
academic use. In making clear how the contents of this revised work are related to the continuing research of the
Cambridge Group, I have decided to make use of its composite
character. The main body of the text, the original essay somewhat amended and extended, continues to be a personal interpretation, addressed to the general reader and to the would-be
initiate into demographic and social structural history. But in
the appended section containing a description of the Files of
the Cambridge Group, many of the results of our co-operative

research are briefly reported upon. The Notes themselves, though their original numeration has been for the most part retained, have occasionally been provided with subject headings and have been extended to refer to the relevant Cambridge Group research files, as well as to the publications which have appeared on the topics concerned in the last five years. I have not gone so far as to supply references for Chapter 9, which deals for the most part with the early twentieth century, in view of the fact that this subject is only dealt with in a summary fashion here and for comparative purposes only. The scope of this whole section has been widened to cover a little of the work done in France, and a very little of the work done in the United States. Some further material from France and the United States has been incorporated into the text itself, and a glance or two has been made in the direction of Scotland, a country not included in the Cambridge Group collections. The book has been slightly altered, then, in the direction of international comparison, which will I hope make it more useful.

Nevertheless it is not by any means as international in flavour as the whole work of the Cambridge Group now is, nor can it be said to cover anything like all our present activities. There are two major advances of direct relevance to the subject of the book which I have had to decide, with regret, could not be incorporated into the present revision.

The first is the research, now in course of publication, into the one hundred more complete lists of inhabitants of English communities dating from between 1574 and 1821. A few of the results of that work are cited here in the form of references to the first of the articles on this subject by the present writer being published in *Population Studies* under the title *The Size and Structure of the English Household over Three Centuries* (see the issue of that journal for July, 1969). The full presentation of the new evidence and conclusions would have meant a far more extensive modification of the present book than seems justifiable and will have to be postponed until the position is reached when the full treatment of family and community in pre-industrial England can be contemplated.

Some of this material will in fact appear in the publication of the first results of a more wide-ranging departure in research at Cambridge which has grown out of the studies for *The World we have lost*. An investigation is being carried out on the com-

parative history of the domestic group since the later Middle
Ages mainly in five areas; these are England, France, Serbia
(now part of Jugoslavia), Japan and the society of the United
States, especially in its colonial phase. The evidence now
revealed, which was presented at a meeting in Cambridge in
September, 1969, only hints at an enormous potential area
of enquiry, but it is sufficient to provide a frame of comparative reference for the development of the English household
over time. We can now see that living in the extended household, excepting always a tiny minority mainly of the privileged, was probably no more the characteristic of most
Western European social structures in past time than it was
of England itself, and that the nuclear or conjugal family-
household was very widespread, far into the past, for nearly
all of the societies discussed at Cambridge.

All these studies, with an explanatory introduction by the
present writer, will be incorporated in a volume with the title
Family and Household in the Past, sent to the Cambridge Press
in 1971 for publication in English, and perhaps in French at
a later date. It is in this context that an attempt will be made
to tackle directly the issues raised by those studies and this
present book for the sociologist of the family. A summary of
the results is given in my article in *The Journal of Social
History*, Fall 1970.

A few references to these studies will be found in the Notes
section, especially to that done at the Cambridge Group itself
on the city of Belgrade in 1733, whose social and familial
structure form a fascinating contrast to that of the England
of Alexander Pope, Robert Walpole and King George II. But
the full outcome of comparing the history of the English
family and household with their history in other countries
must wait till the volume itself appears.

Some results of another study in progress at Cambridge
have, however, been included here. These are the illegitimacy
figures which now form part of Chapter 6. This chapter has
been extended not only to cover other forms of sexual incontinence, but to pursue a little further the extraordinary
story of what actually constituted marriage in traditional
England and how its form and procedures may have affected
rates of pre-nuptial pregnancy.

Chapter 5 has also been prolonged in order to take in recent
work on the plague, which was quite inadequately dealt with

in the original. Most of the new material even on bastardy and on the plague will, however, be found in the Notes, and it will be noticed that little attempt has been made to include work on the actual history of predominantly demographic matters; rates of population growth, birth rates, death rates, relations of population change with economic change, migration, and so on. This is because such topics are very effectively dealt with in a widely available book written for the general reader in 1969 by my colleague at the Cambridge Group for the History of Population and Social Structure, Dr E. A. Wrigley, under the title *Population and History* (Weidenfeld and Nicolson, World University Library, available in translation in a series of other countries, see Book List).

It would be impossible to mention here all the names of persons to whom I am indebted for the revisions to this book. Indeed the list of those acknowledged in 1965 has had to be abbreviated here in order to accommodate this rather wearisome explanation about the second edition, and I hope those whose names are no longer mentioned will not suppose that their help has been forgotten. But I would like to record my obligation to my other colleague in the Cambridge Group, Dr Roger Schofield, and to John Harrison once again, for his marvellous solicitude with the text, and to Professor Barbara Laslett, of California. One further acknowledgement is required.

It is not often that organizations like the Social Science Research Council can be adequately thanked for what they do, but I must here pay my tribute to this new British institution for its loyalty to research into the past of English social structure, and name Michael Young, Jeremy Mitchell and Andrew Schonfield. Though the Gulbenkian Foundation continues its generosity to the Group, and has made possible the beginnings of work on the comparative history of the family, the Council now keeps us going.

Peter Laslett
20 Silver Street, Cambridge
November 1970

English Society before and after the coming of industry
Chapter 1

The passing of the patriarchal household: Parents and children, masters and servants

---

In the year 1619 the bakers of London applied to the authorities for an increase in the price of bread. They sent in support of their claim a complete description of a bakery and an account of its weekly costs.[1] There were thirteen or fourteen people in such an establishment: the baker and his wife, four paid employees who were called journeymen, two apprentices, two maidservants and the three or four children of the master baker himself. Six pounds ten shillings a week was reckoned to be the outgoings of this establishment of which only eleven shillings and eightpence went for wages: half a crown a week for each of the journeymen and tenpence for each of the maids. Far and away the greatest expense was for food: two pounds nine shillings out of the six pounds ten shillings, at five shillings a head for the baker and his wife, four shillings a head for their helpers and two shillings for their children. It cost much more in food to keep a journeyman than it cost in money; four times as much to keep a maid. Clothing was charged up too, not only for the man, wife and children, but for the apprentices as well. Even school fees were claimed as a justifiable charge on the price of bread for sale, and sixpence a week was paid for the teaching and clothing of a baker's child.

A London bakery was undoubtedly what we should call a commercial or even an industrial undertaking, turning out loaves by the thousand. Yet the business was carried on in

[1] *See page* 258.

the house of the baker himself. There was probably a *shop* as part of the house, *shop* as in *workshop* and not as meaning a retail establishment. Loaves were not ordinarily sold over the counter: they had to be carried to the open-air market and displayed on stalls.[2] There was a garner behind the house, for which the baker paid two shillings a week in rent, and where he kept his wheat, his *sea-coal* for the fire and his store of salt. The house itself was one of those high, half-timbered overhanging structures on the narrow London street which we always think of when we remember the scene in which Shakespeare, Pepys or even Christopher Wren lived. Most of it was taken up with the living-quarters of the dozen people who worked there.

It is obvious that all these people ate in the house since the cost of their food helped to determine the production cost of the bread. Except for the journeymen they were all obliged to sleep in the house at night and live together as a family.

The only word used at that time to describe such a group of people was 'family'. The man at the head of the group, the entrepreneur, the employer, or the manager, was then known as the master or head of the family. He was father to some of its members and in place of father to the rest. There was no sharp distinction between his domestic and his economic functions. His wife was both his partner and his subordinate, a partner because she ran the family, took charge of the food and managed the women-servants, a subordinate because she was woman and wife, mother and in place of mother to the rest.[3]

The paid servants of both sexes had their specified and familiar position in the family, as much part of it as the children but not quite in the same position. At that time the family was not one society only but three societies fused together; the society of man and wife, of parents and children and of master and servant. But when they were young, and servants were, for the most part, young, unmarried people, they were very close to children in their status and their function. Here is the agreement made between the parents of a boy about to become an apprentice and his future master. The boy covenants to dwell with his master for seven years, to keep his secrets and to obey his commandments.[4]

---

[2] *See page* 258.   [3] *See page* 259.   [4] *See page* 259.

Taverns and alehouses he shall not haunt, dice, cards or any other unlawful games he shall not use, fornication with any woman he shall not commit, matrimony with any woman he shall not contract. He shall not absent himself by night or by day without his master's leave but be a true and faithful servant.

On his side, the master undertakes to teach his apprentice his '*art, science or occupation with moderate correction*'.

Finding and allowing unto his said servant meat, drink, apparel, washing, lodging and all other things during the said term of seven years, and to give unto his said apprentice at the end of the said term double apparel, to wit, one suit for holydays and one suit for worken days.

Apprentices, therefore, and many other servants, were workers who were also children, extra sons or extra daughters (for girls could be apprenticed too), clothed and educated as well as fed, obliged to obedience and forbidden to marry, often unpaid and dependent until after the age of twenty-one. If such servants were workers in the position of sons and daughters, the sons and daughters of the house were workers too. John Locke laid it down in 1697 that the children of the poor must work for some part of the day when they reached the age of three.[5] The children of a London baker were not free to go to school for many years of their young lives, or even to play as they wished when they came back home. Soon they would find themselves doing what they could in *bolting*, that is sieving flour, or in helping the maidservant with her panniers of loaves on the way to the market stall, or in playing their small parts in preparing the never-ending succession of meals for the whole household.

We may see at once, therefore, that the world we have lost, as I have chosen to call it, was no paradise or golden age of equality, tolerance or loving kindness. It is so important that I should not be misunderstood on this point that I will say at once that the coming of industry cannot be shown to have brought economic oppression and exploitation along with it. It was there already. The patriarchal arrangements which we have begun to explore were not new in the England of Shakespeare and Elizabeth. They were as old as the Greeks, as old as European history, and not confined to Europe. And it may

[5] *See page* 259.

B

well be that they abused and enslaved people quite as remorselessly as the economic arrangements which had replaced them in the England of Blake and Victoria. When people could expect to live for so short a time, how must a man have felt when he realized that so much of his adult life must go in working for his keep and very little more in someone else's family?[6]

But people very seldom recognize facts of this sort, and no one is content to expect to live as long as the majority in fact will live. Every servant in the old social world was probably quite confident that he or she would some day get married and be at the head of a new family, keeping others in subordination. If it is legitimate to use the words exploitation and oppression in thinking of the economic arrangements of the pre-industrial world, there were nevertheless differences in the manner of oppressing and exploiting. The ancient order of society was felt to be eternal and unchangeable by those who supported, enjoyed and endured it. There was no expectation of reform. How could there be when economic organization was domestic organization, and relationships were rigidly regulated by the social system, by the content of Christianity itself?

Here is a vivid contrast with social expectation in Victorian England, or in industrial countries everywhere today. Every relationship in our world which can be seen to affect our economic life is open to change, is expected indeed to change of itself, or if it does not, to *be* changed, made better, by an omnicompetent authority. This makes for a less stable social world, though it is only one of the features of our society which impels us all in that direction. All industrial societies, we may suppose, are far less stable than their predecessors. They lack the extraordinarily cohesive influence which familial relationships carry with them, that power of reconciling the frustrated and the discontented by emotional means. Social revolution, meaning an irreversible changing of the pattern of social relationships, never happened in traditional, patriarchal, pre-industrial human society. It was almost impossible to contemplate.

Almost, but not quite. Sir Thomas More, in the reign of Henry VIII, could follow Plato in imagining a life without privacy and money, even if he stopped short of imagining a

[6] *See page* 260.

life where children would not know their parents and where promiscuity could be a political institution. Sir William Petty, 150 years later, one of the very first of the political sociologists, could speculate about polygamy; and the England of the Tudors and the Stuarts already knew of social structures and sexual arrangements, existing in the newly discovered world, which were alarmingly different from their own. But it must have been an impossible effort of the imagination for them to suppose that they were anything like as satisfactory.[7]

It will be noticed that the roles we have allotted to all the members of the capacious family of the master-baker of London in the year 1619 are, emotionally, all highly symbolic and highly satisfying. We may feel that in a whole society organized like this, in spite of all the subordination, the exploitation and the obliteration of those who were young, or feminine, or in service, everyone belonged in a group, a family group. Everyone had his circle of affection: every relationship could be seen as a love-relationship.

Not so with us. Who could love the name of a limited company or of a government department as an apprentice could love his superbly satisfactory father-figure master, even if he were a bully and a beater, a usurer and a hypocrite? But if a family is a circle of affection, it can also be the scene of hatred. The worst tyrants among human beings, the murderers and the villains, are jealous husbands and resentful wives, possessive parents and deprived children. In the traditional, patriarchal society of Europe, where practically everyone lived out his whole life within the family, though not usually within one family, tension like this must have been incessant and unrelieved, incapable of release except in crisis. Men, women and children have to be very close together for a very long time to generate the emotional power which can give rise to a tragedy of Sophocles, or Shakespeare, or Racine. Conflict in such a society was between individual people, on the personal scale. Except when the Christians fought with the infidels, or Protestants fought with Catholics, clashes between masses of persons did not often arise. There could never be a situation such as that which makes our own time, as some men say, the scene of perpetual revolution.

All this is true to history only if the little knot of people making bread in Stuart London was indeed the typical social

7 *See page* 260.

unit of the old world in its size, composition and scale. There are reasons why a baker's household might have been a little out of the ordinary, for baking was a highly traditional occupation in a society increasingly subject to economic change. We shall see, in due course, that a family of thirteen people, which was also a unit of production of thirteen, less the children quite incapable of work, was quite large for English society at that time. Only the families of the really important, the nobility and the gentry, the aldermen and the successful merchants, were ordinarily as large as this. In fact, we can take the bakery to represent the upper limit in size and scale of the group in which ordinary people lived and worked. Among the great mass of society which cultivated the land, and which will be the major preoccupation of this essay, the family group was smaller than a substantial London craftsman's entourage. There are other things we should observe about the industrial and commercial scene.

It is worth noticing to begin with, how prominently the town and the craft appear in the folk-memory we still retain from the world we have lost. Agriculture and the countryside do not dominate our recollections to anything like the extent that they dominated that vanished world. We still talk to our children about the apprentice who married his master's daughter: these are the heroes. Or about the outsider who marries the widow left behind by the father/master when he comes to die: these unwelcome strangers to the family are the villains. We refer to bakers as if they really baked in their homes; of spinsters who really sit by the fire and spin. A useful, if a rather arbitrary and romantic guide to the subject in hand, is the famous collection of Fairy Tales compiled by the brothers Grimm in Germany nearly 150 years ago, where the tales we tell to our children mostly have their source.[8] Even in the form given to them by Walt Disney and the other makers of films and picture-books for the youngest members of our rich, leisurely, powerful, puzzled world of successful industrialization, stories like Cinderella are a sharp reminder of what life was once like for the apprentice, the journeyman, the master and all his family in the craftsman's household. Which means, in a sense, that we all know it all already.

We know, or half-remember, that a journeyman might

[8] *See page* 260.

sometimes have to spend a year or two on his journeys, serving
out that difficult period after he was trained and capable of his
craft, but before he had made, or inherited, or had the prospect
of marrying, enough money to set up as master by himself. It
takes a little reflection to recognize in this practice the reason
why so many heroes of the nursery rhymes and stories are on
the road, literally seeking their fortunes. We have to go even
further to search here for the origin of the picaresque in
literature, perhaps for the very germ of the novel. And
conscious analysis, directed historical research of a kind only
recently supposed to be possible and necessary, has had to be
done before even a few fragmentary facts about the tendency
of young people to move about could be recovered. It has been
found that most young people in service, except, of course,
the apprentices, seem to have looked upon a change of job
bringing them into a new family as the normal thing every
few years.[9]

This feeling that it is all obvious is a curious and exasperating feature of the whole issue, for it means that the historian
has not hitherto felt a clear call to examine it as a subject. He
has supposed that he knows it already, by rote if not by understanding. This means that the force of the contrast between
our world and the world which the historian undertakes to
describe has hitherto been somewhat indistinct. Without contrast there cannot be full comprehension. One reason for feeling puzzled by our own industrial society is because the
historian has never set out to tell us what society was like
before industry came and seems to assume that everyone
knows.

We shall have much more to say about the movement of
servants from farmhouse to farmhouse in the old world, and
shall return to the problem of understanding ourselves in time,
in contrast with our ancestors. Let us emphasize again the
scale of life in the working family of the London baker. Few
persons in the old world ever found themselves in groups
larger than family groups, and there were few families of
more than a dozen members. The largest household so far
known to us, apart from the royal court and the establishments of the nobility, lay and spiritual, is that of Sir Richard
Newdigate, Baronet, in his house of Arbury within his parish
of Chilvers Coton in Warwickshire, in the year 1684. There

[9] *See page* 260.

were thirty-seven people in Sir Richard's family: himself; Lady Mary Newdigate his wife; seven daughters, all under the age of sixteen; and twenty-eight servants, seventeen men and boys and eleven women and girls.[10] This was still a family, not an institution, a staff, an office or a firm.

Everything physical was on the human scale, for the commercial worker in London, and the miner who lived and toiled in Newdigate's village of Chilvers Coton. No object in England was larger than London Bridge or St Paul's Cathedral, no structure in the Western World to stand comparison with the Colosseum in Rome. Everything temporal was tied to the human life-span too. The death of the master baker, head of the family, ordinarily meant the end of the bakery. Of course there might be a son to succeed, but the master's surviving children would be young if he himself had lived only as long as most men. Or an apprentice might fulfil the final function of apprenticehood, substitute sonship, that is to say, and marry his master's daughter, or even his widow. Surprisingly often, the widow, if she could, would herself carry on the trade.

This, therefore, was not simply a world without factories, without firms, and for the most part without economic continuity. Some partnerships between rich masters existed, especially in London, but since nearly every activity was limited to what could be organized within a family, and the lifetime of its head, there was an unending struggle to manufacture continuity and to provide an expectation of the future. 'One hundred and twenty family uprising and downlying, whereof you may take out six or seven and all the rest were servants and retainers': this was the household of the Herberts, Earls of Pembroke in the years before the Civil War, as it was remembered a generation later by the sentimental antiquarian of the West Country where the Herberts were seated, John Aubrey of the *Lives*. It is wise to be careful of what men liked to report about the size and splendour of the great families in days gone by: £16,000 a year was the Herbert revenue, so John Aubrey claimed, though 'with his offices, and all' the Earl 'had £30,000 per annum. And, as the revenue was great, so the greatness of his retinue and hospitality were answerable.' These are impossible figures, but we know that Lord William Howard kept between forty and fifty servants at Naworth Castle in Cumberland in the 1620's on a much

[10] *See page* 260.

smaller revenue. 'And as late as 1787, the Earl of Lonsdale, a very rich, mine-owning bachelor, lived in a household of fifty at Lowther in Westmorland, himself that is and forty-nine servants.'[11] All this illustrates the symbolic function of the aristocratic family in a society of families, which were generally surprisingly small as we shall see. They were there to defy the limitation on size, and to raise up a line which should remain for ever.

We may pause here to point out that our argument is not complete. There was an organization in the social structure of Europe before the coming of industry which enormously exceeded the family in size and endurance. This was the Christian Church. It is true to say that the ordinary person, especially the female, never went to a gathering larger than could assemble in an ordinary house except when going to church. When we look at the aristocracy and the church from the point of view of the scale of life and the impermanence of all man-made institutions, we can see that their functions were such as make very little sense in an industrial society like our own. Complicated arrangements then existed, and still exist in England now, which were intended to make it easier for the noble family to give the impression that it had indeed always persisted. Such, for example, were those intricate rules of succession which permitted a cousin, however distant, to succeed to the title and to the headship, provided only he was in the male line. Such was the final remedy in the power of the Crown, the fountain of honour, to declare that an anomalous succession should take place. Nobility was for ever.

But the symbolic provision of permanence is only the beginning of the social functions of the church. At a time when the ability to read with understanding and to write much more than a personal letter was confined for the most part to the ruling minority, in a society which was otherwise oral in its communications, the preaching parson was the great link between the illiterate mass and the political, technical and educated world.

Sitting in the 10,000 parish churches of England at every service, Sundays and Saints Days, holy days, that is, or holidays as we now call them, in groups of 20, 50, 100 or 200, the illiterate mass of the people were taking part in the single group activity which they ordinarily shared with others

[11] *See page 261.*

outside their own families. But they were doing more than this. They were informing themselves in the only way open to them of what went on in England, Europe, and the world as a whole. The priesthood was indispensable to the religious activity of the old world, at a time when religion was still of primary interest and importance. But the priesthood was also indispensable because of its functions in social communication. This, perhaps, was one reason why the puritan layman insisted so strongly upon a preaching clergy.

When we insist on the tiny scale of life in the pre-industrial world, especially on the small size of the group in which nearly everybody spent all their lives, there are, of course, certain occasions and institutions which we must not overlook. There were the military practices, an annual muster of the able-bodied men from every county, which took place after harvest in Tudor times.[12] There were regular soldiers too, though not very many of them; variegated bands of the least promising of men straggling behind the banner of some noble adventurer. Much more familiar to Englishmen, at least in the maritime areas, must have been the sailors; twenty, thirty, even fifty men at sea, sometimes for days, or even weeks on end.

Lilliputian, we must feel, when we compare such details with the crowds we meet in our society. The largest crowd recorded for seventeenth-century England, that is the Parliamentary Army which fought at Marston Moor, would have gone three, four or even five times into the sporting stadium of today.[13] Other organizations and purposes which brought groups of people together were the Assizes in the County Towns; the Quarter Sessions of the County Justices; the meetings of the manorial courts in the villages, of the town councils in the towns, of the companies or craftsmen there, each one to a trade or occupation; the assemblies which sometimes took place of clergy or of nonconformist ministers. Most regular of all, and probably largest in scale and most familiar to ordinary men and women were the weekly market days and the annual fairs in each locality. Then there were the 2,000 schools in England, one for every fifth parish but very few large enough to have more than a single teacher, and the two universities, with less than 10,000 men between them.[14] Then there was Parliament itself. All these occasions and

[12] *See page* 261.   [13] *See page* 261.   [14] *See page* 261.

institutions assembled men in some numbers for purposes which could not be called familial. Women too assembled, though, save to the markets, they came as spectators rather than as participants.

The fact that it is possible to name most of the large-scale institutions and occasions in a sentence or two makes the contrast with our own world more telling than ever. We have only to think of the hundreds of children sitting every day, all over the country, in their classrooms, the hundreds and thousands together in the factories, the offices, the shops, to recognize the difference. The detailed study of the pre-industrial social world makes this question of scale more critical still. Wherever the facts of economic life and technology required a working group different in size and constitution from the working family, there was discontinuity. Hence the crew of a ship, the team of workers on a building, the fifty or sixty grown men who might be required to work a mine or an armaments manufactory, were all looked upon as exceptional. As indeed they were, so much so that the building trade had had its own society from medieval times, and the miners were a community apart wherever they were found.[15]

Not only did the scale of their work and the size of the group which was engaged make them exceptional, the constitution of the group did too. In the baking household we have chosen as our standard, sex and age were mingled together. Fortunate children might go out to school, but adults did not usually go out to work. There was nothing to correspond to the thousands of young men on the assembly line, the hundreds of young women in the offices, the lonely lives of housekeeping wives, which we now know only too well. We shall see that those who survived to old age in the much less favourable conditions for survival which then were prevalent, were surprisingly often left to live and die alone, in their tiny cottages or sometimes in the almshouses which were being built so widely in the England of the Tudors and the Stuarts.[16] Poor-law establishments, parochial in purpose and in size, had begun their melancholy chapter in the history of the English people. But institutional life was otherwise almost unknown. There were no hotels, hostels, or blocks of flats for single persons, very few hospitals and none of the kind we are familiar with, almost no young men and women living on their own.

[15] *See page* 262.   [16] *See page* 262.

The family group where so great a majority lived was what we should undoubtedly call a 'balanced' and 'healthy' group.

When we turn from the hand-made city of London to the hand-moulded immensity of rural England, we may carry the same sentimental prejudice along with us. To every farm there was a family, which spread itself over its portion of the village lands as the family of the master-craftsman filled out his manufactory. When a holding was small, and most were small as are the tiny holdings of European peasants today, a man tilled it with the help of his wife and his children. No single man, we must remember, would usually take charge of the land, any more than a single man would often be found at the head of a workshop in the city. The master of a family was expected to be a householder, whether he was a butcher, a baker, a candlestick maker or simply a husbandman, which was the universal name for one whose skill was in working the land. Marriage we must insist, and it is one of the rules which gave its character to the society of our ancestors, was the entry to full membership, in the enfolding countryside, as well as in the scattered urban centres.

 But there was a difference in scale and organization of work on the land and in the town. The necessities of rural life did require recurrent groupings of households for common economic purposes, occasionally something like a crowd of men, women and children working together for days on end. Where the ground was still being tilled as open fields, and each household had a number of strips scattered all over the whole open area and not a compact collection of enclosures, ploughing was co-operative, as were many other operations, above all harvesting, and this continued even after enclosure. We do not yet know how important this element of enforced common activity was in the life of the English rural community on the eve of industrialization, or how much difference enclosure made in this respect. But whatever the situation was, the economic transformation of the eighteenth and nineteenth centuries destroyed communality altogether in English rural life. The group of men from several farmsteads working the heavy plough in springtime, the bevy of harvesters from every house in the village wading into the high standing grass to begin the cutting of the hay, had no successors in large-scale economic activity. For the arrangement of these groups was

entirely different in principle from the arrangement of a
factory, or a firm, or even of a collective farm.

Both before and after enclosure, some peasants did well:
their crops were heavier and they had more land to till. To
provide the extra labour needed then, the farming householder, like the successful craftsman, would extend his working
family by taking on young men and women as servants to live
with him and work the fields. This he would have to do, even
if the land which he was farming was not his own but rented
from the great family in the manor house. Sometimes, we have
found, he would prefer to send out his own children as servants
and bring in other children and young men to do the work.
This is one of the few glimpses we can get into the quality of
the emotional life of the family at this time, for it shows that
parents may have been unwilling to submit children of their
own to the discipline of work at home. It meant, too, that
servants were not simply the perquisites of wealth and position. A quarter, or a third, of all the families in the country
contained servants in Stuart times, and this meant that very
humble people had them as well as the titled and the wealthy.
Most of the servants, moreover, male or female, in the great
house and in the small, were engaged in working the land.[17]

The boys and the men would do the ploughing, hedging,
carting and the heavy, skilled work of the harvest. The women
and the girls would keep the house, prepare the meals, make
the butter and the cheese, the bread and the beer, and would
also look after the cattle and take the fruit to market. At
harvest-time, from June to October, every hand was occupied
and every back was bent. These were the decisive months for
the whole population in our damp northern climate, with its
single harvest in a season and reliance on one or two standard
crops. So critical was the winning of the grain for bread that
the first rule of gentility (a gentleman never worked with his
hands for his living) might be abrogated.

We have hinted that a fundamental characteristic of the
world we have lost was the scene of labour, which was universally supposed to be the home. It has been implied in the case
of industry and in towns, that the hired man who came in
to work during the day and went home to his meals and at
night was looked on as exceptional. Apart from the provisions
about journeymen, who were, in fact, the focus of whatever

[17] *See page 262.*

difficulty in 'labour relations' was experienced at this time in
the towns, no standard arrangement has been found which contemplated any permanent division of place of living and place
of employment. That such divisions existed, and may even
have been commonplace in town and in country, cannot be in
doubt. There is evidence that a clothmaker in a big way, in
the city of Beauvais in France at any rate, would have
machinery in his house for more men than could possibly have
lived there. It is thought that men walked in from the villages
to Beauvais to do their day's work, just as men used to walk
from the villages to the towns to work on the building sites in
Victorian England. In those areas of England which first
became industrial, there are signs that, like those in Beauvais,
they too must have contained economic units which had to be
supplied by daily wage labour. It came also, maybe, from the
surrounding country, but certainly from the grown sons of
families living in the town as well, young men, perhaps,
even older men and married men, who cannot have been
working where they lived.[18] But when all this is said, the
division of dwelling place and working place was no recognized
feature of the social structure of the towns which our ancestors
inhabited. The journey to work, the lonely lodger paying his
rent out of a factory wage or office salary, are the distinguishing marks of our society, not of theirs. We are forced to
suppose that in industrial and commercial matters the working family was assumed to be self-sufficient in its labour, in
spite of the vicissitudes of the market.

But the level of activity in agriculture is fundamentally
rhythmic, and its labour demands inevitably vary with the
time of the year, the weather in the week, as well as with the
prices of its products on the market. To work the land at all,
especially as we have already hinted with the climate and
geology of England, provision had to be made for a pool of
labour, which the farming family could use or not as the
farmer himself should decide. The manner in which this
economic necessity was provided for shows how well the
traditional, patriarchal structure of society could be adapted
to meet the needs of a particular economy. It has to be traced
in the life stories of the men and the women who lived in the
villages and worked the land, or who pursued those occupations which were settled in the countryside, and were as much

[18] *See page* 263.

a part of its life as what went on in the stables and the barns. Let us begin with the life cycle of a poor inhabitant of an English village.

A boy, or a girl, born in a cottage, would leave home for service at any time after the age of ten. A servant-in-husbandry, as he might be called if he were a boy, would usually stay in the position of servant, though very rarely in the same household, until he or she got married. Marriage, when and if it came, would quite often take place with another servant. All this while, and it might be twelve, fifteen or even twenty years, the servant would be kept by the succession of employers in whose houses he dwelt. He was in no danger of poverty or hunger, even if the modest husbandman with whom he lived was worse housed than his landlord's horses, and worse clothed than his landlord's servants. 'His landlord's horses,' wrote a contemporary of the lowly husbandman, 'lie in finer houses, than he, and his meanest servant wears a cloth beyond him.' But the husbandman had his own servant, nevertheless, for when he said family prayers after a day's exhausting toil 'the wife is sleeping in one corner, the child in another, the servant in a third'.[19]

But poverty awaited the husbandman's servant when he got married, and went himself to live in just such a labourer's cottage as the one in which he had been born. Whoever had been his former master, the labourer, late servant in husbandry, would be liable to fall into want directly his wife began to have children and he lost the earnings of his companion. Once he found himself outside the farming household his living had to come from his wages, and he, with every member of his family, was subject for his labour to the local vagaries in the market. Day-labourer was now his full description, for he earned what money came his way by contracting for work a day at a time with the gentlemen, yeomen, and husbandmen of his village. This was a source of the variable casual labour needed to keep agriculture going, and the poor cottager could expect mainly seasonal employment at a wage fixed, as indeed his wage as a servant had been fixed, by the justices of the peace. Two forms of wage were laid out in the published tables, with and without meat and drink. The day-labourer visiting a farm for his work could claim his place at the table along with the servants living-in; it might be said

[19] *See page* 263.

that he was made a member of the working family for that day
by breaking bread with the permanent members. It was almost
a sacramental matter.

But his own casual earnings were not the only fund on which
the labourer had to live. There was the produce of the little
plot of land lying round his cottage to begin with. Elizabeth's
government had decreed that it should be four acres in size
though this cannot have been anything like a general rule.
Then there were the pennies thrown to his children for bird
scaring, or catching vermin, or minding sheep – the little boy
blue who burst into tears in the nursery rhyme might easily
have been of nursery age. But above all, there were the earnings of his wife and the whole of his little family at 'industrial'
occupations.[20] A little family because every grown child would
have to leave, and because death came quickly. It was the
cottagers of England who carried on the great woollen industry of England, spinning the yarn which the capitalist clothiers
brought to their doors. Industry, in fact, kept the poor alive
in the England of our ancestors, and the problem of poverty
in their own opinion could only have been solved by the spread
of industrial activity. Though men did not seem to have seen
it in quite this way, the existence of industry also helped to
ensure that enough people lived on the land to meet the
seasonal demands of agriculture.

The men and women whose livelihood came from crafts,
agricultural and industrial, lived under the same system of
servanthood until marriage. So indeed did the merchants and
the shopkeepers. Not all households took part in this system
all the time. At any moment a quarter or a third of the households of a community would contain servants, and a similar
proportion would have children absent from home and in service. The households which remained would at that point in
time be unaffected by the system of service, but many of
them, perhaps most, would at other stages of their development either yield up or take in servants. This is the sense in
which it could be said that service was practically a universal
characteristic of pre-industrial English society.

Industry at this time was carried on not only by individual
productive units, like the bakery in London, but by the *put-
ting-out* system, in which several households were set on work
by one middleman, the clothier-capitalist we have referred to.

[20] *See page* 264.

Much of it was done in the spare time of the farming population, not simply by the labourers, but by the farmers and their families as well, the simpler operations, that is to say, the sorting and carding and spinning of the wool. But the weaving, the dyeing and dressing of the cloth was usually the work of families of weavers, shearmen or dyers who did nothing else for nine months of the year. If they worked on the land of the villages where they lived it was only in harvest-time, from late June, when the haymaking began, till late September when the last of the wheat or the barley would be brought home.

Hence it came about that the English village contained not simply the husbandmen, the labourers and their families, with the smith, the ploughwright, the miller and the men who plied the agricultural trades, but textile workers too. In the Midlands there were nailers and miners, and everywhere everyone might also work on the land, during the crisis of harvest-time. Such are the rough outlines of the system whereby the independent household was preserved, yet made to collaborate with other independent households in the working of the land, and in the production of cloth. Capitalism, we must notice, was a feature of the system, that store of wealth and raw materials in the hands of the clothier which made it possible for him to give work to the villagers and yet not move them from the village. In the world we have lost, then, industry and agriculture lived together in some sort of symmetry, and the unity of the family was in no way in jeopardy.

The bourgeoisie, wherever it has got the upper hand, has put an end to all feudal, patriarchal, idyllic relations. It has pitilessly torn asunder the motley feudal ties that bound man to his natural superiors, and has left remaining no other nexus between man and man than naked self-interest, than callous cash-payment. It has drowned the most heavenly ecstasies of religious fervour, of chivalrous enthusiasm, of philistine sentimentalism, in the icy water of egotistical calculation. It has resolved personal worth into exchange value, and in place of the numberless indefeasible chartered freedoms, has set up that single, unconscionable freedom – Free Trade. In one word, for exploitation veiled by religious and political illusions, it has substituted naked, shameless, direct, brutal exploitation.

The bourgeoisie has stripped of its halo every occupation hitherto

*honoured and looked up to with reverent awe. It has converted
the physician, the lawyer, the priest, the poet, the man of science,
into its paid wage-labourers.*

*The bourgeoisie has torn away from the family its sentimental
veil, and has reduced the family relation to a mere money-relation.*

These were the fervent words used by the most penetrating
of all observers of the world we have lost when they came to
pronounce on its passing. The idyllic patriarchalism and the
exploitation which Marx and Engels had in mind in this
passage from the *Communist Manifesto*[21] written in 1848 is
recognizable in the arrangements we have been discussing in
this introductory chapter. The ending of the system which
ensured that however he was paid, however little he owned,
or however close he was to the point of starvation, a man
usually lived and worked within the family, the circle of
affection, released enough dissatisfaction to account for all the
restlessness which has marked the progress of the industrial
world.

The factory won its victory by outproducing the working
family, taking away the market for the products of hand-
labour and cutting prices to the point where the craftsman
had either to starve or take a job under factory discipline himself. Usually in fact he had to watch his sons and daughters go
and do so, for the factory system won no swift and final
triumph when the Industrial Revolution eventually appeared.
The seamstresses were working in the garrets right up to the
twentieth century, and the horrors of sweated labour which
so alarmed our grandfathers took place amongst the out-
workers, not on the factory floor. It was not a transformation
which affected only commerce, industry and the towns, for the
hand-work of the cottages disappeared entirely, till, by the year
1920, rural England was an agrarian remnant, an almost lifeless shell. The process was not English alone, at any point in
its development, and its effects on the Continent of Europe
were in some ways more obviously devastating than ever they
were amongst our people. But ours was the society which
first ventured into the industrial era, and English men and
women were the first who had to try to find a home for themselves in a world where the working family, the producing
household, seemed to have no place.

[21] *See page 265.*

But Marx and the historians who have followed him were surely wrong to call this process by the simple name of the triumph of capitalism, the rise and victory of the bourgeoisie. The presence of capital, we have seen, was the very circumstance which made it possible in earlier times for the working family to preserve its independence both on the land and in the cities, linking together the scattered households of the workers in such a way that no one had to make the daily double journey from home to workshop, from suburb to office and factory. Capitalism, however defined, did not begin at the time when the working household was endangered by the beginnings of the factory system, and economic inequality was not the product of the social transformation which so quickly followed after. Though the enormous, insolent wealth of the new commercial and industrial fortunes emphasized the iniquity of the division between rich and poor, it is doubtful whether Victorian England was any worse in this respect than the England of the Tudors and the Stuarts. It was not the fact of capitalism alone, not simply the concentration of the means of production in the hands of the few and the reduction of the rest to a position of dependence, which opened wide the social gulf, though the writers of the eighteenth and nineteenth centuries give us ample evidence that this was observed and was resented – by the dispossessed peasantry in England especially. More important, it is suggested, far more likely a source for the feeling that there is a world which once we all possessed, a world now passed away, is the fact of the transformation of the family life of everyone which industrialism brought with it.[22]

In the vague and difficult verbiage of our own generation, we can say that the removal of the economic functions from the patriarchal family at the point of industrialization created a mass society. It turned the people who worked into a mass of undifferentiated equals, working in a factory or scattered between the factories and mines, bereft for ever of the feeling that work was a family affair, done within the family. Marxist historical sociology presents this as the growth of class consciousness amongst the proletariat, and this is an important historical truth. But because it belongs with the large-scale class model for all social change it can also be misleading, as we shall hope to show. Moreover it has tended to divert attention

[22] *See page* 265.

c

from the structural function of the family in the pre-industrial world, and has impeded a proper, informed contrast between our world and the lost world we have to analyse.

But this is not the only consequence of the failure to look realistically at the familial texture of society at the time of our ancestors, and Marxist historical convention is not the only source of the distortions. Historians have to talk all the time about nations, countries, the units of historical narrative, the arena of historical change. The logical difficulties of defining change in such a way that nations can change autonomously, like chemical elements or compounds, are formidable by themselves. But the historian does not seem to have got even as far as this before he loses his realism. What does the word *England* mean, for the year 1640, shall we say?

Not every single person alive in the country in that year: no historian, however simple-minded, could possibly suppose such a thing. But only the recognition that people came not as individuals, but as families, makes it possible to begin to come closer to the facts. England was an association between the heads of such families, but an association largely confined to those who were literate, who had wealth and status, those, in fact, who belonged, with their families as part of them, to what we have already called the ruling minority. Almost no woman ever belonged to England as an individual, except it be a queen regnant – scarcely a woman in the ordinary sense – or a noble widow and heiress or two, a scattering of widows of successful merchants and yeomen. No individual under the age of thirty was likely to be a member, except in the very highest reaches of society, and very few men who had never been married.

It is problematical how far the mature male heads of families amongst the mass can be counted as part of England for historical purposes: in so far as they had a role at all, it was a negative rather than a positive one, a limitation on what the ruling minority could do rather than an independent source of action and of attitude. We shall return to the relationship between the gentry and the rest, and attempt to make a rough sketch of what the whole was like, though much will have to be left uncertain. It goes without saying, of course, that no one in a position of 'service' was an independent member of society, national or local, and individuals in this position themselves made up 10 per cent or even 15 per cent of the population. Such men and women, boys and girls, were caught up, so to speak, 'subsumed' is the ugly word we shall use, into the personalities of their fathers and masters. They were subsumed in exactly the way that all children were subsumed by their fathers, and children – unmarried individuals still living at home, not out at service – made up two-fifths and more of the entire population. 'Subsumption' then was a very widespread characteristic of traditional society and it could well be extended to cover the relationship between the great household in a village community and the ring of smaller households ranged around it, sited on the landlord's estate, engaged for the most part in working his land. That same contemporary whose words we have quoted on the husbandman and his servants had this to say about the husbandman and his lordly neighbour:

A just fear and respect he must have for his landlord, or the gentleman his neighbour, because God hath placed them above him and he hath learnt that by the father he ought to honour [the reference here is to the Fifth Commandment, Honour thy Father . . .] is meant all his superiors.[23]

In other parts of the world, indeed in some parts of Central and Northern Europe, it is reported that the satellite households in a village community were literally subjected in a patriarchal manner to the great household at the centre. But though no arrangement of this kind has been traced in our country, we can claim with confidence, that anyone who uses the word *England* without remembering the existence of subsumption is scarcely using it with understanding. A very considerable number of existent individuals must moreover be looked upon as null, as having no function, not even as subsumed into units which did have a function. These were the paupers, anyone who was in receipt of charity for his upkeep, or who had ever been in such a position. This body was surely as much a proletariat as ever there has been in the age of industrialism.

Capitalism, then, is an incomplete description and historians' language is marked by many other incomplete descriptions too, of which their use of the names of countries is but one example. The historical distortions which come about

[23] *See page* 265.

from the use of *capitalism, the rise of the bourgeoisie,* and so on, have arisen from a faulty sense of proportion which we can only now begin to correct. With the 'capitalism changed the world' way of thinking goes a division of history into the ancient, feudal and bourgeois eras or stages. But the facts of the contrast which has to be drawn between the world we have lost and the world we now inhabit tends to make all such divisions as these into subdivisions. The time has now come to divide our European past in a simpler way with industrialization as the point of critical change.

The word alienation is part of the cant of the mid-twentieth century and it began as an attempt to describe the separation of the worker from his world of work. We need not accept all that this expression has come to convey in order to recognize that it does point to something vital to us all in relation to our past. Time was when the whole of life went forward in the family, in a circle of loved, familiar faces, known and fondled objects, all to human size. That time has gone for ever. It makes us very different from our ancestors.

A One-Class Society
Chapter 2

---

*Social divisions and power relations amongst
nobility and gentry, townsmen and peasants*

A one-class society may appear at first sight to mean one
where there is no inequality, because everyone belonged to the
same class. But it has already been laid down that this cannot
have been so in the pre-industrial world, at least in Europe.
The *ancien régime*, as the historians call it, was marked by a
very sharply delineated system of status, which drew firm
distinctions between persons and made some superior, most
inferior. There were various gradations, all authoritatively
established and generally recognized. If class were simply a
matter of social status, of the various degrees of respect in
which men are held by their fellows, then it could not be said
that the world we have lost was a one-class society. On the
contrary, it would have to be described as a society with a
considerable number of classes, as many as there were distinct
steps in the graduated system of status.

But when the word class is used, in conversation and by
historians, it does not merely refer to status or to respect. The
distribution of wealth and power is also at issue. This is
obvious when the phrase class-conflict appears. For it nearly
always seems to imply the clash of groups of persons defending
and enhancing not simply a common status but also interest
and power. The emphasis is on the solidarity of classes as
groups of persons which act in championship of their conflict-
ing aims. Such classes have a further characteristic in ordinary
usage: they are nation-wide.

It is in this sense that we shall claim that there was, in
England at least, only one class in pre-industrial society. A
distinction will be drawn between a status group, which is the
number of people enjoying or enduring the same social status,
and a class, which is a number of people banded together in

the exercise of collective power, political and economic. The argument will be that there were a large number of status groups but only one body of persons capable of concerted action over the whole area of society, only one class in fact.

It is unfortunate that an introductory study of this character should have to be concerned with anything as difficult, contentious and technical as the question of class. It is unfortunate also that the only vocabulary which is open to us to discuss it should be that designed for nineteenth- and twentieth-century society. 'Status groups' and 'class' do not fit at all well as descriptions of sets of people belonging to Stuart England, and most of the rest of the terminology used by sociologists is inappropriate too. These expressions have implications belonging to rather different social structures. But literary critics, even novelists have talked about traditional England in these terms, as well as historians and sociologists. We cannot direct our attention to the everyday life of our ancestors and the scale on which they lived it out without any notion of the overall shape of their society, its macro-structure as it might be called, in contrast to its micro-structure where, as we have seen, the family was the key. The macro-structure of Stuart society moreover has become a subject of world-wide discussion because a good part of the contemporary world has to believe in a particular version of what is called The English Revolution for political reasons. Class conflict in the age of Charles I and Cromwell is not simply a matter of social antiquarianism.

There is a sense, of course, in which the phrase 'class-conflict' might be appropriate to pre-industrial society, even if it did contain only one class. For the conflict could be between those who were included within it and everyone else. Perhaps if the expression were always used in this very restricted sense, it would be acceptable as a rough description of what went on. It is certainly no part of our purpose to deny that conflict existed at this time. But historians have not in fact used the phrase in such a restricted way, or in any very closely defined fashion at all. When they have discussed rising and falling classes they have obviously had in mind interaction of a very different kind. Sometimes, perhaps not very often because their language has been so vague, they have made the precise error of confusing a status group with a class and have proceeded as if status groups could rise, fall, conflict, be self-conscious, have a policy. Let us leave these generalities for a moment and look more closely at status symbols and systems in our industrial society as well as in that of our ancestors.

We now inhabit a world of immeasurable wealth and many of us are possessed of a power and a consequence never before known on such a scale. Our society is therefore marked by an intense search after status and after symbols to express it. The most important of those symbols is a personal title, an addition to a man's name, proclaiming who he is, how much success he has had and how much he ought to be respected. There is a whole study of the part which titles and other less satisfactory and specific symbols of status have to play in our contemporary world and on its social, economic, even its political stage. The difficult problem for us in our day is to find out how status and its symbols are to do their necessary psychological work unless they belong to a recognizably coherent system. This used to exist in pre-industrial times but change since then has been so rapid and profound that it survives today only in a form so attenuated that it can hardly fulfil its functions any longer.

The reasons for this are complex, but the most obvious is that we want contradictory things – a system of status and universal social equality. It is easy to illustrate the difficulties. Some issues of relative social importance can still be settled fairly simply; we can put a managing director, for example, on a level with a lieutenant-colonel, though it begins to be a little puzzling when we consider whether the executive secretary of a professional society, say of electrical engineers, is in the same category of status. When it comes to extremes, our status system breaks down altogether. We have no intelligible method for relating a world-ranking pop musician and a cardinal-archbishop. We know that they are both influential people, and must be treated with due deference, but we cannot relate them satisfactorily one to another.

We cannot weigh them up against each other, but even if we could we have no set of symbols universally recognized which could give even a rough expression of their relative importance. The pop-star can, and will, collect as many signs of superiority as possible, of an enormously variegated sort, but none of them help very much when we compare them to the traditional titles of the senior and successful cleric. For the symbolic superiority of a cardinal-archbishop belongs to an ordering which the master of the media of our day can never hope to share. This ordering is an inheritance from the world we have lost.

'Lost' may not be quite the proper word here, and for two reasons. One is that in some contemporary societies and for certain purposes, the status system of the traditional, pre-industrial world is still in use with all its necessary symbols: near imaginary use perhaps we ought to say, since the effectiveness both of the traditional status and its trappings are so much reduced. Just as the English still seem to want to live in the structures of the pre-industrial world, prizing the thatched cottage and the half-timbered house as the proper place for the proper Englishman to dwell in, so also do the English go on awarding the symbolic titles which belong to the status system of the world we have lost. We go on creating knights and barons, setting up industrial peerages, and calling cricketers and jockeys 'Sir', though we no longer understand the system which informed these honorifics and are uneasily aware that their distribution may not correspond to the true distribution of consequence in our society. This is typical of the way in which the world we have lost is in some sense still present with us, or at least of the difficulty we have in becoming conscious of its ghostly persistence, and so addressing ourselves to the problem of putting something else in its place.

But the second reason why the word 'lost' is somewhat paradoxical when we talk of the system of status and its symbols in the pre-industrial world is that elsewhere it was not a case of losing but of rejecting. Titles of honour were deliberately obliterated, first in the United States, then in France and so successively in other European countries, at their 'revolutions'. Great Britain is one of a handful of countries which has not yet found it proper to abolish them by law. The subject of status and its symbols is, therefore, of particular interest to English historians. Here is something in our present which we know to affect the lives of everybody, since the hierarchy of status we preserve so meticulously is by no means confined to titles of nobility and marks of gentility, yet which can only be explained by reference to a past we have nearly forgotten. This is one of the ways in which our country, which was the first to be industrialized and to lose most of the economic nstitutions of the traditional Europe, has nevertheless clung

for longest and with most affection to little, unrelated frag-
ments of the world we have lost.

We live, in England, among the material remains of a
patriarchal society of peasants and craftsmen: those stately
churches, spacious manor houses, farmsteads, cottages, mill-
houses, bridges, all built for itself by the familial social order
which is the subject of this essay. We find them interesting,
often quaint and picturesque, and always, if we are honest,
a little puzzling too. We are puzzled in exactly the same
way when we try to decide whether to put 'Esq.' or 'Mr' on
a letter. If we ask ourselves why we use these abbreviations
at all, we find that we do not quite know. Yet these are the
most common of all status symbols and we use them every day.

We call each other *gentlemen* as well, although we have some
difficulty in deciding what the word means. Defining *gentleman*
indeed, and disputing about the qualities which go to make
one, is a favourite pastime of those who write impressionists'
accounts of social history. The rest of us, if ever it occurs to us
to decide, dismiss the expression as having by now no meaning
at all. It can no longer be defined by contrast since everybody
expects to be called a gentleman, and to be addressed in
writing as *esquire*. So it is not difficult to guess that the descriptions 'Mister' and 'Esquire' must once have implied that
the person addressed was in fact a gentleman. But further
than that we usually cannot go.

There could be no more vivid illustration of our dim and
partial understanding of the pre-industrial world. In that
society of peasants, craftsmen, labourers, husbandmen, and
a very few gentry and nobility, the word *gentleman* meant
something tangible, substantial enough, if uncertain in precise
definition. It was a grade amongst other grades in a carefully
graduated system of social status and had a critically important use.

The term gentleman marked the exact point at which the
traditional social system divided up the population into two
extremely unequal sections. About a twenty-fifth, at most a
twentieth, of all the people alive in the England of the Tudors
and the Stuarts, the last generations before the coming of
industry, belonged to the gentry and to those above them in
the social hierarchy. This tiny minority owned most of the
wealth, wielded the power and made all the decisions, political, economic and social for the national whole. If you were

not a gentleman, if you were not ordinarily called '*Master*' by the commoner folk, or '*Your Worship*'; if you, like nearly all the rest, had a Christian and a surname and nothing more; then you counted for little in the world outside your own household, and for almost nothing outside your small village community and its neighbourhood.

'Nothing' is too strong a word perhaps, and in every society, however constituted, even the smallest unit, the weakest influence, is of some account, has to be allowed for in the general social process. The plain Richard Hodgsons, Robert Boswells, Humphrey Eltons and John Burtons of the English villages, the labourers and husbandmen, the tailors, millers, drovers, watermen, masons, could become constables, parish clerks, churchwardens, ale-conners, even overseers of the poor. They had something of a public life, within the tiny boundaries of the village, and this might give them a minor consequence in the surrounding villages. If they happened to be technically qualified, they might even cast a vote at an election. But in none of these capacities did their opinion matter very much, even in the last. They brought no personal weight to the modest offices which they could hold. As individuals they had no instituted, recognized power over other individuals, always excepting once again those subsumed within their families. Directly they acquired such power, whether by the making or the inheriting of wealth, or by the painful acquisition of a little learning, then they became *worshipful* by that very fact. Then and then only could they know anything substantial of the world, which meant everything which went on outside their own localities, everything rather which was inter-local, affecting more communities and localities than one.

To exercise power, then, to be free of the society of England, to count at all as an active agent in the record we call historical, you had to be a gentleman. When you came to die you had to hold one of those exceptional names in a parish register which bore a prefix or a suffix, about one name in fifteen or twenty seems to have been the average. The commonest addition to a name to be read in a register is *Mr*, for the word 'Master', and *Mrs*, for the word 'Mistress', applied to the maidens as well as the wives and widows. *Gent.* and *Esq.* are rare amongst the additions, as is the word *Dame*, the designation of their wives, and *Knight* and *Baronet* are, of course, much rarer still. The reader with the whole population in his mind, as distinct from the reader with an eye only for the interesting and attractive, will, of course, occasionally come across the titles *Lord* or *Lady*, and the ceremonious phrase 'The Right Honourable the . . .' which was often used to introduce them. But the higher titles of nobility are absent for all practical purposes when the whole population is under review. They are rather like the four-leaved clover to the collector of flowers, or perhaps the winning ticket numbers in a national lottery; one knows they must exist because the system demands it, but one never sees them. Nevertheless, page after page, year after year, decade after decade in the books recording, conscientiously, the burials in an ordinary English parish church will show some title or other for 3 per cent, 5 per cent or at most 10 per cent of the names, never very much more unless the parish had extraordinarily aristocratic or even Royal connections. All the rest of the entries are for simple names and surnames.[24]

Yet the history books we read are studded with much grander titles, and no one seems to appear in them who was without any title at all, except perhaps in the cursory chapter heading 'social'. Which is one way to show again that *England* in the pre-industrial era meant a small minority of the English, small, select and special. Not everyone who belonged to the majority of those who were nobodies felt this exclusion; contemporaries comment often enough on the rich yeoman, for a yeoman was the rank or status immediately below the critical divide, who refused to 'bear the port or mien of a gentleman'. But if the yeoman himself did not wish it, his son or grandson would find it difficult to resist the temptation and the pressure to assume the title and responsibility of gentry. Most of those on the way up in the world needed little persuasion, for when a man was successful the reward was tangible and important, and the higher a family went the more remarkable the difference was from the situation in which its rise began. The great nobles of the traditional world lived a life of superiority which we can no longer imagine, because we no longer possess so clear and overt a system of status.

However lofty the traditional social structure was, the point of transformation was the change which came with the transition from the commonalty to the gentry. Here was a society which has no devices for the saving of labour, none that is

[24] *See page* 266.

when we compare it with our own. The simplest operation in everyday life needed effort; drawing the water from the well, striking steel on flint to catch the tinder alight, cutting goose-feather quills to make a pen, they all took time, trouble and energy. The working of the land, the labour in the craftsmen's shop, were infinitely taxing. The surviving peasantry in Western Europe still shock us with their worn hands and faces, their immeasurable fatigue. Yet the primary characteristic of the gentleman was that he never worked with his hands on necessary, as opposed to leisurely, activities.

The simple fact of leisure dividing off this little society of the privileged – it had to be little at a time when the general resources were so small – is the first step in comprehending the attitude of our forefathers to rank and status. The law of the land laid it down how long common men should work and how little they should rest:

And be it further enacted by the authority aforesaid, That all artificers and labourers being hired for wages by the day or week shall, betwixt the midst of the months of March and September, be and continue at their work, at or before five of the clock in the morning, and continue at work, and not depart, until between seven and eight of the clock at night (except it be in the time of breakfast, dinner or drinking, the which times at most shall not exceed two and a half hours in a day, that is to say, at every drinking one half-hour, for his dinner, one hour, and for his sleep, when he is allowed to sleep, the which is from the midst of May, to the midst of August, half an hour at the most, and at every breakfast one half-hour). And all the said artificers and labourers, between the midst of September, and the midst of March, shall be and continue at their work from the spring of the day in the morning, until the night of the same day, except it be in time afore appointed to breakfast and dinner.

This was laid down in 1563 in the famous Elizabethan Statute of Artificers,[25] as it is usually called, which made compulsory by law the common practice of the time. At the County Assizes, the judges had to inquire whether there were workers who 'do not continue from Five of the Clock in the Morning till Seven at Night in the Summer and from Seven till five in the Winter'.[26] No mention of sleeping-time here, even in the heat of the harvest. Still Breughel's sleeping har-

[25] *See page 267.*   [26] *See page 267.*

vester was an ordinary working man acting on his rights; he
was no visionary, no drowsy peasant drunkard.

Although those in work for wages lived a life of rough,
incessant toil – no Saturday afternoons, none even of the safe-
guards of the early Factory Acts – not all the common people
were caught up in productive work. This is outstandingly
evident from Gregory King's famous table of the structure of
English society, reproduced on pages 36–37. It was drawn up
in the 1690's and applied to the year 1688. It divides up the
population of the country in such a way as to show that more
than half the people then alive were dependent – 'Decreasing
the Wealth of the Kingdom' is the expression appearing in
King's *General Account*.[27]

King's calculation was made on extensive and probably
fairly reliable evidence, and was the only one ever worked out
by a contemporary for a European society in wholly pre-
industrial times. It is now supposed that the reason why so
large a proportion of the population could not wholly support
itself was because there was not enough productive work to
do.[28] The more impressionistic writers in Gregory King's time
and before it did not hesitate to call everyone below a certain
level by insulting names: the *rascals*, or *rascality*, the *proletarii*.
In the 1560's Sir Thomas Smith, a respected lawyer, spoke his
mind in this way, and his is an instructive comment on the
common people of England in their relation with their social
superiors.

For this observer, English society had a fourfold division:

1. '*The first part of the Gentlemen of England called* Nobilitas
   Major.' *This is the nobility, or aristocracy proper.*
2. '*The second sort of Gentlemen called* Nobilitas Minor.' *This is
   the gentry and Smith further divides it into Knights, Esquires
   and gentlemen.*
3. '*Citizens, Burgesses and Yeomen.*'
4. '*The fourth sort of men which do not rule.*'

We shall concern ourselves in due course with the relationship
between these four divisions. Our present interest is in Smith's
detailed description of the lowest of them. These are his
words:

The fourth sort or class amongst us is of those which the old

---

[27] *See page* 267.   [28] *See page* 267.

Romans called capite sensu proletarii *or* operarii, *day labourers, poor husbandmen, yea merchants or retailers which have no free land, copyholders, and all artificers, as tailors, shoemakers, carpenters, brick-makers, brick-layers, etc. These have no voice nor authority in our commonwealth and no account is made of them, but only to be ruled and not to rule other, and yet they be not altogether neglected. For in cities and corporate towns, for default of yeomen, inquests and juries are impanelled of such manner of people. And in villages they are commonly made churchwardens, aleconners, and many times constables, which office toucheth more the commonwealth.*[29]

Even though Smith was prepared to use the word *proletarii* of these people, the old Roman expression meaning those able to produce nothing but offspring, *proles*, as their contribution to society, it does not appear that this description includes the humblest of all. These 'low and base persons' as Smith goes on to call them may not have made up the complete whole of the majority of the population which was 'decreasing the wealth of the kingdom' and some of them may have been increasers. The really large groups of lowly persons are not mentioned by Smith. Though King's 'labouring people' appear, his 'cottagers and paupers' are not mentioned at all. The truly poor, the begging poor, had no craft and could never have become constable or ale-conners, as could the proletariat of Sir Thomas Smith.

Begging was universal, as it is today in some of the countries of Asia; beggars at the door, outside the churches, in the market-places and wandering along the roads. Men sometimes took fright at their numbers, especially in Tudor times, and the savage laws against sturdy vagabonds have become notorious in the textbooks. Everyone knows that Elizabeth made each parish responsible for its own poor, and that when a pauper could be identified as from another community, he or she was sent along the highway from place to place until the place of settlement was reached. These outcasts have left their sad traces in the registers of deaths in our churches: 'a poor walking woman buried', 'a wandering beggar lad', 'a poor woman name unknown who had crept into Mr Miller's barn'.

Yet crowds of destitute people were not typical of poverty in the old world in quite the way that queues of unemployed

[29] *See page* 268.

are typical of industrial poverty. The trouble then, as we have hinted, was not so much unemployment, as under-employment, as it is now called, and once more the comparison is with the countries of Asia in our own century. Too many members of a family were half-busied about an inadequate plot of infertile land; not enough work could be found for the women and children to do round the cottage fire, in some districts none at all, for there was no rural industry in them. Everywhere work of all kinds varied alarmingly with the state of the weather and of trade, so that hunger was not very far away, as we shall see. Starvation, we perhaps ought to add at once, cannot yet be shown to have been a present menace to the poor in Stuart times.

No one could call a life of this sort a life of leisure, even if it was not a life of ceaseless toil for everybody, and leisure as has been said was a mark of the gentleman. The most celebrated Elizabethan definition of a gentleman comes from Harrison's *Description of Britain*, published in 1577. Besides the sons of gentlemen already recognized, he says:

Whosoever studieth the laws of this realm, who so abideth in the university giving his mind to his books, or professeth physic [that is medicine of course] and the liberal sciences, or beside his service in the room of captain in the wars, or good counsell given at home, whereby his common-wealth is benefitted, can live without manual labour, and thereto is able and will bear the port, charge and countenance of a gentleman, he shall for money have a coat and arms [coat of arms, etc.] bestowed upon him by the heralds (who in the charter of the same do of custom pretend antiquity, service and many gay things) and thereunto being made so good cheap, be called master, which is the title that men give to esquires and gentlemen, and reputed for a gentleman ever after.[30]

Any professional man, any university graduate, any officer in the royal forces, therefore, was a gentleman in England by that very fact, and the business of coats of arms, ancestry and public service could all be assumed; the heralds who were responsible would make it all up if required. Harrison is a little obscure when it comes to the matter of the money necessary to attain gentility, but popular opinion was much more straightforward: 'In England gentry is but ancient riches.' The historian is always coming across families which

[30] *See page 268.*

obey this simple rule. If a family had the money for long
enough, just over one succession was generally sufficient, it
graduated to the gentry. By money here is meant means
sufficient to enable a family to live without doing manual
work.

Gentility and its ranks were objective realities as well as
honorifics: they counted for example when taxation systems
were devised. The Poll Tax, imposed in 1660 for the first time
was graduated according to rank: a really ordinary person
paid only 6*d*. a year, but a gentleman paid £5, an esquire paid
£10, a knight £20, a baronet £30, a baron paid £40 and his
heir £30, a viscount £50 (£35), an earl £60 (£40) and a duke
£100 (£60).[31] The time when you could be legally compelled to
dress according to your rank was passing, though private
correspondence is full of resentment at common people wearing the clothes reserved to the socially superior. But the distinction between those who were and those who were not
within the gentry was still of overriding importance. It could
be said without much distortion of the very elusive facts that
this distinction in the eyes of our ancestors was only less
significant than the sharpest of all distinctions, that between
the Christian and a heathen. Indeed the very phrase 'A Christian and a gentleman', a typical survival of the values of that
vanished world, suggests such a comparison. It also leaves
open the possibility that a man could in some sense be a
gentleman without being a Christian.

The system of status does not seem to have prevented social
mobility. Movement into the select minority was straightforward enough in Harrison's view; a man simply had to have
the necessary qualifications and be acceptable to those already
there. But this is not the end of the matter. A great deal more
will have to be found out about the family background and
economic resources of men who were able to get entrance to a
university, or to a profitable profession, or to commissioned
rank in the army and so on, before it will be clear exactly how
often gentlemen were recruited in this fashion. All that can be
said with much confidence is that it did happen and that it was
noticed and accepted by contemporaries.

When we come to consider social mobility rather more
closely, we shall find ourselves having to assume that it must
have been going on all the while in pre-industrial England, if

[31] *See page* 268.

only because of vital statistics. The scale of this movement may have been small and it undoubtedly varied from time to time, but it went on in both directions, downwards as well as upwards. In fact rather more people must have descended than ascended in society. Social mobility is always most pronounced at the frontiers, so to speak, and in traditional society this meant at the crucial divide between the minority which ruled and the mass which did not rule. The fact that this movement was constantly happening was one of the circumstances which made it possible for the single ruling group to maintain its supremacy and to adapt its membership to changing conditions.

In such a situation it seems hardly likely that simple upward motion in society can have been the final effective cause of political strife and civil commotion. There were other reasons for social mobility than vital statistics; obviously an incompetent family above the line of division which mismanaged its affairs and dissipated its fortune was likely to go down, and a family of capable people below the line which was making money was likely to go up. In spite of the elaborate arrangements to maintain the community of the privileged in their position, which was far easier to ensure in that agrarian society than it is in our own industrial society, interchange due to such influences could not be entirely prevented, and presumably happened most often at times of pronounced economic change. It is possible therefore that periods of particularly intense economic change might have been marked by unusually pronounced social mobility, and this might conceivably have led to unrest and conflict, particularly if there was any blockage, so to speak, any threat of resistance from those unwilling to be replaced. But if what is called the English Revolution was like this, then it was very different from a conflict of classes as that term has ordinarily been used. It leaves little room for the rise of a class, the capitalist or middle class as a group of persons. Even some of those who wish to retain a modified version of the rise-of-a-capitalist-class view of social development in pre-industrial times have begun to recognize that the capitalists as a group of persons capable of coming into conflict with other groups of persons are unlikely ever to be identified in England under pre-industrial conditions.[32] Rather it is now supposed that the

[32] *See page* 268.

D

Gregory King's Scheme of the income & expence of the several families.

Number of Families	Ranks, Degrees, Titles and Qualifications	Heads per Family	Number of Persons
160	Temporal Lords	40	6,400
26	Spiritual Lords	20	520
800	Baronets	16	12,800
600	Knights	13	7,800
3,000	Esquires	10	30,000
12,000	Gentlemen	8	96,000
5,000	Persons in greater Offices and Places	8	40,000
5,000	Persons in lesser Offices and Places	6	30,000
2,000	Eminent Merchants and Traders by Sea	8	16,000
8,000	Lesser Merchants and Traders by Sea	6	48,000
10,000	Persons in the Law	7	70,000
2,000	Eminent Clergy-men	6	12,000
8,000	Lesser Clergy-men	5	40,000
40,000	Freeholders of the better sort	7	280,000
120,000	Freeholders of the lesser sort	5½	660,000
150,000	Farmers	5	750,000
15,000	Persons in Liberal Arts and Sciences	5	75,000
50,000	Shopkeepers and Tradesmen	4½	225,000
60,000	Artizans and Handicrafts	4	240,000
5,000	Naval Officers	4	20,000
4,000	Military Officers	4	16,000
500,586		5⅓	2,675,520
50,000	Common Seamen	3	150,000
364,000	Labouring People and Out Servants	3½	1,275,000
400,000	Cottagers and Paupers	3¼	1,300,000
35,000	Common Soldiers	2	70,000
849,000		3¼	2,795,000
	Vagrants; as Gipsies, Thieves, Beggars, &c.		30,000
	So the general Account is		
500,586	Increasing the Wealth of the Kingdom	5⅓	2,675,520
849,000	Decreasing the Wealth of the Kingdom	3¼	2,825,000
1,349,586	Neat Totals	4 1/13	5,500,520

of England calculated for the year 1688*

Yearly income per Family		Yearly income in general	Yearly income per Head			Yearly expense per Head			Yearly increase per Head			Yearly increase in general
£	s.	£	£	s.	d.	£	s.	d.	£	s.	d.	£
3,200		512,000	80	0	0	70	0	0	10	0	0	64,000
1,300		33,800	65	0	0	45	0	0	20	0	0	10,400
800		704,000	55	0	0	49	0	0	6	0	0	76,800
650		390,000	50	0	0	45	0	0	5	0	0	39,000
450		1,200,000	45	0	0	41	0	0	4	0	0	120,000
280		2,880,000	35	0	0	32	0	0	3	0	0	288,000
240		1,200,000	30	0	0	26	0	0	4	0	0	160,000
120		600,000	20	0	0	17	0	0	3	0	0	90,000
400		800,000	50	0	0	37	0	0	13	0	0	208,000
198		1,600,000	33	0	0	27	0	0	6	0	0	288,000
154		1,540,000	22	0	0	18	0	0	4	0	0	280,000
72		144,000	12	0	0	10	0	0	2	0	0	24,000
50		400,000	10	0	0	9	4	0	0	16	0	32,000
91		3,640,000	13	0	0	11	15	0	1	5	0	350,000
55		6,600,000	10	0	0	9	10	0	0	10	0	330,000
42	10	6,375,000	8	10	0	8	5	0	0	5	0	187,500
60		900,000	12	0	0	11	0	0	1	0	0	75,000
45		2,250,000	10	0	0	9	0	0	1	0	0	225,000
38		2,280,000	9	10	0	9	0	0	0	10	0	120,000
80		400,000	20	0	0	18	0	0	2	0	0	40,000
60		240,000	15	0	0	14	0	0	1	0	0	16,000
68	18	34,488,800	12	18	0	11	15	4	1	2	8	3,023,700
									Decrease			*Decrease*
20		1,000,000	7	0	0	7	10	0	0	10	0	75,000
15		5,460,000	4	10	0	4	12	0	0	2	0	127,500
6	10	2,000,000	2	0	0	2	5	0	0	5	0	325,000
14		490,000	7	0	0	7	10	0	0	10	0	35,000
10	10	8,950,000	3	5	0	3	9	0	0	4	0	562,500
		60,000	2	0	0	4	0	0	2	0	0	60,000
68	18	34,488,800	12	18	0	11	15	4	1	2	8	3,023,700
10	10	9,010,000	3	3	0	3	7	6	0	4	6	622,500
32	5	43,491,800	7	18	0	7	9	3	0	8	9	2,401,200

* See note 27, page 267.

Chart of Rank and Status   Stuart England

	Grade	Title	Form of Address	Status Name	Occupational Name
GENTRY — NOBILITAS MAJOR (Greater Nobility) LORDS AND LADIES	1. Duke, Archbishop	Lord, Lady	Honourable Right Honourable The Lord My Lord My Lady Your Grace (for Grade 1) Your Lordship Your Ladyship, etc.	Noble-men	None
	2. Marquess				
	3. Earl				
	4. Viscount				
	5. Baron, Bishop				
NOBILITAS MINOR (Lesser Nobility) GENTLEMEN	6. Baronet	Sir	The Worshipful, Your Worship, etc.	Gentle-men	[*Professions*] Army Officer, Medical Doctor, Merchant, etc.
	7. Knight	Dame*†			
	8. Esquire	Mr			
	9. Gentleman	‡Mrs			
	Clergyman	[†Sir]	[Your Reverence]		
	10. Yeoman	†Goodman †Goodwife (Goody)	†Worthy	Yeoman	Husband-man
	11. Husbandman				
	12. Craftsman Tradesman Artificer	None	Name and Sur-name Only	None	Name of Craft (Carpenter, etc.)
	13. Labourer				Labourer
	14. Cottager Pauper				None

* Often called *Lady* by courtesy.
† Occasional, obsolescent usage.
‡ For unmarried as well as married women.

whole of the English gentry, in our own terminology the whole of the ruling segment, was imbued with bourgeois values by the middle years of the seventeenth century. According to this view the world of gentleman, parson, peasant, craftsman and pauper was already a 'fully possessive market society', where

General note to scheme of Ranks

The common tendency for a person to be called by a rather higher title than the one to which he was strictly entitled was already present. For example the wives of Knights and Baronets were called *Lady* rather than *Dame*. Usage was stricter amongst the nobility and also somewhat complicated. Any nobleman might be called *Lord* (Lord Norfolk, Lord Shaftesbury), but in the higher ranks the actual grade was almost always specified on each occasion (the Duke of Norfolk, the Earl of Shaftesbury). Most noblemen had titles of honour different from their family names (Anthony Ashley Cooper, Earl of Shaftesbury). Occasionally however the family and the title were identical (Ralph Montagu, Duke of Montagu). Some courtesy titles were in use for their heirs: more usually, the heirs to noble titles would be called *Lord* followed by the family name, but the brothers and sisters of heirs of noble titles were often called plain *Mr* or *Mrs*. They were all entitled of course to the general designation *Honourable* as an additional form of address. The grandsons of holders of titles were quite usually called *Mr* without the *Honourable* and so came to be recognized as plain gentry. Usage below the line of gentry, as is emphasized in the text, was very much more uncertain because what status there was was associated with occupation.

The clerical equivalents given above represent usage, but status was uncertain and some clerics (especially those without benefices) were often regarded as below the line of gentry. The status name applied to all members of a family, that is to say the wife and children of a nobleman, were all noble, and of a Knight all gentle. In the case of the clergy, wives and children were always in an equivocal position. There was a tendency for the occupational name of a professional man to be associated with his status name, so that the son of a merchant would be described as a merchant. Below the gentry line this tendency seems to have taken the form of associating the children with the status below that of the head of the family, so that a yeoman's sons would call themselves husbandmen and husbandmen's sons labourers.

---

conflict must presumably have been due to the internal contradictions of capitalism rather than to the clash of bourgeoisie and aristocrats. If this was so, the rivalries and clashes between Englishmen in Stuart and even Tudor times, intellectual, political and military, can hardly have been of an inter-class character. They must have gone on within the one class.

Social change and development in the pre-industrial world need not, therefore, be thought of in terms of classes which rise, conflict and fall. It perhaps ought to be emphasized once again that this does not mean that opposition of economic interest was absent from that society. No sharper clash of interest, material, economic or even biological, can be easily imagined than that between those with and those without access to the land. In an agrarian economy not far removed from the subsistence level in some areas and in some periods, this might have meant that when harvests were bad some men could count on surviving, whilst others, the landless, could not be so sure. But this confrontation of class interest in the sense that whole unorganized masses of persons were on the one side and a few, concerted persons were on the other, is very different from an overt or covert collision between the rising bourgeoisie on the one hand and the falling feudality on the other. Rather it was an opposition between all those within and all those without the possessing minority which we have already referred to.[33]

The graduated ladder from top to bottom of the social scale has already been referred to as the status system. Status depended for the most part on the position a man occupied on that ladder, though there was some admixture of status which arose from his actual function in society and his personal achievement. Status, that is to say, did not come exclusively from the title a man had inherited or had conferred on him. Nearly all the height of the social ladder was to be found within the ruling minority, within that part of the whole society which contained the nobility and the gentry, though the men below that line did share to some extent in the status system. I have tried to represent the facts in the chart on page 38, drawing the dividing line below Gentleman.

At the very top of the society came the monarchy, but it was related to the whole in many other ways than that of status and its very special position is not our present concern. Under the Throne came the nobility, two hundred families, a thousand people or so, in a population of some five and a half million – by 1690 in Gregory King's reckoning (see Table page 36).[34] Yet most of the gradations in the system of honour were contained within this little gilded network; his Grace the Duke (or the Archbishop), the Marquess, the Earl, the Viscount, and lowest of all, His Lordship the Baron (or the Bishop). These were the *nobilitas major* of Sir Thomas Smith, but described by him as belonging to the gentlemen of England all the same. Every step in the honorific grading was meticulously marked and every noble family strove to mount

[33] *See page* 268.   [34] *See page* 269.

the next one upwards of the glittering steps. Differences in
wealth sometimes made the distinctions unrealistic, for even
in Stuart times a viscount on the coal measures might out-
weigh a marquess on the Northern moors, but it could not
obliterate them.

It cannot be said that the whole society of the nobility ever
acted as a group; their identification with the gentry as a
whole was reality, not a piece of legal fancy. We now know
for certain that a majority of all marriages made by the English nobility from the sixteenth century until the twentieth
were made with commoners, mainly with the gentry.[35] This
may mark off our English titled families from their continental
counterparts, and hierarchy was notoriously less rigid in England than elsewhere in Western Europe. But they had a
remarkable privilege of their own nevertheless which gave
them a defined, active institution and consolidated political
power; they had the House of Lords. It may seem extraordinary to assert that in spite of this the peerage in England
was for all purposes except the details of their status at one
with the rest of the ruling segment, the gentry as a whole, yet
this was undoubtedly the case. To look on the peerage as a
class apart, to see it simply as an element surviving from the
feudal age, resenting, and in rivalry with, the humbler members of the privileged order, is only a partial understanding
of the system of status.

Every system of this type must have its rewards, its goals,
its upper reaches, otherwise it will not work. This, then, was
the important function of the English peerage, to provide the
topmost placements in a society of privileged persons all of
whom were gentry and all of whom were members of a different order than the whole mass of the people. The language
of 'The Estates of the Realm', which made of the Lords
Spiritual, the Lords Temporal and the Commons the constituent parts of Parliament, might seem to imply that the
function of nobility was much more extensive than this. It is
true that in the highly conventional activity of politics, both
at the centre of society round the throne, and in the localities,
titles of nobility had considerable political potential and did
not operate simply as the final goal of political success. It is
true also that the traditional division of Parliament was of
structural importance to its workings and did give the nobles

[35] *See page* 269.

an additional purchase over political decisions because they had their own House.

But the Estates of the Realm never had corresponded at all closely to divisions in English society as a whole and the general history of Parliaments might make a fascinating study in the complicated relationships between social structures and the political systems which they generate. In seventeenth-century England the whole arrangement was recognized as archaic and there was even some confusion about what the Estates were, for the Crown rather than the Lords Spiritual was already being referred to as one of them. What might seem to us the most critical division of all, that between members for the boroughs and members for the counties, was passed over and all members of the Lower House referred to as the Commons. Whatever distinction historians of our own day have seen between the bourgeoisie of the urban areas and the gentry of the countryside, it was decidedly not reflected in the constitution of the estates. It was less so in Stuart times in fact than it had been earlier, for the gentry had taken over the representation of the boroughs from their retained, wage-receiving M.P.s by the year 1700. Andrew Marvell, poet and (what was typical of his age) politico as well, is traditionally pointed out as the last Member of Parliament who received his pay, for representing the borough of Kingston-upon-Hull, until his death in 1678. It is wholly confusing to think, as sociologists tend to do, of class systems of subsequent societies, including our own, as descended in any simple way from the medieval Estates of the Realm.

During the Commonwealth, at the height of what is usually called the English Revolution, the House of Lords was abolished. It is a remarkable fact that the peers as a status group were entirely unaffected by the fundamental change in the political situation of the country. Those that did not go into exile with the royalists, went on living in their magnificent seats, enjoying their social and apparently all their other privileges, even some of their political eminence as individuals. Cromwell's government continued to address them by their titles and ended by attempting to create its own class of peers. This is eloquent testimony to the apparently indispensable function of the English peerage in the traditional English social structure and to the extent to which their order existed independently of the House of Lords itself. Though as a society, as a political group, the peers did not exist under Cromwell, within a century, by the middle of the Hanoverian Age, the English nobility had come to make up a palpable block of political power. These vicissitudes seem to me to indicate that none of the events which occurred to those occupying positions of the highest social status at this time, did much to threaten the solidarity of the ruling minority as a whole, that consolidated block of *gentlemen*, including the nobility, who virtually constituted English political society.[36]

It always seems to have been true that the gap between those who were within and those who were outside the ruling group was greater than the gap between any two orders within the ruling group itself. The differences between say a baronet and an ordinary baron (the lowest type of Lord), who stood above the baronet in the status system, were always smaller in number and degree than the differences between the man who was, and he who was not, a gentleman.

Perhaps this rule was not quite invariable. It would certainly be difficult to argue it in the case of an exceptionally rich and successful yeoman who refused to take on the status of gentleman though his neighbours expected him to do so, and though his son was destined to do so directly the father died. But such cases were few, in spite of what some men of the time said about prosperous yeomen. It is also possible that the centuries from the close of the Middle Ages to the end of Stuart times were marked by an exceptional emphasis on the gentleman as a type of person and on the differences between anyone who could call himself a gentleman and everyone else. The establishment of the Herald's Office and its activities in making Visitations of the counties and recording those who were entitled to gentry could be used to substantiate this claim. When the Visitations ceased at the end of this period, it might perhaps be supposed that the sharp emphasis on gentry was beginning to fade[37].

These considerations might take us a long way from our chosen and rather limited subject, but it can be said that the greater political eminence of noblemen in the eighteenth century as compared with the gentry did not imply any over-all change in the relationship between the ruling minority as a whole and the rest of society. In the Middle Ages when the nobility was of such enormous importance the ruling segment

[36] *See page* 269.   [37] *See page* 269.

as a whole must have been much smaller in size and perhaps smaller in relation to the whole. But it would be surprising if it turned out that it consisted of the nobility alone with no intervening area of privileged persons marked off from the whole.

Baronet, knight, esquire, gentleman – these were the grades below the peerage in Tudor and Stuart times, Smith's *Nobilitas Minor*. All these titles, like the titles of nobility, were honorifics only, not descriptions of function. But we have seen that Harrison does talk of a man's function as qualifying him for gentle status, since a physician, a don, a military officer were gentlemen, he thought, by virtue of doing what they did. Another fiscal measure of the Stuart parliaments, an Act passed in 1694[38] which goes into status to a degree of minuteness which has to be read to be believed, is even more straightforward about who and who was not a gentleman. It imposed a tax to be collected 'upon burial of every Gentleman or reputed Gentleman, or owning or writing himself such'. Phrases of this sort are quite common in legal discussion of the crucial difference between those who belonged to the privileged and ruling minority. In fact a man's reputation as a gentleman depended to a considerable degree on what he did, when it was not obvious to all who knew him that he had been born to that status. The Poll Tax quoted earlier lists a whole range of holders of legal, ecclesiastical and even commercial offices as being liable to taxation at levels corresponding to grades of the nobility and gentry. The equivalent grades were usually rather modest ones, except for certain lucrative legal offices.[39]

Such provisions as these amount to an overt, legal recognition of movement into the gentry, even deliberate provision for ensuring that anyone making money or attaining any form of social consequence should succeed to gentle status. Let us pursue the hierarchy of status below the critical divide, and into the largely undifferentiated mass of ordinary people. Before we do so we may notice that the lowest grades of gentry enormously outnumbered the titled grades. With less than two hundred noble families in his table (page 36), it was reckoned by Gregory King that there were in 1688 eight hundred families of baronets and six hundred of knights, but three thousand families of esquires and twelve thousand of gentlemen. This only makes up a third or more of the full

[38] *See page* 270.   [39] *See page* 270.

number of those who must be reckoned to have composed the ruling segment at that time, a third of the one in twenty we referred to earlier. The other two-thirds must have been those with the title 'master' (*Mr* on our letters), self-reputed or locally recognized gentlemen rather than those living on estates in land. This was what might be called the penumbra of the privileged group and again will concern us when we come to social mobility.

Status amongst the common people, the vast majority, went with occupation in so far as it was marked at all; it was a matter of function, not description. The only status name as such which men recognized below the line, so to speak, was the name 'yeoman' (see the *Chart* on page 38). Even this was to some extent a functional term, since a yeoman had to be a fairly substantial owner (not renter) of land which he had to work himself, for he emphatically did not come under the idleness rule which defined gentlemanliness. Alternatively, and here the much greater vagueness of terms for these lower statuses is already to be seen, such a man might be called a freeholder, a greater freeholder (much more likely to have the alternative title yeoman) or a lesser freeholder (probably a freeholder without the vote, that is with less than 40*s.* a year from his own land). Sometimes, during the final generations of the old order, he might be called a farmer, and this is a functional name altogether. It has survived as the only term we now use for those occupied in agriculture.

Yeoman then, was the status name of the most successful of those who worked the land. This was a name which became sentimentalized very early, whilst the men who had held it under the old order became farmers under the new. It is interesting that there was a *yeoman* status even in the companies of craftsmen in the cities and that it should have come below the status of *master* in those associations. The word yeoman has survived in our vocabulary, whilst the functional name based upon what we call farming, working the land, the word *husbandman* has disappeared. All yeomen were husbandmen, because they worked the land, but not all husbandmen were yeomen by any means, because most of them had neither the qualifications nor the status. Since a yeoman's sons worked the land without owning it, they were often called husbandmen too, and most husbandmen were workers of land they did not own but rented. There was a very special sense in which

even a gentleman might sometimes describe himself, in his
letters, shall we say, as a *husbandman*. For a gentleman had
to direct work on his land, even if he was not supposed to
engage in the labour itself.

Husbandman, then, was an extremely common description
of men in the old world, because it was the description of what
so many of them were engaged in, tending the animals and
tilling the soil. Alongside of husbandmen came all the other
callings, the craftsman. Husbandmen and craftsmen are
given no titles in our table and were addressed always by
simple name and surname, followed where necessary by their
occupational name. The word *worthy* would sometimes be used
as a sort of prefix to their names, though never in quite the
way in which *worshipful* was associated with gentry. Yeomen
would be called worthy more readily, and the occasional use of
this word emphasizes the very considerable variation which
men called husbandmen or craftsmen might show in their
prosperity and importance. There was an enormous difference
between a draper in the City of London engaged in large-scale
cloth dealings and a tailor or a blacksmith in a village, even if
the draper was not substantial enough to be regarded as
worshipful and gentle.

'Mechanick' was the title often given to the meaner handicrafts: John Bunyan, the tinker, was thought of as a 'mechanick preacher'. The craftsmen in the towns must nearly always
have worked on a larger scale than those in the countryside,
but in town and in country the overriding impression of the
grade of craftsman was of its multifarious variety. Miller,
tailor, ploughwright, weaver, plumber, dyer, bricklayer,
carpenter, mason, tanner, innkeeper, all these are still familiar
words and many of them common surnames. Some of the
occupations of craftsmen which the historian finds have disappeared so completely from our memory that the ordinary
reader does not usually recognize them: there were the
fletchers (arrow-makers), badgers (corn-dealers), cordwainers
(leather-workers), whittawers (sadlers). How many readers
would know that hedge-cutting or hedge-laying, was probably
what the *plasher* did, who is listed as living at Clayworth in
Nottinghamshire in 1688?

All these men, and the yeomen too, were described simply
by their Christian and surnames whenever they were mentioned: plain John Hart, husbandman, or James Buckland,

carpenter. It had been some centuries since ordinary Englishmen had lacked surnames, but it can easily be seen how natural it was when surnames came in to call Peter the Smith, Peter Smith. On the Continent of Europe the older naming custom survived longer; in Holland for example the common folk did not acquire second names until the time of Napoleon.

There were three further names of common people: *labourer, cottager* and *pauper*. Only *labourer* in any sense described status or function. A *labourer* could be either of the other two, and a man who called himself that could not call himself a husbandman, because he did not work land on his own account. He could have no other calling-name, because he had no specific calling; he just worked for other people. *Cottager* was a description, not of a calling but of a means of livelihood which was not specific. Getting a living where you, you and your whole family, could make one, and wringing all that was possible out of the land which might be attached to the hovel you lived in. This is an unwieldy description, but it is as short a way as I have found of placing a cottager in the old order. The final term, *pauper*, speaks for itself.

According to Gregory King (see page 36), the largest group of families in England was in fact made up of 'Cottagers and Paupers', 400,000 out of 1,350,000. If we regard these as the lowest in the social scale, in spite of the recognition that 'scale' does not strictly apply below the line, the enormous inequality of life in the world we have lost immediately becomes apparent. Not all of these wretched families must be counted as permanently below the level of subsistence, as the early sociologists used to say, or in what was once called primary poverty. But they were for varying periods in poverty of some sort, in need of relief. In fact that whole half and more of the population which Gregory King described as decreasing the wealth of the kingdom may well be supposed to have been living in intermittent poverty in the England of 1688. Indeed it is probably safe to assume that at all times before the beginnings of industrialization a good half of all those living were judged by their contemporaries to be poor, and their standards must have been extremely harsh, even in comparison with those laid down by Victorian poor law authorities.[40]

There is another important characteristic of King's figures

[40] *See page* 270.

which we must not overlook, because it demonstrates a general principle which was a striking feature of social arrangements as they were in his day. The total number of people he gives as five and a half million, of which we have seen a little over half (2,825,000) were 'decreasing the wealth of the kingdom' and a little under half (2,675,520) were increasing it. But the difference in the number of 'families' (we should now, of course, use the word 'household') between these two halves was very much greater; only 501,000 'families' were in the richer section as against 849,000 'families' in the poorer section. Poor people, therefore, lived in small households, and rich people in big ones, though some members of rich households, the servants, came from poor homes and might themselves die in poverty. The general principle, then, runs as follows: the higher the status of the household or family, the larger it was, and the humbler people were, the smaller were the households they lived in. The majority of households were the small, poorer ones, and the minority the large, richer ones, even though more people in total lived in them than in the smaller ones. Humble families in fact lost some of their members, as servants to richer families. We shall return to the size of the family and household in due course; all we are registering here is its connection with the hierarchy of status.

If the phrase middle class seems to have so many misleading associations when it is used of any part of Stuart society, there was of course a middle range of income and status in the plain numerical sense as there always must be. Indeed the 'middling sort of people' began to enter into social descriptions in Stuart times and it is interesting to find that the term was mostly used of the towns. We must look a little closer at the townsfolk and the bourgeoisie in order to decide the extent to which they can be said to have lived apart from the rest of the population, even though like everybody else they found themselves under the domination of the ruling minority. Can it be said that the two thousand families of 'Merchants and Traders by Sea' which Gregory King estimated as existing in 1688, or ten thousand of them in all if the lesser ones are included, really formed the bourgeoisie in pre-industrial England? Or would it be realistic and useful to call Sir Thomas Smith's third sort of men, 'Citizens, Burgesses and Yeomen' by the title middle class?

Though yeomen and merchants must have come from

the same stock, and though there might seem to be some rough
sort of equivalence in the position of the more modest burgesses with that of the substantial peasantry, Smith is exceptional in linking them together in this way. In the provincial
towns – how insignificant they were will become obvious in the
next chapter – the local grazier who was also a butcher had
already appeared in the sixteenth century and his is a figure
which persisted until the twentieth century. Nevertheless the
towns had a life of their own, small as they were, and any
acquaintance with municipal records will show how intense
such a community feeling could be. It was at the top that the
linkage with society as a whole is to be seen, and it was the
link between the gentry and the merchants which preoccupied
the men of the time.

This is what Harrison says about merchants: 'They often
change estate with gentlemen as gentlemen do with them, by
mutual conversion of one into the other.'[41] William Lambarde, the first historian of an English county, says very much
the same thing of Kent in Elizabethan times: 'The gentlemen
be not here (throughout) of so ancient stocks as elsewhere,
especially in the parts nearest to London, from which city (as
it were from a certain rich and wealthy seedplot) courtiers,
lawyers and merchants be continuously translated and do
become new plants among them.'[42] This interchange was by
no means confined to Kent, and as Harrison said it was not
simply a flow of merchant families into the gentry: the gentry
became merchants too. Westcote, the first to write about the
broad seafaring county of Devon, with its flourishing ports,
says of the merchants: 'Divers of them are esquire's and
gentlemen's younger sons, who by means of their travel and
transmigration are very well qualified, apt and fit to manage
great and high offices.'[43]

Some contemporaries, it is true, do give an impression that
the merchants were a community of their own: 'These, by
reason of the great privileges they enjoy, every city being as
it were a Common Wealth by themselves,'[44] wrote one of them
in 1600, somewhat obscurely and ungrammatically it must be
confessed. There was an interesting and anxious controversy
in the seventeenth century about whether a gentleman's son
could become an apprentice and still preserve his gentle status

[41] *See page* 271.   [42] *See page* 271.   [43] *See page* 271.
[44] *See page* 271.

since apprenticeship, as we have seen, meant serving in someone else's house and actually undertaking menial tasks for a
person ordinarily of lower lineage than his own.[45] But whatever prejudice there might have been, however much snobbery
affected our ancestors, there can be no doubt that gentlemen
did become apprentices in very considerable numbers to the
more profitable trades. There can be no doubt either that the
sons of the manor house married the daughters of the city
merchants, for as much money in the way of a dowry as they
could possibly get, or that the son of a successful goldsmith,
merchant, haberdasher or draper, might marry the daughter
of a country gentleman.

Here we return at once to the authoritarian, patriarchal
family which bound people together with tough, durable bands
of kinship. The gentleman's son who went into the City as an
apprentice, and married City money, remained part of the
family in the countryside. When the gentry of the county
underwent a Visitation from the Heralds, which happened
once in a couple of generations, they registered their sons or
grandsons, daughters, nephews, living in the City along with
all the others married off to other county gentry. So many
gentry got into London in this way that the City of London
had its Visitations too. It is interesting that the families there
very seldom went back more than two or three generations,
for most English merchant families retired to the countryside
as soon as opportunity presented itself. There were English
families which maintained a dual allegiance over many generations, dynasties of prosperous London merchants which
were also gentry in the countryside, seated most often, as
might be expected, in the Home Counties. But these were
few.[46] Londoners who happened to inherit country houses
nearly always seem to have taken up their residence there
and left the City.

It was often the death of an uncle, a great-uncle or a cousin
rather than a father, brother or grandfather which required
that the younger, City Branch should move to the family seat.
We still talk of the City Branch, just as we still talk of county
families, which is one more indication of how our language of
status belongs to an older world. When we come to talk of
social mobility and vital statistics (see below, Chapter 8) we
shall see that even more conspicuous transformations were

[45] *See page* 272.   [46] *See page* 272.

possible. A man might be merely the eldest in the female line
of a minor gentle family, yet end his life as a titled magnate
or even a peer. The point of present importance is the web of
kinship, to use a phrase of the anthropologists, which enfolded
every family in the ruling segment. It was not simply a community of interest, a political or economic grouping, it was a
lineage, a clan. Entry into it was by marriage.

Given that there was no bar to intermarriage, therefore, it
is extremely difficult to see how any enclave could remain
isolated from the rest. The City of London was undoubtedly
a community of its own; so extraordinarily rich and powerful
did it become in the final generations of the old order that
it is understandable that men sometimes described it as a
state within a state. But we shall shortly see how it was
pretty well alone as an urban community, the only area of the
country where rural ways did not penetrate, in the whole of
England. Life in London was different from life elsewhere and
life in the richest London families very different, perhaps,
from life in the country houses whose masters were so much
less wealthy than the Aldermen. But however striking the
texture of social life in the *haute bourgeoisie* might turn out to
be when it is minutely examined, this does not justify us in
calling the city dweller a member of a different class, forming
a conscious, permanent community, capable of seeing itself
as separate from the ruling segment.

The difference in outlook must presumably have been at its
greatest when some city father had risen from truly humble
origins, from well beneath the rank of gentleman. Like the
rest of those who prospered in the towns, of course, he was
called *master*, he was *worshipful*, by virtue of his personal
wealth and power over others. We do not yet know how often
such a thing came to pass, or how essential it may have been
to have come from some gentle or at least yeoman family
before such a career of success as a bourgeois became possible
in the pre-industrial world. It is clear, however, that social
differences of this sort did not outlast more than a generation.
A wealthy clothier, or tanner, or victualler, or perhaps barber
surgeon might, if he lived to see them, feel very different from
his grandchildren in the countryside whom he shared with the
gentleman whose son had married his daughter. But the
grandchildren themselves would not experience any uncertainty of status. Moreover, they might succeed very rapidly to

E

the family fortune because of the short expectation of life. This point is usually put in the form of an admission that families can and do sometimes ascend in the traditional societies, but that it took a generation and more. At that time however several generations might well elapse within the ordinary span of life in our time.

We have been able in this outline of an argument to refer only very little to other members of the *middle class*, as we understand it today. We now think of professional people such as doctors and lawyers, technicians of every description, teachers, architects, civil servants as the important people of this type. It is men like these which the nations of Africa and Asia are so sadly lacking in our century, and not so much the businessmen, who correspond (not very exactly) to the merchants of, say, Elizabethan England. All that can now be said of *professional* people of this sort in the world we have lost is that, just as in Africa now, there were very, very few of them. Those who did exist, belonged to the ruling minority by definition. We have seen William Harrison admitting it and they have been placed accordingly in our chart on page 38.

Conditions on the Continent were often somewhat different from those in England. In Holland, for example, or in Italy, there seems to have been a greater continuity of succession in urban, patrician families, who perhaps did not marry into the gentle families of the countryside so easily and presumably, therefore, did not attain gentle status so often. The status system differed too, for in some countries the nobility does seem to have been more separate from the rest of the privileged community, and provisions for social descent such as existed in England seem to have been lacking. This is a capital point, which might well have been developed, for the rule of status which laid it down that in England the younger son of a baron was plain *master*, *Mr*, just like a successful merchant, certainly led to an acceptance of social mobility not so apparent elsewhere. In all these directions it may turn out that England was exceptional.

Perhaps the phrase a 'one-class society' would fit no other European country as well as it seems to fit pre-industrial England, even with all the complicated exceptions and reservations which have had to be made in the course of this chapter. This title gives rise to no expectation that the workers of the pre-industrial world can be thought of as a community apart from the rest, which is a further advantage over the usual phraseology. Detailed analysis of the working force, or the labour force as the economists say, cannot be undertaken here and it is one more of the subjects which will have to be pursued elsewhere for itself alone. There was a considerable number of wage-earners even before large-scale industry made the wage packet the almost universal form of payment and support. Indeed there is evidence that even in Tudor times well over a half or even two-thirds of all households received some part at least of their income from wages. Nevertheless the paupers, when they were fortunate enough to receive wages, the labourers, the artificers, even the husbandmen and the yeomen who pocketed such payments from their employers were in a very different position from the worker in the factory, the shop or the office. They did not all share a common work situation by any means, as do the members of the working class in the contemporary industrial world.

A considerable part of the labour force, moreover, cannot have been householders at all. These were the servants living in the households of their masters and the grown and growing children still at home and at work at the bench or in the fields. Most of them were young, but some of them were as old as the heads of their households, and a very few even older, unmarried and now largely unmarriable. They were separated into the myriad familial cells which went to make up the society. Here we return once again to the minute scale of life, the small size of human groups, before the coming of industry. Working persons were held apart from each other by the social system. Many or most of them were subsumed, as we have said, within the personalities of their fathers and masters. If it had not been for the terminology which was invented for a society like our own, it would never have occurred to us even to wonder whether they could be thought of as a community, a class of their own.

The working families were poor, and we have seen men of the time openly talking of them as the proletariat. 'Miserable men,' Westcote calls them, 'in regard of their labour and poverty.'[47] Everyone was quite well aware throughout the life of that social order that the poorer peasantry might at any time break out into violence. Talking about the 'pulling and contest' after money at a time of deflation, John Locke said

[47] *See page* 272.

in 1692 that this struggle usually went on between 'the landed men and the merchant'.

For the labourer's share, being seldom more than a bare subsistence, never allows that body of man time or opportunity to raise their thoughts above that, or struggle with the richer for theirs (as one common interest), unless when some common or great distress, uniting them in one universal ferment, makes them forget respect, and emboldens them to carve to their wants with armed force, and then sometimes they break in upon the rich and sweep all like a deluge. But this rarely happens but in the mal-administration of a neglected or mismanaged government.[48]

Journeymen out of their time, but unable to set up for themselves; small masters miserably dependent on the capital of rich masters; husbandmen pinched for their rent by avaricious landlords; these were likewise looked upon as dangerous men who might sometimes become desperate.

But the head of the poorest family was at least the head of something. The workers did not form a million *outs* facing a handful of *ins*. They were not in what we should call a mass situation. They could not be what we should call a class. For this, it has been claimed, if the expression can be used at all, was a one-class society. It must be clear that the question of how the *élite*, the ruling segment, was related to the rest is not an easy one to answer. A great deal of patient, intricate work of discovery and analysis will have to be undertaken by the historians before they can begin to decide such issues as these. They will have to show an imaginative sensitivity to all those subtle influences which enable a minority to live for all the rest. When they come to do this, it is the symbolic life of our ancestors which will be the most difficult to handle, and especially their symbols of status.

[48] *See page* 272.

The Village Community
Chapter 3

The scale of life in cottage, farmstead, manor house and church

Nothing seems more poignant and appropriate to us than that Falstaff should have died babbling of green fields. Indeed we still think of our English surroundings in this way; lush little meadows and, more commonplace still, the group of thatched cottages, standing in irregular relationship with manor-house, inn and church. This is a picture of England which the Englishman goes to make sure about when his holidays come round, and which foreigners see when they look on us from outside, especially from the North American Continent.

It is now an entirely false picture, of course, and by this time most of us surely know quite well that it is false. Nevertheless, its persisting attractiveness, the effect it still has on our national image of ourselves is one further example of the influence upon us of the lost world which vanished with the coming of industrial, urban life. In our day, at least four Englishmen out of every ten live in cities. Over half of us live in towns of 50,000 inhabitants and more,[49] which are so vast that none of our rural ancestors would recognize his surroundings as human, should he find his way there through some impossible chronological vagary.

London even then was a city on an industrial scale, though industry, as we use the word, did not exist there. The inn in Eastcheap where Falstaff lay plucking at the sheets, his nose sharp as a pen, was quite a long way from green fields, perhaps a mile and a half or two miles, probably as far as it was possible to get. By the end of the pre-industrial era London was undoubtedly the biggest city in Europe and, if men had but known it, with only Tokyo as its rival as the biggest city in the world it was still smaller than the Rome of the ancients,

[49] *See page* 273.

which was the largest city men then knew about. One Englishman in every ten lived in London, which actually topped the
half-million mark by the end of the seventeenth century.[50]
But urban, mass living in an environment entirely man-made,
if no way machine-made, ended at that point in England. If
three-quarters and more of our people live in cities today, then
in Tudor and Stuart times the position was exactly the reverse.
When Elizabeth reigned, Charles and Cromwell fought the
Civil War, and William and Mary came to the throne after
the Glorious Revolution, some three-quarters of the whole
people lived in villages.

These villages were, moreover, small even on the standards
of the villages we still know. It is difficult to be certain what
was the scale of each settlement, and a great deal of work
has still to be done on the elementary facts about the human
geography of our country in its historical dimension. It is
quite certain that there was no average size in the sense
that most villages could be expected to contain roughly the
same number of people. There were large villages and little
villages, just as there were great and small towns and cities:
the composition and organization of settlements varied enormously, from region to region and even to some degree within
the same limited area. But the numerical mean or average,
that is the number of places divided into the total population
in England and Wales in late Stuart times, was very probably
as small as 200 or smaller. The only example which can yet
be quoted of an appreciable number of places in the same area,
yields even smaller figures. This is the Wingham division of
the county of Kent in 1705 where there were forty separately
named places in the collection of lists of inhabitants, with a
total of 6,411 people: the average, or mean, size of a settlement was thus 160 people. Much of the Stuart population
lived out their lives in settlements so small that in the
twentieth century we should regard them as miniatures,
curiosities.

But even in the Wingham area, there was one community
of 1,172 people, and 42 per cent of the people lived in settlements larger than 400 people. Like all figures, those we have
presented for the whole country, and for this particular area,
are deceptive to some degree. Though the figure for the actual
national average was scarcely 200 and the median or middle

[50] *See page* 273.

sized, settlement perhaps as low as 150, yet just as in Kent in 1705, a considerable minority presumably lived in larger places, with perhaps 500 or more inhabitants.[51] It is possible then, to give a rather different impression for the country as a whole, when it is remembered that a quarter of the people were living in London and the towns. Something like two-thirds of the whole population of the country can be supposed to have dwelt in settlements of 500 or more, and a tenth of them in a real city on the twentieth-century scale. But when we make the gross comparison with our own day which is the general object of this superficial survey, these different angles of view change the prospect very little. Life in a community of 500 or 600 souls can have been very little different from life in a community of 300 or 400, in contrast to life in a modern industrial centre of 50,000 or more.

The facts of the minuscule scale of living in the world we have lost, therefore, are almost as conspicuous for the size of the communities in which men dwelt as they are for the size of the group in which they lived and worked. England, apart from the phenomenon of London, may have been exceptionally laid out, more blanketed by its fields than many other areas of Europe. It can now be shown that English villages were much, much smaller than the settlements which their inhabitants established in the New World, for example. But though the details of the distribution of persons between villages, hamlets might be a better word, have still to be worked out, there can be little doubt about the figures. Gregory King reckoned that there were 530,000 people living in London in 1688, nearly 10 per cent of the population of the country; 870,000 living in 'The other Cities and Market Towns', that is nearly 16 per cent, and 4,100,000 living in 'The Villages and Hamlets', over 74 per cent. Since we already have some idea of the scale of life in London we must look at these last two categories separately, because the difference in order of magnitude between London and the rest is truly impressive.

Gregory King does not specify the number of 'Cities and Market Towns' in his table, but Professor Glass has discovered in King's workings a table of some 800 places which he seemed to have had in mind as accounting for the 870,000 people in his second category.[52] This would make the mean size of an English city, or local town-centre, only a little over

[51] *See page* 274.   [52] *See page* 274.

1,000, not much more than one five-hundredth of the size of London. The height of the step between London and the next level of size is, perhaps, even more surprising, from half a million, to about 25,000 to 30,000. This was reached only by four places, probably Bristol, Norwich and York were three of them. These four giants among the provincial cities contained no more than $11\frac{1}{4}$ per cent of the population which lived in places which could be called in any sense urban. Below them came 10 cities of about 18,000 people, 30 cities (or 'great towns' as King is careful to say) of about 2,200 and then 100 of about 1,300 inhabitants. The majority of the town-dwelling population outside London, if the adjective town-dwelling is permissible at all, lived in 250 places of some 900 people and 400 further places of something over 650. Between them these two classes of 'town' contained well over a half of all those outside the capital not dwelling in villages or hamlets.

England, therefore, was decidedly not an urban country before the arrival of industry. If King and the other men of his day who discussed the matter are to be trusted, and such evidence as has yet been surveyed all points in the same direction, England was a large rural hinterland attached to a vast metropolis through a network of insignificant local centres. There was little to correspond with the great provincial towns of France. After the really big cities of Paris, Lyons and Marseilles, came Rouen, Orleans, Amiens, Bordeaux, Rheims, Angers, all six of which had between 35,000 and 50,000 people and more.[53] Even Beauvais, a medium-sized clothing city, had some 15,000 or 20,000, and the relatively minor provincial capital of Aix-en-Provence numbered 27,500 people in 1695 when a fairly accurate count was made.[54] We may compare this with an almost contemporary census of similar reliability, carried out with the knowledge, and perhaps the co-operation, of King himself, in his own birthplace, Lichfield in Staffordshire.[55] A cathedral city and a county centre, it contained 2,861 people in the same year, 1695.

Our country had no city-states, like Italy: no Florence, no Venice, not even a Frankfurt-am-Main, or a Salzburg. Even London, for all its fantastic size, could not be called a civic site: it was then, as it has sadly continued to be, except in select areas and for a brief period under the Georges, a dis-

[53] *See page* 275.   [54] *See page* 275.   [55] *See page* 275.

orderly sprawl, as much of a haphazard muddle as any English rural village. We are right to think of the world we have lost as a bucolic world, in our country at least, even if we are wrong to go on believing that we ought all to be living in the countryside still.

This is the justification for our talking almost exclusively about rural life and village institutions in the pre-industrial world in England. The scale and quality of the experience of our ancestors must have been determined by them: urban living cannot have been anything like as important to them as it seems to have become in our folk memory of the past and in most historians' accounts of it. There is another and quite accidental reason why village life will have to occupy us so largely. Our evidence mostly comes from rural villages, and even purely demographic study may, for technical reasons, have to be confined to village life for some time to come. We shall find ourselves from time to time, however, remarking here on rural/urban differences, particularly between London and the rest of the country.

Sometimes it is surprising that these differences were as small as they seem to have been, but Gregory King's own writing is proof that the men of the time were well aware that society did vary between town and country. The whole of King's *Observations* is marked by attempts to distinguish rural from urban figures, and he provides tables showing that in London and the towns there were more married couples, more servants, more widows and fewer children than in the country. Our preliminary evidence in some cases contradicts even Gregory King but we shall not be able to claim that we know enough to pronounce in general on the contrast between town and country.

When we talk of England as being almost entirely a landscape of green meadows and wide-open fields with village communities scattered amongst them, it is a network rather than a scattering that we have in mind. The very large numbers of small settlements in which so much of the population lived were in fact all connected by the local rural centres. They were independent as communities, but their independence implied the existence of communities larger than themselves. Though these larger villages and towns turn out to be so small as compared with the provincial cities of the rest of Western Europe, they were nevertheless differently constituted from the others because they were centres of exchange as well as of communication. The whole pattern must therefore be thought of as a reticulation rather than as a particulation, a web spread over the whole geography is the metaphor which will come most easily to the mind. We shall use the same expression for the society of the gentry which did so much to maintain unity and consciousness over the complete area. But the bondages which come from roads, rivers, markets, fairs and neighbourhood were always present too.

The word *settlement* is right for the villages and hamlets of our country. They were in fact the knots of households originally set down by the first colonizers of the island, still being inhabited and run by their successors after a thousand years and more. Many, perhaps even most of them, bore, and still bear, the names which had got stuck when the site was being cleared and the earliest dwellings set up. Such names are Woolpit in Suffolk, for *wolfpit*, or Caldecote, which appears in several counties and means a fold for the sheep from the cold.

Each group of farmsteads was surrounded by the land which had been laid out for it, presumably enough to support the inhabitants. In some areas, therefore, where the land was rich and even and easy to till, and where the rivers flowed together, settlements came thick and fast. Norfolk has no less than 660 ancient parishes, and in that most prosperous of the shires in earlier times, there were 969 medieval churches; you can sometimes see ten spires or towers from one vantage point.[56] Yet even in Norfolk, on the Breckland, there are miles and miles of desolate landscape where few dwelt and where the settlements are well out of sight of each other. In the highlands of England, the whole area north and west of the famous line drawn from Bristol to the Wash, church was separated from church by five, seven or even ten miles. Yorkshire, which is more than twice as big as Norfolk, had but 459 parishes in Stuart times, Cornwall only 61. Westmorland only 26, and Lancashire, the county where industrial transformation was to be at its most sudden and intense, not more than 64.

Parishes are not settlements. There are often several distinct hamlets in one parish, or more than one parish in a village. About three settlements to two parishes is, perhaps, about

[56] *See page* **275.**

right. These parish figures, therefore, are only very rough indications of the variation between size, density and structure of settlements found in various parts of the country, especially between the highland and lowland zones. In the highlands, chapelries had grown up to accommodate the growing population which had often already appeared in response to early industrial activity, especially the making of wool and cloth. Yet, even in these regions parish and settlement were sometimes congruent, or rather the parish covered an area comprising only one hamlet, or two, as in the lowlands. This was so at Widecombe-in-the-Moor, in Devonshire, from whose boundaries Dartmoor still stretches away as far as the eye can see. Life amongst inhabitants of that parish, or of Greystoke in Cumberland, locked in the mountains of the Lake District, was one thing. Life in the large and prosperous village of Colyton on the Devon seaboard, or in the single little bunch of housesteads which went to make up Cogenhoe in Northamptonshire, two hundred people on only 800 acres yet with their own church and rector, was another thing again.

The villages of Greystoke, Colyton and Cogenhoe[57] come into the story many times, for they are amongst the ten or a dozen village communities which have been examined in some detail for the purpose of this essay. But the subtler elements which went to make up the differences between community and community have not yet been reached. It is not yet known how much effect the final origin of the inhabitants might have had on the way they arranged their community life, laid out their fields and worked them, or conducted their religious worship. For the highlanders in Britain, as everyone remembers, are Celtic by descent, and the lowlanders are Saxon.[58] Another difference in the texture of local life which certainly had a part to play was the extent to which it was *industrialized*, in the old meaning of the phrase, how many of the households were wholly or partly working for the clothier, or the nailer or how many of the menfolk worked the mines. So powerful was this force becoming that in many places it may have been decisive, overriding differences in origin, or tradition, even the influence of geographical position.

There were differences between village communities which came from recent agricultural history as well, and these have taken pride of place in the story which historians have had to

[57] *See page* 275.　　　　　　　　[58] *See page* 276.

tell. Most important of all have been questions of enclosure. Did this settlement once work its land as open fields, co-operatively, until some grasping or enterprising Tudor land-lord managed to bring about enclosure? To enclose a village meant that the inhabitants had to abandon their co-operative customs, and break up their great open fields into little, hedged plots, one single piece to each landholder and, of course, the largest by far for the landlord himself. Or was the open field, co-operative system then still in force there? Or had the land, perhaps, as in Kent or in East Anglia, always been enclosed? These are clearly fundamental questions to ask of any village community in the traditional world, since work-ing the land was the fundamental activity of all its members, and co-operating for the purpose a powerful link between the constituent households. But no very large proportion of the cultivated land had been enclosed by the years 1700–10,[59] which is the final decade of the old world for our purposes. Where enclosure had taken place, moreover, even recently, the differences it had made from the point of view of the life of the community were perhaps less than might be expected.

Enclosure could not destroy the distances between the com-munity and its neighbours. Though the detailed arrangements for the working of the land were no longer undertaken at the manor court, and though that court might be dying as an institution, nevertheless, the community still had its affairs to run co-operatively. The church had to be administered, or perhaps two churches in the same village. The poor law had to be carried out; the roads had to be kept up; the constable appointed to maintain the peace. The more important the common responsibilities of any community, presumably, the stronger the association between its members, because each one's interest is engaged. But living together in one township, isolated, spatially, from others of comparable size, of very much the same structure, inevitably means a communal sense and communal activity, even if that activity is trivial and symbolic, as it is in the *social club* which we treasure so much in our day.

The strength of this sense of community in the English villager can be seen when he removed himself beyond the ocean, and settled again, surrounded by the alien, virgin land, which required new household groupings. In the final years of

[59] *See page* 276.

the traditional order in England, when the English were establishing their townships on the eastern seaboard of the North American continent, the village community at home was of course the model. The men from the ancient enclosed villages of East Anglia and the newly enclosed communities of the Midlands showed no less communal sense, no greater unwillingness to serve the new community, than the men from villages where the immemorial open fields still lay undisturbed under the wide, grey English sky. Open-field villagers would sometimes insist on the open-field system for a new township in Massachusetts. But it is not recorded that those from elsewhere would welcome this return to the ancient co-operative system.[60]

There is very little reason to believe, therefore, that the *husbandry*, that is the working landholders, of the English village community who went out to join the Puritan commonwealth which grew up on the rocky soil of New England were seeking refuge from the enclosing landlord. Nevertheless they were certainly disinclined, in their surroundings, to allow a gentry to grow up amongst them, and quite determined to have no truck with ecclesiastical dignitaries. However, gentle folk were never entirely absent from any part of the American colonies, even from quintessentially Puritan Massachusetts; in the southern areas, as everyone knows, the gentry were much more prominent and even the Anglican hierarchy took root. The plantation-owners of Virginia looked upon themselves from the very beginning as the overseas branches of English county families, and there is evidence that the gentry did indeed take the intiative in opening up the leafy green plain between the Atlantic and the Appalachians though they had great difficulty in settling it.[61] Indeed, the role of the gentry in the creation of America must have been an important one, if the analysis of English society presented here is at all accurate. Still, at the American Revolution, as we have seen, all this disappeared from the official life, political and social, of the new United States, and has had to be pieced together by subsequent historians. The pattern of Puritan society in Massachusetts became the pattern of American society generally, in this as in so much else. It was a pattern which no doubt came to some extent from the life of the English towns, but whose major origin can be clearly seen

[60] *See page 276.*   [61] *See page 277.*

in those villages of Stuart England where no gentlemanly household was to be found and where the yeomen and the husbandmen ran everything themselves.

It would be easy in our own century to exaggerate the extent to which the new Englishmen of the American continent deliberately rejected the system of status established amongst the old Englishmen of Europe, for we are so interested in social differentiation, and so apt to seize upon every sign of social resentment or of disaffection. But there can be no doubt that the social hierarchy deeply affected the lives of ordinary people in the Old World. The presence, or absence, of the gentry in an English village made a vital difference. Without the gentry, or any member of the ruling minority in their midst, the members of an English village community were indeed free to run their own affairs, almost as free, it might seem, as the members of the townships set up in New England. Galby, in Leicestershire, never had a resident squire, and the free villagers have been traced for centuries, running their community as they would.[62] Many communities like this must have been present, scattered amongst the villages where the manor-house was the largest building, apart from the church, and deference to its occupants the first principle of village life. Perhaps a fifth of all the village communities of England may have been in this position.

The surprising thing about this figure, on reflection, is how small it is. The gentry were, at most, a twentieth of the population, yet they managed to spread themselves over two-thirds of the countryside. This is a rough estimate and it would, perhaps, be best if the source of it were given here. In 1680, a survey was published with the following title:

> *Index Villaris; or, An Alphabetical Table of all the Cities, Market-Towns, Parishes, Villages, and Private Seats in England and Wales.*

The author of this large and on the whole remarkably reliable work, compiled among other sources from the records of the Hearth Tax, was John Adams, an eminent early maker of maps of our country and acquainted with Gregory King.[63] He gave each entry in his index a marking to indicate noblemen's seats: those with one, two, three or more than three, gentlemen's seats: those which had gentry in numbers unknown to

[62] *See page 277.* 　　　　　　　　　[63] *See page 277.*

the compiler; and those which had no gentry at all. Rough calculation from the evidence painstakingly recorded in this book shows that titled families, aristocratic or merely genteel, were indeed widespread.

If the English settlers in America felt that you could not move in the old country without coming up against the honourables and the worshipfuls, this survey shows that they had some justification.

It must be used with caution, of course, even if the original information was reliable. Noblemen had more seats than one: the same work names no less than twelve houses for Henry Somerset, Duke of Beaufort, Marquess and Earl of Worcester,

Number of named places	%	Description of titled residents		
13	2·3	Noblemen		
360	64·0	Gentlemen	33 (5·9%)	Baronets
			5 (0·9%)	Knights
			85 (15·1%)	Two Gentlemen or more
			174 (30·9%)	One Gentleman
			63 (11·2%)	Gentlemen, number unspecified
106	19·0	No titled residents recorded		
83	14·7	Not clear		
562	100·0			

Lord Herbert of Chepstow, Raglan and Gower. He had Worcester House in the Strand, in London; Badminton and Wollaston Grange in Gloucestershire; Monmouth Castle, Chepstow Castle, Raglan Castle, Chepstow Grange and Tintern Abbey in Monmouthshire; Crickhowel Castle and Tretower Castle in Brecknockshire and Swansea Castle in Glamorgan. The Duke of Norfolk had ten seats, including one in the very centre of the city of Norwich, castles in four English counties and Norfolk House in London. One earl had nine seats, and one baron had eight. No family could possibly occupy so many houses at any one time, but in the villages where they stood, these baronial mansions spoke eloquently of the power of their owners. If you grew up under the shadow of a castle, or outside the walls of a lordly park, you knew who ruled England, even if the place was in the hands of tenants.[64]

[64] *See page* 277.

Though by such means as this, the nobility managed to be present in something like every fortieth village, the baronets, knights, esquires and gentlemen were literally everywhere. Some counties had more in proportion than others; in some they were richer, in some they were more aristocratic; but they were to be found over the whole countryside, and in the towns and cities too.[65] Even in those villages we have mentioned where the yeomen held sway, dominating manor and church and deciding everything for themselves, there might well be some land held by an absent gentleman. And if there were none in the settlement, there would be some in the next hamlet, or village, and not far away a gentlemanly seat. The families of the ruling segment pressed, like the atmosphere, evenly, over the whole face of England. It is time to look at the actual constitution of a village community to see how it felt.

On April 7th, 1676, the curate of the parish of Goodnestone-next-Wingham, in Kent, made his reply to the Archbishop of Canterbury, who wanted to know how many people lived under his care, and how many came to communion.[66] He chose to answer in unexpected detail, and presented his list under the following five heads; families of gentlemen, families of yeomen, families of tradesmen, families of labourers and families of poor men. There were 62 households at Goodnestone in that year, and they contained 276 people; the average size of household, therefore, was 4·45, quite a normal figure for pre-industrial England, though below the average. But the average is deceptive. This is how the households went:

Goodnestone-next-Wingham, Kent, April, 1676

Status of households	No.	Mean size of house- hold	Range of sizes	Numbers of persons	Numbers of children	Numbers of servants	Numbers of kin
Gentry	3	9·0	22,3,2	27	7	15	1
Yeomen	26	5·8	12–2	151	64	34	3
Tradesmen	9	3·9	8–1	35	16	2	0
Labourers	12	3·2	6–2	38	15	0	0
Poor Men	12	2·1	6–1	25	11	0	1
Totals	62	4·45	22–1	276	113	51	5

[65] *See page* 277.   [66] *See page* 278.

Approaching two-thirds of the people, 178 out of 276, were
living in the households of the gentry and the yeomen.
Though the tradesmen, the labourers and the poor people
made up 33 of the households, a clear majority, they contained less than one-third of the inhabitants. In this village the
number of children, the number of servants and the number
of kin per household went down it will be seen with social
standing. So did the mean size of household.

As we have already said, variation of size of household
with social status was a universal law of society in the traditional world before the coming of industry. It did not mean
that most people were born of rich parents whose families
or households were accordingly large, in a society where, as
we have seen, social consequence went with size of household.
Quite the reverse, for, in the village community of Goodnestone, no less than 51 persons, men, women and children, were
servants, born in a humbler family, and yet living in another,
more substantial one. This is 18·2 per cent of the whole
population,[67] an offering, so to speak, of the children of the
poor to those above them. But not always an offering to the
ruling minority, to the gentry. In Goodnestone, the three
gentle families had 15 servants between them, certainly a
large number but the yeomanry had more; 14 of the yeomen
households had servants, 34 in number, and even the tradesmen had two, a girl in one household and a youth in another.
More than half of the 33 men and boys and the 18 women
and girls who were servants in this community were serving
the yeomenry, and they were serving them in husbandry, on
the land and in the land-working households, not as personal
menials, not as housemaids or cooks or kitchen helpers. They
had left their parents back at home with their younger
brothers and sisters, or even alone in the cottages. Five of the
12 labourers' families consisted of man and wife alone, their
children gone, or yet to be born: if they had gone, we now
know where they were.

Gentlemen, yeomen, tradesmen, labourers and paupers,
these were the social orders in the community according to the
curate of Goodnestone. But they do not quite conform to the
titles we have laid down in our last chapter; husbandmen are
missing here, included, no doubt, among the yeomen by their
curate. Once more, the vagaries of titles might mislead us, if

[67] *See page* 278.

F

it were not possible to prompt our reading of this revealing document from scores of others like it.[68] This peculiarity might obscure from us just how the inhabitant of Goodnestone would think of his community as a shape, as a society ranged in an order which was used by the priest in charge when he wrote out all the names.

Looking at the parish under his spiritual care, he saw first and foremost the huge family of 22 people living at the manor-house. The head of the household was Edward Hales, Esq., who seems to have been a tenant of the London merchant family of Pennington, owners of the manor of Goodnestone, and, no doubt, of most of the land in the village.[69] In the squire's household there was his wife, six children and fourteen servants, eight men and boys and six women and girls. Also in Goodnestone were two other small households of gentry, whom we may imagine as satellites to the Hales. These brought up the total of people born of gentle blood in this community to 12. Only these individuals out of the 280 in his parish belonged, like the parson himself, to the fully literate minority, the people with some knowledge of the world beyond the parish of Goodnestone and this particular area of the county of Kent. But the land in the parish was not worked by the family of Hales, though the eight men and boys in the manor house must have tilled a good-sized manor farm, with the daily help, when it was required, of some of the twelve labourers living in the village. Most of the land was actually run by a dozen substantial families of yeomen and husbandmen whether or not it belonged to the squire. There were two families called Neame, one with 14 and the other with 7 in the household; three called Wanstall, 8, 8 and 3; William Tucker with 10, Richard Fuller and Stephen Church with 9 apiece, and John Pet with 8. These dozen families contained over a hundred people, a quarter of whom were servants, mostly young men. Squire and the larger yeomanry almost constituted the village community of Goodnestone-next-Wingham in 1676.

Not completely, of course, for over half its members have yet to be considered. There were 14 more families of the smaller yeomen or husbandmen, the nine tradesmen, and a dozen each of labourers and of paupers. There was, in addition, an institution which we have not yet mentioned, a hospital

[68] *See page* 278.   [69] *See page* 278.

for the destitute, with one man and three women in it, bringing total population up to 280. It is not true to say that
nobody apart from gentry and yeomanry counted for anything in the village community, though the pauper families
and the hospitallers can be dismissed as of no positive account
whatsoever. Each of the yeomen, the tradesmen and even the
labourers might have had some public life, as we have already
seen. The male head of a labourer's household could occupy
office in the village, and it is possible that by more than the
usual back-breaking, unremitting toil, some cunning and
intelligence, and above all considerable good fortune in the
wives he married, in the relatives who died, a man of the grade
of husbandman or labourer might, in his lifetime, become a
substantial yeoman. We know that this happened, and we
know that over the generations there was an astonishing
interchange between the names of those peasant households
which were prospering and those which were languishing. In
the one community where we can actually trace the fortunes
of each homestead at six separate points in one decade, the
period between 1618 and 1628, we witness a considerable
change in the size of some of them from year to year.[70]

But at any one time, and for any important purpose which
could have a political effect beyond the little area of the
village, these smaller households can be disregarded. The
tradesmen, it is true, added a little variety to village society;
there were two families of carpenters at Goodnestone, and one
of these had a servant; two of brickmakers; one each headed
by a weaver; a shoemaker; a hempster (probably a tailor), and
a solitary woman calling herself a grocer. She is a little exceptional, but otherwise it is a normal list of occupations for a
rural community, in the old world, if a little short: no smith
of any sort is surprising, and it is to be supposed that the
specialized agricultural callings like shepherd, or thatcher, or
drover, are included here under the *Labourers*, perhaps even
some under *Yeomen*.

There was, evidently, no inn at Goodnestone, and the priest,
a curate, seems to have lived outside the village. This, again,
was quite an ordinary thing, but a resident married parson,
with his wife, children and servants, would have had a substantial effect on the little society there, and so might a prosperous hostelry on a highroad.[71] The most important possible

[70] *See page* 278.   [71] *See page* 278.

difference would have been the absence of the family of Hales: a decision to live temporarily, or permanently, elsewhere would have considerably altered the social balance, as would the death of the head of the family whilst his son was still a minor. But while the estate continued to be a whole, some tenant would occupy the great house, and the man in authority there, along with those at the head of the table in the twelve substantial yeomen households, ran the village. Nearly three hundred people went to make up the body of the community, but by far the most important member was its head, the squire, and a dozen or fifteen other mature, male heads of household provided all the other working parts.

A different opinion is possible on this point. The walls round the squire's park, the keepers who kept the villagers from his game, the separate pews, high box-pews in the eighteenth century, which he and his household occupied in church, also operated to cut him off from the village community. An absentee, or a minor, a politician on the county or the national level, perpetually preoccupied with business more important than the fixing of the parish poor-rate or the upkeep of the river-bridge, could not be looked upon as the leader, the metaphorical father of village society. The literature of the Tudor and Stuart age is full of laments about the decay of housekeeping which meant, amongst so many other things, holding open-house for the tenantry. There are endless exhortations to the gentry to keep away from the city and the court. There must have been some grounds for the conviction that the country gentry were leaving their own people unsupported, without means of access to that greater world in which the gentry alone could freely move. But no choice between two such different opinions can be made for Edward Hales, Esquire, and the village of Goodnestone; the evidence will not yield it.

Social description, in fact, is a difficult and intricate task, often tedious to the reader. It is necessary to talk in terms of one community, for generalized statements lack the stuff of life, yet no community is entirely typical. We may have spent too much time already on our chosen village, and there are communities now open to examination whose working can be reconstructed in far greater detail. But the shape of society at Goodnestone is particularly well-marked, and it is a convenient model for all the rest. Each of the 40 villages in

Kent in 1705 whose listings we have referred to before, seems
to have been constructed, with variations, very much on this
model, and so were villages all over the country.[72]

Shepherdswell, for example, though it had fewer people
than Goodnestone, 160 instead of 280, contained more large
families: one of 15, one of 13 and one of 10. There was a group
of 6 working families, as we have called them, which each had
6 or 7 people, and the average overall was 5 to a household.
At Hugham, the average was even higher, at 5·7, and out of
187 people there was one family of 20, one of 17 and two of 11.
Lest it should be thought that these large households containing so many working servants, land-working servants, were
typical of Kent only, and of the early eighteenth century, they
may be compared with the situation at Ealing in 1599.[73] In
this still rural village the Goodnestone pattern was quite
evident: 404 people in 85 families, an average of 4·75: a
gentleman's family of 21, dominating all the rest, and 20
working families of between 7 and 11 apiece. In another village
which we have got to know well, Clayworth in Nottinghamshire, the landed gentry had smaller establishments, between
7 and 10 apiece.[74] There were four of them in this village of
about 400 people, and some of the yeomen (called 'Freeholders' and 'Farmers' here by the parson who described
them) had families of a similar size. But the working families
at Clayworth can easily be separated from those whose masters
lived without manual exertion, and this distinction is generally
obvious from the first glance at a list of members of a village
community in pre-industrial England.

This sufficiently illustrates the difference in scale in these
communities. In all but one of the whole number of English
villages we have been able to examine there was a number,
often a large number of servants, though the proportion in
service varied for reasons which we think we can now begin to
understand. The percentage could be as low as 4 and as high
as 25, or even more, which begins to rival the rich London or
Norwich parishes of the 1690's where nearly a third of all the
people could be servants.[75] It has recently been shown that
the figures from Goodnestone do seem to be representative
of the whole of England before the coming of industry, not
simply the countryside, but of the towns as well, and even

[72] *See page* 279.   [73] *See page* 279.   [74] *See page* 279.
[75] *See page* 279.

in some respects of the capital itself. In the table below figures for size of household, for mean size of groups of children, mean proportion of households with kin and with servants, are given for one hundred parishes coming from the whole of England between the years 1574 and 1821. In reading the table, however, the column headed N for each household constituent shows the number of parishes out of the whole hundred for which we were able to obtain the information.

One Hundred English parishes 1574–1821; size of household, groups of children, proportion of kin, proportion of servants by social status.

	Size of House- hold		Mean Size of Groups of Children		Mean Proportion of Households with Kin		Mean Proportion of Households with Servants	
	N	Mean Size	N	Mean size	N	(Means of proportions)	N	(Means of proportions)
Gentlemen	26	6·63	26	2·94	16	27·6%	18	81·1%
Clergy	25	5·83	12	3·53	12	25·0%	16	81·2%
Yeomen	21	5·91	17	2·76	9	17·0%	14	71·9%
Husbandmen	35	5·09	33	3·10	14	17·3%	21	46·8%
Tradesmen and Craftsmen	40	4·65	42	2·90	18	12·3%	25	23·3%
Labourers	33	4·51	32	2·70	16	7·9%	21	2·2%
Paupers	16	3·96	13	2·34	6	7·7%	26 ⎫	
Others	39	3·72	37 ⎫ 2·31		18	15·0%	⎬ 13·9%	
Not stated	19	4·29	⎭				26 ⎭	

It will be seen that there was one difference between Goodnestone and the villages making up this sample of one hundred, which is in the mean size of groups of children. This goes down with social status at Goodnestone, but not so regularly at the other places. Nevertheless, the association of few children with modest position and resources is almost as marked a feature of social structure in the traditional world as the association of smaller families generally with the poor. It was not simply a matter of the poor offering up their children to the rich as servants; they probably also had fewer children born to them, and of those which were born, fewer survived. It is likely that works on the expectation of life and size of the biological family will confirm what early impressions seem to show, which is that poor men and their wives could not expect to live together long enough to have as many offspring as the rich. This loss of potential labour-power was a matter of consequence, for it always must be remembered that the actual work on most of the plots of land was done by the working family, the man, his wife and children.

At harvest-time, of course, there was a difference: the individual farming family could no longer cope with the work. From the making of the hay in June until the winning of the corn and pease in late September, every able-bodied person in the village community was at work on everyone's land. How much co-operation there was is difficult to say, but when the crisis of the agricultural year came round, right up to the time of mechanized farming, the village acted as a community. When all was in, there was harvest home.

It is usual, in most places, after they get all the pease pulled or the last grain down, to invite all the workfolks and their wives (that helped them that harvest) to supper, and then they have puddings, bacon, or boiled beef, flesh or apple pies, and then cream brought in platters, and every one a spoon; then after all they have hot cakes and ale; for they bake cakes and send for ale against that time: some will cut their cake and put it into the cream, and this feast is called cream-pot, or cream-kit; for on the morning that they get all done the workfolks will ask their dames if they have good store of cream and say they must have the cream-kit anon.[76]

This was the Yorkshire custom in the 1640's when it was necessary, at harvest-time, to go even beyond the carpenters, the wheelwrights and the millers, in order to bring in the sheaves off the fields. The richer men had to make a home in the barns during harvest for folk, pastoral in their ways, who came down from the wild moorland. Migration of labour at harvest was common enough in the eighteenth century, but eating and drinking together was a universal characteristic of rural life at all times. Whatever the churchwardens or the overseers of the poor did, when the church-bell was rung in celebration, or the churchyard mowed, there was an entry in the ill-written accounts for ale drunk on the occasion.[77] The meticulous, unpopular Rector of Clayworth in the last

[76] *See page* 279.   [77] *See page* 279.

quarter of the seventeenth century, entertained the *husbandry* of the two settlements in his parish separately to dinner every year.

When the curate of Goodnestone returned the names of all his parishioners in April, 1676, 'according to their families, according to their quality and according to their religion', he did as he was bid and told his lordship, the bishop, how many of them had been to holy communion that Eastertide. With only sixteen exceptions every person in the community known by their priest to be qualified for the sacrament had actually taken it at some time during the festival, which fell in that year between March 19th and 26th: 128 people communicated that is to say, out of a population of 281. Even the defaulters had promised to make amends at Whitsuntide, all but the one family in the village which was nonconformist. But William Wanstall, senior, one of the absentees, was given no such grace; he had been 'excluded the Holy Sacrament for his notorious drunkenness, but since hath promised reformation'. Francis Nicholson, the priest-in-charge, was evidently a devoted pastor, for he could give an account of every one of the absentees. Mrs Elizabeth Richards, the widowed head of one of the households of gentry, was excused as 'melancholy', and Barbara Pain since she was 'under a dismal calamity, the unnatural death of her husband', who had left her at the head of a yeoman family, three children and two servants.[78]

This rather exceptional record of communicants draws attention to a feature of the village community and of the whole of the world we have now half-forgotten which has scarcely been mentioned so far. All our ancestors were literal Christian believers, all of the time. Not only zealous priests, such as Francis Nicholson, not only serious-minded laymen, but also the intellectuals and the publicly responsible looked on the Christian religion as the explanation of life, and on religious service as its proper end. Not everyone was equally devout, of course, and it would be simple-minded to suppose that none of these villagers ever had their doubts. Much of their devotion must have been formal, and some of it mere conformity. But their world was a Christian world and their religious activity was spontaneous, not forced on them from above. When Francis Nicholson refused the cup to William Wanstall, in March, 1676, the scores of other people in the church that

[78] *See page* 279.

morning no doubt approved of what he did, as no doubt
Wanstall deserved this very public rebuke. When William
Sampson, the formidable Rector of Clayworth, did exactly the
same thing in April, 1679, to Ralph Meers and Anne Fenton
'upon a common fame that they lived and lodged together,
not being married', he also had the community behind him.
He knew what he was doing too, for Anne Fenton's first baby
was christened two months' later, only a week or two, presumably, after she had married Ralph Meers.[79]

It has been shown only very recently how it came about that
the mass of the English people lost their Christian belief, and
how religion came to be a middle-class matter. When the
arrival of industry created huge societies of persons in the
towns with an entirely different outlook from these Stuart
villagers, practically no one went to church, not if he was
working class and was left untouched by religious emotion.[80]
Christianity was no longer in the social air which everyone
breathed together, rich and poor, gentleman, husbandman,
artificer, labourer and pauper. So much has been written
about the abuses of the clergy in earlier times, so much about
the controversies and doubts, about the revivals, especially
the Wesleyan revival, that the religious attitude of common
folk has been lost sight of. Perhaps the twelve labourers who
lived at Goodnestone in 1676 did not know very clearly what
Our Lord's Supper meant, and the thought of being reported
to the church court by the churchwardens may have influenced
them, but every single one of them took communion. Their
descendants in the slums of London in the 1830's, '40's and
'50's did not do so: they already looked on Christianity as
belonging to the rural world which they had lost. It was something for their employers, something for the respectable,
which, perhaps, they might go in for if ever they attained
respectability and comfort. This was not true of the hard-
working, needy, half-starved labourers of pre-industrial times.

At Clayworth, at that same Eastertide of 1676, an even
greater proportion of the villages took the sacrament than at
Goodnestone, 200 out of 401. How powerful the effect of even
formal Christianity could be is shown by an anecdote which
Sampson records of a servant-boy there whose mother died.
The meagre wages of servants, some fifty shillings a year for a
skilled woman and five pounds for a grown man, were subject

[79] *See page* 279.   [80] *See page* 279.

to tithe in this village, and the Rector was in combat with masters, maids and men for the money. This poor lad let his side down by coming and paying 'fully for his wages at one farthing i' the shilling. The occasion of his mother's death brought him to an honest mind.' But later in his ministry, Sampson found that the number of communicants went down to about 125, though the population did not seem to fall. This is about the same proportion as at Cogenhoe, in 1612, when the Rector there recorded 63 'Communicants upon Easter Day', just over half the qualified adults.[81] In judging the numbers we have quoted, it is proper to remember that until 1690, after which religious dissent could be pleaded, the law of church and state made attendance at service and at communion compulsory for everyone. But ecclesiastical punishments were not formidable, and it is known that in many places numbers were much lower, even before the 1690's.

Perhaps it is more than usually dangerous to judge of religious life from the few scattered records of this sort which have so far been found and examined. Perhaps it may turn out in the end that Christianity was ceasing to be the most important activity of all communities of men and women before ever industrialization transformed the social scene. It must not be forgotten that Christianity did have rivals of sorts, particularly amongst the common people, who would sometimes consult sorcerers and witches, who still believed in fairies and in other pagan, pre-Christian rites and practices. Nevertheless once men began to differ over religion, the life of the community was affected, and the whole history of the seventeenth century, local and national, was perpetually vexed by the quarrel between the puritan and the traditionalist, just as Tudor England had been disturbed by the Reformation itself. But the separatists were Christians too. The intensity of their convictions and the fierceness of their protest testify to the secure hold which Christianity had over everyone. The failure of the Puritan Commonwealth in England is too easily interpreted as a weakening of Christian beliefs. After all, the Puritan policy succeeded in New England, where far fewer of the settlers have turned out to be Puritans than was once supposed.

Every meeting of the village community took place in the Church, if there was a church or chapel close enough. At

[81] *See page* 280.

Clayworth every Easter Monday, the village community met there and chose the three churchwardens, two for the *town*, that is Clayworth itself, and one for Wiseton, the separate hamlet within the parish; we have seen that many, perhaps most, parishes were geographically divided like this. Two overseers of the poor were chosen for Clayworth as well as two 'burrough men', who might elsewhere be constables, but here they had agricultural duties too. Only male heads of households were eligible to serve, but gentlemen, freeholders (or yeomen), husbandmen and labourers are all found recorded as selected for each office in the Clayworth Town Book.[82]

This function of the church building as a meeting place for all the purposes of the community, must be stressed. Here they were, these farming householders, not all of whom could read, sitting in the building put up by their fore-runners many centuries before, and which they, in their turn, annually repaired and even beautified. In the place where they came so often to Christian service they chose their neighbours for the traditional offices, secular and spiritual. When English villagers found themselves in America, one of the first buildings which they put up for the new village was the *Meeting House*, for the town meeting had a great deal to decide in starting all anew. The *Meeting House* was also, of course, the Christian church of the village being born.[83]

The only public appearance of women and children, almost their only expedition outside the circle of the family, was at service in Church. Wives and maidservants might take and sell their poultry and their eggs to market, or even their apples and cherries, but otherwise they stayed at home. It has already been emphasized that ordinary people did not usually find themselves in a group inside a building, larger than the household, except in church. For the menfolk, especially for the substantial ones, there were the occasional meetings of the manor-courts, which still controlled agriculture over most of the countryside. In some places, these meetings were perhaps as important as the Easter Monday gathering in the Saxon-towered church of Saint Peter at Clayworth every year. For the men, too, there were the alehouses, much too famous in popular history as the poor man's parliament. The single village inn seems in fact to have been rare; most drinking was done in the cottages of people having permission from the

[82] *See page* 280.   [83] *See page* 281.

magistrates to keep an alehouse, on the strict understanding that there was to be no tippling and that no liquor was to change hands during time of divine service.[84] The alewife, for it was often a widow brewing for sale what most women had to brew for their own households, did not even have to have a painted sign, in that age when a sign was all that an illiterate could recognize. All she had to do was to hang a bush outside her door.

But the renowned English inn was not the creation of Samuel Johnson and Charles Dickens. Outside London it was the hostelry for travellers, placed on the important roads and common in a country where travel was so painfully slow, but not intended first and foremost for the local people. It could be a large and important institution, on the scale of life which was then the rule, and have an effect on the locality. An ale house at Harefield in Middlesex in 1699 – it was one of four in this village and not granted the title of inn by the man who made the list of the community – was kept by John and Catherine Baily, and they had in their house the largest family of grown and growing children we have yet traced in pre-industrial England. They had twelve children alive, aged from two to twenty-eight; the two eldest had left home, but of the ten who were left, six were above the age of twelve, all old enough to help run the family establishment, with their aunt, Catherine Baily's sister, who lived there as well. No need of any servants for John Bailey, who was also a smith. Meanwhile his potential rival, the New Inn at Harefield, was marked 'Empty not finisht'.[85]

There was plenty of drinking done in the village community, and not all of it in celebration of some activity or meeting. Men like Goodman William Wanstall, the excommunicated drunkard of Goodnestone, are met with fairly often. (*Goodman* was used of a substantial householder who was not a *Mr* and *Goodwife*, or *Goody* for his partner or his widow.) There is a famous legend from Malmesbury, in Wiltshire, of Sir Thomas Hobbes the curate of St Mary's about the time of the Spanish Armada and father of Thomas Hobbes, the great philosopher. (*Sir*, as Shakespeare used it, could mean a clergyman as well as a knight.) 'Trafells is Troumps', he is supposed to have bawled out to his congregation one Sunday morning, starting suddenly from his slumber in the pulpit, after all Saturday

[84] *See page* 281.   [85] *See page* 281.

night playing cards with the citizens of that little market-town. Trafells was a word for clubs. Whether this happened or not,[86] it would be wrong to think of the alehouse at this time as playing the part which it came to play for working men in early industrial towns, where it was to be the only meeting place at their disposal, and almost the only social institution. In Francis Place's world the public house was in place of the church as well as the alehouse in the pre-industrial village.

In 1688 parson Sampson made a second list of all the inhabitants of the village of Clayworth, twelve years after the one which like the curate of Goodnestone, he had drawn up for the ecclesiastical census of 1676. This time he wrote it out, not alphabetically, *ad evitandam invidiam* – to avoid envy – as he did the first, but in order of social importance like most of the other listings we have found. The gentleman's family had returned into residence after a minority and Sampson could boldly begin: 'Mr Thomas Wawen, Lord of the Soil.' So the young gentleman was, in spite of the fact that nothing like half of the land at Clayworth belonged to him.[87] His over-lordship consisted in the traditional position of the lord of the manor, and in the power which he had over the tenants of the land he did own.

Like every other landlord, Thomas Wawen was to some degree bound by manorial custom which had the force of local law, and general custom too. These might tie his hands as to the length and conditions of his leases, even the amount of his rents. Custom, what his neighbours, the village generally, thought, as well as universal expectation, would inevitably influence him in making the many other decisions open to him. He had to decide, to begin with, how much of his land he would keep under his own hand, as the saying was, and work from his house with his servants. Then he had to determine how much he would rely on those servants, or how much work he would get done by labourers coming in from the village and working their day's work on his land. Another decision to be made was whether he would feed such day-labourers during their working-time or pay them extra so that they could bring their own food. If he had to *table* them, then his housekeeping would have to be on a scale to correspond with his obligations. The only way for him to avoid having his

[86] *See page* 281.   [87] *See page* 281.

workers in his house altogether would be either to let all his
land and buy his provisions, a possible but not very easy
prospect, or to make arrangements for one or other of the local
husbandmen, workers of the land, to come and undertake all
the operations on his home farm.[88]

A landlord who lived away from the community in another
of his houses, or one who lived in London in hired accom-
modation and took no responsibility for running any of his
land, would of course tend to let as much of his estate as he
could. His bailiff or his tenant would, no doubt, also get as
much of the work done as possible by putting it out 'to task'.
The economically-minded amongst the owners of land, moreover, might reckon precisely how much more profitable it
would be to make one choice or another amongst those we
have listed. But the social duty of every 'Lord of the Soil' was
made quite plain to him: he was expected to reside in his
manor-house or at least in one of those he owned. He, or his
resident tenant, was also firmly expected to work as much of
the home-farmland as possible, maintain a household-full of
servants and keep up a table for the day-labourers. It was not
by any means a matter of custom alone. Raising crops and
tending stock go on in the night as well as the day, and this
gave the household servant system a permanent advantage.
Before the coming of the bicycle and the paved highway,
there was a fixed distance from the labourer's cottage beyond
which a full day's work was out of the question – it took too
long to get there and back. These were some of the conditions
which made it impossible for the landowner to act as entrepreneur in the modern fashion, to run their land as our farmers
do, using daytime labour alone, hired from outside the house,
on the model of the business or the factory.

Even in the twentieth century the limits to economic
rationalism in farming are still in evidence, in the socialist as
well as in the capitalist areas of the world. But three hundred
years ago, this issue could scarcely arise. Working the land,
managing, nurturing a 'family' were then one and the same
thing, and could no more be 'rationalized' than the cherishing
of a wife or the bringing up of children. Even the nobleman
with several seats in the countryside, and with a strong pre-
ference for living in his London house on his rents, recognized
this sometimes irksome fact. Hence the feeling about the

[88] *See page* 281.

'country' in opposition to the 'Town', and hence a great deal
of aristocratic guilt and ambivalence. Hence, also, the plots of
many of our English dramas, of the Elizabethan age, or of the
time of the Restoration: and many of the emotional assumptions and overtones of our literature. 'I wish you were married
and living in the country,' said Lord Rochester, the rake, to
the cur which had bitten him. Even he could find no worse
an imprecation.[89] Smaller men, right down to the humblest
husbandman, or the labourer on his cottage patch, had no
occasion to see any separation whatsoever between keeping
house and working the soil.

The village community was, as we have said, the group of
households at the centre of a particular area of cultivated
land. It might or might not be a manor, have its own church,
or have one owner. If it did have a single owner, he might
work it all himself, with one large household,[90] or, at least, as
one estate. More probably, he let it out, either in large parcels,
or in some large lots and some small (presumably the most
usual), or all in small holdings. Apart from the large landowner or landowners, a village might, and usually did, contain
a mixture of freeholders and tenants, again some in a big and
some in a small way. There would also be a number of families,
often a sizeable minority, with only a scrap of land round
a cottage, or no land at all. The accepted view seems to be
that these were on the increase as the eighteenth century
drew near, but the demonstration of this for the whole country
would be a very difficult undertaking. These were the families
not only of the labourers and the paupers, but of most of
the craftsmen as well, the masons and the ploughwrights, the
weavers, the tailors, the cobblers, the carpenters and the
rest.

But whatever the official description and the distribution of
property and the numbers of the callings represented in it, as a
community the village consisted of households in association.
To the facts of geography, being together in the one place,
were added all the bonds which are forged between human
beings when they are permanently alongside each other; bonds
of intermarriage and of kinship, of common ancestry and
common experience and of friendship and co-operation in
matters of common concern. Consequence within the community went with weight of responsibility and with wealth;

[89] *See page* 282.   [90] *See page* 282.

its expression was the size of the agrarian household which a
man had to keep in operation.

The difficulties of talking about typicality have already been
mentioned, and what follows must be read with that in mind.
Most of the yeomen, husbandmen, labourers, artificers and
paupers, from whom we nearly all descend, lived in the village
community which we have attempted to describe. They grew
up in a society of 300, 400 or 500 strong, perhaps more often
in a hamlet separated from other hamlets which made up the
parish, than in a village which was one group of houses side by
side. From their earliest years, they must have been conscious
of the standing of the family into which they were born, within
a group of other families, sometimes ten, sometimes twenty,
more often thirty, forty or fifty altogether. If they came from
the lower families, within a dozen years of birth they might
find themselves as servants in the larger families. If they
grew up in more prosperous and important households, they
would always be conscious that there were other people round
them who were not their brothers and sisters, servants who
were not often blood relatives at all. Only a small number in
the middle can have been outside this interchange of persons as
servants. This was the motion up and down which gave verti-
cal structure to the whole. It demonstrates how the village
community was a patriarchal matter, even if it cannot itself
have been a family.

There are complications which go beyond the present purpose and uncertainties which are inevitable in social descriptions in this attempt to analyse the village community. It
may be thought surprising that no very clear distinction for
sociological purposes can be drawn along the jurisdictional
lines which our ancestors themselves laid down and insisted
upon. The truth is that for our purpose a group of households
did not have to be a parish, or a manor, to be a unit, and the
complications of definition do not finally matter when we try
to make an imaginative judgement of the social experience of
individuals. The fact, to which we shall come in due course,[91]
that so much geographical movement went on between village
communities, makes very little difference either. To be a social
unit conscious of itself, and removed, distinct from others, it
was not necessary for the village community to be cut off from
interchange with its companions. On the contrary; it was in

[91] *See page* 282.

perpetual negotiation with its neighbours, and this was an essential feature of its individuality. But each village community, we have claimed, played a part in the whole national community of the country only through the gentry. We have also stated that no group inside a village could possibly have threatened the supremacy of its ruling structure. These are questions to which we shall have to return.

Births, Marriages and Deaths
Chapter 4

Misbeliefs about child brides and extended family households amongst our ancestors

---

> *My child is yet a stranger in the world*
> *She hath not seen the change of fourteen years*
> *Let two more summers wither in their pride*
> *Ere we may think her ripe to be a bride.*

Capulet says this in the second scene of Romeo and Juliet. But whatever he said and whatever he felt, his child Juliet did take Romeo to husband at about her fourteenth birthday. Juliet's mother left her in no doubt of her opinion.

> *Well, think of marriage now; younger than you,*
> *Here in Verona, ladies of esteem,*
> *Are made already mothers. By my count*
> *I was your mother much upon these years*
> *That you are now a maid.*

So she had been married at twelve, or early thirteen, and all those other ladies of Verona also. Miranda was married in her fifteenth year in the *Tempest*. It all seems clear and consistent enough. The women in Shakespeare's plays, and so presumably the Englishwomen of Shakespeare's day, might marry in their early teens, or even before, and very often did.[92]

Yet this is not true. We have examined every record we can find to test it and they all declare that, in Elizabethan and Jacobean England, marriage was rare at these early ages and not as common in the late teens as it is now. At twelve marriage as we understand it was virtually unknown.

Some of the evidence for these blank statements will have to be presented here and we shall have to discuss what constituted marriage, leaving *espousals* to a later chapter. An espousal was a promise which became marriage as we understand it if sexual intercourse took place. People could marry by licence as well as by banns in England then, just as

[92] *See page* 283.

they still can in the Church of England today. They had
to apply for the licence to the bishop of the diocese they
lived in, and very often they were required to give their
ages; the reason was that no one under 21 could married by
the Church without his parents' permission: it was a
grave sin to do so at an older age without good reason.
We have examined a thousand licences containing the ages of
the applicants, issued by the diocese of Canterbury between
1619 and 1660 to people marrying for the first time.[93] One
woman gave her age as 13, four as 15, twelve as 16: all the rest
were 17 and over, and 966 of the women got married for the
first time after the age of 19, that is nearly 85 per cent. The
commonest age of first marriage for women in this sample was
22, and the median age – the age below which as many got
married as got married above it – was about $22\frac{3}{4}$: the average,
mean age was about 24. Bridegrooms were something like
three years older than brides, though some of the unions
recorded show an extraordinary discrepancy in age. Only ten
men married below the age of 20, two of them at 18, and the
most common age was 24; the median age was something like
$25\frac{1}{2}$ and the mean age over $26\frac{3}{4}$.

Put in the familiar form we use in conversation, the average
age of these Elizabethan and Jacobean brides was something
like 24 and the average of bridegrooms was nearly 28. Surely
these figures by themselves ought to be sufficient to dispel
belief that our ancestors married much younger than we do.

But the literary references are so straightforward, and
Shakespeare at least so influential that we must go further:
there seems to be some desire in our day to believe in this
particular mistake. Did the gentry marry early? – after all
Romeo and Juliet were not ordinary people.

It is more difficult to answer this question, because the
numbers are so small. The table on page 86 summarizes results
of the analysis already referred to, and it will be seen that
gentle brides were younger than the others in this area in the
middle years of the seventeenth century, but bridegrooms of
much the same age as the rest of the population. When the
first marriages of peers are added, this contrast is made a little
sharper, but it cannot be said to be very impressive, and
further research has not confirmed these early results. Later
in the century gentry seem to have been a little older at first
marriage than craftsmen, and the age at marriage of peers

[93] *See page* 284.

went up. No class of the population as far as we can see seems to have married at anything like the ages suggested by Shakespeare's plays.

Mean age at first marriage

	Mean age of Bridegrooms	Mean age of Brides
All applicants for licences, Diocese of Canterbury, 1619–60	26·65	23·58
(1,007 bridegrooms, 1,007 brides) Standard deviation	4·61	4·12
Gentry only amongst Canterbury applicants	26·18	21·75
(118 bridegrooms, 118 brides) Standard deviation	4·41	3·60
Marriages of nobles,* from about 1600 to about 1625 (325 brides, 313 bridegrooms)	19·39	24·28
Marriages of nobles,* from about 1625 to about 1650 (510 brides, 403 bridegrooms)	20·67	25·99

* Kindly communicated by Mr T. H. Hollingsworth, of the University of Glasgow.[94]

There are substantial differences in this table and the more detailed figures bear them out although they must not be exaggerated. The slightly lower age at marriage for gentlemen is statistically significant and the larger margin for gentlewomen more decidedly so. More notable is the contrast in age gaps between partners, a mean of 3·06 for ordinary folk but 3·97 for gentry, and it seems quite certain in statistical terms that this cannot be due to chance. The details show that twice as many well-born girls married before twenty than in the rest of the sample.

The mean age at marriage, all marriages, in our day is 28 or 29 for men and 25 or 26 for women. Better evidence will be available very soon for traditional England, but when everything now known is added to that presented here the conclusion is inescapable. It is not true to say that in earlier times, in the world we have lost as we have called it, people, either ordinary or privileged, married much younger than we marry now. In fact they were very much older in relation to their expectation of life.

[94] *See page* 285.

Juliet's mother's statement is a little extraordinary in quite another way. It is believed by the experts that the age of sexual maturity in women has fallen surprisingly during the last two or three generations in Western countries, and is falling now, perhaps even more rapidly. In Sweden in 1905 girls began to menstruate at 15·7 years, by 1949 the age had fallen to 14·1. In the United States the age of menarche as it is called was already as low as 14·1 years in 1904, but in 1951 it was 12·9. In Norway, which has the longest record yet published, it was 17·1 in 1850 and 13·5 in 1951, and the age in England in the later year was just about the same.[95] If Lady Capulet and her daughter were sexually mature and capable of having children at an earlier age four hundred years ago than women are today in most countries, then they must have been very exceptional indeed. And if what is known of the age of menarche in Norway in 1850, is any indication of what it was in Elizabethan England, it is impossible that the general age of marriage can have been anything like as low as twelve or thirteen. The elementary facts of life were against it.

It should not be long before we have very much better factual foundation for statements of this sort, which may seem a little odd as an approach to the everyday life of our ancestors, but which do concern their habitual behaviour and the whole course of their lives. Before this point is pursued, there is even more to be said about Romeo and Juliet and the facts about sexuality which are at issue in that drama.

First of all there is the possibility that Shakespeare was deliberately writing a play about love and marriage amongst boys and girls. Scholars have discovered that he actually reduced Juliet's age; in the poem containing the plot for the play, Arthur Broke's *Romeus and Juliet*, published in 1562, Juliet was sixteen. Four years later another author who told the story, William Painter in his collection of novels *The Palace of Pleasure*, made Juliet eighteen years old. When Shakespeare came to adapt it thirty years afterwards he may possibly have had to reduce the heroine's age to suit the boy-actor who was to play her part, but some of his other heroines seem to be mature enough, Viola in *Twelfth Night* for example. The insistence on Juliet's being a young girl looks quite deliberate.

Now it is possible that Shakespeare's heroines were as young

[95] *See page* 285.

as he portrayed them in the Italian society from which his stories so often come. It is now known that in Tuscany at about the time when the action of *Romeo and Juliet* is supposed to have taken place, the girls could have been as young as fourteen at marriage, though the men would more likely have been nearer thirty, and there are passages in the English drama which suggest that marriage for women in their middle teens was a familiar fact. In Henry Porter's comedy *Two Angry Women of Abington*, 1599, the heroine, Mall, is speaking at the age of fourteen:

> *Good Lord, thought I, fifteen will ne'er be here,*
> *For I have heard my mother say that then*
> *Pretty maids were fit for handsome men.*
> *Fifteen past, sixteen and seventeen too,*
> *What, thought I, will not this husband do?*
> *Will no man marry me?*

Mall certainly seems to have been nubile well before her wedding-day: the hint of uncertainty as to the age when a girl would be physically fit for marriage must be noticed. Another character in the drama of that decade makes a rather different complaint: 'They study twenty years together to make us grow straight as a wand, and then marry us off to men we do not like' (Lyly, *Mother Bombie*, 1594). Shakespeare himself gives us further examples of child marriage: Marina in *Pericles* is fourteen years old when she is taken to the brothel, rescued and betrothed to Lysimachus, and Perdita in the *Winter's Tale* is sixteen.[96]

It is true that children did marry in Tudor England, though under exceptional circumstances, and the marriage was of a kind we should scarcely recognize. One quite explicit case has been recorded from even earlier years, where a noblewoman 'married' at a time of life when she could not have been capable of sexual intercourse. Margaret, Lady Rowecliffe, first had a husband in 1463 at the age of four, but had lost him by the age of twelve, when she was given another one. The bridegroom's father then undertook that 'they should not ligg togeder til she came to the age XVI years', which is the plainest indication I have seen of the time at which a woman of late medieval times could be expected to be sexually mature. Both these early marriages should properly be called

[96] *See page* 286.

espousals de futuro, the meaning of which will have to concern us. Life was uncertain amongst commoners as well as amongst aristocrats. The head of the household at any one time had to be so much concerned with the succession, that the marriage partner to be taken by the heir apparent was always a matter of the first importance where there was an estate and name to be safeguarded.

In 1593, Robert Furse, of Moreshead in Devonshire, a substantial yeoman on his way up in the world and engaged like every other yeoman of ability in building up his family, matched his son at the age of nine years and three months to Susan Alford, an orphan and the ward of a kinsman: the marriage was to take place at the age of fifteen. In this instance either death intervened or one or other of the children exercised the undoubted right not to carry out the bargain made for them by their parents and guardians, for no marriage took place. This was obviously a fairly usual arrangement, and the postponement of the actual union must be noted.[97]

The records of the diocesan courts, which deal with disputes over marriage, contain numbers of cases of affianced minors, some of whom did actually live together and were expected to have done so. Frederick Furnivall, that marvellous Victorian literary antiquarian, published in 1897 for his Early English Text Society a volume with the title *Child Marriages, Divorces and Ratifications, etc.*, which may itself have done much to foster the tradition that the marriage of children was an ordinary occurrence in Tudor times. In the single Diocese of Chester between the years 1561 and 1566 he found documents concerning about thirty couples married young, some of them at a very early age indeed; there were matches between babes-in-arms, matches between teen-agers, matches between children entirely unwilling to live with each other. One poor lad of eleven or twelve, according to the testimony of his bride of thirteen or fourteen, was brought to bed with her weeping to go home with his father, 'and there lay still till in the morning . . . with his back towards her all night'. 'He never touched her bare skin,' so he himself affirmed.

We could scarcely expect the exuberant Furnivall to put these intriguing facts into any sort of numerical proportion. If we do it for him we can estimate that well over 10,000

[97] *See page* 286.

weddings must in fact have taken place in the diocese of Chester during the six years in question. These wretched children cannot, therefore, have made up one-half of one per cent of all persons marrying in that area in that period. In nearly all the documents which Furnivall prints it is made plain that the settlement of property was at issue. None of the married children mentioned lived together until late in their teens, and it is hinted that some were not fit to do so even then.

Child-marriages of this kind may well have been commoner in the sixteenth century than in the seventeenth. But whatever their nature and purpose they cannot be called representative of the marriages of the great majority who had no land, no houses and no property worth assuring in this peculiar fashion. The possibility still remains that it was part of Shakespeare's dramatic intention to make Romeo and Juliet, and perhaps some of his other heroes and heroines too, younger than was usual in his day. If anything, legal and biographical evidence of the kind presented by Furnivall tends to give substance to the claim that literary evidence may be systematically deceptive in these matters. Certainly some of the witnesses to the Chester cases remarked in surprise and disapproval of the youth of the parties concerned; they knew they were talking of extraordinary people. The Elizabethan writers certainly give no hint that this was what they were doing. But then poets, dramatists and novelists are seldom commenting on ordinary people. Even when the effect they strive for is precisely this, they often succeed in making heroes and heroines completely out of the ordinary.

It is true, and very important to the social historian, that the spontaneous assumptions in the literature of any age, the behaviour of the minor characters, the conventions against which irony and humour must be understood, reveal with great precision facts of considerable interest about the structure of society. We shall find ourselves arguing in something like this way from time to time in this essay. But it is indeed hazardous to infer an institution or a habit characteristic of a whole society or a whole era from the central character of a literary work and its story, from *Pamela*, for example, or from Elizabeth Bennett in *Pride and Prejudice* just as much as from Juliet or Viola. The outcome may be to make people believe that what was the entirely exceptional, was in fact the perfectly normal. This is what seems to have happened with the Capulet ladies and the Elizabethan age of marriage. It is easy to see how a very similar distortion might come about if some future historian used *Lolita* or *West Side Story* as a source book for our own sexual habits, uncorrected by other evidence, unliterary and statistical.

This is a cogent argument in favour of statistical awareness, and of the sociological imagination, in studies of this sort. Conventional historical or literary inference is not enough. Statistical awareness provides the point for a further reflection on Lady Capulet, and her daughter. It is, in fact, just possible that the 'Old Lady', as some of her speech headings called her, could have been physiologically mature enough to conceive the young one in her thirteenth or her fourteenth year. But it could have happened, so it may turn out, only because of her privileged circumstances and particular physique.

Elizabeth Manners married the second Earl of Exeter in 1589 at thirteen years old, a month or so either way; she had a child at about fourteen years five months.* Lady Capulet and her companions amongst the matrons of Verona could have been just like this young English noblewoman of Shakespeare's own day – though a little more precocious even than she. Moreover none of the figures which have been mentioned must be thought of as precise indications of the one age only at which women reached maturity. They are all *median* ages, the middle point about which *actual* ages range themselves.

The particular physique of individuals, and also probably their general level of health and nutrition, would decide whether the age of maturity fell below or above the median. The figure of 17·1 for a sample of Norwegian girls in 1850 does not mean that sexual maturity amongst them never arrived at 15, 14, or even 13 or 12. It only states that it arrived as many times before 17·1 years as it arrived after that age. Juliet then could conceivably have been capable of bearing children even though the median age of the menarche for girls of that age generally was in her day four or five years later than the age she had reached when she met Romeo. But it also means, of course, that a considerable proportion of her contemporaries, particularly the girls in humble families,

* *I owe this entirely to the researches of Mr Hollingsworth and it is reproduced with his permission.*

would have had to wait until the age of 18, 19 or even 20 before the arrival of maturity.

All this may seem to be an unnecessary complication of the task of the sociological historian at this early stage in his studies, and to have very little to do with an introductory essay of this type. But everything we can get to know about differences between the privileged people and the rest in pre-industrial times is of significance, and perhaps especially in this matter, for the following reason. The fall in the age of the menarche in the twentieth century is a puzzle to the physiologists, and is susceptible of more than one explanation, or may be due to a combination of more than one set of circumstances. The better feeding and superior living conditions generally of our own day look as if they must have something to do with the fact that adult height has been increasing by a centimetre a decade all over Western Europe since 1850. Certainly there must be some connection between nurture and physical achievement in order to explain why there was a difference of three and a half inches in height and eleven and a half pounds in weight between the boys from the poorest and the boys from the best-off working-class homes in the city of York in 1899.[98] When these considerations are taken back into pre-industrial society, the implications are clear. Only the privileged few fed as well, or lived as comfortably, in earlier times as we all do now, though the health of even the best provided for was exceedingly precarious even then. It begins to look, therefore, as if only people like Lady Capulet and her daughter could ordinarily hope to be mature enough to marry, or to have children anyway, at thirteen or fourteen.

Now if this was true of all privileged people in the world we have lost, of all members of the ruling stratum as we have called it, in relation to the rest, and of the gentry as a society in relation to those below them in the scale, then it implies a very remarkable contrast between the two sections of the population. The privileged were no doubt taller, heavier and better developed than the rest just as they were in Victorian times. But in the Elizabethan age, and in pre-industrial times generally, gentlemen may have had beards and broken voices earlier than the rest of the population, and ladies may have become full women more quickly.

In spite of the great uncertainty of the evidence, we have

[98] *See page* 287.

spelt out syllable by syllable the analysis of this particular element of the effect upon us today of our dim, half-knowledge of the past of our society in order to provide one example of the type of evidence used throughout this study. It must be obvious how little progress has yet been made in exploiting that evidence and how much more can and will be known as time goes on. At present there is a perpetual challenge to the imagination to find illuminating questions to ask of the evidence and ways of answering them properly.

The delusion about marriageable age is, perhaps, the most conspicuous of all the errors we seem to want to make about everyday life in the old world, but is not the only one. More far reaching in its consequences for the view we take of ourselves, and the plans we make for our society and its welfare, is the supposition which has already been extensively discussed, that the family group in the pre-industrial world was large. It is erroneously believed that it was large because it contained whole groups of kinsfolk living together. The impression seems to be that sons and daughters stayed with their parents after marriage and had their children there: therefore the family group must often have been multi-generational. What after all does patriarch mean if not the ancient, bearded head of such a family group? It is assumed that when a woman's husband died she returned to her original family group and was supported by it. A widowed mother might live with her married daughter, or a family would support various in-laws. It is also said that there would also be extended households of another type, because two married couples would often find it more convenient to share one establishment, just as perhaps they shared one plot of land. In any case, and this seems to be the most deep-seated and important generalization of all, in the familial, patriarchal world the family was the source of welfare. Sickness, unemployment, bereavement were all the responsibility of the family, and so to a large extent was education. To fulfil all these functions the family in the old world would have had to be large. Something like this seems to be the general impression of family life among our ancestors.

But their families were *not* large; at least the average family was relatively small. In fact the evidence we now have suggests that household size was remarkably constant in England at 4·75 persons per household at all times from the late sixteenth until the early twentieth century. The general rule which governed the size and the constitution of the family has yet to be laid down.

This rule is as follows: no two married couples or more went to make up a family group; whether parents and children, brothers and sisters, employers and servants or married couples associated only for convenience.[99] When a son got married he left the family of his parents and started a family of his own. If he was not in a position to do this, then he could not get married, nor could his sister unless the man who was to take her for his bride was also in a position to start a new family.

But it has been insisted that marriage was an act of profound importance to the social structure. It meant the creation of a new economic unit as well as a life-long association of persons previously separate and caught-up in existing families. It gave the man full membership of the community, and added a cell to village society. It is understandable, therefore, that marriage could not come about unless a slot was vacant, so to speak, and the aspiring couple was fit to fill it up. It might be a cottage which had fallen empty, so that a man-servant and a womanservant could now marry and go to live there as cottagers. For the more fortunate it would be a plot of land which had to be taken up and worked by some yeoman's or some husbandman's son, with his wife to help him. It might be a bakery, or a joinery, or a loom which had to be manned anew. This meant that all young people ordinarily had to wait before they were permitted to marry, at least in England, and probably in Western Europe as a whole. This may have been a characteristic which distinguished the west and the north of Europe from the east and the south. Once it is realized that our English ancestors had the same rule as we have, or would like to have, no two married couples in one family, then size of family and age at marriage are seen to be linked together, and linked with a third extremely important circumstance, expectation of life.

In the village of Cogenhoe in 1628 there were 33 families; 6, nearly one in five, seem to have had resident in-laws. This is the highest proportion we have so far found in an English pre-industrial community. At Clayworth in 1676, 7 out of 98 families had in-laws, not one in twelve, but in 1688 the proportion had fallen to 3 in 91. Only 13 out of the 176 households at Chilvers Coton in 1684 had in-laws, which is

[99] *See page* 287.

about $7\frac{1}{2}$ per cent. By no means all of these in-laws were parents of the husband or wife at the head of the household: in fact only one case of this occurred at Clayworth in the lists of 1676 and 1688, and only 3 at Chilvers Coton in 1684. In all the communities for which evidence has so far been recovered the presence of children living at home after marriage was even rarer than the presence of parents living with married children. There were three such families at Chilvers Coton out of the 176, there were none amongst the 86 families living at Ealing in 1599, none at Clayworth in either 1676 or 1688; there was one at Cogenhoe in 1620, but none in the other five years in the record. What was true in these villages is now known to have been true for dozens of others. Living with in-laws can only have been occasional in the world we have lost. It is impossible that it can have been the ordinary expected thing to do.

We have only to think for a moment of our immediate acquaintance and neighbourhood today to recognize how much more often families contain in-laws now than they did in the communities we have discussed. In Woodford in 1957, 23 per cent of all people of pensionable age who had at least one married child shared their dwellings with a married couple, one of the partners being a son or daughter. In Bethnal Green in 1954 the proportion was 21 per cent.[100] When we compare these seventeenth-century English peasant communities with the peasant communities which have survived into contemporary Western Europe, the result is even more surprising. In the eastern part of the Netherlands, peasant farming still survives. During the early 1950's, no less than 25 per cent of farms there were being worked by married couples living with their in-laws.[101] This compares as we have seen with the quite low percentage in those seventeenth-century English communities we have so far examined. There may be many reasons for this startling change; much more research will have to be done about the family then and now before we can be certain why this has taken place. An obvious cause is the lengthening of life. In Stuart England very few people lived with their in-laws, because they less often had in-laws to live with. A couple seldom had their parents living with them, because their parents survived less frequently to an age where this might become necessary.

[100] *See page* 287.   [101] *See page* 287.

It might be added that they probably had less difficulty about housing. This is not quite a distinct reason, because we ourselves would find housing easier no doubt if we all lived shorter lives. But it seems nevertheless to be true that the relative cost of housing in pre-industrial times was less, perhaps considerably less, than it is now. The humblest dwelling of all, a cottage for the labouring poor, could, it seems, be put up new for less than three years of the annual income of a labourer, and the justices of the peace seem always to be authorizing or ordering such undertakings as if they were a casual matter. Landlords and overseers of the poor would put them up apparently as a matter of course, and one of the persistent, if probably baseless, traditions of the village community was that if a poor man could build a cottage on the *waste*, the common grazing land, of a manor overnight, he could occupy it undisturbed. This tradition reflects the restrictions which stood in the way of building. It needed the permission of the justices to convert a house into a cottage, to divide a cottage between families or to turn a barn or part of a barn into a dwelling.[102]

Where lists of the houses in a village have survived, however, some seem always to have been vacant, especially in the later seventeenth century. This is a feature of the Hearth Tax returns of the 1660's, '70's and '80's.[103] Not that homelessness was unknown in those years or at any time in that era of endemic poverty and wretchedness. One Simon Gibbs, writes the clerk to the Justices of Warwickshire in January 1667, 'is destitute of an habitation for his wife and five small children, having long lain out of doors'. A cottage was ordered to be erected on the common of his village.[104]

But the housing standards and the housing difficulties of our ancestors go beyond the very restricted ground which can be covered here. It will be obvious by now how crucial expectation of life turns out to be when comparing our own everyday experience with that of our ancestors. Though we are not in a position to contrast the two in any detail, and shall not make much progress until family reconstitution has been undertaken on a large scale, the table printed opposite has something to tell us.

Life expectancy at birth in seventeenth-century England seems to have been in the low thirties – it may have quite

[102] *See page* 287.   [103] *See page* 288.   [104] *See page* 289.

Expectation of Life: Pre-Industrial England[105]

At age 0	Colyton, Devon (Wrigley) High mortality	Low mortality	Midpoint	England and Wales (Gregory King)	USA 1955 (UN Yearbook) both sexes
1538–1624	40·6	45·8	43·2	1690's	
1625–1699	34·9	38·9	36·9	32·0	
1700–1774	38·4	45·1	41·8		

At age	Breslau 1690's (Edmund Halley) both sexes	Haiti 1950 (UN Yearbook) both sexes	Egypt 1936–8 (UN Yearbook) Male	Female	India 1441–50 (UN Yearbook) Male	Female	UK 1960 (UN Yearbook) Male	Female	USA 1955 both sexes
0	27·5	32·6	35·6	41·5	32·4	31·7	68·3	74·1	69·5
1	—	38·3	42·1	48·1	39·0	37·3	69·0	74·6	70·4
5	—	40·1	49·7	58·3	40·9	40·9	65·2	70·8	67·7
10	40·2	38·9	46·9	54·5	39·0	39·4	60·4	65·9	61·9
20	33·9	34·4	39·8	46·1	33·0	33·0	50·7	56·1	52·3
30	27·6	29·3	33·0	38·2	26·6	26·1	41·3	46·4	42·9
40	22·0	24·4	26·1	30·8	20·5	21·1	31·8	36·8	33·7
50	17·0	19·8	19·4	23·4	14·9	16·1	22·9	27·7	25·1
60	12·3	15·5	13·3	16·3	10·1	11·3	15·3	19·2	17·5
70	7·7	11·8	7·9	9·5	6·5	7·5	19·5	6·5	11·3

105 See page 288.

closely resembled life expectancy in India or in Haiti in the
1950's. But the evidence for Colyton, surprising in this as in so
many other ways, shows that for an English village it could
vary quite markedly from period to period, and could reach
the forties in the favourable demographic conditions in the
sixteenth and eighteenth centuries. The paradox to be found
in all life tables, that expectancy rises after the first and
dangerous year, is seen to have been very pronounced in
Breslau in the 1690's. There, children aged 10 could apparently
expect to live thirteen years longer than newborn babies.
This old effect, due to high infant and child mortality, would
undoubtedly have been a feature of the life table of Halley's
own country, had he been able to carry out the first such demographic exercise for England rather than for a foreign city. But
in the late seventeenth century England may have resembled
Haiti, or Egypt or India rather than Breslau. Englishwomen
probably lived longer at all ages than Englishmen in pre-
industrial times, for this is the normal circumstance, though
the Indian figures in the table happen to be an exception.

This table, and especially the evidence of Colyton should
warn us not to exaggerate the brevity of life in earlier times.
Even if Halley's Breslau estimates are too optimistic for
Englishmen of his day at ages upwards of ten, it is still quite
likely that a man of twenty-one could have something like
thirty years to live, pretty much the same time as a newborn
baby. If he married at thirty – not an unlikely age as we have
seen – he could probably expect to live twenty-five years with
his wife. This was a substantial period as lifetimes went then,
but not long enough to ensure that he would see his own son
married. There may turn out to be a startling contrast here
between England and her colonial daughters. Life in the
Plymouth colony in its early years has been estimated to
last for 45·5 years, and men to live longer than women.

Perhaps the early Americans (and Dutch peasants now)
differed from our English ancestors mainly because they lived
to be so much older. Nevertheless there are stray pieces of
evidence which go to show that even when she did survive her
husband, a widowed Englishwoman could not always rely
on her children to give her a home. At Clayworth in 1676
dwelt the little craftsman's family of Bacon: Francis Bacon
the father, Joan Bacon his wife, Nicholas, Anne and Francis
their children. His occupation was that of cooper, maker of

barrels, which were the only important form of packaging in the old days. In 1688 his son Nicholas had succeeded him as the cooper at Clayworth, since Francis Bacon himself had been buried on April 25th, 1685. The Bacon family now consisted of Nicholas, his wife Elizabeth, and two of her children, Elizabeth and Gervas Welter. Nicholas had married Elizabeth Welter as a widow on June 1st, 1686; their own twin children, very probably conceived before their marriage, had died as babies in 1687. Now Nicholas's mother Joan and his sister Anne were still alive and in Clayworth in 1688, but not in the family home. They were being supported in the 'Common-Houses on Alms' – paupers in a charitable institution in fact. Anne Bacon was a delinquent, far more blameworthy than the unfortunate women who attract so much attention in our day: in July, 1687, she had had a bastard child by a married man. Little Naphtaly Loversage (the father was Nicholas Loversage, a shepherd's son) died a six-month-old baby.

It is true that Nicholas Loversage made an honest woman of her directly his first wife died, which was very soon after the Rector drew up the list of parishioners in May, 1688. But we have no evidence that Loversage gave house-room to his new wife's mother, and there is nothing to explain the behaviour of his wife's brother Nicholas in turning mother and sister out of the family cottage when he himself got married, leaving them to the mercy of the parish poor-law overseers and to charitable relief. It may be unfair to condemn Nicholas Bacon, for the full circumstances never will be known; indeed it is unusual that so much should have been discovered about the very private lives of these obscure villagers who lived so long ago.[106] The Bacons and Loversages look a shiftless, irresponsible lot, though Gervas Welter, father of Nicholas Bacon's two step-children, was a blacksmith, and blacksmiths, shepherds and coopers were respectable enough occupations. In the twentieth century it is tempting to speculate on the emotional effect of this break-up of marriages and homes on the children, on Nicholas's naughty sister Anne, and on his wife's two orphans. But it may be unwise to go as far as this. The emotional pattern of that society has vanished for ever, and people may then have had quite a different attitude to sudden death, orphanage, widowhood and living with step-parents.

[106] *See page* 288.

H

Nevertheless the step-mother and her evil influence is so conspicuous a feature of the fairy tales and of the literature as a whole, that it seems to correspond to something important in the lives of those who repeated them. The lonely old widowed woman, witch in possibility and sometimes in fact, is a familiar figure too. It cannot be without significance that 35·5 per cent of all the children alive in Clayworth in May, 1688, were orphans in the sense that one parent or other had died whilst they were still dependent. It must be significant too that something like a half of the solitaries were widows, – it is understandable that not much detailed evidence is yet available on the very small proportion of people in the old world who had to live alone.[107] In the face of facts like these, therefore, it may become difficult for us to go on being so sorry for ourselves because of the vast numbers of broken homes, and solitary, neglected people, which we think of as characteristic of high industrialism in our day. The society of the pre-industrial world was inured to bereavement and the shortness of life. It clearly had to be.

There are other elementary facts about births, marriages and deaths which may seem to be almost as surprising as the ones already cited. It is natural to think, for example, of the traditional marriage arrangement and ceremonial in the terms of Shakespeare's plays. We might contrast those famous accounts with the words of the same contemporary who recorded the details of harvest home in Yorkshire in the 1640's. He must be talking of the gentry, perhaps substantial yeomen too.

Concerning our Fashions of our Country Weddings

Usually the young man's father, or he himself, writes to the father of the maid to know if he shall be welcome to the house, if he shall have furtherance if he come in such a way or how he liketh of the notion. Then if he [presumably the woman's father] pretend any excuse, only thanking him for his good will, then it is as good as a denial. If the motion be thought well of, and embraced, then the young man goeth perhaps twice to see how the maid standeth affected. Then if he see that she be tractable, and that her inclination is towards him, then the third time that he visiteth, he perhaps giveth her a ten-shilling piece of gold, or a ring of that price; or perhaps a twenty-shilling piece, or a ring of that price, then 10s the next time, or the next after that, a pair of gloves of 6s. 8d. a

[107] *See page* 288.

pair; and after that, each other time, some conceited toy or novelty of less value. They visit usually every three weeks or a month, and are usually half a year, or very near, from the first going to the conclusion.

So soon as the young folks are agreed and contracted, then the father of the maid carrieth her over to the young man's house to see how they like of all, and there doth the young man's father meet them to treat of a dower, and likewise of a jointure or feoffment [this was what was settled on her] for the woman. And then do they also appoint and set down the day of the marriage, which may perhaps be about a fortnight or three weeks after, and in that time do they get made the wedding clothes, and make provision against the wedding dinner, which is usually at the maid's father's. Their use is [it is usual] to buy gloves to give to each of their friends a pair on that day; the man should be at the cost for them, but sometimes the man gives the gloves to the men and the woman to the women, or else he to her friends and she to his. They give them that morning when they are almost ready to go to church to be married.

Then so soon as the bride is tired [attired] and that they are ready to go forth, the bridegroom comes, and takes her by the hand, and saith: 'Mistress, I hope you are willing', or else kisseth her before them, and then followeth her father out of the doors. Then one of the bridegroom his men ushereth the bride, and goes foremost, and the rest of the young men usher each of them a maid to church. The bridegroom and the brides brothers or friends tend at dinner: he perhaps fetcheth her home to his house a month after, and the portion is paid that morning that she goes away. When the young man comes to fetch away his bride some of his best friends, and young men his neighbours, come along with him, and others perhaps meet them in the way, and then there is the same jollity at his house. For they perhaps have love? wine [sic – as in original] ready to give to the company when they light [alight], then a dinner, supper and breakfast next day.[108]

It sounds rather like the marriage rites which anthropologists record of alien societies, and there are clear signs, if only in passing, of things like the bride-price and the betrothal, which, as we shall see, was separated from the later marriage. What may be most surprising is that the married couple did not go away together after the feast in the home of the bride, but

[108] *See page 289.*

weeks later. The point which will have to be considered in due course is whether or not sexual intercourse was permissible or condoned, by the church or the opinion of the village, between the contract and the marriage ceremony, or between the ceremony and the actual departure.

The marriage customs of Stuart Yorkshire may have differed widely from those elsewhere in England and Wales, and a great deal of work would have to be done to discover quite how the mass of the people got married; the really lowly people that is to say, the mere husbandmen, the artificers, the labourers, the paupers. Ralph Meers, the servant in the house of the Wawens at Clayworth in 1676, could surely not have afforded the rings, the sovereigns or half-sovereigns when he married Anne Fenton, his fellow servant, and set up as a labourer. There can have been no portion to speak of for Anne, though she may well have saved her wages, all of them, at 30*s*. or £2 a year against that wonderful day, and no question of a horse for them to alight from at the cottage door.

The marriages of truly modest folk, as for example the Bacons and Loversages, may well have often been less public and regular than those of the better off. Apart from clandestine marriages, performed by shady clergymen in places of worship, not usually parish churches, without licence or banns, there were the common law marriages. These were, and are, consensual unions, recognized by authority for certain purposes, as today for social welfare. In earlier times it seems probable that the clergy, some, if not all, would recognize them as legal and not stigmatize the offspring as bastards. There is reason to believe that common law marriages may have been more frequent in the late seventeenth century and early eighteenth century, than at other times. The exact nature of these marriages is not yet clear, nor is their relationship with the 'Handfastings' consummated by intercourse which are discussed in Chapter 6.

It would certainly be out of the question to think of Nicholas Bacon behaving like the bridegroom in Best's account when he married Elizabeth Welter, the widow, or to suppose that they had to take such care to have the permission of their parents, since both of their fathers were dead, and, in any case, a widow disposed of herself in marriage. There was no smiling father to go to the church when Anne Bacon married Nicholas Loversage the summer after their baby boy died. In fact something like one-quarter of all marriages were remarriages. Although the evidence we have goes to show that it was not the custom either for boys or for girls to await the death of the father or mother before getting married, many bridegrooms and brides were orphans nevertheless; in Manchester in the years 1653–7 over half of the girls marrying for the first time were fatherless.[109] Many of them presumably came from the houses of their step-fathers, or step-mothers, but these examples should do something to revise sentimental notions about marriages in earlier times, and to underline the difference made by shorter life. You could not with any confidence expect to see your grandchildren in the world we have lost.

The figures given for the proportion of remarriages and of fatherless brides are provisional once again, though they too will very soon be supplemented from more exhaustive work. The scarcity of grandchildren will be much more difficult to substantiate for any given individual, because every birth to a son or daughter away from the parental home would have to be traced. But some confidence can be placed in a provisional figure for the proportion of households in any community which contained grandchildren either of the head, or of anyone else living there. These were the multigenerational households which many people have wrongly supposed to have been characteristic of society in pre-industrial times. In general only a little over one household in twenty had a generation depth of more than two. At Ealing in 1599 no household contained a grandchild, only one in Clayworth in 1688, and none in 1676; only one out of 176 in Chilvers Coton in 1684. Society as a whole was forced to rely upon its oral memory for many important things, since writing was so restricted an accomplishment; only an old man could tell a young one who took up a holding, whether it ever flooded, perhaps only a man with many, many years at one job could make a mill of a particular type. Yet resident grandparents were uncommon, and conversation across the generations must have been relatively rare, much more so than it is today.

An illusion must be guarded against here nevertheless. Though so few people reached the age of seventy, it was regarded as the allotted span of life all the same. Some attained it, and those who did were observed to be in very old age; this is how the phrase must be understood. Some

[109] *See page* 289.

husbands and wives lived long enough to see their great-grand-
children, and even occasionally their great-great-grand-
children too. But the consequence which men attached to
being very old at that time, though very understandable in
view of its relative rarity and possible usefulness, made them
exaggerate their ages. Anyone who has read parish registers
is aware of this, for every now and again a particularly vener-
able age will be recorded at burial, and examination will
sometimes show how much the old man had added to it to
impress his neighbours.

The heavier mortality of that age made for more frequent
remarriage. Records of the number of times people had been
married unfortunately only rarely survive, but it so happens
that the listing of the people of Clayworth in 1688 was carried
out with such care that this information can be worked out
from it. There were at that date 72 husbands in the village,
and no less than 21 are recorded as having been married more
than once: 13 of them had been married twice, 1 a number of
times unspecified, 3 three times, 3 four times and 1 five times.
Of the 72 wives, 9 had been previously married; 1 of the 7
widowers and 1 of the 21 widows are known to have been
married more than once. This is spectacular confirmation for
one single community of a law which seems to obtain for the
whole pre-industrial world, that once a man reached the marriage age he would tend to go on getting married whenever
he found himself without a wife. At Adel in Yorkshire one old
man married his sixth wife in 1698 and his seventh in 1702.[110]
The law holds for women too, but is weaker in their case,
because widows found it more difficult to get husbands than
widowers to get wives. Together with the much marrying
majority of the older people there may also have been a small
community of persons who did not marry at all.

We have given this celibate community the name of the
nubile unmarried, and it seems probable that a fair proportion
of its members were servants. But discussion of this very
interesting issue soon becomes too complex for the present
purpose.[111] The relatively low expectation of life combined
with the relatively high age at marriage had an effect on the
personal experience of men and women of the time which was
of more general importance for the structure of their society
than is obvious at first sight.

[110] *See page* 289.   [111] *See page* 289.

These two circumstances implied a relatively short duration of marriage. Once again care must be taken not to exaggerate its importance and we have seen that expectation of life in the middle years was surprisingly long in relation to expectation of life at birth. Nevertheless when a man married in the old world he cannot have had on average much more than 27 or at most 30 years to live, whereas today the expectation is more like 45. This means that a 'generation' now lasts half as long again as it used to do and the passing of a 'generation' was of much greater importance then.

For the breaking up of a marriage by the death of the husband brought the end to an undertaking almost as surely as the beginning of a marriage meant its foundation. When a wife died, this result can rarely have followed, though the importance of a capable woman at the head of a farming or even a craftsman's household is easily overlooked. Replacing her with someone approximately suited to her duties with the children and in household management generally must often have been a difficult matter. But when the husband and the father died, everything on which the family depended was put in jeopardy. The effect would vary, of course, with the point of his career when catastrophe came, with the number, age and capacity of his sons, the vigour and determination of his widow and her attractiveness as a possible wife for someone else. 'Attractiveness' here must be read almost exclusively as an economic advantage, for when the land she now controlled was freehold and enough to live well upon, she would have had very little time to wait for a new husband. Alternatively it might pass to the late man's son or other heir who, perhaps, was already helping to work it, again without making much difference to the undertaking.

But if the land had been leasehold and the lease had been for life; if there was no son left of the right age, or daughter ready to be married to a man who could take over; if the undertaking had been a commercial or industrial one, with the proper successor not immediately to hand; under all these circumstances and many more, the day of the end of the marriage would also be the day of the end of the family enterprise, or at least the end of a particular régime, of a generation. It is obvious how much more *permanent* in this sense agricultural and landed activities were than commercial, industrial and urban ones. But on the land the passing of a generation meant a crisis in each farming household, of a kind which our economic institutions are now much less likely to undergo. This implied a surprisingly high rate of turnover, so to speak, in institutions as well as in persons. How quickly people succeeded one to another in the same small settlement will be seen in due course.

The end of the marriage of course meant the end of child-bearing, and this was one of the important factors in keeping down the number of children in a family. It is not true that in peasant society in England or in France a married woman would have a baby every year. For one thing fecundity goes down with age and the French have shown that it declined and came to an end sooner then than now. Moreover the much longer period of suckling babies inhibited conception to a marked degree.[112] Only in the sense that deliberate inter-ference with procreation seems to have been absent amongst the villagers whom he decided to study for the purpose can it be said that the French demographer Louis Henry found himself able to examine what is called natural fertility amongst the peasantry of his native country in the seventeenth and eighteenth centuries. Natural fertility exists where birth succeeds birth as quickly as the wife is physiologically capable of maintaining the succession. The maximum number of births even under these conditions is considerable, with an upper limit of 23, even if no twins are born. He actually discovered an instance of 21 births to a woman, but this was not in a French village, but amongst the bourgeoisie of the city of Geneva. The record for our country so far is 18 births to an alderman's wife in the little town of Banbury in Oxford-shire, between 1597 and 1623.

In the course of these researches, which can be said to have been the foundation of contemporary scientific historical demography, Henry diagnosed the existence in Genevan society of deliberate limitation of births, taking place as long ago as the later seventeenth century.[113] The demonstration was statistical: the numbers of children being born to wives was shown to vary not exclusively with the age of the mother, as it does under natural fertility, but with the length of the marriage as well. If a woman had married early, and had had all the children she wanted, then her fertility would be less in her later married years than that of a woman of her age who

[112] *See page* 290.   [113] *See page* 290.

had not been a young bride. Moreover the overall pattern of birth intervals in Geneva at this time and thereafter already resembled the one shown by birth intervals in our own late twentieth-century society, where contraception is certainly very widespread. It should be noticed that the proof was numerical, and no evidence as to methods of avoiding conception entered into it.

It was surprising to find that the Calvinist citizens of Geneva had adopted this practice so early. Even more surprising, however, and of profound importance for the study of family life in the world we have lost, was the demonstration by Dr E. A. Wrigley ten years later, in 1966, that the birth schedules of Colyton, an ordinary English village, also exhibited the tell-tale pattern, and at an even earlier period.[114] This result of the first successful process of family reconstitution in our country showed that family limitation seems to have begun in the village in the mid-seventeenth century and to have continued until the early eighteenth century. Later on, which may seem the most surprising thing of all, it disappeared. To put a vulgar point upon it, the peasants and craftsmen of Colyton could take it, or leave it alone. Coitus interruptus (withdrawal before ejaculation) is assumed to have been the main method used, but once again no literary evidence of its prevalence in the village has been found, or is necessary.

No French rural parish has so far been discovered to have been affected in this way before the last decade of the eighteenth century, though in 1969 family limitation was reported to have been present in a small French town in the 1770's. As might be expected, mean numbers of children per marriage were smaller in the period of limitation at Colyton. Women marrying before 30 had 6·4 children before the mid-seventeenth century, between 4·2 and 4·4 during the next hundred years or so, and 5·9 after that until 1837. Cruder methods confirm these figures for many other English parishes, for the division of the total of births by the total of marriages during a given period is some sort of measure of fertility. This figure comes out at 3·6 for 24 parishes over the period 1581–1810, and it rarely reaches 5 for any individual community over any prolonged period of time. In spite of what may be a profound difference in their marital conduct, the inhabitants of French villages seem to have had much the same general

[114] *See page* 290.

average of children per marriage as their English counterparts.[115]

The facts and figures under discussion imply that fertility in
England was high in the late sixteenth and earlier seventeenth
centuries, low for a hundred and more years after that
and high again from the mid-eighteenth century. This is
amply confirmed by the monthly totals of baptisms, marriages
and burials for each of the five hundred parishes or so now
held by the Cambridge Group for the History of Population
and Social Structure, and together they suggest very strongly
that total population followed the same course – rising between the early Tudors and the Civil War, static in some areas
and even falling in others until about 1750 and then rising
again, very steeply almost everywhere. These changes went
on without mothers generally ever giving birth as frequently
as is often supposed to be usual in pre-industrial peasant
society. But it is not yet quite clear how far English demographic development was free by the time of the Tudors and
Stuarts of that ultimate sanction over population and its
growth, exhaustion of the food supply.

This fateful issue must be left to our next chapter. Probably
the most conspicuous feature of traditional society to be
gathered from its vital statistics is its overwhelming youthfulness. Gregory King calculated that above 45 per cent of all
the people alive in his day were children, with some variation

Comparative age table, percentages

Age group	Ealing (Pop. 427) 1599	Lichfield (Pop. 2861) 1695	Stoke-on Trent (Pop. 1629) 1701	England and Wales (From Gregory King) 1695	England and Wales 1821	Ceylon 1955	England and Wales 1958
0–9	20·6	24·2	28·1	27·6	27·9	29·4	14·8
10–19	28·8	21·5	19·8	20·2	21·1	21·0	13·2
20–29	13·4	13·8	14·3	15·5	15·7	16·7	14·8
30–39	12·7	15·9	13·9	11·7	11·8	13·4	1·1
40–49	7·0	10·2	8·7	8·4	9·3	10·0	13·9
50–59	10·5	6·4	6·9	5·8	6·6	6·0	13·2
60 and above	7·0	8·0	8·4	10·7	7·3	3·5	16·9

[115] *See page* 290.

between town and country; there were, he reckoned, 33 per
cent in London, 40 per cent in the other urban areas and 47
per cent in the villages. It will be a long time before we can
confirm or criticize these figures from a wide sample of Stuart
population, but the table opposite shows that King's estimates of age composition were about right for three of the
communities we can examine. They fit in to all our other
preliminary evidence and place Stuart England alongside such
twentieth-century Asian communities as Ceylon.

When it comes to the average age, King's figure of 27½ for
the whole country in his day is perhaps a little high. It was
25·7 years at Ealing, and 26·4 at Lichfield and 25·9 at Stoke.
The median age, the age at which the population divided,
shows more variation from place to place, as might perhaps be
expected. The 1,107 people living at Buckfastleigh in Devon
in 1698 had a median age of as high as 25·1 years; at Lichfield
it was 27·7, at Ealing 22·2 and at Chilvers Coton in Warwickshire in 1684 (population 780) it was as low as 20·12. The best
estimate at present for a general average age of a pre-industrial English community is 25·4.[116]

We must imagine our ancestors, therefore, in the perpetual
presence of their young offspring. A good 70 per cent of all
households contained children – this figure is remarkably constant from place to place and date to date – and there were
between two and a half and three children to every household
with them. Sometimes the numbers in those groups of five and
above could reach a quarter of the whole number of children
in a village, though most children always lived in groups
smaller than this. In the pre-industrial world there were children everywhere; playing in the village street and fields when
they were very small, hanging round the farmyards and
getting in the way, until they had grown enough to be given
child-sized jobs to do; thronging the churches; for ever cling-
ing to the skirts of women in the house and wherever they
went and above all crowding round the cottage fires.

The perpetual distraction of childish noise and talk must
have affected everyone almost all the time, except of course
the gentleman in his study or the lady in her boudoir; incessant interruptions to answer questions, quieten fears, rescue
from danger or make peace between the quarrelling. These
crowds and crowds of little children are strangely absent from

[116] *See page* 291.

the written record, even if they are conspicuous enough in the pictures painted at the time, particularly the outside scenes. There is something mysterious about the silence of all these multitudes of babes in arms, toddlers and adolescents in the statements men made at the time about their own experience. Children appear, of course, but so seldom and in such an indefinite way that we know very little indeed about child nurture in pre-industrial times, and no confident promise can be made of knowledge yet to come.

We cannot say whether fathers helped in the tending of infants or whether women and girls, sisters and aunts as well as mothers, did it all as women's peculiar business. We do not know how the instruction of children was divided between the parents, though it is natural to suppose that boys at least would learn how men behaved and how they worked the lathe, the plane, the plough, the loom from watching their fathers all and every day. Such letters as they learnt, and the stories of the past, traditionally came to them at their mothers' knees, and their religious training too. But there is nothing as yet to confirm that this tradition is wholly correct. We are even more ignorant of what happened when the children left the house and went out to play; whether it was in family groups, or whether it was neighbourhood gangs, even village gangs, embracing rich and poor, the privileged along with the rest. We do not know very much about what they played, or even about what they were encouraged to play or to do.

We know a little about what they were taught when they went to school, which was almost all Christianity and a little classics, and about the rigour of their treatment there. But very few of them went to school, and we can only suppose that when they were at home they were as peremptorily treated as they would have been in the classroom. The most important material object in the world of the child may well have been the rod, but these myriads of children have left almost nothing material behind them. A cradle or two in most old houses, a hobby horse, a whipping top and one or two other traditional toys, that is all, and most of these once belonged to little gentlemen and gentlewomen, not to the ordinary children, our own ancestors.

The Stuart gentry seem to have dressed their children like themselves, at least for the purpose of having their pictures painted. The peasants and craftsmen appear to have done the same. But we cannot say how far children were universally thought of as little adults, though the notion of a world of the child distinct from the world of the grown-up seems to be no older than the early Victorians. Nothing can as yet be said on what is called by the psychologists toilet training, and reckoned by them to be of great importance in the formation of personality; there seems no likelihood of our discovering whether indeed it varied from Puritan to Anglican, from gentry to peasantry, from town to country. We do not even know for certain how babies were carried about. It is in fact an effort of the mind to remember all the time that children were always present in such numbers in the traditional world, nearly half the whole community living in a condition of semi-obliteration, many of them never destined to become persons at all. Indeed a number of them can never have handled a penny which they could pocket and call their own, even if they actually survived to the age of twenty-one.

Immaturity implies authority, and those who cannot look after themselves have to be commanded. The authoritarianism of traditional social life and educational practice becomes a little easier to understand when the youthfulness of so much of the community is borne in mind. A very high proportion of dependent bodies, mouths to feed and clothes and fuel to find, energy to summon up for the heavy work or rearing children, weights down the active members of society. This is of crucial significance when it comes to the chances of technical and economic progress, and finally of industrial transformation. It is so in Asia in our day and it must have been so in England and in Europe before 1700. A great deal of time and ingenuity has gone in trying to reconstruct the story of the growth of population over the years of first industrialization, and the time has now come to turn attention to its age-composition before and during that little-understood process.[117]

But a glance at the tables on page 108 will show that no simple result is to be expected from such a study. The England of 1821, when economic transformation was in full cry, was almost exactly the same in its age composition, in the relationship between youth and age considered merely in terms of numbers present, as it had been in Gregory King's time. No easy contrast can be drawn between the world we have lost and the world we now inhabit when it comes to

[117] *See page* 291.

births, marriages and deaths. Nevertheless these neglected
numerical facts have a great deal to tell, even in the crude
and inchoate form in which they are so far available to us. It
is remarkable too how much we can learn from trying to find
out whether our Elizabethan forerunners really did marry
their wives as young as Romeo married Juliet.

Did the Peasants Really Starve?
Chapter 5

Famine and pestilence in pre-industrial society

'The starving peasantry' is a common phrase, especially in popular literature. The words bring to mind a picture in simple black and white of conditions as they were in the bad old days of the reformer and the good old days of the sentimentalist. Perhaps 'starving' should not be taken to mean actually dying of lack of food; rather, badly fed and clothed, wretchedly housed in hovels, miserable in general. Still, in our own day the phrase has reverted to its grimmer meaning, reminding us of the contrast between the rich, industrialized parts of the world where food is plentiful, and the poorer areas, where industry has not yet got a hold and where literal starvation does occur.

It is therefore of considerable importance to decide how far famine was an endemic feature of the world we have lost and how far England as a country was exposed to it in the generations which led up to the industrial revolution. Did the peasants really starve, in Hertfordshire and Hampshire, in Cumberland and Cornwall, just as they sometimes starved in the area called the Beauvaisis in France, which surrounds and includes the ancient cathedral city of Beauvais?

There can be no doubt that the peasants and the craftsmen living in this region were liable to starve at times during the seventeenth and early eighteenth century, and that starvation also occurred in other parts of France. It is not yet quite clear how far these people can be taken as typical of the whole of that country, and of the whole period before the arrival of industry, all over Europe. The Beauvaisis may have been particularly vulnerable because it was a region gathering only one harvest a year and dependent upon a single crop for food.

It was also given over to the production of woollen cloth, heavily industrialized in the old sense. Where the peasants kept cows, starvation was less likely, and this may have been the English case, for all its close resemblance to the situation in the Beauvaisis.[118]

If the state of the evidence about starvation amongst the French peasantry is somewhat uncertain, it is to be expected that the situation in England should be still more obscure. We do not yet know whether the men and women of the villages and towns of our landscape in the old days lived out their lives in present or distant fear that their food supply might some day run out. Because the subject is of such over-riding interest and significance, it seems worth while to present such early evidence as we already have, though most of it is negative. If in fact this fear was present among them it must have had an effect on many of the features of their lives which have been discussed so far.

The fund of food was obviously related to the age at marriage. This was a point fully recognized by Thomas Malthus, the pioneer of studies of this sort. A society conscious that its food resources might be outstripped by the growth of its population will have to control the rate of formation of families if starvation is to be avoided, and this means that marriage will have to be postponed. It also means that the procreation of children outside marriage must be strictly forbidden, and this implied authoritarian sexual morals. These we shall discuss in due course. But the possibility of starvation by no means implied that every marriage must lead to the formation of a new household: rather the reverse. It might be thought that the economies which could come from living in large households, multi-generational groups of kin, would have been an influence against the existence of small households of one married couple and their children. Since we now know that small households were the rule, and that men and women were prepared to postpone marriage to a late age in relation to their life-expectancy in order perhaps to maintain that rule, then we can conclude that this feature of their social structure was of some significance. But its importance is enhanced if it can be shown that there was a danger of starvation.

The characteristics of society in the world we have lost, therefore, play in with each other in a variety of ways, and

[118] *See page* 292.

each part of our subject is also our whole subject. In this superficial survey we can only touch on the principles and open up possibilities. It must be pointed out that the risk of starvation would not necessarily show itself in conspicuous events, the famines of the history books. Perhaps perpetual undernourishment, or undernourishment lasting for several disastrous harvests, might be its usual manifestation.

The influence of climate, good and bad years, mild and severe winters, must be stressed as we think of these things. Where the less fortunate members of a society are at the mercy of the weather and around the margin of subsistence, the tendency will surely be that the fluctuating situation will occasionally become extreme. We should therefore expect catastrophe from time to time, when famine would openly appear. This is what happened in the Beauvaisis and this is why it seems legitimate to suppose that the inhabitants of that area, living in perpetual awareness that the day might come again when they would not be able to get enough food to keep alive, would behave accordingly. We have said that the economic geography of that area of France in some ways resembled that of England, in fact of Britain as a whole. It is known that Scotland suffered from famine in Stuart times, though its occurrence has yet to be systematically studied.[119] The question of starvation amongst the English is an intricate, if undecided, problem.

We may begin our presentation of the rather fragmentary evidence by citing a contemporary, a rare example of a peasant speaking for himself, or in this case for herself. The account she gives is enlightening for many reasons. What follows is a passage from the diary of John Locke, dated March 1st, 1681.

This day I saw one Alice George, a woman as she said of 108 years old at Alhallontide last [November 1st, 1680]. She lived in St Giles parish in Oxford and hath lived in and about Oxford since she was a young woman. She was born at Saltwyche [? Salwarp] in Worcestershire, her maiden name was Alice Guise. Her father lived to 83, her mother to 96, and her mother's mother to 111. When she was young she was fair-haired and neither fat nor lean, but very slender in the waist, for her size she was to be reckoned rather amongst the tall than short women. Her condition was but mean, and her maintenance her labour, and she said she

[119] *See page 292.*

I

was able to have reaped as much in a day as any man, and had as much wages. She was married at 30, and had 15 children, viz. 10 sons and 5 daughters baptized, besides 3 miscarriages. She has 3 sons still alive, her eldest John living the next door to her, 77 years old the 25th of this month. She goes upright though with a staff in one hand, but yet I saw her stoop twice without resting upon anything, taking up once a pot and another time her glove from the ground.

Her hearing is very good and her smelling so quick that as soon as she came near me she said I smelt very sweet, I having a pair of new gloves on that were not strong scented. Her eyes she complains of as failing her, since her last sickness, which was an ague that seized her about 2 years since and held her about a year. And yet she made a shift to thread a needle before us, though she seemed not to see the end of the thread very perfectly. She has as comely a face as ever I saw any old woman and age hath neither made her deformed nor decrepit.

The greatest part of her food now is bread and cheese or bread and butter and ale. Sack [sherry] revives her when she can get it. For flesh she cannot now eat, unless it be roasting pig which she loves. She had, she said, in her youth a good stomach [appetite] and ate what came in her way, oftener wanting victuals than a stomach. Her memory and understanding perfectly good and quick, and amongst a great deal of discourse we had with her and stories she told she spoke not one idle or impertinent [irrelevant] word. Before this last ague she used to go to church constantly on Sundays, Wednesdays and Saturdays. Since that she walks not beyond her little garden.

She has been ever since her being married troubled with vapours [either flatulence or depression] and so is still, but never took any physic but once about 40 year since, viz. one pennyworth of Jollop [aperient] which the apothecary out of kindness making a large pennyworth wrought more than sufficiently. She said she was 16 in '88 [1588], and went then to Worcester to see Queen Elizabeth, but came an hour too late, which agrees with her account of her age.[120]

Locke was a practising physician, an exact recorder and very reliable witness, so that we can believe that this is what Goody George did tell him, and that this was her true physical condition. We may, nevertheless, have our reservations about

[120] *See page* 292.

the ages she gives, particularly that for her grandmother, in view of the tendency to exaggerate which has been noticed. If she did have eighteen pregnancies after the age of thirty (this is obviously a round figure in the account and she may have been twenty-seven, twenty-eight or twenty-nine at marriage) then she is something of a record for English women of her time, and difficult to parallel even in France where so many more cases have been investigated. But most of her story rings true.

Women did work with men in the field, especially at harvest. 'The best sort of women-shearers [sickle-wielders]', says the Yorkshire farming-book quoted twice before, should have 'mowers' wages'; 'we should do them an injury if we should take them from their company and not make them equal to those in wages whom they can equalize in work.'[121] Her church attendance is probable enough, as has been seen, though it may come as a surprise to see how often our ancestors held their services. It is not without its interest that she lived alone next door to her son. She was another of the solitary widows we have already referred to, but like so many of the citizens of Bethnal Green today she had managed to get within an easy walk of a member of her family. A superficial survey of a city like Lichfield shows that this was common enough then, though perhaps not in anything like the degree that it has been found in twentieth-century working-class areas: in a street of some sixty-five households, only fifty-two surnames were counted in Lichfield in the survey of 1696.[122]

But her statements about what she ate, what she liked and how often she had to go without are the most interesting. The whole account reads rather like an explanation of how much she had to do to keep her stomach full. Still, she does not mention starvation or anything of that kind. John Graunt, the first man in history to study burial returns, was sceptical about starvation in England in his time. 'Of 229,250 which have died,' he wrote in 1662 referring to burials in London over twenty recent years, 'we find not above fifty-one to have been *starved*, excepting helpless infants at nurse, which being caused rather by carelessness, ignorance, and infirmity of the milch-women, is not properly an effect, or sign of want of food in the country or the means to get it.'[123]

If there was so seldom any lack of food to keep people alive

[121] *See page* 292.   [122] *See page* 292.   [123] *See page* 293.

in the huge city of London with its mass of paupers, surely the possibility of starvation can be dismissed out of hand for the years which Graunt had surveyed. But it can still be asked why he went to the trouble of denying that starvation ever happened. In order to be sure of what it is that is being sought after, it would be useful to see quite what is meant by the French historical demographers when they write of crises of subsistence occurring in French villages. They occurred when the price of bread rose so far that peasants and craftsmen could no longer afford to buy enough to eat, and became liable to starve.[124]

The crises in the villages of the Beauvaisis came at irregular intervals: 1625, 1648–53, 1693–4 were some of the dates. The parish registers of these communities, and of the churches of the city of Beauvais itself, would show a sudden rise in burials; double, or even treble the normal would be entered. Towards the first peak in mortality, marriages would drop and conceptions would go down too; they have to be reckoned by subtracting nine months from the date of birth, and the year used is the harvest year. From August 1st to July 31st. Conceptions in fact tended to disappear, because lack of nourishment inhibits ovulation. By the time the second peak in mortality came, for these crises were often though not always doubleheaded, the poor would be eating grass off the fields and offal from dung-heaps in the streets, dying perhaps more often from the effects of things like this and from the onset of endemic diseases than from starvation as such. The rich, though they might suffer from the infections spread about in this way, would not be affected by starvation.

Professor Goubert, the French historian of these lugubrious events, chooses this story to show what might happen to one family.

There was a family in Beauvais in the parish of Saint-Etienne in the year 1693 named Cocu: Jean Cocu, weaver of serges, and his wife with three daughters, all four spinning wool for him, since the youngest daughter was already nine years old. The family earned 108 sols a week, but they ate 70 pounds of bread between them. With bread up to $\frac{1}{2}$ a sol a pound, their livelihood was secure. With bread at 1 sol a pound, it began to get difficult. With bread at 2 sols, then at 3·2, 3·3 and 3·4 – as it was in 1649, in 1652, in 1662, in 1694, in 1710 – it was misery.

[124] *See page* 293.

Crisis in agriculture was nearly always intensified by crisis in manufacturing: it certainly was in 1693, so work began to fall off, then income. They went without; perhaps they were able to lay their hands on a coin or two saved up for a rainy day; they pawned their things; they began to eat unwholesome food, bran bread, cooked nettles, mouldy cereals, entrails of animals picked up outside the slaughter-houses. The 'contagion' manifested itself in various ways; after hunger came lassitude, starvation, 'pernicious and mortifying fevers'. The family was registered at the Office of the Poor in December, 1693. In March, 1694, the youngest daughter died; in May the eldest daughter and the father. All that remained of a particularly fortunate family, fortunate because everyone in it worked, was a widow and an orphan. Because of the price of bread.[125]

That one of the symptoms of starvation could occur in the British Isles is evident from the Scottish State Papers of 1700, and referred to the year 1698. 'Since the commencement of this Tack [that is period of excise] many have dyed, for want of bread, and have been necessitate, to make use of *wild-runches draff*, and the like for the support of nature.' But distressing as this account is, especially since it apparently refers to the whole kingdom of Scotland in the very last years of its autonomy, it may not have been as serious as what had happened in Beauvais five years earlier. It does not bear the full series of signs of the classical crisis of subsistence, and cannot do so because it appears that demographic readings do not exist in Scotland for the relevant years.

In order to demonstrate that the crisis of subsistence was a possibility in England at the same time as it was obviously a possibility in France, and presumably in Scotland too, we should have to show that three conclusions can be certainly drawn from at least one English parish register at a time when the price of food was particularly high. The first is that there was a sudden, sharp increase in mortality; the second is that at the same time there was a corresponding fall in conceptions and perhaps in marriages; the third is that the stated cause of death of some of those buried was in fact starvation or diseases caused by malnutrition. There are other features associated with such crises which have to be looked for also,

[125] *See page 294.*

such as an increase in infantile mortality and in abortions.
But any register showing the three listed features at any time
of dearth must be taken as providing proof that in that parish
the inhabitants were undergoing a crisis of subsistence.

It must be said at once that only one such English instance
has so far been found. Although very little concerted work has
yet been possible on the subject, Graunt seems to have been
right when he claimed that starvation was extremely rare in
England as a stated cause of death. But the simplicity of this
negative conclusion is obscured by the exasperating rarity of
parish registers which give any indication as to why the
person buried died. The third, and most conclusive, of the
features listed, therefore, is almost universally absent from the
English evidence, and the other two are seldom found in as
extreme a form as they are to be seen in France. Nearly all of
the English registers which have been studied so far yield
entirely negative conclusions; they contain no examples of
harvest years where a conspicuous rise in burials was accompanied by a corresponding fall in conceptions and in marriages.

We may here be faced with a sociological discovery of the
first historical importance, that our country in the seventeenth
century was already immune from these periodical disasters,
whereas France and Scotland were not. Perhaps the English
peasantry were justified rather later on in despising the French
for eating black bread and wearing wooden shoes. We do not
yet know, though it should not be long now before we shall find
out. Let us take the wool-weaving parish of Ashton-under-Lyne
in Lancashire as an example of an incomplete crisis of subsistence, occurring during the harvest year 1623–4. Its incom-
pleteness, its difference, that is to say, from the classical
French model, consists first in the fact that the evidence is
imperfect, owing to gaps in the register, and second in that
not all of the symptoms are present in a very clear or pronounced form.[126]

The harvest year 1623–4 was one of bad crops and high
prices all over the country: the weather was very nasty. The
textile industry was in the depth of depression, just as it was
in Beauvais 1693–4. There had been a sudden rise in burials at
Ashton two years before 1620–1, but after this they returned
to their average of about seventy-five a year. In the harvest
year 1623–4 184 people were buried, over two and a half times

[126] *See page* 294.

the normal, and conceptions fell from an average of about 105 to 60. Unfortunately causes of death are not given and the words 'famine', 'starvation', etc. do not appear. These events could provisionally be classed as an English crisis of subsistence though not a severe one. They are confirmed in a general way by what is known to have been happening in a wool manufacturing area in Yorkshire at the same time.[126]

The one parish which undoubtedly did suffer this disaster, experienced it during these same months in the early 1620's when the situation at Ashton-under-Lyne was so gloomy. The register of the church of Greystoke in the Cumberland hills contains 474 baptisms during the decade 1610–19, with extremes of 40 and 58, 368 burials (20 and 61) and 96 marriages (6 and 15). The expected average then must have been about 47 baptisms, 37 burials and 10 marriages every year. Even here alas, there is a chasm in the register from December 1st, 1620, to June 16th, 1622, so that the full story of the crisis cannot be told and we cannot reconstruct the harvest year over the critical months.[127]

In the calendar year 1623 no less than 161 people were buried in the churchyard at Greystoke, which is over four times the expected number. Only 20 babies were baptized, which is almost down to half the average, and marriages fell about as much, to 4. We cannot say how conceptions behaved at the height of the crisis, but in the worst period for burials, which was September to November, 1623, there were only 3 conceptions, no marriages and 62 registered deaths. We know that some of these deaths were due to starvation, for the entries actually confess this melancholy fact.

Extracts from the Register of Greystoke 1623
29th January: '*A poor fellow destitute of succour and was brought out of the street in Johnby into the house of Anthony Clemmerson, constable there, where he died.*'
27th March: '*A poor hungerstarved beggar child, Dorothy, daughter of Henry Patteson, Miller.*'
28th March: '*Thomas Simpson a poor, hungerstarved beggar boy and son of one Richard Simpson of Brough by Mandgyes house in Thorp.*'
19th May: '*At night James Irwin, a poor beggar stripling born upon the borders of England. He died in Johnby in great misery.*'

[127] *See page 295.*

12th July: '*Thomas, child of Richard Bell, a poor man, which child died for very want of food and maintenance to live.*'
11th September: '*Leonard, son of Anthony Cowlman, of Johnby, late deceased, which child died for want of food and maintenance to live.*'
12th September: '*Jaine, wife of Anthony Cowlman, late deceased, which woman died in Edward Dawson's barn of Greystoke for want of maintenance.*'
27th September: '*John, son of John Lancaster, late of Greystoke, a waller by trade, which child died for want of food and means.*'
[*The register tells us that he was baptized on October 17th, 1619, so he was four years old.*]
4th October: '*Agnes, wife of John Lancaster, late of Greystoke, a waller by his trade, which woman died for want of means to live.*'
27th October: '*William child of Lancelot Brown, which Lancelot went forth of the country [the district] for want of means.*'

The fells of Cumberland, with their scattered flocks of sheep and their thin crops of cereals, were very different from the sad Beauvais plain, though they may have suffered as badly from too great a press of people dependent upon a textile industry stricken with depression. 'The smallness, barrenness, and the multitude of inhabitants in the habitable places of this country is . . . far incomparable to the other counties of the kingdom,' declared the justices of the neighbouring county of Westmorland in the year 1622, then already attempting to make some headway against the conditions which were to have such a tragic effect at Greystoke.[128] The deaths which took place there were not, as was usual in France, predominantly of children, in spite of the impression which may be created by the extracts we have printed here.

But if these dismal details are to be made the most of, we must notice the fact that there were two cases of a mother and child both dying of famine at almost the same time, and that one of these pathetic families was without a shelter. Wandering beggars, like the miserable James Irwin, were, as we have already said, a feature of the countryside at all times, and most noticeable under the Tudors. They may perhaps have attracted more attention than is numerically justified, for it will be seen that Gregory King's table provides for only 30,000 of them in the whole population. A significant thing for the

[128] *See page* 294.

study of men's attitude to the means of keeping themselves
and their families alive is the action of Lancelot Brown,
named in the last entry, who appears to have left the starvel-
ing hillsides of Cumberland to try to find subsistence in some
more fortunate part of England.

His child died nevertheless, and perhaps the loss of the
breadwinner, rather than exhaustion of the food supply, must
be held to be the immediate, if not the final, cause of death.
We cannot yet tell, any more than we can say whether or not
the wandering father would have found much more favourable conditions anywhere in the highland zone of England in
the dreadful season 1623–4. Other parish registers show a
pattern similar to that at Ashton-under-Lyne, and some of
those which run unbroken through the troubled years 1640 to
1660 reveal what may turn out to be a terrible climacteric
about 1645, just as the war between King and Parliament was
reaching its crisis. At Colyton in Devonshire it is reckoned
that something like a quarter of the thousand and more
inhabitants were buried during the calendar year 1645; but
there the words 'great sickness' appear in the register.[129]

The task of isolating deaths due to starvation from those
which can be ascribed more confidently to infectious diseases
has still to be undertaken for any parish. Perhaps it will not
be long before we are able to make use of medical advances in
the study of nutritional diseases which demonstrate that their
casualties show a particular pattern of mortality as to age of
victim, sex and time of year at which death is most likely.
Certainly pellagra, which is the most conspicuous deficiency
disease amongst corn-eating populations such as those of
seventeenth-century England, has been shown to have such
a pattern. It would of course be necessary to be able to distinguish this from the mortality pattern of the plague, to be
discussed shortly, in order to infer which one of these two
was the cause of any particular excess of deaths. A register
which contains no more information than date of burial, sex
and maturity of the corpse would permit this to be done.[130]

When entries like those from Greystoke are found, or when
the clerk of the rich metropolitan parliamentary parish of St
Margaret's, Westminster, records the causes of death during
the summer months of the year 1557 and ascribes 16 out of
181 to 'famine', we can be fairly certain that individuals were

[129] *See page* 295.   [130] *See page* 295.

dying of lack of food. This must have been true at Wednesbury in Staffordshire in 1674, where the register reads under November 22nd: 'John Russel being famished through want of food (Josiah Freeman being overseer), was buried with the solemnity of many tears.' Food prices were very high in the area at about that time, and the mid-1670's resembled the early 1620's in many respects in this region. But poor John Russel's fate was obviously thought by his indignant neighbours to have been due to the neglect of the overseer of the poor.[131]

In the extreme conditions which wrecked the family of Cocu in Beauvais it seems probable that no system of poor relief could have been effective, and the arrangements in that city were apparently exceptionally good. Transfer payments, as the economists call them, between the prosperous and the dependent could never have prevented crises of subsistence of the kind found by the French historical demographers, and which may have occurred in seventeenth-century Scotland as well. There was simply not enough food to go round at such times, and poor people were inevitably in danger from high prices. More efficient means of distribution between country and country, region and region, even village and village might have mitigated the crises, and a really ambitious policy of storage could have gone far towards eliminating them. Everything in the French evidence points to the absence of adequate stocks of corn and of the means of distributing it when it was wanted. It would have been necessary to have had an accurate idea of the numbers of people who had to be fed in order to make quite certain that food would never run out, and there are indications that counts of the population were in fact carried out for the purpose in some cities: at Ypres in the 15th century, for example, or perhaps at Coventry in the year 1520. The story of what Joseph did in preparation for the Seven Lean Years in Egypt might well have been written for the administrators of the pre-industrial world.

Once we are alive to the real possibility of famine the perpetual preoccupation of the authorities of that era, governmental and municipal, with the supply of food for the poor takes on a new significance. The insistence on fair prices for all victuals and especially for bread is a reminder that people might starve even where supplies were available, if they had

[131] *See page* 295.

exhausted their savings and lost their employment, or even sometimes if taxation had pressed them too hard. Hence the strict control of all dealings in breadstuffs and all handlers of them, especially buyers and sellers of wheat. The stocks of corn so conspicuous in the records of Tudor and Stuart London were examples of a policy which had to be pursued all the time and in deadly earnest.[132] It was indeed a matter of life and death, and felt to be so by King, Mayor, Justice of the Peace and Overseer of the Poor alike. Right up to the time of the French Revolution and beyond in Europe the threat of high prices for food was the commonest and most potent cause of public disorder. It was dangerous when overseers were as neglectful as Josiah Freeman of Wednesbury, and during the years of scarcity in the early 1620's corn was stored locally. The harvest year 1623–4 was in many places the worst of a succession of bad harvest years, and in this it is typical of the crises detected in France. It may also be typical of these black periods that this one should have ended in an outbreak of plague.

At this point arises the most difficult of the many questions which will have to be settled before we can make up our minds about the issue which confronts us. We have to decide whether liability to starvation, extinction owing to an insufficient supply of food, must be taken as a defining characteristic of the world we have lost, and fear of such catastrophe an attribute which all our ancestors shared, but which we no longer experience, at least not in respect of ourselves. Are many of the deaths which are put down by historical writers with such facility to the plague, pestilence, endemic diseases, in fact to be attributed to lack of food? If not always to a famine, to a sudden-felt visitation of the sort so far discussed, then more often to months and months, or even years, of under-nourishment?

Only quite recently have we begun to be able to distinguish the effects of one disease on past populations from the effects of other diseases, and so from starvation. The bubonic plague is undoubtedly the worst killer of pre-industrial populations, though some of its visitations, as reported by the men of the past, may well have been mixed up with typhus and other things, or not have been plague at all. The exact nature of bubonic plague and the extraordinary mechanism by which

[132] *See page* 295.

it spreads is now completely understood. Although there is still some doubt about agents of transmission, times have changed since Charles Creighton, the greatest authority on epidemics in English history, died in 1927 still believing that plague was due to an exhalation from the corrupted earth.

The usual mode of entry of the bacterium is through the bite of a particular species of rat flea, which preys for the most part on a particular species of rat – the black rat. This flea will only attack mammals other than rats when it is 'blocked', that is to say so crammed with the plague bacteria that it can no longer digest. Human beings seem to be the creatures most vulnerable to such plague-fraught fleas, and the dogs and cats which were regularly exterminated during outbreaks of the disease in England died innocently and needlessly. It is necessary for a heavily infected rat population to persist in order for blocked fleas to appear, and only under these conditions can the disease persist through the winter, at the time when the fleas are dormant. As with epidemics of other diseases, mortality was heaviest at the beginning of an outbreak, when virtually every victim died, and went down somewhat as the weeks went by and cases multiplied. The virulence of the infection, and the odd, almost arbitrary way in which humans contract it, can be judged from the fact that no more than 12 per cent of rat fleas ever get 'blocked', and that the bacteria are active only between 60° and 75°F. Cool weather, therefore, or a real heat wave, interrupts an epidemic.[133]

This medical evidence obviously provides some grounds for separating plague deaths from other deaths. Bubonic plague is a disease of the late summer, though it appears in the spring, and will be found where rats are both abundant and likely to be in contact with the infection. This was most probable in sea-ports (London, Southampton, Bristol are notorious), river-ports (Cambridge was often attacked), and trade centres generally, and much less likely in the 9,000 English country villages. Records confirm this diagnosis, which, it must be noticed, does not allow of spread by contact between humans directly, only via rats and their fleas. But there do seem to be cases where heavy mortality, apparently caused by bubonic plague, occurred at times of the year other than late summer, and there is still a question as to whether

[133] *See page* 295.

the even more dangerous pneumonic form, which can be spread direct from person to person, was still active in England in the sixteenth and seventeenth centuries. There is also a chance that plague-infected body lice, or *Pulex irritans*, the ordinary man-haunting flea, if really abundant, could spread infection without benefit of rats. Body lice also carry typhus, and this can flourish outside the temperature range which limits the spread of the plague.

The great unsolved mystery about bubonic plague is why it disappeared from England after the 1660's. The reduction and virtual extinction of the notorious house rat or black rat has often been supposed to be the cause, but the reasons for the departure of these creatures is not known, and there are other possible explanations for the fading away of bubonic plague.[134] Nevertheless there is no doubt that whilst it was prevalent it could and did inflict terrible disasters on cities, towns and plenty of villages too. Wherever there is a tenfold increase, or even a trebling, of burials in a parish register in the months between May and October, and particularly in July to September, then bubonic plague can be presumed, especially in the presence of the other circumstances mentioned. Marriages and baptisms fall only a little, and this provides some indication of presence of plague rather than famine, but the simultaneous occurrence of typhus or other infections often confuses the issue. As might be expected, London suffered worst, and through the capital the whole country was injured. It has been reckoned that the Great Plague of the late summer of 1665 struck a blow as ruinous to the population of London as did the atomic bomb to that of Hiroshima in 1945. But 1563 seems to have been the worst plague year for London, followed by 1625, and from 1625 comes a heartrending story out of Malpas, a Cheshire village. In one small hamlet there, the parish register tells us, everyone died and the last full grown man to fall sick actually dug his own grave in the yard of the house and buried himself in it.[135]

Visitations of the plague as well as crises of subsistence are peculiarly awful to read about in our day and in our country, where food shortage is virtually unknown and where infectious diseases have lost their killing capacity almost entirely. But the attitude towards death may have been very

[134] *See page* 295.   [135] *See page* 296.

different in earlier times where nursing mothers and wage-earning fathers were much more likely to die and where babies perished in such large numbers also, in addition to the old and the chronically ill. A contemporary realist might have said that very many of those who perished would have died anyway within a few years. He could also have pointed to the undoubted upsurge in marriages and then in births, together with the low level of burials, which succeeded the catastrophe, and did something to make up the losses.

Of course, such an outlook was impossible then, just as it was impossible for the connection between rats, fleas and bubonic infection to be understood. No Stuart Englishman, not even Locke or Graunt, would have thought of vital statistics in such a way. It takes a complete transformation of attitude to recognize what a death-rate might be, and why it is important: only a handful of people ever developed anything like that attitude in the world we have lost, and even they did not get very far. It has been recently shown that some authorities could control plague infection to a surprising degree, but by rule-of-thumb methods, never by scientific insight.[136] The ordinary feeling about the black years, amongst the peasantry at least, was to behave as if they had never happened; there are many records of the more serious-minded of their contemporaries remarking on this very natural reaction.

Whatever its nature, and however it was related to diet and the means of subsistence generally, the important fact about the plague in England in the final years before the coming of industry is that it faded into insignificance, earlier here than in France. The Great Plague of the history books and popular memory, the visitation of London and much of the country in 1665–6, was the last in our country which can be compared in its catastrophic effects with the French demographic crises. It is impossible as yet to conjecture whether this disappearance could be related in any way with the remarkable developments which Professor Goubert goes on to trace out in eighteenth-century France after the 1740's, at least for the area of Beauvais. Crises of subsistence ceased to occur, infantile mortality went down, and the precarious balance between increase and decrease of population gave way to a steady upward trend. This transformation led to the disappearance of the old demographic régime, as he calls it,

[136] *See page* 296.

and the succession of the modern demographic régime, in which all in Western Europe and highly industrialized countries still live. The alteration of the relation between population and the means of subsistence, if it did indeed occur in France generally before the year 1750, happened without benefit of industrialism on the modern scale.[137]

Perhaps these facts from France should persuade us that liability to starvation without warning cannot be counted as a defining characteristic of the world we have lost in the same way as the facts of the scale of life which have been discussed already. The mild, retiring English clergyman, Thomas Malthus, first formulated the population and subsistence law in the form used by all subsequent economists. This was as late as 1797, when large-scale industry was already under way in his own country, for the first time in history anywhere, and he did not admit that this economic transformation made his law obsolete. It was fashionable until quite recently to claim that Malthus was wrong in his persistence, but the awful fate of Ireland in the decade after his death, during the Great Famine as it is called, is surely a sufficient demonstration that the crisis of subsistence was not abolished all over the British Isles by the coming of industry. It may nevertheless be deceptive to read the circumstance of Ireland and Irish society in the 1840's too easily back into the pre-industrial past of our own country. Let us return to the situation of the English village community before the year 1700, for there are further circumstances affecting it which have a bearing on the question of whether the peasants really starved in England in the old days.

The operation of what Malthus called the prudential check may first be noticed once again. This kept population within the resources of food by postponing marriage. In spite of the possibility that women reached sexual maturity rather late, if they had all begun to have children immediately they had become fecund, the number born to each marriage would have been far more than the eight which has been laid down for the average when uninterrupted, and the five for marriages overall. For this reason the age at marriage provides a very sensitive indicator of social conditions. It may record the effects of economic expansiveness, or men's appreciation of it. It may sometimes record the failure of the prudential check to operate

[137] *See page* 296.

on young immigrants to new industrial towns, at a long remove from the traditional, authoritarian atmosphere of the village. Nevertheless, it is by no means clear that earlier marriage for the mass of the people was always the permanent result of the growth of urban centres and of industry, and it is not yet known whether we should seek here for the reason why population so often rose as European countries became industrialized. But it is obvious that a knowledge of the age of marriage and its variations is of the greatest importance to historical analysis; the mistake about the typicality of Juliet is not a trivial mistake at all.

Infantile mortality is a very well-known and much used index of welfare, and certainly varies with adequacy of nourishment. The French crises of subsistence, as has been stated, were marked by very sharp increases of deaths amongst the new born, and in abortions too, though abortions are very difficult to reckon even from French parish registers. It so happens that Ashton-under-Lyne is one of the very few places where burials of abortions are registered in our parish books at the relevant time, and they were higher in the early 1620's than at any other time when the clerk recorded them, reaching nearly 7 per cent of births in 1623.[138] But even at this level they did not much exceed the rate of nearly 6 per cent which can be derived from John Graunt's extracts from the London bills of mortality for the early 1630's, and neither figure is as high as the estimated rate for our own day.[139]

More marked at Ashton during the years of crisis was the peak in the total of 'nuncupative' babies, or 'chrissoms' as they were called, who had to be buried. Chrissoms were those who died before there was time to baptize them; they were put into a grave wrapped in the christening cloth which had been prepared for the ceremony at the font. Our ancestors had other curious and to our generation rather ghoulish customs. In some places when a mother died in childbed the baby was christened on her coffin.[140] Chrissom children buried numbered nine in the crisis year 1623–4 at Ashton, when fifty-eight was the total of those conceived. They were even more numerous in 1621, the first of the two years of high mortality, when they reached nearly a fifth of all conceptions. The increase in babies buried in the first year of life can also be

[138] *See page* 296.   [139] *See page* 296.
[140] *See page* 296.

seen at Greystoke at the same time, at its worst when persons
were actually dying of starvation.

Infantile mortality has a wider significance than its relationship with periods of want and starvation in the traditional
world. It enters into our general attitude in the twentieth
century towards the world we have lost, because of the widespread belief that industrialization in its early stages had a
disastrous effect on the health of the newly born. It seems to
be supposed that only recently and in only the most advanced
industrial countries has the mass of the population been able
to go back to anything like healthy, natural conditions under
which the peasant woman had her babies, and therefore only
recently has the tragic waste of infant life which comes from
industrial conditions begun to be stemmed. Historians have
sometimes referred in an ominous way to some isolated index
for the mortality of babies in an early industrial suburb, and
the national proportion of 153 per thousand dying in the first
year of life in the decade 1841–50 has occasionally been cited
as an indication of a general deterioration. What evidence we
now have on the issue points to a somewhat different
conclusion.

The French historical demographers, in fact, tend to suppose that a figure much greater than 150 per thousand, a figure
nearer to 200 per thousand and probably even higher, was
typical of rural villages in pre-industrial France in normal
times. Since this may seem a startling proposition a few of
their results are listed in the table which follows.[141] They have
been worked out after intensive study of their more detailed
and reliable parish registers, and using the methods of family
reconstitution which are only now coming into use in England.
Even these figures from France may not state the true position all over the country, and there were, as we have seen,

Infantile Mortality, France and Belgium

Crulai, Normandy	1675–1775	210–230
Auneuil, Beauvaisis,	1656–1755	288
Saint Laurent-des-Eaux, Sologne	1st Quarter 18th century	326
Paris Region	1750–1789	230
Vieuxbourg, Belgium	1700–19	206·7
	1720–1739	193·9

[141] *See page* 297.
K

enormous variations in infantile mortality from time to time, in accordance with nutrition and with general health. But it seems unlikely that the figures cited, or the general average, exaggerate the probable mortality amongst the newly born. If anything it may understate it, for even in France the sharp eye of the curé might occasionally fail to observe an unwanted baby stealthily disposed of, or a careless family might fail to report it.

In England we have found it difficult to confirm an infantile mortality as high as 200 per thousand. Our best figures so far come from Wrigley's reconstitution at Colyton, and give an infantile mortality rate of 120 to 140 in the second half of the sixteenth century, 126 to 158 in the first half of the seventeenth, 118 to 147 in the second half, 162 to 203 in the first half of the eighteenth century and 122 to 153 between 1750 and 1837. Cruder methods provide a rate of almost 300 in the 1660's for the parish of Wem in Shropshire, and at Ashton-under-Lyne the minimal rate certainly rose above 200 in the years of crisis in the early 1620's to which we have already referred.[142] Though it was 176 for the six years 1629–34, it never reached 200 for any prolonged period in the seventeenth century.

The largest sample available known for any European country for so early a date is contained in Graunt's study of the bills of mortality in London. His tables can be made to yield a rate of infantile mortality of over 200, but only on the assumption that all those he records as 'Chrissomes and Infants' at their burial were in fact less than twelve months old. Between 1629 and 1632, for example, there were 9,277 such burials out of a total of 36,024 baptisms, which would mean a rate of 257 per thousand. Even this estimate leaves open the question of whether any of those he classifies as dying of 'Convulsions' or 'Teeth and Worms' were in fact under one year of age.[143] We can reckon infantile mortality fairly accurately and with interesting additional details at Clayworth during the pastorate of William Sampson. It is interesting to find that in his village over the whole period the rate was on average 215, not so very different from that at Crulai. Since such information is still rare it might be as well to present it in full, together with some rough indication of the prices the villagers were paying for the wheat,

[142] *See page* 297.   [143] *See page* 297.

rye or barley they made into bread, those of them, that is to
say, who had to buy their food rather than living off their
own crops.[144]

---

*Registered Infantile Mortality at Clayworth, Notts, rate per thousand live
births. (With a crude index of prices of cereals.)*

1680–1682	385	Price Index 1676–85	64·5 (1682	77·0)
1683–1685	300			
1686–1688	350			
1689–1691	242	Price Index 1686–96	53·4 (1690	43·7)
1692–1694	185			
1695–1697	168			
1698–1700	117	Price Index 1696–1701	68·4 (1698	103·5)
1701–1703	174			

If it had not been for the very unfavourable years in the
1680's, it will be seen, registered infantile mortality even here
would have been on a somewhat lower level than it seems
ordinarily to have been in France at the same time. Nothing
can be made of the vague tendency of the level of local cereal
prices to vary with the numbers of babies dying. But it is not
without interest, that the number of baptisms, marriages
and burials as a whole shows that there was something of a
demographic crisis in the years 1678–81 with its peak of
thirty-one burials in 1679, whilst the average during Sampson's time was under five overall. He never mentioned hunger
during the twenty-eight years he lived in Clayworth, but he
does record November and December, 1679, as 'sickly months',
when, after 'a very wet time about autumn . . . the quartan
ague was almost in every house and none in some escaped
it.'[145]

Mortality at Clayworth interests for other reasons which
will appear in the next chapter, but it would be difficult to use
it even as a token demonstration that the liability of infants
to die in their first year of life was increased by the coming of
industry in England. The truth seems to be that infantile
mortality was unlikely to have been higher under Queen
Victoria than it was under the Stuarts, and the first rough
indications are that it was lower; fewer babies certainly died
in industrial England in the 1840's than in peasant France in
the 1670's, '80's or '90's. No doubt the early industrial suburbs
did show a lamentable death-rate amongst the very youngest

[144] *See page* 297.   [145] *See page* 297.

of their inhabitants, and the conspicuous fact about them
was that in the areas of the same cities where the richer people
lived infantile mortality was very much lower even in the
early twentieth century. It seems true to say that a baby
born into the Gorbals of Glasgow in 1879 probably had a
better chance of surviving to its first birthday than a baby
born into the entirely rural, open-field village of Clayworth
in the fairly prosperous county of Nottinghamshire in 1679.

It is not possible to give precise reasons why the peasantry
found it so difficult to keep their babies alive, or whether the
food supply was the governing influence. The relation between
the amount and cost of food and the variations in the level
of mortality, of men and women as well as children, must
remain an open question for the time, along with that of
whether crises of subsistence were a present possibility in the
English towns and countryside. One further plaintive query
may be addressed to the historians of England, rather than
to the slightly exasperating records of their doings left by our
predecessors.

Why is it that we know so much about the building of the
British Empire, the growth of Parliament, and its practices,
the public and private lives of English kings, statesmen,
generals, writers, thinkers and yet do not know whether all
our ancestors had enough to eat? Our genealogical knowledge
of how Englishmen and their distant kinsmen overseas are
related to the Englishmen of the pre-industrial world is truly
enormous, and is growing all the time. Why has almost nothing been done to discover how long those earlier Englishmen
lived and how confident most of them could be of having any
posterity at all? Not only do we not know the answers to these
questions, until now we never seem to have bothered to ask
them.

Personal Discipline and Social Survival
Chapter 6

With notes on the history
of bastardy in England

Prone as we are to be sentimental about our ancestors, we are also quite prepared to believe that they were often wicked people, at least on the standards which they set for themselves. When bastardy comes into the conversation, we suppose that country people, and our forefathers in general, were far more likely than we are to bring illegitimate children into the world and far more tolerant of bastardy as a condition. It is widely supposed too, that no shrewd, hard-working peasant or craftsman, to whom strong, hard-working sons and daughters were a tangible asset, would ever undertake to marry a girl unless he knew from his own sexual experience that she was capable of bearing children. If she did prove barren (this implies) no marriage would take place, and the poor girl would live out her life as a reject.

This element of suspicion in our attitude to the world we have lost is probably complicated in its origins. So sudden and complete has been the desertion of the countryside for the cities in our recent history, that it was perhaps natural for people to suppose that those who remained behind were, and are, the inferior people – in aptitude and intelligence, and therefore, presumably, in moral calibre. Though this impression is faulty in its supposition of what actually happened, since the towns and cities have been recruited far more from their own natural increase than is often thought, it has had some little justification from surveys of the condition of rural communities in recent times; the village idiot, who was also a half-wit and a degenerate, is not entirely a fiction.[146] But

[146] *See page* 298.

to this must be added the outlook every emigrant tends to adopt towards those who lacked the energy and foresight to leave with him. He has to assure himself that the people he, his father or his grandfather had lived amongst in the green countryside, in the idyllic village community, were also people without initiative, inbred and not entirely desirable.

This unappealing attitude may perhaps seem to be confirmed to some degree by the suggestion a French historical demographer made to explain the occasional conditions of crisis which concerned us in the last chapter. These periods of disastrous death-rates, of rising infant mortality and of high rates of abortion, were, he thinks, also periods when bastardy was commoner and when more children were conceived before marriage; they may therefore possibly be explained as intervals of moral collapse as well as of scarcity of food and widespread infectious disease. At these times, so the suggestion goes, the peasantry broke free to some extent from the strict rule of sexual continence outside marriage which the Church universal and established opinion prescribed for everybody at all times. Hence a dangerously large number of children with no hope of survival, leading to infanticide as well as to a sudden growth in numbers of children not within the familial system.[147]

This hypothesis has met with little approval from other students of the problem. Its rejection is due to more than a dislike of its apparent desire to convict the suffering populations of moral obliquity. Though we shall find the issue of prenuptial conception – the tendency of brides to be already pregnant when it came to the celebration of the marriage in Church – is a complex and interesting one, in England at least the general proposition is easily disposed of. Our English ancestors cannot have been generally guilty of sexual irresponsibility of the kind which has just been described.

The peasants and the craftsmen of Tudor and Stuart times seem on the whole to have been cautious about the procreation of children and the formation of families. All the facts we have surveyed about the late age of marriage amongst them, and the circumstances which surrounded every decision to set up a new household, seem to imply that they were well enough aware that the fund of food and conveniences of life were strictly limited even if starvation did not ordinarily have

[147] *See page* 298.

to be reckoned as a possibility. Their marked success in finding themselves new partners when they were widowed is another sign of recognition that the position of a child was precarious indeed without a father's support, or a mother's care. Neither the relatives, nor even the parents of those who had irregular children were prepared to shoulder the burden as often as we perhaps expect them to have done.

It might perhaps be better to say that it was custom, traditional conduct and the regulations of the Church which took these dangers into account, rather than the deliberate reflection of men and women, whose only action was to do as others did and as always had been done. The code of moral behaviour in the traditional world can be looked upon from this point of view as an essential part of the workings of the general social scheme. If the shape of the society was to be maintained then Pauline morality had to be maintained.

It is essential to realize that these norms of conduct were enforced by a constituted authority, that is to say the established church, with its spiritual courts, its executive officials called *apparitors* and its humiliating and very public punishments. Anyone who committed or tried to commit a sexual act with anyone not his spouse, whether or not conception took place, ran the risk of a summons to the archdeacon's court – the lowest in the hierarchy of spiritual courts – a fine, and then penance in church at service time, or in the market place. If a person about whom a *fame of incontinency* had got abroad (that is a suspicion of a sexual escapade) ignored the summons or refused the punishment, then excommunication followed. This meant exile from the most important of all social activities, isolation within the community.

The lay courts and lay authority could be invoked for the more serious offences, and this often happened for the begetting of bastards. The official punishment for the most scandalous acts of all, homosexual intercourse or intercourse with animals, consummated physically, was condemnation to death. Almost no case of this kind is known to scholars, and probably a very great many of the lesser offences went unpunished, but there can be no doubt that much reporting, summoning and writ-executing was always going on. You could not let fornication take place in your house, or allow a bastard to be born there, or as much as offer a job to an excommunicate, without running these risks. It was not wise to rely on the silence of your friends and neighbours because the courts upheld what was thought to be right. The system had the support of the community, at least until the time of Charles II and in many places, in Scotland especially, for generations after that. Sexual irregularity was disliked and condemned as a public disgrace; it is only necessary to read what the witnesses said in the spiritual courts about it to recognize this fact.[148]

Even the more light-hearted beliefs we have entertained about this intriguing subject seem to be unjustified. The tumultuous weeks of Charles II's Restoration to the throne do not seem to have been marked by any perceptible increase in the conceptions, legitimate or illegitimate, recorded by implication in the registers of baptisms nine months later. Nothing in the documents confirms that there was a change in sexual habits to correspond with that licence and licentiousness which has always been associated with the Restoration as a whole period of time.[149] The very interesting literary thesis recently advanced by Mr David Foxon, which would place the beginnings of prurience in the decade 1651–60, perhaps gains some support from the fact that the illegitimacy ratios, as will be seen from the table printed below, reached a nadir in that decade. They continued low for the rest of the century and for well on into the eighteenth century too, but sexual prurience did not decline with the rise of illegitimacy in the later eighteenth century, and was surely at its height when bastards were most common, that is to say, under Queen Victoria.[150]

The impression left by the beginning of research into the sexual conduct of the men and women of pre-industrial England is that regulation of sexual behaviour was on the whole successful. Less difference than might be expected has yet been found between town and country, gentry and commoner. It is an astonishing fact that registered illegitimacy was actually lower in English cities than in the countryside in the nineteenth century, but earlier than that the differences are too slight to impress the general observer. Hypocrisy was presumably as widespread then as it always is, and indifference to religious sanctions was no doubt common and getting commoner. Fornication and adultery took place of course, and were often conveniently camouflaged by the low fertility

[148] *See page* 299.   [149] *See page* 299.   [150] *See page* 299.

of very young women and by the regularity with which babies came to married women in the ordinary course.[151] It can be assumed that much was concealed from the neighbours, and more from the parish priests, probably more in Protestant England than in Catholic France.

Certainly the English of Stuart times seem to have been less stringent about base-born children than the French of Bourbon times. Whores seem to have been an acknowledged feature of the social scene; the earnest ministers might deplore their existence, but when they talked of behaviour in a wife which might lead a husband to seek satisfaction elsewhere they accepted the brothel as a fact.[152] At Wem the fluctuations we can observe in the illegitimacy rate seem to have been due to some extent to increases and decreases in the number of bastards born to women who had more than one, often two and sometimes even four or six. This interesting result, which can already be confirmed for other parishes and may be a general one, suggests that bastard bearing was not spread throughout the community at large. There are even signs that it could run in families, and that having had a bastard was certainly no necessary bar to subsequent marriage, even for women. But by and large men and women lived what the respectable call respectable lives. They were chaste until marriage came, or perhaps until it was in certain prospect in the very near future, and then they begot children very quickly indeed. Thereafter they cohabited and they only seem very rarely to have indulged themselves outside marriage. It is an extraordinary thing that we can investigate these, the most intimate doings of our predecessors and discuss them with some confidence, whilst many of their more public actions and attributes are still mysterious and will probably remain so. In doing so we are observing the purchase over what they allowed themselves to do of a whole social system.

Its operation can be seen in the *presentments* made by the churchwardens of each parish to the spiritual courts of those actions or suspected actions of members of the community for which he or she was required to give satisfaction to the church and to society. These reports, and the lively discussion of them in the courts by those accused and the witnesses, certainly give an impression of widespread immorality, or

[151] *See page* 299.   [152] *See page* 300.   [153] *See page* 300.

attempted immorality, in the parishes whose records have been preserved and examined. But it is quite impossible to gain any sort of numerical impression from evidence of this kind; we have only to imagine the result of an attempt at estimating the extent of extra-marital intercourse from the records of our own divorce courts to recognize this fact. Even the proportion of baptisms marked *illegitimate* in the parish registers is an exceedingly uncertain indicator. Numbers of baptized bastards may well have to be multiplied fifty, seventy or even a hundred times and more[154] in order to guess at the number of sexual lapses which lay behind them. What is worse, this large but indefinite multiplier may be expected to have varied with the length of cohabitation. It may have varied also from time to time, place to place, and perhaps social class to social class, both of man and of woman. By sexual lapses responsible for such illegitimacy as can be observed, acts of fornication only are at issue for we know nothing numerical whatever about acts of adultery in past time, almost nothing about them in our own time. The one twentieth-century figure for adulterine bastards, that is birth to married women of children procreated by men who are not their husbands at the time, suggests that these numbers may not have been negligible.[155]

If the records of the church courts are filled with notices of sexual incontinence, those of the magistrates courts are studded with measures taken in punishment of unmarried mothers, and sometimes of unmarried fathers too, with provision for the upkeep of the child:

Jane Sotworth of Wrightington, spinster, swears that Richard Garstange of Fazarkerley, husbandman, is the father of Alice, her bastard daughter. She is to have charge of the child for two years, provided she does not beg, and Richard is then to take charge until it is twelve years old. He shall give Jane a cow and 6s. in money. Both he and she shall this day be whipped in Ormeskirke.

So ordered the Lancashire justices at the Ormskirk Sessions on Monday, April 27th, 1601, though the language they used was Latin and lengthier. At Manchester, in 1604, they went so far as to require that Thomas Byrom, gentleman, should maintain a bastard he had begotten on a widow, and be

[154] *See page* 300.   [155] *See page* 301.

whipped too. On October 10th, 1604, he was whipped in Manchester market-place.[156]

Not many 'gentlemen' can ever have suffered this indignity. But the frequency of these cases in the records, even the number of times behaviour of this character has appeared in the present essay, must not be allowed to create the impression that illegitimacy was commonplace, more often to be met with than it is in our own day. The trouble taken over each instance by spiritual and lay authorities makes it clear that it was an irregularity, a breach of the norm, and when their care grew less obvious in later Stuart times, the figures in the records of baptism marked 'illeg.', 'base', 'spur', or plain 'b.' for bastard did not increase. They grew less.

Illegitimacy is recorded in the parish registers, with a consistency which makes it seem clear that where they appear at all the entries must be taken seriously as an indication of the extent of the practice. This in itself is a demonstration of the power of the clergy and of public opinion because it must have taken some courage to offer a base-born child to the priest for baptism, though something must surely be allowed for the mother's concern for the baby's immortal soul. Evasion may have been common of course, and it is probably wise to reject as testimony those parish registers, or those periods of registration, in which bastardy appears not at all, or only at very long intervals. The fall in the number of illegitimacies which might come under a strong-minded parish priest, a man like William Sampson, could have been due to the fact that the unmarried pregnant girls evaded registration, rather than to the success of the parson in enforcing the code. Nevertheless detailed study of entries for bastards in the registers makes them look reliable as indicators of the extent of illegitimacy. Where such events are recorded at all, that is in about a fifth or a third of English parishes, figures tend to confirm each other. The well-marked pattern of variation over time displayed in the table below is found in every one of the 100 and more registers which so far have been analysed for the purpose.

The historical study of illegitimacy is interesting and difficult; it is much better pursued comparatively between countries. The English figures over the period since the late sixteenth century presented here are so far the only ones to

[156] *See page* 302.

cover so long a duration of time in the past in any country and the fluctuations they record are certainly intriguing. Perhaps everyone would have expected the dramatic drop coming with the Puritan ascendancy in the 1650's. But who

---

Ratios of illegitimacy, sixteenth–twentieth century

Registered baptisms, percentage marked illegitimate, England and France

24 English Parishes, 1581–1810 (From Laslett and Oosterveen)

				Mean percentage of illegitimate baptisms:		
1581–90	3·7	1701–10	2·0	Whole period	1581–1810	3·6
1591–1600	4·5	1711–20	2·0	Earlier high	1581–1630	4·0
1601–10	4·3	1721–30	2·6	Middle low	1651–1720	1·7
1611–20	3·6	1731–40	2·9	Later high	1741–1810	5·1
1621–30	3·7	1741–50	3·5			
1631–40	2·4	1751–60	3·6	*French Parishes*		
1641–50	2·1	1761–70	4·7	*Crulai*, Normandy (Henry)		
1651–60	0·5	1771–80	5·3	1604–1699	0·6	
1661–70	1·6	1781–90	5·4	1700–1749	0·5	
1671–80	1·6	1791–1800	8·0	1750–1799	0·9	
1681–90	1·8	1801–10	6·3	Paris Region, 41 villages.		
1691–1700	1·9			1740–1789	0·5	

Registered births, percentage marked illegitimate, England and Wales, France, USA. Nineteenth and twentieth centuries.

England and Wales		*France*	*England and Wales*	
1811–50	5·3–7·0	4·5–7·5	1900–40	3·9–5·4
1851–80	4·7–7·6	7·2–7·5	1941–45	5·4–9·3
1881–1900	4·2–4·7	7·8–8·2	1947–60	4·7–5·4
			1962	6·6

USA, 1965; White, 4·0; Coloured, 26·3.   Both, 7·7.

---

would have guessed that after this the rate of bastardy would fail to go up again in the supposedly dissolute society of Restoration England, and remain at a low point for the whole period up to the 1720's. Even more puzzling, perhaps, is the enormous difference between English illegitimacy ratios before 1800 and those which have been recovered for certain periods and areas in France. French villages seem to have had about a fifth or even less a proportion of all illegitimate births than English villages did in the eighteenth century. There is piquancy too in the fact that illegitimacy ratios in respectable nineteenth-century England were on a high plateau, so to speak. Indeed, bastard babies must have been commoner between 1810 and 1850 than at any other time in our past for which details are known, before our own permissive generation.

This evidence comes from a special, though introductory, study of illegitimacy which is being composed at Cambridge.[157] Obscure as some of the issues are, it should be quite clear even at this stage how difficult it would be to conclude from the data we now have that illegitimacy was higher in traditional England than it is in our country today. The figures we have recovered show that it varied from region to region as well as from period to period. In the west and in the north the earlier peak in bastardy ratios, at the turn of the sixteenth and seventeenth centuries, was higher than the later peak or plateau which came in the late eighteenth century and continued to the late nineteenth century. At Ashton-under-Lyne the ratio for the period 1594 to 1640 was 6·8 per cent and in one year, 1594, it reached 16·6 per cent. At Rochdale it was nearly 10 per cent in the last decade of the sixteenth century, and at Prestbury in Cheshire it was about 16·0 per cent for each successive decade from 1571 to 1599. These are remarkable recordings, but it must be remembered that at the same time in central, southern and eastern England, though there was a rise at this earlier period, levels were generally very much lower, with early seventeenth-century peaks of 2·5 or 3 per cent, and figures not reaching 5·0 per cent until the late eighteenth century. Since at the present time illegitimacy rates in England are well over 5·0 per cent and rising, bastardy was very unlikely to have been commoner in the England of the world we have lost than it is now, particularly when we remember the facts about efficient contraception in our day.

Some of the stereotypes about this practice do seem however to be confirmed by the preliminary figures, particularly the belief in Victorian times that bastardy was then more frequent in France than in England. The comparison between the figures in the two countries in earlier times is complicated by the habit which French peasant mothers seem to have had of abandoning their bastards as *enfants trouvés* in the cities. This did happen in England, but on nothing like the same scale, and it makes French village records suspiciously low, and those of the cities extremely high. It will be seen that

[157] *See page 301.*

French bastardy rates rose dramatically at the turn of the eighteenth and nineteenth centuries, the increase beginning with the great French Revolution and continuing with growing urbanization and industrialization. This development, which has been known to scholars for many years although earlier French figures are still fragmentary, must have helped to establish the account of the course and causes of fluctuations in illegitimacy, which the newly recovered English figures seem so clearly to contradict.

In our own country, as has been seen, bastardy in urban areas appears not to have been greater than that in the countryside, and may even have been smaller. Registered illegitimacy at St Margaret's, Westminster, between 1539 and 1648 never exceeded 2·5 per cent, and was consistent, in spite of population growth and instability. The parish of St Augustine at Bristol, largely peopled with maritime persons, also had a low rate at about the same time.[158] Perhaps these figures should be treated with caution, but this evidence faces us with an intriguing dual possibility. It looks as if there was a significant difference between England and France in respect of babies born outside marriage, with the prize for continence going to the Catholic country rather than to the Protestant, Puritan, ascetic English. It also looks as if it may be difficult to demonstrate that the wicked, worldly city of London, the despair of the earnest preachers, was, along with the other English towns, more given to sexual irregularity than the countryside.

The rise of English illegitimacy ratios in the late sixteenth and later eighteenth centuries came at times when the population was itself increasing, as we have seen, when perhaps the age of marriage was generally a little lower and when more people were getting married. They were times, in fact, when we might suppose that conditions were favourable, certainly not times of frequent dearth. In France the low rate of bastardy is understandably used as evidence for the stability of the rural social structure. But it will be much more difficult to use illegitimacy rates as indications of social dislocation in England if it does turn out that they tended to be highest in times of prosperity and not conspicuously higher in towns than in the countryside. Numbers of bastards should no longer be thought of as the necessary outcome of political

[158] *See page* 301.

crisis or even the movement of armies in England. The illegitimacy rate certainly does not seem to be positively related to scarcity of food and demographic crisis.

Suicide is the most usual index of social demoralization, of *anomie* as the sociologists call it. If ever we could get to know anything reliable about it in these earlier times, it would probably be an even more sensitive index than it is now, marking the relationship between personal discipline and social survival. Killing yourself was a far graver sin in the traditional world than fornication or adultery, and it was punished by the denial of Christian burial. We need go no further than the story of Hamlet to discover this fact.

Isolated records of suicides in the parish registers have occasionally been commented upon, and the extraordinary custom of burying the offending corpse at the crossroads was not abolished until 1823. At Ashton-under-Lyne there seems to have been a more humane attitude. On June 11th, 1683, for example, the following entry appears in the register for that parish.[159]

Roger Peake of Treehouse Bank, who hanged himself in his own barn the 9th day and was stolen into the churchyard and buried on the north side about one of the clock in the morning.

In hugger-mugger they had to inter him, just as they did Ophelia.

The parson must have connived at this neighbourly defiance of the church's rules, since the register is so frank about it. Suicides appear with what looks like fair regularity in the Ashton register throughout the seventeenth century. Most decades passed with only one suicide or none at all, but in the 1610's and the 1680's there were two, whilst in the 1620's there were four. Nothing like a suicide rate can be guessed at from figures of this isolated character, but it is at least worth remembering that the 1620's were times of depression in the textile trade, and of dearth; the probable crisis of subsistence at Ashton itself in 1623 and 1624 has already been discussed. The actual years in which suicides occurred there, however, were spread evenly out over the decade; 1623, 1625, 1626 and 1628.

Suicide in this one settlement, then, does not seem to have been very closely associated with demographic crisis, though

[159] *See page* 301.

it might possibly be connected with economic fluctuation. The French sociologist Durkheim introduced the concept of anomie and established suicide as the most sensitive indicator of that condition. He noticed that suicide increased at times of economic depression, but he also related it to many other social phenomena which are often thought of as leading to disintegration of social life. Urbanization is one of them, and it so happens that a little can be said about suicide and the life of cities in Stuart England because Graunt's study of the bills of mortality can be made to yield a suicide rate of sorts for the middle decades of the seventeenth century, and the bills themselves could be used to continue the series up till the end of the eighteenth century. Taking the population as 400,000, a working minimum, something like 2·5 people per hundred thousand 'Hanged and made away with themselves' during the twenty years preceding 1660 for which Graunt prepared figures. This is a low rate as compared with those which obtain today, when a figure of 10 per 100,000 inhabitants is regarded as favourable, and when in a city like San Francisco the rate can rise as high as 25·9, as it did in 1950. It is probable, however, that many or even all of the people classified in the Bills of Mortality as lunatic at death were in fact suicides, and if this was so the suicide rate might well have been as high as 4 or 5 per hundred thousand in London in Graunt's day.[160]

Though we have no means of comparing these very vague estimates with suicide rates in rural England at that time, these first, preliminary figures do make two things clear. One is that suicide was a known and even a familiar phenomenon in traditional society and is not a peculiarity of our own highly urban, industrialized era. The literature of our ancestors could be used to confirm this essential fact, but it is very important that such evidence should now be related to actual happenings. The second point is that the enormous growth of London in Stuart times with all the disorganization of the pattern of people's lives which it must have brought with it does not on the face of it seem to have been accompanied by a suicide rate which was high on our own standards. Further work might establish some correlation between urbanization and anomie in pre-industrial England, but unfortunately so few parish registers record suicides that a credible rate for rural

[160] *See page* 301.

areas may never be a possibility. It is perhaps worth mentioning that suicide rates in London varied from year to year and decade to decade as they did at Ashton-under-Lyne. The years 1648, 1657 and 1660 seem to have been the bad ones in the seventeenth century. In the eighteenth century suicide in London was consistently higher than in the seventeenth, and from about 1735 it shows a steady tendency to rise.

Perhaps too much attention has been given to these particularly sketchy and unconvincing figures, especially since it seems so unlikely that we shall ever be able to follow Durkheim into those subtleties of social analysis of the incidence of suicide which would so illuminate the society of our ancestors. The last of the possible indices of demoralization is far more easily prepared, though its interpretation turns out to be much more difficult. This is the proportion of the chosen brides of English peasants and craftsmen who had been got with child before ever they took their parts in the rites of matrimony performed inside a Christian church.

It is quite a simple matter to work out a very approximate index for this phenomenon. All that has to be done is to observe the date on which a marriage was performed and then look up the date at which the first child was brought to the font for baptism. Over a given period the number of those baptisms which take place eight months or less from the date of marriage provides the index of pre-nuptial pregnancy, when divided into the number of marriages which are certainly known from entries in the register to have given birth to children in the parish. In England we find that there was an interval of something like a fortnight on average between the date of birth and date of baptism, in the period from which our recordings come. In the table overleaf, therefore, a column has been added for a period of eight and a half months.

Less work has been done as yet on this point in France than on illegitimacy, and the figures for Crulai may be exceptionally low. But it is known that they vary very considerably in that country between parish and parish, just as they obviously do in England. The group of villages from the Ile de France may be exceptional too, and the figures are of later date. But they are well below those from Wylye and nowhere near those for Colyton. So the indications are that the French rates may have been lower than the English ones though the difference may turn out to be nothing like as marked as it is in the case of

illegitimacy; It is also obvious that our record today is not all
that different from that of our ancestors, except perhaps in
some rural areas such as Gosforth. It is unlikely that their

Pre-nuptial pregnancy (England and France).[161]

	Percentage of first baptisms recorded (in months from date of marriage)					
	1–8	*8½*	*9*	*10*	*11*	*12*
Cartmel (Lancs.)						
1660–75 (173 cases)	13·2%	17·8%	24·7%	35·6%	47·7%	57·5%
Wylye (Wilts.)						
1654–1783 (76 cases)	28·9%	34·2%	40·0%	48·5%	63·0%	66·4%
Clayworth (Notts.)						
1650–1750 (127 cases)	10·2%	13·4%	15·7%	22·0%	44·9%	49·8%
Colyton (Devon)						
1538–1799 (976 cases)	46·2%		61·3%		83·4%	
Crulai (France)						
1674–1742 (323 cases)	9·5%		20·3%	33·0%	42·2%	45·4%
3 villages in the Ile de France Late 18th century (206 cases)	19·9%		35·9%	47·1%	54·4%	63·6%
Gosforth, Cumb. 1920–50 (247) (Farmers only)	40% (53·2%)					
England and Wales 1938	18%					
1950	16%					

% of all brides pregnant at marriage.

behaviour in this respect will turn out to be any 'worse' than
ours is now.

Once we start asking for the reasons why Catholic France
had a different record of bastardy and pre-nuptial pregnancy
from that of Protestant England we find ourselves in the midst
of an intricate discussion which would soon take us a long way
from our present purpose. It must always be remembered that
it is community opinion, social consensus, which is at play
when defiance of the norm is being dealt with. Perhaps these
standards were in fact less exacting here than across the
Channel. But some importance must surely be attached to
the different positions of the clergy in the two countries. The
curés of the French villages, celibate and officially without
possessions, were no doubt much closer to the everyday lives

[161] *See page* 301.

of the peasants than the beneficed rectors, the substantial, housekeeping vicars and sometimes conscientious but seldom respected curates of the English Church. The English clergy moreover had to depend far more than the French upon opinion and conscience to keep discipline. In so far as the English Puritans were responsible for sexual prurience – their responsibility has probably been greatly exaggerated – this may be one of the reasons. They tended to emphasize subjective authoritarianism in sexual matters because they could not rely to any extent on the church courts, which is plain from the records.

But, as we have already noticed in respect of illegitimacy, the English had not become lax enough to imply anything like free love. The most regular feature of the above table is found in the percentages in the final column which show how many fertile women had their first baby within the first year of marriage. More than half were born within twelve months, and the full figures show that in both countries by the second anniversary three-quarters or four-fifths of all these couples had produced a child. In maintaining a fairly late age of marriage, our ancestors were in fact holding down the number of births, and it is difficult to assume any degree of promiscuity among single people. Although women may have become mature rather later than they do today, being low in fertility until the early twenties, any general approach of sexual licence would have led to a far higher rate of bastardy than has yet been observed, even in England. Moreover more than half of those babies who arrive early had been conceived within the three months before the marriage ceremony and not earlier. If there had been any form of trial marriage in our country, this proportion would presumably have been lower. Babies would surely have arrived within a month or week or two of the ceremony, not occasionally but as a regular thing.

Nevertheless, these first results of study show that premarital pregnancy was common in England, so common in Colyton and Wylye that it hardly seems possible that an affianced couple was everywhere expected to maintain chastity until after the church celebration was over. We saw how difficult it was to tell from the account of marriage in a Yorkshire rural area in the 1640's exactly when it was that a man and woman caught up in the process of getting married actually began to cohabit. The fact seems to be that in many places in England in the sixteenth, seventeenth and eighteenth centuries, and perhaps in France too, the people in the parishes had a different view of marriage and of the time when its privileges began, from that of the clergy. The church scarcely condoned this difference, but it was only relatively successful in obliterating it, even in France.

The contrast which was possible between community opinion and official doctrine on this point is obvious from the following quotation from the proceedings in the Registry of the Archdeaconry at Leicester, the case in question dating from July, 1598.[162]

The common use and custom within the county of Leicester, specially in and about the town before mentioned (Hoby and Waltham) and in other places thereunto adjoining for the space of 10, 20, 30 or 40 years past hath been and is that any man being a suitor to a woman in the way of marriage is upon the day appointed to make a final conclusion of the marriage before treated of. If the said marriage be concluded and contracted then the man doth most commonly remain in the house where the woman doth abide the night the next following after such contract, otherwise he doth depart without staying the night.

It is plain that no ceremony in church, no ecclesiastical marriage, is in question here, but a contract to marry – an espousal, a troth plight, a *handfasting* as it was called in some localities – what we would term an engagement. The custom of Leicestershire and of a particular group of villages implies two rather surprising features of peasant behaviour. One is that marriage procedures were looked upon as liable to differ considerably from place to place, and even conceivably in the same place from time to time. The other is that in this particular custom sexual intercourse did not have to await the conclusion of the church marriage; it was expected to take place directly the contract was definitely concluded. Brides in Leicestershire at this time must normally have gone to their weddings in the early, and sometimes in the late, stages of pregnancy.

The same seems very likely to have been true of the Mary Gillett who is found testifying to her marriage-in-progress to the Oxfordshire archdeacon's court in 1598.

[162] *See page* 302.

*She doth and hath used the company of William Whit, who is
contracted to her before witnesses and meaneth to marry her as
soon as he is out of service.*

Living together before the church ceremony, as would seem
evident, they were apparently confident that having been
contracted before witnesses was a defence against any charge
of immorality. Sixty years earlier, in the diocese of Ely, Joan
Wigg was careful not to contract herself before witnesses,
though she admitted she had privately promised to marry
John Newman of Royston, Hertfordshire. When he brought
such witnesses to hear her testify to the contract she burst out:

*John Newman, I marvel what you mean. You follow some evil
counsel. I cannot deny but I have made a promise to you to my
husband; but shall we need to marry so soon? It were better for
us to forebear and [have] some household stuff to begin withal.*

This was about 1535. Joan Wigg was clearly a prudent girl.

Espousals cannot be discussed in any length here, and a
special study would be necessary in order to decide how widespread was the customary assumption that they permitted
cohabitation and to estimate their consequent effect on vital
statistics. It is suggested that their persistence in England has
given rise to the belief in the existence of trial marriage
amongst our peasantry. Marriage contracts of this sort were
abolished in the Catholic world by the Papal Bull confirming
the decree of the Council of Trent in 1564, making privy
contracts null and void and directing that all marriages should
be performed by a priest in the church of the parish where one
of the parties dwelt. This would help to explain the apparently stricter discipline maintained in France. Though by then
very little used, at least formally, espousals were in a sense
officially abolished here by the act of 1753, usually called
Hardwicke's Marriage Act. The assumption that an agreement
to marry meant freedom to copulate clearly persisted, however, in spite of the fact that 'pre-nuptial fornication' was
an offence punishable in the Archdeacons' court. This body,
so given over to sexual offences that people called it 'the
bawdy court', proceeded against pregnant brides even in the
eighteenth century. There is some doubt as to what authority
in church law was at issue in this matter, and even more so
in Scotland, where the ferociousness of the Kirk Sessions at

this late date in dealing with parents who brought babies to
be baptised within nine months of marriage makes melancholy
reading. Folk opinion at this time in a remote Cumberland
parish was evidently in no doubt of what was permissible,
if we can trust a passage in the guide to one of the churches –

> 'The Kirk of Ulpha to the pilgrim's eye.
> Is welcome as a start'.

*A story often told by the old folks, relates how a certain parson,
before the days when marriages must necessarily be held in church,
gathered together those living together and not yet legally united,
and performed the wedding ceremony over seventeen such couples
who assembled at Frith Hall on one day in the year 1730 for that
purpose.*[163]

Frith Hall was the largest house in that scattered hamlet on
the Duddon.

In spite of local variations in the words used and the actions
taken, it is possible to make the following tentative generalization about espousals or contracts in England in relation to
marriage. A contract publicly entered into before witnesses
and marked by two overt actions, the kissing of the woman
by the man and the presentation of gifts – often a gold ring,
or, oddly enough, half a gold ring – constituted a binding
marriage, provided only that the couple then proceeded to
sexual intercourse. In the Roman Church after 1564 such an
action between an affianced couple was a grave sin. In the
English church it was a much less serious matter. In extreme
Protestant practice, amongst the sects in America as well as
here, the whole issue was different. For the nonconformists
marriage consisted simply of a promise followed by consum-
mation: church ceremony was irrelevant. Since in our day
Puritanism is closely associated with sexual authoritarianism
perhaps an example ought to be cited from the works of an
English Puritan divine on this interesting point. William
Gouge had this to say in 1622:

*I would advise all Christians that desire a blessing and good
success on their marriage to be contracted before they are married.
Contracted persons are in a middle degree betwixt single persons
and married persons: they are neither simply single, nor actually
married. Many make it a very marriage, and thereupon have a*

[163] *See page* 303.

*greater solemnity at their contract than at their marriage: yea
many take liberty after a contract to know their spouse, as if they
were married: an unwarrantable and dishonest practice. The
laudable custom of our and other churches showeth, that at least
three weeks must pass betwixt contract and marriage. For the
contract is to be three times published, and that but once a week
before the wedding is celebrated.*

If three weeks and more were added to the figures in the table
we have printed, the intervals between marriage ceremony and
first birth in Crulai and in an English village would begin to
look a little more alike. Gouge's advice in favour of a definite
contract confirms what is known from other literary and legal
evidence, that the formal practice was on the way out in his
time. The informal act of affiancing no doubt continued without document or sworn witnesses, but marked by social celebration and having the same effect on the behaviour of the
parties. The really significant revelation in this passage is in
the words used about sexual intercourse during the period of
the contract, whilst the banns were being called and the
actual marriage ceremony prepared. Though ascribed to the
temptation of Satan, though 'unwarrantable and dishonest',
such an action was not described as sinful.

No hard-headed peasant would have let his daughter get to
the point of espousal until a firm agreement had been made
between the two families. Still some risk remained that the
banns might be forbidden from the body of the congregation
on one or other of those three successive Sunday mornings.
William Perkins was a better-known spokesman of the Puritans in the years of their rise to power in the seventeenth
century, and he also skirts round the awful word 'sin' when he
reaches this point, though he used it freely enough elsewhere.
He talked in frowning disapproval of affianced couples 'seeking
to satisfy their own fleshly desires, after the manner of brute
beasts' but he goes no further than that.[164] Towards the end
of the seventeenth century the nonconformist view of marriage
as a personal matter, not a sacrament of the church at all,
evidently grew much more influential in our country. In 1680
one, William Lawrence, a Scottish Presbyterian, published a
long treatise insisting that all ecclesiastical matrimony was
unnatural outrage, and that indissoluble partnership between

[164] *See page* 303.

man and woman began whenever the first sexual union took place, needing neither witness, nor confirmation, nor any public celebration. It is true that this highly unconventional book ends on page 422 with the confession 'By the interruption of the Press I am compelled to break off this book abruptly'.[165] Still the outlook he defended is close to the secular conception of marriage so prevalent in our own century. In registering his protest against what might be called the authoritarian orthodoxy being established in his time, he cannot be said to have been expressing anything like relaxation of moral discipline or anomie in English or in Scottish society.

The marriage customs of the English peasantry may have been variable and complicated, much more so than those of their Catholic French contemporaries, but they expressed and maintained personal and social discipline nevertheless. Still it remains the case that pre-nuptial conception may never provide the sort of index of social dislocation in England which it perhaps already provides in France. When they discovered that the proportion of brides having babies within eight months of marriage rose to 30 per cent at Sotteville-les-Rouen towards the end of the eighteenth century, the French historians might have concluded justifiably that some important social difference had appeared there to bring about so marked a contrast with the record elsewhere.[166] The marked general rise in this index in England in the eighteenth century may perhaps come to be interpreted in the same way. The significant fact of such detached figures as those from Colyton may not be so much that nearly two-thirds of the brides had children baptized within eight months as that one-third of those already pregnant were delivered within three months of the ceremony. It seems as if the young men in that parish found themselves making honest women of the girls rather more often than was necessary elsewhere, and this might possibly have important implications about the age of marriage and the effectiveness of regulation.

The consideration of the relationship between personal discipline and social survival must be left at this point. It may perhaps be felt that the evidence at present available is almost as challenging and inconclusive as it had to be on the subject of starvation. But the belief that the defiance of Christian injunction and social regulation was very common in the

[165] *See page* 303. [166] *See page* 303.

world we have lost would be difficult to sustain in the face of the figures we have quoted and it seems unlikely that 'moral' breakdown can have been of much importance in bringing about demographic crises. In trying to decide what significance is to be attached to figures of bastardy and pre-nuptial pregnancy amongst our ancestors, there is one salient fact which must never be overlooked. Enforced chastity affected a a far greater proportion of people's lives than it does today. This was because so many of them were too young to be married, the age of marriage being relatively high, and because marriage if and when it came was likely to last for a shorter time.

It may have been noticed that no room has been found to discuss the best known of all vital statistics, birth-rates, marriage-rates and death-rates. Crude rates of this sort, numbers per thousand of a population being born, married or dying in a period of twelve months, are somewhat deceptive indices. They have some usefulness, especially when the crudity is refined out of them, but they are extremely difficult to obtain for the time before the census gives totals, because to calculate them at all the total numbers at risk have to be known. When these numbers can be obtained at all, death-rates generally turn out to be high, marriage-rates about the same as ours, and birth-rates very high in comparison. These rates also varied from place to place and time to time; it will be many years before any accurate general impression will be available and this will come from the application of the complex process of family reconstitution to suitable parish registers. Even then statisticians will prefer to use more revealing measures, such as age-specific fertility and mortality. Nevertheless it may perhaps be just worth while glancing at the birth- (baptismal), marriage- and death- (burial) rates where they are known with something like twentieth-century accuracy. Thus we can take Clayworth and Cogenhoe as examples. In 1676 Clayworth had 401 people and 412 in 1688; Cogenhoe had 185 in 1618, 180 in 1628 and varying numbers in between.

The birth- and death-rates were high at Clayworth over the relevant years, the baptismal rate being about 35 or 37 per thousand and the burial rate 40 or 42. These are both above the peak rates reached in Victorian times, when the birth-rate was about 35 over the whole country and the death-rate in the

20's. Clayworth seems to have experienced very high mortality indeed, even if no demographic crises can be confirmed for these years, though we have seen that something very like it occurred between 1678 and 1680. In Cogenhoe on the other hand between 1613 and 1628 rates were lower; the baptismal-rate was somewhere between 26 and 35, the burial-rate as low as it is today, at 13½ to 18; nowadays both rates vary at about this level for the whole country. The experience of these communities then, as to general mortality and fertility, is contradictory and tells us very little about conditions in the world we have lost as a whole, except that, as might be expected, they could be extremely unfavourable. They illustrate, in fact, the uselessness of trying to argue overall from a sample too small to be free of extreme random variation.[167] But there is another and more important reason why they are of interest to us.

We have to admit that we are still at an inconclusive stage in answering questions about starvation and comparative sexual discipline. Our colleagues in France are something like half a generation ahead of us in the study of these questions, but we have been able to demonstrate one striking and entirely unexpected feature of the life of the English village community at that time. The turnover of population in these settled, agricultural, traditional communities was remarkably high. No less than 61·8 per cent of the people living at Clayworth in 1688 had not been there in 1676, and something like 50 per cent of those living in Cogenhoe in 1628 were not there in 1618. Most of the movement was clearly local and larger areas would show much less. In these two communities, people were moving to and fro, society was changing, whole households were coming and going and both villages were in perpetual exchange with their neighbours. All this went on quite independently of the level of birth- and death-rates, though if this were the opportunity, it could be demonstrated how intimately this movement must have been connected with the low expectation of life. In fact every feature of pre-industrial society could be shown to fit in with this somewhat unexpected characteristic of peasant society, and especially the migratory activities of servants.

Some of these details of life at Clayworth and Cogenhoe have been printed in a preliminary form. These are the first public

[167] *See page* 303.

results of the attempt now being made to understand the
social structure of our peasant forefathers in something like
numerical form. We may finish this chapter of our essay by
quoting the concluding paragraph of what was written about
these two villages when these facts were announced in 1963.

*In spite of sudden change of this sort, and of the more gradual
change which came about through the succession of son to father,
nephew to uncle, kinsman to kinsman, the impression of permanence in the constituent households which composed a Stuart
community is easy to understand. Nearly half of the heads of
households at Clayworth had either died or had left the village by
1688, nevertheless their successors presided over units of persons
which were mostly recognizably the same. And at Cogenhoe,
where eight out of thirty-three households failed to survive a
decade of change, it is still true that over three-quarters of them
did survive, often with different heads, with a membership sometimes extensively revised, but still the same households, inhabiting
the same buildings, working the same fields. The system, that
familial, patriarchal system which dominated and gave structure
to pre-industrial society, had succeeded in maintaining permanence in spite of the shortness of life, the fluctuations of
prosperity, the falling in of leases, the wayward habits of young
folk in service, and the fickleness of their employers.*

*The institutions of the old world must be looked upon in this
way, as expedients to provide permanence in an environment
which was all too impermanent and insecure. The respect due to
the old and experienced, the reverence for the Church and its
immense, impersonal antiquity, the spontaneous feeling that it
was the family which gave a meaning to life because the family
could and must endure, all these things helped to reconcile our
ancestors with relentless, remorseless mortality and mischance.
But they must not deceive the historian into supposing that the
fixed and the ancient were the only reality: an unchanging, unchangeable social structure may well be essential to a swiftly
changing population.*

*The historical observer in an inquiry of this sort can only feel
himself to be in the position of the scientist in his bathyscope,
miles beneath the surface of the sea, concentrating his gaze for a
moment or two on the few strange creatures who happen to stray
out of the total darkness into his beam of light. Where have they
come from, and what will happen to them? he cannot help asking*

himself. What did happen to poor little Copperwhite Mastin, son of Elizabeth Mastin, spinster, and seven months old in May 1688, the only bastard alive in Clayworth? Or to the Coles household, thirteen strong, which appeared at Cogenhoe in 1623, no doubt as tenants of the leased-out manor, was there in 1624, but had disappeared by 1628? Even more puzzling and challenging is to ask whether these two communities are in fact typical of the whole. On this the historian can only talk as the scientist might. Here are two examples of communities in motion, two tiny globes of light disposed at random a little way down into the great ocean of persons who lived and died in our country before records of persons in general began to be kept. These samples may be ordinary enough, but they may be quite extraordinary. We cannot yet tell: we may never be able to tell.[168]

Elizabeth Mastin was a widow's daughter. We may not know enough yet to decide whether the English peasants literally starved, but we do know what was likely to happen to a fatherless boy who, because his parents had broken the disciplinary rules, had no regular home in the world we have lost. He was almost certain to die before he was mature, just as so many millions will die in our own world, unless the age-old problems of subsistence and population are somehow finally resolved.

[168] *See page* 304.

Economic organization and political awareness

In spite of the smallness of its scale and the simplicity of its economics, the society we have been describing was a highly complex arrangement of persons. Moreover, the whole structure was subject to conflict and change. Up to the end of the feudal era proper, civil strife was commonplace all over Europe. Shakespeare still preserves for us the interminable quarrels of the fifteenth century, when the houses of York and Lancaster embroiled baronage, knighthood, church, citizens and people in a dreary contest for dynastic power, only occasionally a matter of open fighting and never as dramatic as Shakespeare had to make it out to be.

But the contest which sticks in the imagination and which the whole world immediately associates with civil war and revolution in our country is the last which ever occurred, that between Roundhead and Cavalier, when Charles I was defeated and beheaded by the Puritans. The years between 1640 and 1660, when desultory fighting turned into desperately serious campaigns, and constitutional crisis led to usurpation and to an irregular régime, is now conventionally called the Puritan Revolution. After the much less romantic embroglio of 1688–9 the whole English Revolution had run its irregular course. This *English Revolution*, needless to say, along with the *French*, *American* and *Russian Revolutions*, is one of the great historical realities in accepted parlance.

In this interlude between our discussion of the personal, everyday life of the traditional world and the brief description we shall attempt to give of its political workings, it is necessary to analyse the reasons for the Civil War and to ask whether the word Revolution can justifiably be used of seventeenth-century England, if anything of Social Revolution is intended. This necessity arises from the persistent preoccupations of the historians, rather than from the subject itself. It is always interesting and important to know the circumstances under which a society will be at war with itself, but social description can be undertaken without entering into the issues of any particular crisis however fundamental it may have been. Dwelling on the seriousness of the differences over which men fought at Naseby and Sedgemoor has helped to distort the shape which that society has taken up in the minds of men in our time. But since this question is so often put to the evidence by historians and learners alike – 'What was it in Stuart society which led to political disaster and fighting?' – it can scarcely be evaded here.

The historian, as we shall see in our final chapter, is something of a nuisance to the sociological inquirer, just because it is his habit to ask questions of this blank and simple sort. What is much more confusing is that he expects to be able to get swift and straightforward answers to them. In the present case, because of the form which an answer is ordinarily expected to take, the question itself is not simple at all. Along with a request for the social origins of a particular political crisis, there is usually also a demand for a descriptive response of a kind which would relate the English Revolution with the long-term social transformation which finally gave rise to the modern, industrialized world. Can any connection be traced, it is required to know, between Cromwell and his Roundheads on the one hand, and the social forces which led to the dethronement of the patriarchal family in economic organization on the other? Or between the Glorious Revolution of 1688 and the coming of the factories?

We shall not attempt to deal in this preliminary essay with the course of the secular, overall change which brought about the contrast between our world and the world we have lost. Our subject is rather the comparison of the two, and all that we shall need to do is to dwell briefly on the England of the early twentieth century in order to point the contrast as sharply as we can. The task of the present chapter will have to be entirely analytical, therefore, and at a rather more academic level than the rest of the book. The reader who wishes simply to get to know some of the facts about the comparison as such may safely pass it by.

The subject begins with a curious uncertainty as to the actual nature and extent of that contrast itself. This uncertainty attaches to the most conspicuous feature of all in the industrialized world – the factory, that instrument of mechanical and mass production. No one seems quite to know exactly when the factory appeared.

Final origins of things like this are in fact much more difficult to trace than might be supposed. Like the source of a river, the institutional story as you trace it back first branches into numbers of streams of similar size, so that you are puzzled to say which is the one you should follow, and then finally disperses into the runlets and the raindrops of the distant and misty heights of time.

The *ergasterion*, or slave work-centre, where these human chattels were congregated for collective work in the Ancient World is one such tributary. Another, in the analysis laid out by the great sociologist, Max Weber, is the *fabrica* or cellarden, found in the medieval town as the collective property of a group of masters, or deep in the countryside as part of the lord's property in a manor. Though Weber and the more learned and cautious of the other writers express surprise at the absence of evidence for factories in earlier times, when they get to Tudor England they feel at last that they are on firm ground.[169] Listen to this:

> *Within one room being large and long*
> *There stood two hundred looms full strong*
> *Two hundred men, the truth is so,*
> *Wrought in these looms all in a row.*
> *By every one a pretty boy*
> *Sat making quils with mickle joy.*
> *And in another place hard by*
> *An hundred women merrily,*
> *Were carding hard with joyful cheer*
> *Who singing sat with voices clear.*
> *And in a chamber close beside*
> *Two hundred maidens did abide*
> *In petticoats of Stamell red*
> *And milk white kerchers on their head*
> *These pretty maids did never lin*
> *But in that place all day did spin.*

[169] *See page* 305.

And so on; 'quils' were needed by the men for the loomwork, as was the carded twine: the maidens who did not 'lin' did not neglect their work as they sat in the coarse (Stamell) red petticoats. Here was a building large enough for two hundred looms, with two hundred men, a hundred women, two hundred boys and a hundred girls all employed by Jack of Newbury, the famous clothier of England. The poem comes from the novel by Thomas Deloney, published in 1619 and dedicated to the Clothworkers Company of London. Jack's great establishment, Deloney tells us, became so famous that it was actually visited by the reigning King and Queen, Henry VIII and Katherine.[170]

It all looks very much like a factory, and this piece of verse has often been quoted by historians and other authorities as suggesting that factories existed before the coming of modern industry.[171] Jack of Newbury has been classed with the large-scale clothiers, one of whom is known from historical documents to have made use of buildings which may well have been of factory size. This was Stumpe of Malmesbury, who took over the abbey in that Wiltshire town, deserted and forlorn after the dissolution of the monasteries; he negotiated for Oseney Abbey at Oxford also. But intensive search has yielded no other examples, and nothing directly is known about what actually went on in those immense workrooms, so strikingly different from the little shops at the side of the house where the individual Tudor weaver worked, if he did not have his loom in the *hall*, that is the living-room, of his cottage. Deloney's description has filled in a very important gap in the account of social and economic organization as its development has been traditionally reconstructed.

But the fact seems to be that this Jack of Newbury was as much of a myth as Jack and the Beanstalk, and the 'factory' he is supposed to have set up as deceptive as Juliet's marriage, if it is used as a guide to the actual institutions and real behaviour of our ancestors. Throughout Deloney's ribald and formless work, the manufactory is referred to as a *household*: he tells us at one point that 'This great household and family had its own butcher, who killed ten oxen a week for its members to eat.' It soon becomes plain that Deloney was engaged in making up a story about a fabulous clothier's household for the diversion of the London clothworkers; his subject was

[170] *See page* 305.   [171] *See page* 305.

a Panurge amongst craftsmen, not perhaps capable of drowning a whole city when he made water as Rabelais's character could do, but certainly recognizable in the master-baker with whom this book began, built on Gargantuan lines, with his household enlarged to impossible size. To cite the Royal visit to the 'factory' as evidence of its importance to English economic development is to overlook the further and incredible fact that the King took away some of the poor children working for fabulous Jack. Some of them were made Royal pages and others the King 'sent to the Universities, allotting to every one a Gentleman's living', an interesting piece of make-believe. This fragment from that fascinating half-world between literature and folklore, does not show after all that factories existed in Tudor times. What it does show is that the successful clothier could be idealized as a hero and his household poetically exaggerated. But it was a household still.

This may set us on our guard once more against literary evidence as a literal guide to the social structure of the past. It would be impossible to prove that factories were entirely absent in the world we have lost, but we can say with confidence that large-scale undertakings for the purpose of manufacturing goods are conspicuously lacking in all descriptions of life in England before the late eighteenth century. The traveller of that time was particularly interested in objects and institutions of exceptional size; royal palaces, cathedrals, bridges, vessels of outstanding dimensions are always being commented upon, along with every 'curious engine' which that inventive age brought forth. From Leland to Defoe, in the books of Evelyn, Pepys, Locke and such an exceptional horsewoman as the peripatetic Celia Fiennes, things seen are meticulously recorded even by measure. Some authors, especially Defoe, show a special interest in manufacture and manufacturing processes. Yet not one book can be made to yield a description of what we should call a factory.

Approaches to that peculiarly industrial form of social and economic organization certainly existed before the great Industrial Revolution, and some of them were listed in the first chapter. Mining, building, shipyards, saltworks and a whole list of other forms of manufacture certainly brought together dozens and sometimes scores of workers and placed them under some sort of discipline. Contracting for military and naval operations, turning out tapestries and other articles of

M

refined manufacture needed for monarchical and aristocratic purposes led to the establishment of royal workshops all over Europe, and in England to such institutions as the Mineral and Battery Works set up by Queen Elizabeth. But a complicated system of definitions has to be adopted before it can be decided how far such institutions could be called factories, and the part which all of them put together had to play in the whole economy of the country was exceedingly small. Interestingly enough the closest approximation is to be found in the municipal workhouses, established under a succession of Acts of Parliament and as part of various bursts of energy on the part of municipalities to 'set the poor on work'. In its prehistory the factory was associated with poverty and destitution, just as manufacture generally was universally regarded first and foremost as a means of keeping people occupied who would otherwise be idle, perhaps even keeping them alive when otherwise they might die.

A great deal of post-industrial history has had to go by before this association could be outgrown and before the factory could take its place as a human grouping in its own right, still perhaps the typical institution of the industrialized world though said by some to be at the end of its career in that position. When at last a document appears which belonged to an organization justly described as the first English factory the emphasis on poverty and remedies against it are a conspicuous feature.

Winlaton iron mill at Swalwell in the County of Durham, where ironmaster Ambrose Crowley began work in about 1691, turned out metal for the Navy in William III's war with the French; within a few years Crowley was literally employing workmen by the hundred. The 'Law Book' which he left behind makes it evident also that many of those workers were banded together in one building; certainly they were treated by him as a single labour force, a platoon in an industrial army.[172] The provisions against poverty were many and various and there was a Clerk of the Poor who also ministered at a chapel for the workpeople and kept school for their children. Something of the atmosphere of the factory as it was deliberately established in the close-knit, patriarchal society of Japan under the Meiji emperors in the 1890's is already present here.

[172] *See page* 305.

But the point which impresses the twentieth-century reader in this lengthy and complicated document is the extraordinary mixture in its provisions of elements of the old order with those of the new, the family workshop with the communal workroom. Much of the actual production for Ambrose Crowley was obviously still being done in the homes of the workmen under conditions which had prevailed since the beginnings of history. The problems of disciplining those who did work together on the premises and of co-ordinating the efforts of everyone were evidently exceedingly difficult; they seem to have become an obsession of this earliest factory-owner and organizer to have left his records behind him. The resistance which had to be overcome, if resistance it can be said to have been, was not that of machine breakers, for there seem to have been extremely few machines to break. It was rather the reluctance of an immemorial social order to accommodate an institution so alien in its assumptions about the way in which people should spend their lives.

In the present state of the evidence the arrival of the factory in the earliest country to become industrialized must be firmly placed in the middle and late eighteenth century and it is exceedingly difficult to imagine the discovery of documents in such quantities as to make it necessary to revise this conclusion. Those changes of scale, that sense of alienation of the worker from his work, that breach in the continuity of emotional experience in which we have sought for the trauma inflicted at the passing of the traditional world, cannot be referred to Tudor or to Stuart England. When factory life did at last become the dominant feature of industrial activity it condemned the worker, as we can now see, to the fate previously reserved for the pauper. But the threat of this did not become apparent until the early nineteenth century.

It is still possible, however, that those lesser changes in scale which went forward five or six generations before large-scale industrial organization began may have had some little part to play in the political malaise which then prevailed. An exhaustive understanding of politics and social change in the world we have lost, ought presumably to take every little influence into account which might have made more difficult the preservation of political stability. Perhaps the intensification of trade and commerce could be called divisive, because of the differing relationships it presumably brought with it, and because of the operation at long last of an institution entirely alien to the traditional structure, the joint stock company. This new principle of economic organization was present before 1700; the East India Company and the Bank of England had already set up the model for those institutional instruments which were to bring into being 'business' as we know it. The impact they can have had before the early eighteenth century was infinitesimal in relation to the whole of commercial and industrial activity. Still, in the vocabulary of current expressions favoured by historians 'the commercial revolution of the sixteenth and seventeenth centuries' is a recent but fairly respectable phrase: if there was such a thing, it must supposedly have had some effect on politics.

It could be shown, however, that enormous commercial expansion was possible under the old order without a change in the scale of institutions or even of undertakings, and that the major social outcome of growth of this sort was in the mobility which it gave rise to. The same can be said of manufacturing activity and wealth, as it is known to have developed in Tudor and Stuart times, even though mining was growing so fast and other industries too. There was another area of social relationships which can be thought of in the same way, though it may turn out that here expansion in size was in fact accompanied by a change in structure of much greater strategic significance. This was governmental administration. Samuel Pepys of the Navy Office may prove to have a claim to be a forerunner of industrial England as important as that of Samuel Smiles.

If, as we shall try to show, social mobility was a constant feature of traditional society, then neither commerce, industry nor bureaucracy need be thought of as always disruptive because of their expansive tendencies. But there was one current in economic development which affected many more people than all these put together, in ways which clearly led to unrest. Although we were disposed to minimize the enclosure movement as a solvent of the village community, there can be no doubt of the social displacement which it caused, even though only a small proportion of villages was concerned. Any considerable change in land-distribution, anything which bore on the crucial question of access to the means of growing food, was bound to be important. But even when all these influences are added together it seems entirely unlikely that a situation which could be called a social crisis or which might lead to social revolution, could have been brought about by them. Discussion of why civil war happened in seventeenth-century England which is confined to such slight effects as these lacks all conviction.

The truth is that changes in English society between the reign of Elizabeth and the reign of Anne were not revolutionary. The impression left by an attempt to survey the fundamental framework during these generations is of how little, not of how much, evolution seems to have taken place. Nothing in economic organization or in social arrangements seems to have come about which would have led of itself to political crisis, and the changes that did go on seem to have been gradual over the whole period rather than sudden.

This is a hypothetical claim of course and no historian can prove a negative, especially in an area so elusive as the development of social structure. He can be certain of only one thing, which is that interpretation will always incline to exaggerate the new discovery about social change into a revolution. The vagaries in the fortunes of the nobility, for instance, or the success of a particular textile innovation, or the possibility of marked progress in literacy and education will tend to be made into that one crucial social change which explains everything. But once it is recognized that the rise-of-a-capitalist-class interpretation can be misleading as well as informative, and that social mobility was present in the traditional world, then the idea of a social revolution however occasioned becomes an embarrassment rather than a help towards understanding political breakdown.

It might be very different, if for example, the few facts so far discovered did indicate the possibility of fundamental change in the size, structure and function of the family and household over this period. Or if the growth of town life had looked as though it must have led to social dislocation on an impressive scale. Or if there were unmistakable evidence of class-consciousness and collective resentment building up over the generation in question amongst a group of persons increasing in power, number and organization, though always frustrated in their expressed aims.

None of these things seems to have happened. There were changes in all these respects, perhaps some overall changes in the atmosphere of family life. The movement of population and the transformation of environment associated with the enormous growth of London must surely have led to *anomie*, even though there does not seem to have been an obvious increase in suicide, and so on. But these long-term, gradual tendencies cannot in principle have been the cause of political upheaval in the middle of the seventeenth century. The famous ructions which led to the execution of Charles I and the exile of James II, the two outstanding episodes in 'The English Revolution', seem therefore to have little relevance to the passing of the world we have lost, to that contrast between our world and the world of our ancestors which is the subject of this essay.

Nevertheless it is understandable that historians should always strive to relate political frictions to what is called 'underlying social change'. If this is to be done, great care must be taken to avoid the pitfalls which words like 'underlying' or even words like 'expressing' carry with them when society as a structure is contrasted with its political and intellectual life. Religious and political beliefs have tended to be looked upon as displaced symptoms of something in the material structure of society, manifesting itself in what is called ideological terms. It will be a long time, so it seems, before historians recognize that no simple, powerful, universally adaptable mechanism capable of bringing about such effects ever existed in any society.

If we are to understand how violence and military contest did fit in with social arrangements we may be able to learn from the attitude which professional sociologists are now developing towards social conflict. After long years of insisting that stability was the normal state of human society, and that integration was the function of every distinguishable element in the social structure, they are now prepared frankly to accept the existence of conflict as a permanent and even a necessary element in every social system. Some emphasize the social purposes of conflict to such an extent that conflict itself appears to be functional: 'where there is no conflict, there is no change, no progress', is the point they make. Others feel that this is unnecessary, and suppose that in all societies at all times there are disintegrative tendencies, some of which have the final effect of furthering social purposes and others which do not. If the problem of relating political crisis in Stuart England with long-term, overall change is approached along the lines of this second attitude, these seem to be the conclusions which may be reached.[173]

In the first place the tendencies to disruption and disintegration which were obviously at work at that time need no longer be regarded as abnormal, in the unexpected sense. The unruliness of the Puritan clergy and gentry, the obstinacy of the common lawyers, the arrogance of the parliamentarians in the early 1600's, cease to be things which have to be explained because they existed at all. Historians need no longer go on looking at all contradictions as peculiarly significant, on all conflict as the exception to what is to be expected, and on anything which could be described as 'revolutionary' as very special indeed, requiring the most determined effort of understanding. Once it is realized that all societies, including those as stable as the England which was described in our first chapter, are liable to break down into conflict, sometimes armed, it becomes possible to look at political violence with a cooler eye. This can be done not only in our country in the 1640's, but in France in the 1790's, and in Russia in the years after 1917.

Conflict, as has been said elsewhere is a common enough form of social interaction.[174] Since nearly everybody has an obvious interest in preventing differences from becoming collisions all parties will take strenuous avoiding action when collisions threaten. But collisions sometimes take place in social and political life, just as car collisions do, and there is a logical resemblance. When accidents happen on the roads, it makes sense to look for long-term, even 'deep-seated' causes, as well as for the errors of the drivers concerned; the continued growth of traffic, the increase in its speed, the progressive inadequacy of the roads may all have to be analysed. But it does not follow that the more dramatic the crash and important its consequences the more profound its causes must be and the more likely to be the climax of some perennial 'process'.

Now it is natural, though it may not be justifiable, to suppose that great events have great causes. The Civil War and the Puritan Revolution, together with the Glorious Revolution of 1688, are so conspicuous, so interesting, so momentous in their consequences and so fraught with the origins of our liberties and of our political values, ours and those of the rest

[173] *See page* 305.   [174] *See page* 305.

of the world, that they have inevitably been looked upon as cataclysmic, the apex of some mountain-building movement in historical evolution. And this from the very time of their occurrence. 'If in time as in place,' said the acutest of all contemporary observers, Thomas Hobbes, 'there were degrees of high and low, I verily believe that the highest of time, would be that which passed between 1640 and 1660.'[175] The parliamentary struggle and the bloodshed on the battlefields must have been the final outcome of a process going deep down into the social fabric, and extending over many generations, backwards and forwards in time. This assumption comes the more easily to the English because we pride ourselves on the continuity of our political life, and believe it to be unbroken except for these particular events. What could be more understandable than that the historians should have set aside a whole century, from 1540–1640, for the causes of the Civil War, and the whole period 1640–88, or even 1625–1714, for 'The English Revolution'?

But what is true may also be trivial, which is perhaps why the discussion of this portentous question has become by now so tedious. Nothing beyond a fuller demonstration that conflict was everywhere necessarily follows from showing that the causes of war between Roundhead and Cavalier can be infinitely extended into areas 'social', 'economic' or even 'social structural', for every event that ever happened can be treated in this way, and be made to appear culminatory. The simple and over-dramatic question: What was it in English society over these years which led to open fighting? has encouraged the tendency to inflate the importance of the next little piece of evidence on social development into something crucial to catastrophe. Hence the persisting search for the one final cause of disaster, the unwitting acceptance of the stale paradox about the nail in the shoe of the horse of the rider whose presence might have won the battle and changed the world.

But the most constrictive effect of the conventional assumption about the relation of the struggle in Stuart England to social structure and change has yet to be mentioned; it leads us on to the second lesson we can learn from the sociology of conflict.

The habit of expecting to discover that 'revolution' was a

[175] *See page* 305.

geological catastrophe, when a situation of ever-increasing instability suddenly gave way to a situation of rock-like permanence, obscures the possibility that society at that time had what might be called a conflict-mechanism built into it. This oversight is the more extraordinary since the supreme achievement of the whole epoch was the adaptation of a medieval institution into a classic conflict-defining, conflict-restricting and conflict-resolving social instrument, that is to say the Houses of Parliament with their Oppositions, their motions of censure, their parties and their unending, superbly conventionalized political battle.

Once the imagination is set free, there are many possible comparisons in social organization which spring to mind for Stuart England. There are, for example, the segmented societies described by anthropologists. Professor Gluckman's examination of African communities shows how a fight over the dynastic succession is a permanent feature of political life. Far from weakening or destroying the whole, conflict actually confirms its solidarity. This fits some of the features of political life in England aptly enough, from Tudor, to Stuart, to Hanoverian and even to Victorian times.[176] The segmented characteristics of the political community of our country in pre-industrial times, its division into a network of small county communities which were also conflict arenas, will concern us in our next chapter.

The picture of political institutions and political life which might finally be adopted is one where the stream of variation was wide enough to include the 'despotism of Charles I' as one extreme, and the rule of the Parliamentary Army as the other. Both were unlikely to be permanent, but both nevertheless belonged within the definition; each possible, though not as much to be expected, as the traditional King-in-parliament arrangement. But the most useful concept to be borrowed from the sociological study of conflict in industrial, as opposed to pre-industrial, society does not concern itself with extreme situations as such but with the reasons why they alternated with each other. 'Revolution' as meaning a resolution of unendurable social conflict by reshaping society as a whole has been rejected here as impossible in pre-industrial times. But what Ralf Dahrendorf has to say about the process which occasionally brings it about in the twentieth century has its

[176] *See page* 305.

value in understanding irreconcilable conflict as it happened in the seventeenth century.[177]

Political breakdown is only likely to come about when it happens that several sources of conflict become *superimposed* – Dahrendorf's word. To the permanent divisive influences in the society are added specific issues about which the men of the time care so passionately that they are prepared to fight about them. The particular reason why political agreement becomes impossible is often that forces of conflict which at other times tend to modify each other, even to cancel each other out, all conspire together to make compromise impossible. This is no very novel nor perhaps a very subtle way of looking at things, but its important virtue is that each individual conflict, each pair of antagonistic forces, is looked upon as for the most part an independent variable. None of them is taken as an 'expression of' another, or as necessarily 'underlying' one or all of the others.

Of course, a difference of opinion or a collision of interest at one point in the structure will have a greater divisive effect than at another. If the King fell out with the Common Council of the City of London over monopolies (conflict of economic interest with obvious political potentiality) more disruption occurred than when a Bishop insisted that the surplice be worn in all the churches in his diocese (religious conflict with only a slight possibility of affecting any but the participants). But a simple scheme of this sort excludes altogether any explanation which insists that the whole complex interaction was 'really' religious, or 'really' economic, or 'really the rise of a social class', and that the 'real' contradiction was somehow resolved in the process of open violence.

In the particular case we are examining it could be said that the so-called Puritan Revolution happened when a desperately acute religious controversy was superimposed upon a fierce dispute over political organization, and upon much more than that. A number of other sources of conflict were polarized at the same time, and complete knowledge would presumably show that some of them were what we should call conflicts of economic interest; many of them might well deserve the title of challenges by capitalistic organization and the values of a market economy to traditional organization and assumptions. But the discontinuities which had arisen to

[177] *See page* 306.

commercial, industrial and administrative life which were referred to above were decidedly not all of this character, and can only, as we have said, have had additive effect of problematic and perhaps negligible importance. When after a year or two of Civil War the Levellers raised their platform and the Diggers added a tiny scrap of plain communist protest over the distribution of property, then it could be said that something like a conflict over membership of the ruling *élite* became involved. To this limited degree the description 'conflict over a class differential' might be applied to part of the general disagreement.

Using a word like superimposition for all these elements of conflict emphatically does not imply that one underlay all the others, or was expressive of it, or that overt aggressiveness was the displaced symptom of something else. A general release of suppressed resentment was quite apparent in the events of the 1640's nevertheless and there is truth in the claim that, like other movements of political disruption, the whole episode had a certain dynamic of its own. Contemporaries at the time and the observers of our day have reason, moreover, to believe that as the struggle intensified, social structural friction became a little more apparent. When the Clubmen appeared in Dorset, that latent fear of the *jacquerie*, that betrayal by those in superior positions that they were well aware of the resentment of those beneath them, had something tangible to fasten upon. But not all the sources of stress were at play in the struggle, and it is quite unjustifiable to exaggerate their breakdown into a general social structural cleavage. Of this, let it be repeated, there is no indication, and the notion of a social revolution is not permissible.

So much for the relationship of political violence in the seventeenth century to the structure of society in the world we have lost, and to the overall transformation which at the time of the military battles and the constitutional crises was still well in the future. Before we inquire why it was that our ancestors endured the supremacy of the very few, and why it was therefore that they showed so little disposition to challenge authority, social or political, we ought perhaps to complete the story of what happened in seventeenth-century history in a very summary form. We shall have to anticipate what will be said in our next chapter about the county community of country gentry, but the suggested mechanics of constitutional crisis under the Stuarts can be understood in a formal way without knowledge of the nature of political associations as it then existed. We shall be quoting once again from the context in which the comparison of political breakdown with accidents on the roads was first suggested.[178]

The political stability of England in Stuart times depended on two things, on the maintenance of ordered responsibility within each county community of politically active gentry, and on the interplay between those county communities and the central organization, that is the Crown and its institutions. The occasional meetings of Parliament were opportunities for local and national political awareness to be merged for short periods; the politics of Parliament when it was in session were national politics, the stuff of constitutional development. Far greater in extent and absolutely unbroken were the politics played within each county community. It was there, for example, that the collective memory of Parliament was to be found between its sessions.

This last point may need a little explanation, for in our day Parliament is a more or less continuous affair, and intervals of two, five or seven years are a constitutional administrative and political impossibility. Apart from the very brief life of the Short Parliament from April 13th to May 5th 1640, no less than eleven years had elapsed since the last foregathering of Knights of the Shire and Burgesses for Parliamentary towns when Charles I's Long Parliament met in November of that year. The previous experience of 167 of the 547 members of that remarkable assembly, which was to lay down the general lines of the Anglo-Saxon model of representative government, was confined to the three weeks of the Short Parliament: 161 of the remainder were newcomers altogether.

Though many of them had presumably met and discussed parliamentary affairs before, and though the London season had probably brought a good number together for very different purposes, the reason why this new House of Commons was able to take up just where its predecessors had left off must be sought away from the centre of the country. It was at their meetings as justices of the peace, at the Quarter Sessions in the country towns, at Petty Sessions in the smaller places, over their morning draughts as they called them when the militia was exercised or sporting engagements took place,

[178] *See page* 306.

that the gentry of England talked parliamentary affairs. The truly political among them, of course, must have met for the purpose in their own manor houses. But however its continuity was maintained the memory of Parliament was dispersed during the periods when no sessions took place and only became collective again when the M.P.s, new and old, appeared at Westminster with the years and years of conversation with their neighbours, friends and rivals in the shires reverberating in their minds.

In the county community of gentry local offices were intrigued over, parliamentary seats were lost and won, family rivalries were created, intensified and handed down from generation to generation, changing their objects of competition and their ideological content with the times. Continuity was kept up over the whole area of national politics and within each county because differences were resolved by argument and compromise, by the victory in the political struggle of one official, or of one man over others, or of one family or faction over others.

This is only the beginning of an anatomy of political consciousness at that time, and we shall have to go into it a little more closely in our next chapter. For the moment let us turn our attention to what happened to this complex of relationships in the year before the Civil War. As the Tudors gave way to Stuarts, politics, national and local, began increasingly to include the politics of intellectual difference, of argument about theory or something approaching it. This may be recognized as the beginnings of constitutionalism, told however without supposing that the occasional and intermittent life of the House of Commons was the whole political life of the English gentry. In the counties from day to day, as well as in the Palace of Westminster once every three, five or seven years, men differed volubly over issues which were brought up for discussion, as well as combating each other over matters of prestige and office, matters of economic interest and policy, matters above all of family aggrandisement. The overriding issue which was tearing them apart during the early Stuart reigns was of course religion. Differences over the content of the faith and the proper organization of the Christian church set man against man and family against family. Some of them wrote about these bitter controversies, some published what they had written and others even preached about them, so little did the clergy retain their function as the official intelligentsia.

Naturally only a small minority within every community took to argumentation in this way, but politics are always a matter of the articulate, vigorous, able few at work amongst an inert majority. The questions which the vocal ones chose to raise and to become indignant about may not all have been those which most of their companions would have thought the most important. But anyone who resented the activities of the proselytizing Puritan gentleman, or of the fanatical defender of the Ancient Constitution, or of the grim-faced Lecturer expounding the necessity of restoring the constitution of the Primitive Church, found himself drawn into argumentation too. Under such circumstances each county community, and the ruling segment as a whole, found it increasingly difficult to maintain political continuity, to contain their frictions. Even the men who sincerely wanted to be loyal and to maintain traditional arrangements, which for the most part everyone protested he wished to do, became exceedingly difficult to manage. Even if they agreed on fundamentals, as they all perpetually claimed they did, what now interested them was their differences, and there were always arguers on hand to exacerbate them.

As disaster and ineptitude succeeded each other in Charles I's conduct of affairs, the royal task of maintaining assent to policy became hazardous. In the crisis of the 1640's, after long years of difficulty over the national finances, this task became at last impossible. What wonder that the Stuarts wished to dispense with Parliament, and so added to the turbulence by giving the gentry reason to believe that their liberties were indeed in jeopardy. Since two of the Stuart House were in fact Roman Catholic in their personal convictions, it is not surprising that the less scrupulous leaders were able to convince themselves that a Bourbon solution was in store. Government by discussion is not the correct way to describe what went on in Tudor, Stuart or Hanoverian times. But it may be quite accurate and very important to lay it down that government, agreement and civil peace in England did involve the resolution of differences of opinion, which must sometimes be called intellectual. Political breakdown, when it occurred in the 1640's and again in the 1680's, was an event, intellectual as well as political and constitutional, for those with the greatest power to disrupt or to settle English political life.

This analysis might perhaps look like one further attempt to assign a new meaning to that controversial yet appealing phrase 'The Rise of the Gentry'. Certainly the appreciation of political and constitutional issues in something like intellectual terms by the communities of gentry in the counties may turn out to be a crucial development for the conduct of political life in late Tudor and early Stuart times. The communities of gentry themselves had an origin and a history, and it might perhaps be possible to reserve the expression to the story of that particular process. But the associations of the phrase with the pattern of interpretation which has become misleading seem too strong for it to be worth while to keep it at all. It would, if it were possible, be far better to lay 'The Rise of the Gentry' carefully alongside 'The Rise of the Middle Classes', and to place them reverently together in the great and growing collection of outmoded historians' idiom. There they might long exercise the ingenuity and delight the hearts of the historians of historiography.

Once the limitations of this way of thinking about the last generations of the traditional world have been recognized, a different view will have to be taken of its other attributes, some of them even more important to us in the twentieth century. This was after all the 'century of genius' for Englishmen, and the social structure which we have been discussing formed the surroundings of Shakespeare, Milton, Locke and Donne as well as those of Cromwell and Charles I. Even more significant for the world as it has developed since their time are the names of Bacon, Boyle, Harvey and Newton, for this was the era when the new 'natural Philosophy', natural science, came into being. In so far as historians generally, and historians of science in particular, have thought of the final causes for this astonishing departure in human activity, they have tended to suppose that it all was in some sense an expression of the rise of the bourgeoisie, just as the rise of the gentry is supposed to have been.

Only the most ingenious manipulation of the theory of ideology could possibly make such a final explanation sound at all convincing. But though it seems to be unwarrantable to suppose that any overall evolution like 'the rise of the bourgeoisie' was in fact characteristic of England at that time, which means that the new natural philosophy cannot be thought of in any convincing sense as its ideological expression, this does not settle the question of the relation between science and social arrangements. Scientific activity, as has been said elsewhere, during the heroic generations when Englishmen were so prominent in it, was heterogeneous, so various that it can scarcely be called an activity in itself.[179] It has to be sought in the tiny interstices, the nooks and crannies of the social structural whole, for the number of people able to contribute to it was tiny even on the scale of their own small society, and their activities were remote from each other. The study of an activity of this sort is a study of what might be called residues, minutiae, not of a general preoccupation which can be easily associated with the trend of overall, widespread social change.

If, therefore, we are to inform ourselves with any accuracy about the origins of the most remarkable of all our inheritances from the world we have lost, we shall have to get to know the map of English society in Stuart times in very intimate detail, and decide with clarity on the principles of its structure. Very small tendencies, forces of negligible strength may have been the promptings behind this particular intellectual tendency. These residual influences could in principle be related to some process of class formation, though no persuasive evidence of this seems as yet to be forthcoming. When simple-minded argumentation from material and economic substructure or background to cultural and intellectual result is abandoned, the challenge to the imagination and subtlety of the sociological historian is indeed acute.

[179] *See page* 306.

The Pattern of Authority and our Political Heritage
Chapter 8

Literacy, social mobility
and the rule of an elite

Hatfield House at Hatfield in Hertfordshire, seat of the Marquesses of Salisbury, still stands as the embodiment of the political importance of the famous house of Cecil. It is a symbol and an instrument of their enormous political effectiveness, and a reward from the Crown for services rendered.

Typical of political success and of political genealogy in England is that there should be two great mansions belonging to the Cecils, and not one only. The elder line, the actual bearers of the original barony of Burghley, conferred for political purposes by the shrewdest of our monarchs in 1571, still lives at Burghley House, near Stamford, 80 miles from Hatfield, and this family has a Marquisate of its own, that of Exeter. It was the younger son of the first eminent Cecil politician, a son by his second marriage, who rose to be first Minister of Elizabeth's successor, James I, and built Hatfield House, being created by his royal master Marquess of Salisbury.

What the present Robert Gascoyne-Cecil, K.G., 5th Marquess of Salisbury, says and does at Hatfield House is of weight in Hertfordshire, in the House of Lords, in the Conservative Party and in the British Commonwealth. His attitude and actions are not of importance to be compared, of course, to those of his great ancestor and founder of the name and both the lineages, William Cecil, 1st Lord Burghley, Minister to Queen Elizabeth. But they are of consequence all the same.

A little way across the suburbanized Hertfordshire

N

countryside Cassiobury House has long since been blown up to make way for semi-detached residences. This was where the Earls of Essex and of Shaftesbury once plotted the expulsion of the Catholic Stuarts. Nevertheless the political life of the country houses and the pattern of political consciousness which made of the county community of gentry its local instrument, still affects our life and conduct. This pattern did not vanish at once before the advance of the factories, firms, railways, schools and building estates of industrialized society. For the political system which the Cecils, the Churchills, the Pitts and the Walpoles worked in and through became after all one of the most efficient, formidable and humane that the world has ever known. Nevertheless, in spite of certain seemingly happy and permanent survivals like Hatfield House, this powerful political inheritance from the world we have lost was based on a set of social institutions which has disappeared.

So completely have these attitudes, practices and relationships vanished from our society that their surviving physical remains often embarrass us, just as the huge crumbling ruins of the buildings from the late Roman Empire embarrassed the Goths and the Saxons. Where the mansions have not succumbed to the swift and final fate of Cassiobury House, they have been put to incongruous uses.

Something of their prestige-conferring and status-symbolizing virtues are being set to work of course, if rather clumsily. They can be seen at play on the puzzled faces of visitors, as they wander through the stately homes of England each summer, listlessly pursuing a gabble of unknown names and old, unhappy, far-off things not worth the entrance fee to hear about. Elsewhere they are lending a very welcome dignity, of sorts, to brand-new universities, or to university departments of adult and extra-mural education. But to be the scene of earnest, self-improving communion in entirely over-impressive surroundings is scarcely ignominy. Royston Manor, the home of the family of that name in 1676 and in 1688, when Parson Sampson made his lists of his parishioners, certainly survives in the village of Clayworth. But its windows have been boarded up and its rooms are filled with the warm stench and perpetual scrabble of fowls being fattened for broiling.

The last peer to be Prime Minister, as a peer, was a Cecil, and Hatfield House was at the hub of the political life of the country only seventy years ago. The continuing political leadership of the very rich and prestigious is a paradoxical feature of other democratic countries than our own, even of the United States. Therefore the succession in the 1960's of the fourteenth Earl of Home to the office held in the 1900's by the third Marquess of Salisbury should perhaps be looked upon in that light rather than as direct evidence that country house government still persists. But it is surely a sign that that tenacious system is not entirely lifeless even yet.

Nevertheless the political machine of the landed families had its origins in a social situation entirely different from our own. It could only work fully when men's assumptions about political organizations were of a kind which now we can only imagine. This was the time when the great house in the park was the sole centre of political authority away from the Royal Court; when its size and magnificence were the one means of expressing political influence and achievement in monumental form. The influence and achievement in question here attached to the resident family and its reigning head, for in that age these things belonged to families alone. 'Family' here has a dual meaning; the actual group of persons living in a mansion, along with the retinue of servants, and the complex of blood relatives of the same lineage scattered across the face of the county, or of several counties, and inhabiting many seats. For if it was not true that the individual household in the traditional order was ordinarily an extended group of kin living together, it was true that political relationships went with kinship. The Cecils, as Cecils, were a political complex of their own, a very intricate one, from the sixteenth to the eighteenth centuries and beyond.

As a matter of fact the great aristocratic household in the great house was more likely to contain grandparents and grandchildren, nephews and nieces, young married couples not yet in their own establishments, cousins, aunts and in-laws generally than the less conspicuous household. This seems to have been so with the gentry also. For one thing there was room enough and to spare in those rambling and towering structures to accommodate the relatives, and servants in plenty to wait upon them. For another thing rich people had more children and lived longer and so would tend to have more relations alive – the Duke of Omnium's huge establishment was not typical of Victorian life and Victorian politics alone.

Since all these prominent people were well aware of the world, they were likely to know who were their kinsfolk and to be acquainted with them. How important this could be may be illustrated by an incident from the court history of Queen Anne.

In self-defence against the bullying of Sarah Churchill, born Jennings, but known to posterity as the wife of the distinguished soldier John Churchill, Duke of Marlborough, Queen Anne finally took into her favour one of her dressers, Abigail Hill, whose duties were to lie on the Royal bedroom floor at night and empty the slops. Abigail had been given this humble post by Sarah herself, because the duchess had been told that one of her great band of relatives was living in complete penury; Abigail and Sarah were in fact first cousins. No sooner had this high-church chambermaid whom Sarah had raised 'from a broom', been taken into the Royal confidence, than Robert Harley, master as he was of political intrigue, discovered a blood relationship with the new favourite. His actual connection with her has never been worked out. He worked so effectively through Abigail, and in other ways of course, that the final fall from favour of the Churchills was brought about, and also the Treaty of Utrecht in 1713. The French dramatist Scribe once wrote a play about the negotiations for this treaty, which he made out to have been held up because of a cup of coffee being spilt down the dress of Abigail, now the Lady Masham.[180]

Though it underlines the intimacy of kinship and politics, the story of Abigail is in no way typical of the workings of court patronage, and (as we have already seen) the family of the possessing minority is a deceptive guide to the family in general. Once more, since it was families like this which interested people, and since most writers came from them or from those near to them in the social structure, the literary evidence on family and household in the world we have lost is deceptive too. The analytical questions about the role of kinship in political life, as well as the size and structure of the household, must be left to a more academic discussion. Some notion has already been given of the function of the varying size of household within each village community in maintaining social authority, in keeping the hierarchy in being and ensuring submission on the part of peasants and craftsmen. This is

[180] *See page* 306.

obviously of importance when we approach once more the question of the reasons for obedience.

Pre-eminence of the rulers in virtue of the size of their households was only one feature of a system of authority whose overall description, as we have already repeatedly insisted, must be patriarchal. This final chapter on the nature of the traditional world and the contrast it presents with the world we now inhabit, will concern itself first with that un-questioning subordination which marked relationships then, and which marks them no longer. From a short survey of the political education of our ancestors, the conditioning process as we might say, we shall proceed to a brief exploration of the actual mechanics of political life. Three characteristics are important to our purposes: social mobility, geographical isolation of all below the level of gentleman, and illiteracy.

The study of these characteristics belongs to a subject which is still in its earliest phase of development, now known by the ugly phrase political socialization. Only the most general reflections are therefore possible as yet. A beginning may be made with a statement about the predominant tone of social and political life at that time, and of almost the whole of political literature. In this society, subordination and politics were founded on tradition. Therefore critical examina-tion of the reasons why some men were better placed than others was unlikely to come about. This submissive cast of mind is almost universal in the statements made by the men about themselves. 'There is degree above degree, As reason is . . .' 'Take but degree away, Untune that string, And hark what discord follows.' It would seem that once a man in the traditional world got himself into a position where he could catch a glimpse of his society as a whole, he immediately felt that degree, order, was its essential feature. Without degree, unquestioning subordination, and some men being privileged while all the others obeyed, anarchy and destruction were inevitable. Any threat to the established order was a danger to everyone's personality.

There are two reasons why this is what might be expected to have been the almost universal attitude. One is implied by the word *traditional* itself, which meant that the set of stand-ards used to make judgements about society and varying positions within it stayed constant for almost all people at all times. Put into more technical language, it must be presumed that neither peasant, pauper nor craftsman nor even gentleman in the pre-industrial world ever changed his reference group in such a way as to feel aware of what is called relative deprivation.* Directly this assumption is recorded, it raises questions about those occasions on which change of reference group did come about in seventeenth-century English society. It could be argued, for example, that the disturbances caused by the Civil War and especially those connected with the recruitment and activities of the parliamentary army, did bring humble people into contact for the first time with those who were better off and had a more aspiring outlook. Indeed the isolation of individuals from their counterparts in other village communities was so marked a feature of the society we have described that the very fact of bringing them together to share a common, vital purpose for months and years together might be expected to have some crystallizing effect on their attitudes to their social position and political rights.

If for example the literature of the Levellers of Cromwell's army and of the city of London could be shown to have arisen to any extent from such circumstances as these, it would provide a fascinating parallel with events in our own century. National war, conscription and disbandment are now commonly assumed to be associated with intense feeling of relative deprivation and revolutionism. Social mobility in industrial society is also known to have the expected effect on reference groups. Once the opportunity of rising in society is envisaged, and once its actual fulfilment begins to look possible, then men do become aware that they are being deprived of what their superiors enjoy, and may well begin to question the rationale of the established social order. Now that we have reason to believe that social mobility was present in pre-industrial society as well, we must suppose that some discontent and criticism was engendered in traditional societies for similar reasons. Social quiescence, therefore, should not be regarded as quite fully descriptive of England or of Europe three hundred years ago, especially of the kingdom which Oliver Cromwell found himself responsible for.

* *The developing theory of relative deprivation and reference groups is admirably described by* W. G. Runciman *in his book* Relative Deprivation and Social Justice, 1966, *where English social history since 1918 is analysed in these terms.*

Interesting as these possibilities are, they can hardly have been of much importance. The second reason why the society we are so hastily describing must be presumed to have been nearly always socially quiescent is that the phrase stable poverty does on the whole seem to be a fair description of most of its area. It is a commonplace of social observation that stable poverty means resignation to the situation as it is. Such an impression seems the only possible one to gather from Gregory King's table, in spite of the political, military, even commercial and industrial energy which was displayed by the England of his century. Though we have nothing like the amount of evidence which de Tocqueville assembled for the *ancien régime* as it was in France just before the fatal year 1789, it seems entirely unlikely that anything like a revolution of rising expectations could have been contemplated by the peasants and craftsmen of our country in Stuart times. Further information and more determined analysis may modify this claim, but an acceptance of unvarying, even poverty seems to be as much a characteristic of those local village communities we have yet been able to examine as it seems to be of King's description of the whole nation.

Nevertheless it is generally supposed that a society in such a situation will have its share of desperate men, and that the downtrodden pauper if ever he does find an opportunity will express his resentment of the hardships he is forced to suffer. We have mentioned that men were aware how the deprived might take to violence, able-bodied men in civil disorder and neglected, elderly women perhaps in witchcraft.[181] Quite apart from those in extreme situations, some rationale must have been present to settle the doubts of those who were disposed for any reason to question the rightness of arrangements as they were and the duty of submission and obedience. Social superiority and political authority did to some small extent depend for their maintenance on outside sanctions.

The outside support for authority in the traditional world was religious, though 'outside' scarcely expresses its relationship with the social system. We can gain a little somewhat unexpected insight into the way in which attitudes of obedience were inculcated into every personality in the formative years.[182] The stated duty of each parish priest was to teach the children of his flock the catechism. After matins on Sundays

[181] *See page* 307.   [182] *See page* 307.

in every one of the 10,000 parishes of England there gathered, or should have gathered, the group of adolescents from the houses of the gentry and the yeomen, the husbandmen, the tradesmen, the labourers and even the paupers to learn from the priest what it meant to be a Christian. This is what they all had to repeat after him: every single one of them had to get to know it by heart:

My duty towards my neighbour is to love him as myself, and to do to all men as I would they should do unto me: to love, honour and succour my father and mother: to submit myself to all my governors, teachers, spiritual pastors and masters; to order myself lowly and reverently to all my betters; to hurt nobody by word nor deed: to be true and just in all my dealings; to bear no malice nor hatred in my heart: to keep my hands from picking and stealing, and my tongue from evil-speaking, lying and slandering: to keep my body in temperance, soberness and chastity: not to covet nor desire other men's goods: but to learn and labour truly to get my own living, and to do my duty in that state of life unto which it shall please God to call me.

These words are still familiar and evocative because they come from the catechism of the Church of England, originally composed in 1549 and still in use. Some effort of the historical imagination has to be made to recognize how important they were at the time when every living person in England was both a believing, fearing Christian and also by compulsion a member of the national church. 'We hold,' said Richard Hooker, the official spokesman of the established order, 'that there is not any man of the Church of England but the same man is also a member of the Commonwealth. Nor any man a member of the Commonwealth which is not also a member of the Church of England.'

What is more this was the only thing that young people were ever told about obedience, authority and the social and political order. It was solemnly inculcated on one of those few public occasions when, as we have seen, they left the circle of the household and the authority of its master, to find themselves in the church under the authority of the priest. Many of these youths and maidens, moreover, had no means of confirming or revising what the grave minister had to tell them, for they could not read. He had to teach them by word of mouth what they would have to say before the formidable figure of the Lord Bishop when it came to their service of Confirmation.

Lest it should be thought that only the orthodox had this formal lesson so firmly impressed upon them, here are the words adopted for the *Shorter Catechism* in the year 1644, when the Puritan clergy were taking control of the Church of England at the height of the war between King and Parliament.

Question 64: What is required in the fifth commandment?

Answer: The fifth commandment requireth the preserving the honour and performing the duties, belonging to every one in their several places and relations, as Superiors, Inferiors or Equals.

Question 65: What is forbidden in the fifth commandment?

Answer: The fifth commandment forbiddeth the neglecting of or doing anything against the duty which belongeth to every one in their several places and relations.

In this case the English Presbyterians were overtly stating the position universally adopted in the traditional interpretation of the Bible, by separatists and sectarians as well as by the hierarchies, that the duty of Christian obedience rested on the commandment *Honour thy Father and thy Mother.* The puritan preachers urged 'fathers and masters of families' to catechize their children and servants at home, and it was a dissenting preacher who based landlordly rights on the fifth commandment (above, p. 21). What more familiar sentiment for the beneficed rector, the itinerant preacher or the conscientious householder to appeal to when children were being instructed in their Christian duties? Submission to the powers that be went very well with the habit of obedience to the head of the patriarchal family, and it had the extremely effective sanction of the universal fear of damnation to the defiant. 'Short life,' so the doctrine went, 'was the punishment of disobedient children.'[183]

Of course the tenant obeyed his landlord for what may be thought were much more tangible reasons than his early training and his care for the salvation of his soul. He might be evicted if he showed insufficient respect, especially in what was his clear political duty when, providing that he had got a vote, he came to exercise the franchise. His landlord was also very likely to be a justice of the peace, with all the forces of

[183] *See page* 307.

the established order on his side. As for those below the landholders, there was the relationship of menial service, past,
present and to come, which was described when we talked of
the village community. A labourer, or a craftsman, a cottager
or even a lowly husbandman could very well have been a
servant in one of the larger houses in the locality, and his sons
and daughters might in fact be in that position at the time.
Each of them might well have to look to those same substantial
householders for a day's work all his life.

There is no need to labour the point about the familial basis
of society and submissiveness further than this. It may begin
to look strange that any one was ever bold enough to escape
at all, impossible that ideas of individual rights, of the
accountability of superiors, of contract as the basis of government could ever have occurred to the men of seventeenth-
century England.

This is one more of the paradoxes which urgently await
systematic study by the sociological historian. If we are to
begin to understand why it was that a society so static and
authoritarian in its attitude to social discipline, and so strict
in maintaining it, could be at the same time so free and inventive in its political ideas and institutions, we must turn our
attention to the actual mechanism of political life. There can
be no doubt of the strangeness of the contrast between what
men said about the rights of individuals and what those rights
actually were.

*All and every particular and individual man and woman, that
ever breathed in the world, are by nature all equal and alike in
their power, dignity, authority and majesty, none of them having
(by nature) any authority, dominion or magisterial power one
over or above another.*[184]

This is a famous statement made by John Lilburne, gentleman, the Leveller leader in 1646, and it reads very strangely
in view of all that has been said here about universal subordination and inequality.

The Levellers were of course an extraordinary phenomenon.
Their appearance in the parliamentary army and in London
during the later years of the Civil War and the earlier years of
unkingly government certainly provides us with the most
revealing evidence we have or ever shall have of life below the

[184] *See page* 307.

level of the *élite*. Here, if anywhere, we must look for those sentiments which did take all the people into account and were not distorted by supposing that the claims made for the few need never be supposed to apply to the many. There are grave difficulties in deciding exactly how many Levellers there were and how they were placed in society; whether they really were confined to London, the army and a few of the home counties, or whether every intelligent villager with a smattering of education would have supported them if he had been given the opportunity. Perhaps some sort of half-collective life, quasi-political life, of this kind was present well before the Civil War, and maintained itself all the way through the centuries until the Chartists brought Leveller demands again into the public arena, and finally the Labour Party developed them into an attitude which is supported by at least half of those with political personality in our country today.

If anything of this last statement could be shown to have been true, a quite different strand of interconnection between the political outlook of the old world and our own might come into view, this time not confined to the fully literate minority and not providing reasons why we should respect and obey our traditional leadership, but grounds for criticizing and replacing it.

But in the world we have lost, as had already been laid down, an entity like 'England' lived its whole life within the confines of a small, select minority. Even a critic of political arrangements, a man who, like Lilburne, had come to believe that most institutions were the unjust result of conquest and usurpation, of the 'Norman Yoke' thrust upon the free English in the year 1066, himself belonged to that fraction of society which alone possessed political awareness. It was therefore perhaps possible even for him to say things which seemed to affect every living individual without his actually contemplating more than a small proportion of them. Political humanity to John Lilburne presumably meant far more people than it did to John Locke when he wrote out thirty years later something with a marked resemblance to Lilburne's statement in the measured tones which were to make it the classic text for the liberties enjoyed by the gentlemen of eighteenth-century England and the citizens of eighteenth-century America.

To understand political power right, and derive it from its original, we must consider what state all men are naturally in, and that is, a state of perfect freedom to order their actions, and dispose of their possessions, and persons as they think fit, within the bounds of the law of nature, without asking leave, or depending upon the will of any other man. A state also of equality, wherein all the power and jurisdiction is reciprocal, no one having more than another.

Though the cautious Locke omits women, and later excepts children from natural equality, he sounds as if he meant literally all humanity in this statement. Indeed he may well have supposed that he did mean such a thing, provided only that the ordinary assumptions of his day about who was in fact concerned in political matters were maintained by his reader. In fact almost everyone did stay within these limits at that time. Very, very few ever found themselves wondering whether a government literally having consent from every breathing, responsible human could or should exist, so far were the assumptions of twentieth-century democracy from their minds. One of Locke's associates, James Tyrrell, did get into a position where this possibility crossed his path, but it will be seen how peremptorily he dismissed it.

There never was any government where all the promiscuous rabble of women and children had votes, as not being capable of it, yet it does not for all that prove that all legal civil government does not owe its original to the consent of the people, since the fathers of families, or freemen at their own dispose, were really and indeed are all the people that needed to have votes . . . Children in their fathers' families being under the notion of servants, and without any property in goods or land, have no reason to have votes in the institution of government.[185]

Locke and Tyrrell were both answering Sir Robert Filmer, the Kentish squire and apologist for the Crown, who wrote out his defence of absolute monarchy before ever the Civil War came about and called it '*Patriarcha, or the Natural Power of Kings*'. This document, a codification of unconscious prejudice, as it has been called, was addressed to his neighbours, to the other members of the Kentish community of county gentry, and not to the intellectuals of a later generation who

[185] *See page* 307.

made of it the most refuted theory in the history of English politics. Locke, Tyrrell and even Lilburne were as much gentlemen of England as the Filmers of East Sutton Park, though Lilburne was no scion of an established family like the others. Filmer's patriarchalism, for all its oddities and its entirely uncritical acceptance of the Scripture – he really believed that Charles Stuart was the literal heir of Adam among the English and so entitled to exercise upon them all the prerogatives conferred on the first father of mankind – provided a reason for the duty of everyone to obey, whilst his critics could justify the right of only a minority to resist. There is however no need to suppose that Filmer took any more account of the really humble mass of the people than his opponents did. Nobody took much notice of them when politics were in question.

Perhaps Colonel Rainborough came nearest when he made his oft-quoted statement to the victorious Parliamentary soldiery at Putney in 1647, when they were debating the future of English state and society: 'For I really think that the poorest he that is in England hath a life to live as the greatest he.' The response of the weighty champions of authority was just what we might expect: they invoked the fifth commandment: 'Honour thy father and thy mother', said Ireton, Cromwell's son-in-law, 'and that law doth extend to all that are our governors.'[186]

Rainborough's response was nothing like as confident as the emphatic challenge with which he had begun, for he found himself denying that the people of England were bound to obey any [political] parent who had not been elected, though parenthood and election go very uneasily together. What is more we can be fairly certain that Rainborough himself did not really mean all the poor people of the country. Like the rest of the Levellers he presumably excluded both servants and paupers from the franchise. We have seen that together these made up a considerable proportion of the whole population.* But Rainborough had no occasion to refer specifically to them, and like everyone else he seems to have had no very

---

[186] *See page* 307.

* *I owe the point that the Levellers excluded servants and the poor from political society to Brough Macpherson, though I cannot agree with him that the word servant then included many wage-earning householders.*

clear picture of what the *whole* people of England, every single one of them, can have looked like. For even in 1647 the facts of political life and the workings of the political machine were against it.

In our analysis of the political breakdown which occurred in Stuart times something has already been said about that wonderful contrivance, that ingenious instrument for maintaining political participation over the whole area of society. The crucial parts of the mechanism, the community of gentry in each county, has as yet only been examined from this point of view for one county in one year and this happens to have been Sir Robert Filmer's own county of Kent. In sketching the human geography of our country as it was in pre-industrial times, we have already insisted upon the universal presence of the gentry, noble and merely gentle, over its whole area, pressing evenly everywhere, like the atmosphere, or resting like an iridescent film on the entire surface. This was certainly true of Kent in 1640, and the interrelated, interacting inhabitants of the manor houses there can be seen to have been active in every possible direction.

When the Civil War came, it led to the formation of County Committees in Kent and all over the kingdom: once the central administration was withdrawn, that is to say, the local administration took its place as a matter of course. The running, recruitment and financing of the hostilities were conducted on a county basis. But in Kent anyway, the county community was also an intellectual society, which was why Sir Robert Filmer originally wrote his theory of politics for his companions in the manor houses, rather than for publication in London. In fact in his county in his time something like a dispersed university could be said to have been in existence, whose research workers found their material not simply in their own libraries of classical and scriptural authorities, but also in their own boxes of title deeds.

Family relationships kept the whole institution in working order, and the genealogical interrelationships between the manor houses were extensive, complicated and meticulously observed. It is astonishing how distant a connection qualified for the title 'cozen', and obvious that those in London, or in any part of the country where a living was to be got from commerce or from any other activity which a gentleman might take up, was as much a member of the society as those in permanent residence in the country houses. In Kent, in fact, these outliers stretched a very long distance indeed; by the year 1660 quite a high proportion of the county families had offshoots in the plantations of Virginia.

The essay from which this description of Kent is drawn makes the following general reflections about the activity which went on within the communities in the middle of the seventeenth century.

There are two characteristics of English society at that time which may prove to be more important to the world than the tensions which ended in fighting. One is that persistent preoccupation with political speculation which was a dominant trait of intellectual life in England in 1640 and for two generations thereafter. This finally gave us the theoretical presuppositions which now underlie our institutions and those of the whole English-speaking world. The other is that urge to create new societies in its own image, or in the image of its ideal self, which appeared in the self-confident years of Queen Elizabeth, though its first momentous consequences became apparent by about 1640 – when the Colony of Virginia was beginning to show the characteristics of American society in infancy.[187]

Twenty years have passed since these words were written, and the shape of political society in the country as a whole in 1640 seems to have turned out to be much as might have been expected from the rough model worked out for Kent. Though emigration was a special feature of certain maritime shires, and though intellectual interchange may not have been as common between the country seats in other counties, political England does appear to have been a reticulation of such familial networks as the one in which Sir Robert Filmer lived his life.

If we had time we could fill out the details here, beginning with the life of the village community which was earlier described, which was politically isolated save for those at the head of the community; the squire and sometimes the parson were the links between the village and the nation. More important to the present purpose is the manner in which the political game was played between the manor houses and the lordly seats: how even a minor gentleman in a new family might win one of the political prizes if he had the skill; how

[187] *See page* 308.

even an ancient lineage and a baronial estate could not help a lordling with the wrong opinions, or lacking a head for management, intrigue and plain political aggrandizement. Not many of the gentle families were of great political importance at any one time, we may notice, and very few from any one county counted nationally: like other political societies, most of the units were inactive, in reserve for a new occasion, another generation. But each genteel establishment always possessed political potential, and, when crisis came, support or resistance could be expected from almost every cell in the battery.

We cannot dwell on the relationship of our own political universe, with its party caucuses and its central offices, with its state primaries and its national, presidential conventions, to their ancestors in this vanished political arena. Nor can we go further in exploring what happened when passion was released and political potential became active participation, of the kind discussed in the last chapter. One suggestion must be made, in order to fulfil a promise made there. If it is justifiable to look upon the total system, social and political, as having any sort of conflict mechanism as a permanent part of its workings, then the county community must be thought of in that light. For the county community, the local political society, was a permanent, everyday affair, of which any qualified person could make himself an active part, and everyone of suitable status was by definition a member; this was not true of any national institution, and particularly of Parliament whose intermittent life depended on the whim and policy of the Sovereign. It may be remembered, however, that the presence of institutions for conflict does not necessarily mean that *all* friction was institutionalized.

Considerations like this belong rather to a general theory of political and social interaction, than to a comparison of the kind which is our proper subject. Any suggested similarity of Stuart England with the segmented societies of contemporary Africa must be left on one side for the same reason, though once again the community of county gentry turns out to be the important point. Stuart England, and perhaps England at any time before industrialization, might begin to be looked upon as something of a permanent federation of segments, within each of which rivalry, almost entirely symbolic and peaceful, was perpetual, and between which open conflict was always a possibility. On those rare occasions when overt conflict came about, it did not necessarily represent a weakening of the national political consciousness, but rather an assertion and intensification of it. The recognition of this fact makes political and constitutional history read rather differently than it has done, especially the history of 'revolution', in our country and in others.

But this is not the last word to be said about authority in the world we have lost and our political heritage from it. There remain two questions to be touched upon, both of which are rather difficult and have been referred to once or twice before. One is social mobility and the other the extent of literacy. Each is open in principle to numerical investigation of the kind which we have been able to use in a very preliminary way in discussing such things as size of household and sexual conformity. The numerical evidence is much more elusive, however, and has yet scarcely been tackled at all, particularly for social mobility. The considerations then must be very rough and provisional indeed.

The indications they seem to imply for social and political change may be thought to be rather surprising, especially in the case of social mobility. The expectation must be that movement both upwards and downwards was normal rather than exceptional in the society of our ancestors, though it was of course a marginal effect. There is at present no way of telling how great the movement was but it seems certain that it was commoner at some times than at others. Nevertheless some motion both ways, upwards and downwards, seems likely to have been going on all the time. Put into the language of traditional discussion, there always was a rise of the gentry and always a (slightly larger) fall of the gentry, though 'rise into' and 'fall out of' would be a more accurate way of putting it. This expectation arises from what is known and what can be inferred about the vital statistics of the population as a whole in relation to the privileged minority. It is certainly not contradicted by other evidence, and once the possibility that this was the ordinary pattern is recognized, the known facts of all kinds seem to fit in quite well.

Common sense and the little we know indicate that the gentry may well have lived a little longer, and perhaps, though this is uncertain, married a little earlier than the others. They would therefore have tended to have more

o

children, and conception may have occurred more often in their wives, since the habit of putting their babies out to wet nurse made them fecund for longer periods. Though it can be urged against this that gentlemen may well have lived less regularly with their wives, it must also have been the case that their higher living standards made childbirth easier and safer, and so ensured that their offspring would often have survived where those of poorer people would have died. There are possible indications, as we shall see, that the privileged families may have deliberately limited their families. Nonetheless it would certainly seem that they must have more than replaced themselves at every generation.

Hence downward mobility; hence the individuals born into the manor-houses who found themselves marrying into the houses of the yeomanry, the clergy, or even the husbandmen, as well as of the city tradesmen. The numbers of such matches cannot have been large, even when social mobility was at its most intense. But we may suppose that the proportion of those on the way down in the world was never negligible in relation to the size of the privileged minority, and its existence was certainly noticed by contemporaries. An example may be taken from a book published in 1656, *The Vale Royal of England, or the County Palatine of Chester*:

In no country of England, the gentlemen are more ancient and of longer continuance than in this country. I have thought good to set down all such arms, as I find them to bear, or to have borne. And not by order or in degree, but after the manner of the alphabet. It goeth with such matters in this country as in other countrys of England. For riches maketh a gentleman throughout the realm, which is contrary to the manner of some other countries beyond the seas. So you shall have in this country, six men of one surname (and peradventure of one house) whereof the first shall be called a Knight, the second an Esquire, the third a Gentleman, the fourth a Freeholder, the fifth a Yeoman, and the sixth a husbandman.
So convinced was this urbane author of his main point that he put in the margin against this passage: 'Riches maketh Gentlemen in all countries of England.'

He was an acute observer who could recognize that the identity of wealth with status meant that a poor man, even if of gentle birth, might go down in the world. His other statements illustrate many of the claims we have made about the

social order in the English counties, whilst the habit of calling
the shire by the word 'country', which we reserve for the
whole national area must not be missed. The truth of the
observation that the name of the gentle family within a
village community was often the same as that of much
humbler families can be confirmed from many of the listings
of persons in village communities which we have recovered
and examined. Indeed many a gentleman's son at his marriage
called himself a yeoman, just as the yeoman's son often called
himself a husbandman. Although almost unnoticed by the
subsequent historian, social descent was something like an
institution of the traditional order in England.

This may have distinguished our country from the rest of
Europe, as we have already stated and as the writer just
quoted also realized. The complaint that the social system
played cuckoo to the superfluous children in a privileged
family is far more often met with in the perennial form of the
younger brother's lament. Here is one from 1600, written by
Thomas Wilson:

*I cannot speak of the [number] of younger brothers, albeit I be one
of the number myself, but for their estate there is no man hath
better cause to know it, nor less cause to praise it. Such a fever
hectic hath custom brought in and inured amongst fathers, and
such fond desires they have to leave a great show of the stock of
their house, though the branches be withered, that my elder brother
forsooth must be my master. He must have all, and all the rest
that which the cat left on the maltheap, perhaps some small
annuity during his life or what pleases our elder brothers worship
to bestow upon us if we please him, and my mistress his wife.
This I must confess doth us good someways, for it makes us
industrious to apply ourselves to letters or to arms, whereby many
times we become my master elder brother's masters, or at least
their betters in honour and reputation, while he lives at home
like a mome [a buffoon might be our word for this] and knows the
sound of no bell but his own.*[188]

The industrious younger sons of the manor-houses of Kent
were those who went and carved out a career for themselves
and a new future for the family name in the southern colonies
of North America. They were impelled to do so both by the
status consciousness of their elder brothers and by the

[188] *See page* 308.

overriding sense of dynasty which led each successor to a manor-house to identify himself with his lineage, past and future.

Patriarchal custom and authority enabled an unfeeling heir to treat his brothers and sisters badly, and his younger children also. A legal system imbued with such attitudes helped him too, though English law was not as emphatic about *patria potestas* as the Civil or Roman law which Wilson professed. But not all heads of families could find it in their hearts to behave in this way; pride of position often led them into actions which depressed the fortunes of the line.

Here we meet a whole series of possibilities arising out of the vital statistics of each lineage, complicated by all the vagaries of personality and predilection. A man might have a large number of children, mostly sons, whom he could, if he wished, either set up in the City, the Army or elsewhere, reasonably cheaply, or else, if they would stand for it, quietly neglect. On the other hand he might be affectionate and indulgent, unwilling to allow dependents to fall into penury, or unable to prevent them from insisting on a maintenance. In the first case the family fortune would be handed down intact, provided always that he had been a good manager, and in the second it might be dispersed. If daughters predominated amongst his children, inroads into capital would be more difficult to resist, because without dowries daughters, even below the level of the gentry, could not be married at all. Many a bearded patriarch besides King Lear was ruined by his daughters.

This is only the beginning of what went on, and it must be noticed how much difference numbers of births and expectation of life made in any such situation. Economic historians have studied the market in dowries and jointures (these were the amounts which had to be settled on a son's bride to maintain her if he should die) and shown how the price of a good match for a child varied over time. Naturally the situation would be very different for a family where there was only one child, and a male at that; or where a great deal was unexpectedly inherited from the early death of the wife's father and only brother; or where the wife died early, and a new marriage brought in a rich heiress; or where a ne'er-do-well cadet suddenly returned from the Indies with a fortune and added it to the main stock. In the eighteenth century this went on offstage in India perhaps or the Navy, and in Victorian times in New

Zealand, or in South America. This is the stuff out of which the plots of novels and plays were woven; in the end they mostly consist of a study in the ups and downs of the fortunes of a family. The perpetual presence in these stock situations of impoverished relatives now begins to look significant. Not all of the grandchildren, not to speak of the nephews and nieces, could possibly expect the golden prospects of the hero and heroine when finally they settled down to live happily ever after.

But we have learnt to mistrust literary evidence on matters of this kind. It should not be long before we have reliable figures on the differential fertility of the various descriptions of people in the world we have lost, and particularly on the groups of children born and brought to maturity in the manor-houses, for it was this rather than the longer life of each individual which determined that there should be a surplus of gentry.

Nevertheless mortality was exceedingly high there, even amongst the titled people: the mean age at death of all the English artistocrats dying in the sixteenth and seventeenth centuries was in the early thirties. What is more, slightly higher overall fertility emphatically does not mean that every lady had many children who grew up. When we come to analyse the bulk of our evidence on the distribution of children between households, we discover a tendency for gentlemen's and yeomen's households to contain smaller groups of children than those lower in the social scale, always excepting the poorest. This very interesting effect may have come about for reasons other than demographic, but it raises the possibility that those in the upper ranges of society were deliberately restricting the numbers of their children for fear of social descent. But even if no such policy was in operation, it would be wrong to suppose that higher fertility amongst privileged women would always lead to a safe succession in the family. Some died in childbirth, and some lost their husbands after one or two births. Some had sons, perhaps several sons, but none who lived long enough to inherit. Others had daughters only, and some would undoubtedly have been unable to have children at all. Even allowing for re-marriage and collateral succession, the perpetuation of the male line was uncertain.

We may take an example in the history of the baronetage.

This honorific order was instituted in 1611 by King James I so as to create something in between Barons and Knights, and so as to raise money by the sale of the right to the inherited title, *Sir*, which would be borne by each successive male heir of the original Baronet. This inheritance was to descend, of course, in perpetuity in accordance with the established English rules. No woman could therefore inherit the title, and if there was no son, the holder's brother's son would succeed, or, for lack of him, a more distant cousin. Such a cousin had to be related by blood rather than by marriage to the last holder, and the line of succession could not go upwards, that is to say pass through the ancestors of the original baronet. Nevertheless these conventions governing succession would seem to provide excellent chances for the survival of baronetcies over long periods. Yet in 1769, 150 years after their creation, over half of the two hundred and more baronetcies created by James I himself had become extinct for want of a properly qualified heir. With expectation of life as it then was amongst the gentry, therefore, a family line as the English understood it seems to have had only one chance in two of surviving for 150 years. Or, to put it another way, and taking for good measure a generation to last an average thirty years, one half of all family lines existing in any year would have died out by the fifth succession.

This may seem surprising, but preliminary calculations show that the probability of a son being alive to succeed his father under the demographic conditions then prevailing was no higher than eight out of ten, even if the father had a family of five children. This means that the direct male line (not allowing cousins to succeed this time) would die out in one family in five after only one lifetime, given five children in a generation, and in one family in three after two successions. After five successions about three-quarters of direct male lines would be broken, again assuming five children to a generation.

Now if we look at the whole directive minority as consisting of such family lines, and revert again to the example of the baronetcies so as to make it possible for cousins to succeed, we can see that to maintain any elite group over the generations there must be perpetual recruitment into it. In fact, of course, family lines composing the elite in general were not bound by the masculine rule, as titled families had to be,

and we have seen how frequently such families were perpetu-
ated by allowing a man to inherit a manor house or a social
position by marrying a daughter of the final heir. We have
seen also how it was the function of the Crown as the fountain
of honour to intervene in particularly critical cases and permit
a breach of the rules, so that a house could go on existing
with its original name and titles in spite of the failure of heirs.
But even given all these expedients to maintain succession
artificially, it will be agreed that promotion from below must
have been going on continuously, simply in order to maintain
the directive minority at full strength over time. If the elite
expanded, of course, upward promotion would have gone on
much more intensely. Yet all the time it would be probable
that as many or more people were being dropped from the
directive minority as were joining it.[189]

But the facts about the rise of fortunate persons in traditional society are not as clear as those about the fall of unfortunate ones. Some of the people who would otherwise have
lost their status in the ruling segment were certainly able to
step into the places of those required to keep a failing lineage
in being. In this way, for example by the judicious marriage
of a girl destined to become the final representative of a particular name to an impoverished younger son of a flourishing
brood, replacement could take place without social ascent.
But this could only happen to a limited extent, and although
by adoption of surname it might save appearances it could
not save a hereditary title from extinction. In any case it
depended on the efficiency of the market, so to speak, on
being able to find just the partner for your child, or your
nephew, or your ward.

If mismanagement had been a major reason for decline,
moreover, nothing less than the sharing out of property, with
a near-certainty of serious losses, could have saved the day.
No privileged order seems likely ever to have gone as far as
this to preserve its exclusiveness, especially in the face of
pressure from outside of men with money to spare. Least of all
would this have happened in the England which we have
described, and where we know that recruitment went on from
below. Marriage was the approved method of bringing it about,
and it was for the most part marriage which set the seal of familial relationship on the arrival from below of property and power.

[189] *See page* 308.

Much of the mobility must have been what might be called semi-circular. A younger son of a manor-house moved into the town; or had to satisfy himself with a parson's or a yeoman's house and duties in the country. Then after a series of deaths in the family his son or grandson found himself moving back into the family mansion. Often it was a different house from that of his direct ancestors and often the perpetuation of a 'family' in the records found in the county histories is a matter of different branches flourishing and languishing, though the final diminuendo is almost never worth recording. City money was very frequently the reason why an obscure branch became the major line, but careful historical study has shown that it was not the only one and may perhaps have been exaggerated, along with the importance of enclosure and capitalist farming, in its effects on social ascent and a family's fortunes. This semi-circular motion is not particularly special, for all social mobility takes place backwards and forwards, or up and down, just across the specified dividing line.

We have already referred to this whole mazy process as the way in which the bourgeoisie kept on a level with the others in the ruling minority, discriminated against for a time by other, older members of a county community of gentry, but always acceptable after the passing of a generation. When the sparse evidence so far collected is examined for signs of the movement roughly described, it seems to conform well enough. Taking a sample of some fifty bridegrooms and over sixty brides described as belonging to the gentry in the Lincoln marriage licences between 1612 and 1617 we find that almost a third of the men and over two-fifths of the women married outside their social order. When clergy and the obviously bourgeois occupations are taken into account the indication of social mobility is rather less; only about 20 per cent in the case of men though still over a third of the women married outside what we have called the ruling segment. Nearly a quarter of the women and over 15 per cent of the men married into yeomen's families; one gentleman married a daughter of a waterman, another the daughter of a pursemaker, whilst one gentlewoman married the son of a barber, another the son of an apothecary and a third the son of a husbandman.

These fragmentary indications have the disadvantage that they only imply change, not its direction. We do not know

whether the eight clergymen who took gentlewomen to wife
were on their way up in the world, or whether they themselves
were sons of gentry marrying on their own level. Some at
least of them may have been taking a daughter off the hands
of a squire fast succumbing to the burden of trying to maintain too large an establishment for his failing means. The
daughter of an alderman to be found in the sample, and the
merchant's daughter, seem rather more certainly to have
been on their way up in the world. But even they may have
belonged to bourgeois families failing in their fortune, and
have been joining genteel families unable to find better
alliances. We have found gentry marrying people beneath
them in Manchester in the 1650's, allying themselves with
clothiers, drapers, mercers and tanners, even husbandmen. In
the Gloucestershire marriage allegations in the 1660's a
'gentleman' appears who was apparently unable to sign his
own name. He at least seems unlikely to have been climbing
the social ladder.

There is plenty of evidence from other contexts to confirm
what the actual records have to tell us about social mobility.
It would be inconsistent of us to take the literary evidence too
seriously after all that has been said about its capacity to
deceive the social historians. But it is difficult not to mention
the trading and manufacturing families of the city of London
as they are portrayed by the Elizabethan and Restoration
playwrights. Their children seem to have been brought up to
marry into the gentry; the decayed gentleman anxious to wed
city money by fair means or foul is a stock figure too. Still it
comes as a surprise to see 'John Cockeshutt, gent.' licensed in
1591 to the drover's trade by the Lancashire justices.[190]

That particular county may have been exceptional in the
use made there of this most important social description. But
the existence of a considerable number of families and persons
who were either just about to move into or were in process of
falling out of the privileged group is what we ought to expect
in a society arranged as this one was. Some of these people
must have been gentlemen for life. They were persons whose
fathers had been landed proprietors, but whose own sons
would be virtually landless: or those who had risen by their
own exertions but not built up enough to found a gentle line.

John Lilburne may have been a member of this penumbra

[190] *See page* 309.

of the ruling segment as we called it when it was first mentioned, and its possible importance in movements of critical unrest in the social structure opens up a whole vista of possible speculation. It must be repeated, however, that the members of this fringe area of the society were sharply contrasted in their social experiences. Some were on the way up and others on the way down, whilst many of the lineages would be up in one generation and down in another. There would be little justification for making this social area into a 'middle class', certainly not one which could be described as rising or falling as a whole. We cannot linger over the very important issues which social mobility raises, and the whole discussion requires a great deal more evidence and much closer analysis than we have yet been able to undertake. But there is one question which cannot be entirely neglected.

This is the size of the privileged minority, which is after all critical to the fact of social mobility. Did it remain fairly constant in relation to the population as a whole, expanding with a general expansion and contracting in a time of falling numbers overall? We have tended to assume such a steady relationship and the consistency in titles given to persons in, for example, the lists of burials, seems to confirm it. But this is after all a very rough sort of calculation and we do not even yet know whether the numbers of gentle persons and families tended to grow in times of economic expansion and contract in times of depression, as common sense might make us expect.

More interesting and significant perhaps is to ask exactly how the numbers were kept in steady relationship with the numbers of the whole society, if indeed they were. It could be suggested that this was indeed one of the perennial sources of conflict in the social structure, but extremely intermittent in its operation. Whatever the mechanism was it seems to have resembled in its operation the crisis of subsistence which afflicted the peasantry in France. It must thus have made itself manifest quite unexpectedly and then, after doing its work, when conditions changed, vanished again. A society retaining the general shape this one is observed to have done could only afford a certain number of privileged persons, just as with its given resources of food it could only afford a certain total population.

But all this is guesswork only, in a field where guesswork has been only too common. In our present state of ignorance and in the infancy of studies of this sort speculation about possible changes in the structure of the ruling segment, about the probable effects of more small estates and families and fewer large ones, or of more great nobles and fewer small ones, seems premature. Nevertheless generalizations of this kind have confidently been made about such things as the 'rise of the gentry', or 'the crisis of the nobility' and so on. No doubt such events and tendencies were real enough, and their historical implications may have been important. But it must now be clear that it is no more than a preliminary exercise to prove that certain families rose and others fell within the social structure. Only if it could be shown that the movement up or down was truly excessive, very much more than might be expected in view of what was normal, could it enter into any explanation of critical social change. Even then, if something to correspond with revolution is to be supposed, it would also have to be demonstrated that the movement in question was such as to defeat the resources for compromise in the political system. This system, it must be assumed, was adapted to disturbances of such a kind. The same consideration applies to the gentry themselves, and to every other distinguishable part of the ruling minority. Internal changes amongst the gentlemen or the nobility would have had to be truly novel and unexpected if they were to have led to changes in the general shape of the whole society.

The exchange of persons between the privileged minority and the rest shows us something of how the whole was related to the all-important part. This does not go very far towards explaining why it was that those within the network of gentle families, when they thought about politics, believed that they were thinking for the whole society. Far more revealing, however, is the recognition of the situation of most of the great majority of people whose existence, attitudes and desires could be assumed, or ignored, by their supporters. Ordinary Englishmen three hundred years ago lived in an oral culture, that is to say one where most transactions went on by word of mouth, yet they belonged to a society whose politics were run in writing.

This is the most conspicuous reason why the peasants of one village were politically and socially isolated from the peasants of all other villages; and why the literate few could feel that they were thinking for the whole mass. Without access to books, without always being able to write as much as their own names, how could the husbandmen of a village where the politically active gentlemen lived be expected to think at all? And if so many of the landholders were in this mute and unreflecting situation, what about the labourers and the artificers, the millers, the wheelwrights, the weavers, shepherds, drovers, masons, shoemakers? What about the paupers?

More than political communication is at issue here. Inability to read and write amongst ordinary folk makes it quite possible to suppose that the kinship network now studied by sociologists of the family may have been more restricted amongst people living, as we have seen so very many of them did, in the tiny communities of the countryside than it is today among the masses who inhabit our huge urban centres. An illiterate maidservant living ten miles from home was cut off from her parents and her brothers and sisters far more effectively than a factory worker in Coventry is separated today from his father and mother in Glasgow. He has the telephone and very often a motor car quite apart from the railway, and above all the writing of letters for immediate and certain delivery. She could only write – and we have found that illiteracy was particularly common amongst maidservants – if someone would write her letter for her; only send it home if someone happened to be travelling that way; in fact could only communicate effectively by walking home one day, staying the night, and walking back the next, if her master would let her. She could send no Christmas cards to her aunts and uncles and cousins, nor could she attend the gatherings at Christmas, at weddings and funerals, which keep family networks together in our time. It is very doubtful whether her elders could have done very much in that direction either. It must be assumed that each kin-connected household lived closer to each other in terms of miles than they do today, but we have already seen that individuals and families did migrate, and we know that servants married for the most part outside their native villages, though the girls amongst them tried to get closer to home when they set up house. The extended family in this sense must have been more difficult to sustain in the pre-industrial world than it is now, and though lack of elementary learning was only one of the reasons for this, it was of crucial importance.[191]

[191] *See page* 309.

Not all of these men and women, boys and girls were entirely unlettered, and it is now known that more weavers or cobblers could read than husbandmen or even yeomen. It is evident that tradesmen had more occasions to use written and printed material than landworkers did, and the tradition of radicalism amongst the tradesmen reveals at once the possible association between literacy and thinking for yourself politically. Since tradesmen were so much greater in numbers and in importance in the towns than in the countryside, the extent of literacy must have made a great difference between the urban and the rural population. In Norwich in Elizabethan times, systematic arrangements seemed to have been made to provide even paupers' children with some sort of instruction. This attribute certainly divided the sexes; in every type of evidence we possess which bears upon the issue, more men turn out to be literate than women. Every historian has met ladies in very high stations who could scarcely spell, to whom writing was evidently a painful ordeal and this continuing into the nineteenth century. Literacy divided the household in another way too, for, as has been said, reading was no common accomplishment amongst servants, and this is true even in genteel and literary households.

The discovery of how great a proportion of the population could read and write at any point in time is one of the most urgent of the tasks which faces the historian of social structure, who is committed to the use of numerical methods. But the challenge is not simply to find the evidence and to devise ways of making it yield reliable answers. It is a challenge to the historical and literary imagination. What we have to recall, to reconstruct, to make a present reality to ourselves is a time when most men and women could only think, and talk, and sing and play, and till the soil, and tend the beasts and make things, like barrels and ploughs and windmills, whilst only some men could also read and write, and record, and refer again, and criticize, and tell others what was the truth of the matter and what should be done about it. Until recently history had indeed been literally history, the record of men who have been able to leave written records behind them. What has now to be done is to recognize what it means to observe only the literate activity of a society most of whose life was oral, above all to try to get the feel of how the attitude of the illiterate mass affected the literate few, and so was allowed for, taken into account, in the social process as a whole and particularly the process of politics.

After Hardwicke's Marriage Act of 1753 each bride and bridegroom was required to sign or make a distinctive mark in the marriage register, just as they had done in France for 150 years. In 17 Yorkshire parishes, not quite typical of the county perhaps, two-thirds of the bridegrooms wrote their names in the appointed places, in the 1750's. This was true of less than half of the brides. A hundred years later bridegrooms unable to sign had fallen to a quarter.[192] This fragment of evidence reveals a level of literacy of the same order as that from France, where something over a half of men and something over a quarter of women signed the register at the village of Crulai in the 1750's, though the proportions had risen to 80 per cent and 64 per cent by 1790. In France generally this accomplishment grew steadily in the eighteenth century: in the 1680's a fifth of brides and bridegrooms were able to sign the register and in the 1780's over a third.[193] But there was great variation from area to area and work in progress on the English evidence confirms this for our country. A number of sources going back to the sixteenth century are being analysed in addition to the marriage registers starting in 1753.

About a quarter of those applying for marriage licences in the 1660's in Gloucestershire, all men, were forced to sign their applications with a cross. But those married by licence were, as we have seen, more likely to be educated than the population as a whole. In a part of the county of Surrey in 1642, no less than two-thirds of the males over eighteen found it necessary to make marks rather than sign a protestation of loyalty to the embattled Parliament against the King.[194] All this evidence, English and French, presents considerable difficulty to the interpreter, because we do not yet know what the mere ability to sign, often very shakily and sometimes probably by tracing or copying, really meant at these times. It seems likely on the whole that more people could read, if only with difficulty, than could sign their names. In the schools children began by being taught to read, and were not ordinarily allowed to use the pen until their reading ability had been established. It is even possible that some men who

[192] *See page* 309.   [193] *See page* 310.
[194] *See page* 310.

could write their names actually chose on occasion to make a mark instead.

This may explain why the only documents to which Shakespeare's father put his name were marked by him with a cross as his sign. But Isaac Newton's father marked with a cross as well, and by the time he came to beget his illustrious, though posthumous, son in 1642 it is almost inconceivable that he would not have written out his name if he was able to do it. It is worth reflecting on the possibility that the two greatest English intellectuals who ever lived in the world we have lost were nurtured in households whose master in both cases may well have been illiterate. It illustrates vividly enough that social mobility by educational means could take place very rapidly, within one generation, and, as in those two very conspicuous cases, in one lifetime. It would seem that a man born into a bookless household could die as the writer of momentous books.

The more general effects of the disability of illiteracy must be emphasized, as well as the intellectual ones. Literacy is of crucial importance to political activity, indeed to political consciousness, in a society, where, as we have already stressed, politics and administration were largely carried forward in writing. In order to take part in political discussion, habitual reading must have been necessary, as well as daily familiarity with the task of recording by writing. A life of this sort may be supposed to imply the ownership of books, and this was very much less common than even the lowest figure for the proportion of signatories might imply. Unfortunately no reliable indicator of book ownership in former times has yet been found, which can be set alongside the analysis of signatures in marriage registers or in ecclesiastical courts. The one file of data which might be thought to yield this evidence, that is the inventories of persons' goods left at death, seems at the moment unlikely to provide evidence of much importance. Far fewer books are mentioned than can be easily reconciled with what is known of book buying and book handling, though in Leicestershire in the 1620's–40's, 17 per cent of all willmakers left books, and 50 per cent of the gentry. That even modest craftsmen could and did own serious and difficult works has recently been demonstrated in the area of Glasgow in Scotland in the 1750's, where farmers, shoemakers, and even coalhewers, but especially textile workers and above all weavers, are now known to have paid good money in order to buy, and presumably to read serious works of theology.[195]

No woman could sign the marriage register at Crulai in the 1680's, and very few in the early eighteenth century, but the proportion rapidly rose to over a half after 1740: it is known that a school for girls had been opened in the village. Where there were schools undertaking the instruction of a good proportion of the community, male and female, then perhaps we can assume that the monopoly of literate communication held by the ruling minority was broken down to some extent, especially in the eighteenth century. But it would be more than usually misguided to make general statements about effects of this kind before the numerical exercises, only now beginning, have been taken a great deal further. Contemporary statements and the rapid growth of schools in Tudor and early Stuart times have recently been used to make out the case for yet another revolutionary process in England over these years, an educational revolution between 1550 and 1640 which made English society into the best instructed of all societies up to that time, where in certain favoured areas up to a half of the whole population were properly literate. The whole movement has been linked with changes in higher education over the same period of time. These statements seem exaggerated to me in the present state of our knowledge.[196]

There can be no doubt of the development in higher education, the education of the gentry, the clergy and the others, however uncertain the claim about a general rise in literacy may turn out to be. We have already referred to the growth of an intellectual interest in political matters amongst the gentry of England at this time, and the story of the universities over the relevant period is now well known. Interesting evidence is beginning to come to light which links educational change of this kind with social mobility downward from the highest levels. It would seem that in the largely illiterate society of England in early Stuart times there may have been for a generation or so too many highly educated people, and in particular too many university trained clergymen for the number of livings available to support them adequately. This paradox has its parallel in Africa and India in the 1970's, where there is also a surplus of highly educated people in societies although the general educational level is extremely

[195] *See page* 310.   [196] *See page* 310.

low. 'Alienated intellectuals' is the phrase which has been
applied to the unwanted graduate priests of Charles I's reign
but in assessing their possible significance we must once again
bear in mind the fact that such a surplus is exactly what
might be expected to appear from time to time. There is no
necessary connection between the presence of professional
men without a proper livelihood and a general raising of
educational standards, except in so far as they took to teaching the poor their letters as a means of keeping alive. In order
to make a perceptible impression on social and political life,
furthermore, they would have had to have brought about in
large numbers of communities a substantial increase in the
numbers of reading, writing, book-owning households.

If such a hypothetical argument as this is to be pursued, it
might be said that in the eighteenth, though not in the seventeenth century, there may turn out to have been just such a
development. The freeholders of the county of Middlesex,
already to some extent a suburban county, who repeatedly
defied their traditional political rulers and managers in the
1760's to elect the incredible John Wilkes as their member of
Parliament, were beginning to dissolve the immemorial pattern. Wilkite radicalism may therefore rightly be heralded as
a sign of an altered relationship between the common man
and his gentleman superior, in which quiescent political ignorance had begun to give way to demands for a share in the
national political life. If we go back to the technical language,
it could perhaps be rightly said of them that they showed
signs of relative deprivation of political power, taking as their
reference group the members of the ruling minority rather
than their own companions. If this is what took place, it seems
extremely likely that they were better informed than their
ancestors, less completely lost in a world where inability to
share in literate life cut most men off from even contemplating a share in political power.

But Middlesex in the 1760's does not belong in the world
we have lost as we have used that phrase in this essay. It may
be appropriate to bring to an end this hurried survey of that
world with the words scrawled on a piece of paper by a Lud-
dite and sent to a clothier in Gloucestershire in 1803:[197]

Wee Hear in Formed that you got Shear in mee sheens [shearing

[197] *See page* 311.

P

machines] *and if you Dont Pull them Down in a Forght Nights Time Wee will pull them Down for you Wee will you Damd infernold dog.*

Here is a barely literate man, the lilt of his ordinary speech showing through his pathetic attempt to make himself understood in writing, struggling and just succeeding in expressing his passionate resentment. We can look on it as a sign of the terror which the coming of the factories and the machines struck into the hearts of ordinary people, those village craftsmen who have occupied us so much. We can also look upon it as a token of what it meant to live an entirely oral life in a world dominated by reading and writing. Surely this is the most compelling of all the contrasts between our world and the world we have lost.

After the Transformation
Chapter 9

English society in the early twentieth century

i The Working Class since 1901

Rattle his bones, over the stones
He's only a pauper whom nobody owns

When Queen Victoria died at the very outset of the twentieth century one person in five could expect to come to this, a solitary burial from the workhouse, the poor-law hospital, the lunatic asylum. On the whole the second year of our century, 1901, was a prosperous time for the English, one of the twenty good years not marked by Depression or by war to the death which they were to have in the fifty which followed. There was a war going on, it is true, the South African War, which, if men had but known it, was the beginning of the end of the English as a people of commanding world-wide power, but its social effects at the time did not go very deep. The huge coalfields of Yorkshire and Lancashire, the great shipbuilding towns, the acres and acres of factory floor given over to textiles, were made busier by the demand for armaments and uniforms and machinery. Nevertheless something like a quarter of the whole population was in poverty.

Poverty, we must notice, was no vague condition then, nothing like as uncertain as the state of 'decreasing the wealth of the kingdom' has to be for the historian looking back to England in 1688 through the eyes of Gregory King. Families were in poverty 'whose total earnings are insufficient to obtain the minimum necessaries for the maintenance of merely physical efficiency'.

Those precise syllables come from Seebohm Rowntree's book called *Poverty* which appeared in 1901 and which published the sombre results of a house-to-house survey carried out with monumental thoroughness in his native city of York, a railway centre, where the family firm of Rowntree manufactured chocolates as it has ever since. Confectionery is perhaps as representative a light industry of the twentieth

century type, as railways were of the heavy industry of the
nineteenth century, which had given England and especially
the north of England her world-wide manufacturing supremacy. Young Mr Rowntree had done his work in order to find
out whether a reasonably typical provincial city was like
London. He had discovered that 27·84 per cent of the citizens
of York were living in poverty according to his definition. In
London 30·7 per cent of the people were in poverty as his
predecessor and mentor, Charles Booth, had already shown,
London which was the richest city in the world and a fifth
of the whole kingdom.

Englishmen in 1901 had to face the disconcerting fact that
destitution was still an outstanding feature of fully industrial
society, a working class perpetually liable to social and
material degradation. More than half of all the children of
working men were in this dreadful condition, which meant
40 per cent of all the children in the country.

These were the scrawny, dirty, hungry, ragged, verminous
boys and girls who were to grow up into the working class of
twentieth-century England. This was the generation which
was to man the armies of the First World War, although they
were inches shorter and pounds lighter than they would have
been if they had been properly fed and cared for. Those who
were left of them became the fathers and mothers of the working people who endured the Depression of the 1920's and the
Great Depression of the 1930's, and who saw at last the squalid
streets in which they made their homes luridly lighted up by
Hitler's bombs. They were also the men and women who
nurtured the Labour Party, the working-man's party, and
brought it to maturity in the 1920's, and to overwhelming
victory in 1945, stable political power for a few years after
1964. They are still, it could be claimed, the most easily
neglected element in English political and historical consciousness even today.

We might take a very well-known example to demonstrate
this fact, though the tenacious memory of labour politicians
and labour voters for the terrible days of not so long ago
might seem to prove it straightaway. Young Beatrice Potter
was an assistant in Booth's survey, as gifted and extraordinary a member of the governing minority as ever took to
'Social Reform' as the Edwardians called it. But she did not
stop after a year or two with the Charity Organization

Society, and marry one of her own set, compounding for a series of subscriptions to worthy causes as so many of her fellows seem to have done. She became the wife of Mr Sidney Webb, of the London County Council and the Fabian Society, and the two of them founded the London School of Economics as well as the *New Statesman*. As Lord Passfield and Mrs Webb – for the aristocratic Beatrice would have nothing to do with Sidney's silly title – they visited Russia in the early 1930's. Hence the title of their final book, the last of a long series, *Soviet Communism, a New Civilization*. Irreducible poverty, that of London in the 1890's and of all the English unemployed forty years later, had helped to turn them from liberal socialism and a successful movement of gradual reform, into prophets of communism.

In this final mood, and perhaps only then, they ceased to be typical of the attitude taken up by their countrymen to what was ordinarily known in their youth as the 'condition of England question', one question amongst the many others that eminent English political leaders had to deal with. The exact percentages in Booth's and Rowntree's figures make uneasy reading in our generation, when statistics are so much more cautiously handled that two places of decimals almost never appear in sociological percentages. An attempt at a scientific, a physiological definition of poverty, one graduated in terms of the biological needs of an ordinary man in performing his day's physical work, would never be attempted today. It will, therefore, perhaps be doubted whether the shift from 1688 to 1901, from counts of parishioners and Gregory King, to house-to-house surveys, Mr Booth and Mr Rowntree, makes much difference as to reliability. Can we really be so certain that the problem of poverty was still so urgent after a century and more of miraculous economic growth and change? Our traditional picture of England in 1901, the first year of the golden Edwardian age, is altogether lighter than this.

What about the countryside, and the country towns? What about the really prosperous manufacturing areas, which were to make the England of Edward the Seventh more expansive economically than it ever was to be again until George VI was on the throne and Mr Attlee became his Prime Minister? The actual condition of the population as a whole of course will never be known, though in the succeeding two generations many cities were submitted to the treatment given to London and York, using an ever-more realistic criterion of prosperity and poverty. But Rowntree had thought of agricultural England.

Some years were to pass before his analysis of agriculture was to be completed, but in his book on York he pointed out that in 1899 over three-quarters of the population of England lived in 'urban areas'. The time in fact had already almost arrived which we talked of when discussing the village community of the traditional world, when the balance between town and country would be completely reversed, and the typical Englishman would be brought up amongst bricks and mortar, and only the exceptional amongst trees and fields. Moreover Rowntree was probably right to assume that those who had remained in the country after three or four generations of steady emigration from it lived rather below the standards endured by their grandchildren, great-nephews and cousins in the city streets.

In 1903 the little village of Ridgmont in Bedfordshire, over the wall from the great park at Woburn, the seat of the Duke of Bedford, was investigated according to the principles of Booth and Rowntree. The Dukes of Bedford were doing very well in that year, with income tax at elevenpence in the pound and death duties at a maximum of 11 per cent. Like most noble families they had urban as well as rural property, industrial and commercial wealth as well as landed. In fact the Fabian Society alleged that the Bedford Estate was receiving £15,000 a year from Covent Garden at the time that Professor Higgins met Eliza Doolittle outside the Royal Opera House. Still the estate was managed in an exemplary way and Ridgmont was being rebuilt cottage by cottage; the tall red-brick roofs of that time of shapely, if cumbersome, domestic architecture are still to be seen in the village. Yet the investigator found that 41 per cent of the population living there were in poverty, the sort of poverty which left biological need unsatisfied.

We cannot linger long in Ridgmont, though the facts about countryside and town, about inequality in income and about the persistence of the country house as the political instrument of a very different society are all very important to our subject. In October, 1900, the Marquess of Salisbury submitted the name of the Duke of Bedford to Queen Victoria when he was reconstructing the Cabinet, and his Grace declined because of his interest in estate-management: Woburn remained a centre of political power nevertheless. Perhaps the annual income of this great noble family was some £100,000 and it must have ranked with the largest in the country, even with the huge industrial and commercial fortunes, though an English duke might already find it advantageous to marry an American heiress, as the Duke of Marlborough had done in 1895. Here is a splendid contrast with the income of about £50 which was earned by a farm labourer in Ridgmont. In Gregory King's time the average nobleman had £3,000 a year and a labourer £15, and this reveals a very similar disproportion, if a duke in King's generation can be assumed to have had twice the average noble income.

But though agricultural labour was still the biggest occupation in England in the early 1900's, it cannot have been any longer true that the country could be divided, as King divided it into two almost equal parts, with the smaller consisting of families receiving on average no less than six times the income of the families in the larger part. If we refer again to his table printed on pages 36 and 37, we can see that families in the richer section had incomes ranging between £38 and £3,200 a year, with an average of £68 18*s*., and the poorer section a range of £6 10*s*. to £20, with an average of £10 10*s*. We cannot tell how the £6 10*s*. a year which King reckoned to be the resources per family of that quarter of the people in his day whom he called cottagers and paupers compared with Rowntree's £100 a year, or rather less, which he reckoned as what a family needed to be above the poverty line in 1899. Still it is clear that the traditional, agricultural society as it had survived in Ridgmont was not more prosperous than the commercial and manufacturing society of the city of York. Nothing went on in this part of Bedfordshire except the tilling of the soil and the keeping of beasts; rural industry was already almost entirely dead. A few cottagers still plaited straw, but lacemaking had disappeared completely. The making of hats had gone off to the factories of Bedford and Luton. Not so much as a loaf of bread was baked in the village; it all came in horse vans from the towns. And every single village child was living in poverty.

To the historian of an earlier England it is a gross and telling contrast that Ridgmont should have belonged in 1901 to a residual area of rural society within an expanding industrial whole, an agricultural remnant which was already not much more than a fifth and still getting smaller. This made English society different in order from anything which had ever gone before, in Europe or in the whole world. It means that the process of social and economic transformation which we call *industrial revolution* was already virtually complete in our country. This distinguishes the society of England as it now is, very sharply from other societies. English social experience since the death of Victoria is the only lengthy experience any country has ever had of really mature industrialization.

It has been in fact experience not of a state of things exactly, but of a perpetual tendency towards continuous change. For industrialization is not a once-for-all process and it is an English error to suppose that it is. Since 1901 our country has tended to fall progressively behind others in the race to re-industrialize with every new technique, but our history since 1901 has been a history of successive transformation all the same. The question of importance for the contrast we are trying to draw in this essay is the question of welfare. In so far as the industrializing process is to be described above all as a change in the scale of living, such as we dwelt on in our first chapter, only in England does it seem to have been virtually complete by 1901. What has happened since then has been a matter of the levelling up of standards, the lengthening of life, the diminution of poverty, the universalization of education. This may not have been the result of what became so suddenly and shockingly apparent after Booth and Rowntree had done their work. But since that time, intentionally or not, the spread of the benefits has gone on both by political compulsion and perhaps also of itself.

This may seem an easy and too comforting generalization, since the contemporary world is even now discovering that in rich societies great hidden areas of poverty go on persisting. The conclusion that we shall reach about the Welfare State which arose in England out of the attitude which Rowntree represents, will not be that it was completely successful in abolishing want in an industrial society, rather perhaps that it was just the last and most effective way of convincing the conscientious that it had been abolished. But when all this has been said there is a difference between the revelations which have shocked the 1960's about the condition of the old in Britain and of the coloured in the United States. It is difficult for us now to realize what it meant in 1901 for England to have to recognize that after a century of leading the world in economic matters, when she was still undoubtedly the world's greatest political and military power, still in many ways the world's wealthiest power, a quarter of her population was living in poverty, in something like destitution.

If King's figures are comparable with Rowntree's, and if both are somewhere near the truth, then the growth of wealth brought by industry did succeed in reducing dependency and destitution by more than half in two hundred years, from the 1690's to the 1900's. If this was so, then it accomplished a great deal, especially when we remember how little sign has ever been found that progress of this sort was ever possible in the world we have lost, where the text 'the poor ye shall always have with you' was a truth not worth the disputing. But the difference in standard between these two observers, the Stuart pursuivant-at-arms and the Edwardian industrialist with a conscience, is so enormous that this most challenging and difficult of questions must be left on one side for the present as unanswerable.

Unfortunately the same objection, that of a difference in standard, can be urged against the known facts about the subsequent history of poverty in the England of the twentieth century. The truly remarkable thing about Seebohm Rowntree was that he lived long enough to satisfy himself by personal investigation that poverty of the hopeless sort had virtually disappeared. In 1936, thirty-seven years after his first survey of York, he examined the city again. This time he used a much more sophisticated method of survey, impelled as he was by the disaster of unemployment which made him expect rather less of a reduction of poverty by 1936 than he had hoped for. Things were even worse than he feared, for on his new and more realistic standard 31 per cent of the working class of York were still in poverty in the late 1930's, as against 43 per cent in 1899, on the cruder standard he was then using.

But there were other differences between the two years. The greatest individual cause of poverty in 1899 had been insufficient wages, and no more telling indictment of industrialism could be imagined: but by far and away the greatest cause of poverty in York in 1936 was unemployment. When he was eighty years old in 1961, Rowntree was able to publish his last, and, it must be said, his least satisfactory, survey of poverty in the city. Using a new and still more sophisticated poverty line, he found that only 3 per cent of the population were in destitution, and that the great cause of poverty was old age. From being a predominant feature of our social life, poverty, so Rowntree tended to think at the very last, had been reduced to insignificance.

We must notice that the abolition of poverty, if abolition it was, came about not gradually over the years, but suddenly, between the late 1930's and the late 1940's, as part of the foundation and functioning of the Welfare State. Within half a generation of that time, in spite of the warnings of Rowntree's successors as investigators of poverty in our country, we have now begun to think of the problem of industrial society as a problem of affluence, of having too much leisure and too many goods.

This attitude may not survive for long. There are signs that the remainder of the twentieth century may also interpret its social mission as the equalization of wealth between every citizen, whatever his colour and his history. This time the redistribution will have to go on not only within so-called 'rich' societies, but between 'rich' and 'poor' areas of the globe as a whole. But gross and familiar contrasts between our country as it was in 1901 and as it is now are quite immediate nevertheless. If any such superficial attempt as this one to describe the twentieth-century English working class is to be successful it must rely for the most part on the reader to make the comparisons from his own experience. Here is some of the obvious material.

In 1901 people in the upper class could expect to live for nearly sixty years, but those at the very lowest level for only thirty: paupers were still, in fact, as short-lived as the whole population in Stuart times. In 1901 you could tell at sight whether a man belonged to the upper or the working classes – bearing, dress and speech, size, attitude and manner were noticeably different. Some are still alive who remember seeing the Victorian farm labourer in his smock. School teachers then had an average of seventy children in every class. Only two-fifths of the population had the vote, and no women at all. Shop assistants worked an average of eighty hours in every seven days, and many of them lived in dormitories above their work, compulsorily unmarried. Since those who had no separate room were excluded from the franchise, a shop assistant living in voted only if the partitions between the beds in the dormitory reached the ceiling. So conscious indeed was this earlier England of social class that the bath-houses of London displayed the following notice:

Baths for working people, 2d. hot and 1d. cold.
Baths for any higher classes, 3d. cold and 6d. hot.

Of course such a crude method as this cannot convey anything like an accurate idea of what we are trying to show and the choice of poverty as a starting point for our survey has grave disadvantages. It distorts our picture of the working people because it leaves out prosperous workers. A wrong twist may have been given to the evidence a little while ago. It was not those who were sunk in hopeless misery who founded and ran the trade unions, who organized the Labour Party. The submerged tenth, as they were sometimes and too hopefully called, were not pre-eminently the people who created and transmitted the traditional culture of the working men which interests our own generation.

We must never forget that well over half of the workers were above the poverty line at any one time, though we are at the great disadvantage of knowing very little from first hand evidence of how they lived. Poverty was on the consciences of our fathers and grandfathers and it was poverty which they described for us. The working-class family, said Rowntree, pursing up his lips, spent 6s. a week on beer, a whole sixth of their income – hence a very great deal of secondary poverty, which the people could have avoided, and which less sympathetic people blamed them for. Now for 6s. you could get 36 pints of beer in 1901, and a working family in the clear can get a great deal of fun out of 36 pints of beer, even if it did sometimes finally lead to the workhouse.

Nevertheless, as has been said, the most important cause of poverty at the turn of the century was low wages. 'The wages paid for unskilled labour in York,' Rowntree concluded, 'are insufficient to provide food, clothing and shelter adequate to maintain a family of moderate size in a state of bare physical efficiency.' Here, then, was the proletariat of Marxian theory and the Marxian law of increasing misery under capitalism seemingly demonstrated for all to see, in the only mature industrial society then known.

The great puzzle about the English working-class may

therefore seem to be why it was that the active, intelligent and well-paid amongst them did not all draw the correct Marxian inference, why it is that there has been no violent social revolution in England in the twentieth century. It cannot be said that geographical and personal propinquity has been lacking in anything like the way that it was lacking amongst their ancestors in the Stuart countryside. Working-classness has existed since well before 1901. It should become clear as we go on that the issue of revolutionary action was never quite as simple as this might make it seem, and that critical social change has in fact occurred without it. But though revolution in this latter sense is the subject of the last section of this chapter, the problem of the acquiescent attitude of English workers in the twentieth century goes beyond the limits of this essay. Let us turn our attention to the cyclical character of poverty in recent times, not so much the alternation of periods of prosperity and depression as the succession of events in the lifetime of an individual working man. This is one of the interesting points of resemblance between his situation and that of his predecessors in traditional society.

'*A labourer,*' Rowntree tells us, '*is in poverty and therefore underfed:*
In childhood, when his constitution is being built up.
In his early and his middle life, when he should be in his prime.
In old age.
And
The women are in poverty for the greater part of the time when they are bearing children.'

This is how the life cycle of working people went. Very few manual labourers in York in 1899 could have been without neighbours, friends, relatives struggling for subsistence. Infantile mortality was 94 in a thousand in the middle class, but no less than 247 amongst those in poverty. Again the resemblance with Clayworth in the 1670's comes to mind. One baby in every six died in the working class generally – the small coffin on one of the family beds, or on the table, or under the table when the family had a meal. This was a sight every working man must have seen and every working woman grieved for.

The discovery of the cyclic descent into the area of poverty

was the most interesting sociological discovery which Seebohm Rowntree ever made, and has too often been forgotten.
It meant that everyone in the working class had at some time
in his life had personal experience of people living below the
poverty level even if he himself had never been so unfortunate.
It meant in fact that the fear of poverty, the insecurity which
that fear brought with it and the resentment against the
system, all these things went deep down into the character of
the English working man. It is not entirely fanciful to think
of them as an inheritance from the traditional world of
peasant, craftsman and pauper.

Those amongst us who now talk of the bourgeoisification –
the horrid word they use – of the working class should take due
note of this. Those who look for a centre for the sense of community in the working class should note it as well, the sense of
community which is forever being stressed as the heart and
soul of the Labour movement. The positive urge to remake the
world in a way which would abolish poverty has its spring in a
negative attitude, the fear which dominated the lives of
grandfathers, fathers, uncles, aunts and cousins. To call the
prosperous working family of the later twentieth century
simply bourgeois or middle class is a superficial historical misconception. It is rather the working family of the 1900's, of the
1920's or the 1930's with something of the horror of poverty
removed. 'Workingclassness' in the social development of
England in the twentieth century has, therefore, an obvious
justification in attitude, in instinctive response, though of
course it has many other defining characteristics. It has an
immemorial history too.

So much for the English working class since 1901. For all
the over-simplification which is inevitable when complicated
description has to be done by allusion, it must be obvious that
no such phenomenon could ever have existed in the world
before the coming of industry. The probable resemblances and
direct descents are fascinating to contemplate nevertheless.

ii   The Solid Middle Class

The solid middle class is a very familiar expression. It is
surrounded by a cluster of clichés which reappear when the
English think of themselves as a society, and look back on
their history, particularly their recent history – the backbone

of the nation, the salt of the earth. The idea of a middle class
which was the anchor of a community's stability is not a recent
one. Aristotle first suggested the notion and it has been applied
to almost every political system and situation known to the
historian. We have seen how commonly the expression has
been used of England before 1700. But Victorian and Edwardian England is usually looked upon as the outstanding
example of apotheosis of the middle class as a community and
a culture. The decline of that solid middle class has sometimes
been made into an account of the social development which
has gone on in England since the twentieth century began.
Meanwhile the working class has also been supposed to have
begun to become like the solid middle class, to be taking on its
attitudes and values.

But when the evidence is closely scanned it turns out to be
somewhat misleading to think of a solid middle-class community as existing in England in 1901, and even more so to
suppose that social development since that time has been the
story of its decline. The word *community* is the important word
here. There most certainly was a lump of persons in English
society in the age of Arnold Bennett and Thomas Hardy and
George Meredith, to which they applied the phrase 'the solid
middle class'. The question is whether it can ever have been
so nation-wide a community.

The very fact that the phrase has been in perpetual use
gives the solid middle class an independent existence of sorts.
The people we shall be examining were, at least as individuals,
solid in the substantial sense of the word. They were substantial because they were rich and had big establishments, and
because they bulked very large in all the affairs of the nation.
What we shall find is that the notion of a community at one
level, more or less homogeneous in its consistency and composed of fairly equal units, is a very questionable one. The
twentieth-century working class which has just been discussed
has these two characteristics, although it is much less usually
referred to as solid. But the facts about the middle class are
rather different. Fortunately these facts are no longer guesswork and riskily made inference as they had to be when we
were talking of the seventeenth century. By and large the
evidence is reasonably well known.

Arnold Bennett recognized something of the truth in the
suggestive and inexact way which is typical of the literary

artist and which we have had to become so wary of. In February, 1909, this highly representative author wrote one of his many essays speculating about who bought and read his books:

'When my morbid curiosity is upon me,' Bennett says, 'I stroll into Mudies or the Times Book Club, or I hover round Smith's bookstall in the Strand. The crowd at these places is the prosperous crowd, the crowd which pays income tax and grumbles at it.' In February, 1909, we may notice, income tax stood at five per cent of earnings. 'Three hundred and seventy-five thousand persons paid income tax last year,' he continues, 'paid it under protest. They stand for perhaps a million souls, and this million is a handful floating more or less easily on the surface of the forty millions of the population.'

We ought perhaps to underline Bennett's words about income-tax payers being only a handful of the population: 'floating on the surface' is very significant too. His description continues thus:

Their assured, curt voices, their carriage, their clothes, the similarity of their manners, all show that they belong to a caste, and that the caste has been successful in the struggle for life. It has been called the middle class, but it ought to be called the upper class, for nearly everything is below it. I go to the stores, to Harrods, to Rumpelmeyer's, to the Royal Academy, and to a dozen clubs in Albemarle Street and Dover Street, and I see again just the same crowd, well-fed, well-dressed, completely free from the cares which beset at least five-sixths of the English race. I do not belong to this class by birth. I was born slightly beneath it. But by the help of God and strict attention to business I have gained the right of entrance to it.

In one nostalgic Edwardian image after another Bennett goes on to list the notorious characteristics of the solid middle class. He talks of its sincere, religious worship of money and success – the world, he says, is a steamer in which the middle class is travelling saloon. He talks of its barbarism, the barbarism which toasts the architect *and the contractor*, and might as well toast the poet *and the printer*. He talks of the dullness, the humourlessness, the unresponsiveness of that 'great, solid, comfortable class which forms the backbone of the novel-reading public'. How appropriate Rumpelmeyer's is, that Mayfair shop which catered only for the carriage trade, and which has not survived to share in our day the fate of the other exclusive Edwardian emporia.

Here, then, is the solid middle class of Edwardian times as a contemporary saw it. Here too we may notice a distant reminder of the shadow of poverty which we have just considered, that other community within the nation which had not been so successful in the struggle for food, housing, clothes and freedom from perpetual insecurity. Bennett's openness in telling his readers that he had not been born into the solid middle class is interesting, but should not be counted as all that revealing; although a solicitor by his best description, his father had kept a pawnbroker's shop at one time, at Hanley in the Potteries. His other uncertainties and inconsistencies are interesting too, for rather a different reason.

He talks sometimes of the *upper* class, as if that were the better term, of a *caste* rather than a *class*. Yet he is prepared to believe that a million people belonged to it, as if the crowd of faces which he saw so often at Rumpelmeyer's or the Clubs could possibly belong to as many as a million people. He was wrong about the figures, as will appear in a moment, but his instinct in thinking of the income tax in order to calculate the size of his potential readership was apt enough. If Bennett had been taken more seriously, if his hint about consulting the income tax returns had been acted upon and the figures they contained had been prominently displayed, then perhaps the numerical fallacy, as it might be called, about the solid middle class would never have come into currency. The other part of this particular illusion, that of a community on one level, might have been avoided too.

By the numerical fallacy about the solid middle class of Bennett's time is meant the uncritical supposition that the middle class can then have contained a sizeable section of the English population, an eighth, shall we say, perhaps even a fifth or a quarter, or a third of the whole population. It did not. It consisted at most of about a seventeenth. If we rely on the income tax figures by themselves it was even smaller. Only one person in twenty-five was rich enough in England, in 1909, when Arnold Bennett wrote his essay, to enjoy the famous middle-class standard of living. The resemblance to the figures we have quoted for the privileged minority in the pre-industrial world may simply be a coincidence, but a very interesting coincidence it is.

Income is not the only way to measure such things as *class-membership*, and these few numerical facts do not prove that only this tiny minority regarded themselves as belonging to the middle classes. Quite the reverse. The truth seems to be that for the whole of this century some millions of people have been aspiring to live as only a few hundred thousand of people could in fact afford to live. The secret of the historian's stereotype about the solid middle class is imitation, what might be called in Arnold Toynbee's expression *mimesis*. Only if imitation, mimesis, is taken to constitute 'solidity' can the phrase the solid middle class be made to apply to any substantial part of the population, not only in Arnold Bennett's day but for most of the time since.

Decline of the middle class, which is how the historian has tended to look on social history since that time, could unfortunately mean many things. It is as elusive a phrase as the rise of the gentry. But if its possible qualitative meaning is disregarded and its numerical meaning only is retained, then it is completely untrue of England in the earlier twentieth century. There has been a completely uninterrupted growth in the numbers of those who could be called middle class in the economic sense since the year 1901. This growth was slowed down but not interrupted by successive depressions, and it has never been more rapid than it has been since 1945.

The numerical fallacy about the solid middle class, then, is very easy to see and to dispose of. More difficult is the fact that historians have allowed it to persist, as have some of the social scientists in spite of their repudiations. To see why the facts have been difficult to appreciate, we must glance at the figures of middle-class occupations as well as of middle-class persons.

It is difficult to decide how much money was needed to maintain the suburban villa which we associate with the solid middle class of Bennett's time, to pay the servants, to educate the children – five or six of them – to run the carriage, and to pay for Bennett's books. Seven hundred or a thousand golden sovereigns a year, shall we say, together with the expectation that the value of money would never go down. Though the precise numbers of tax-payers is not known for that period, it is known that there were about 280,000 households in England and Wales in 1909 with £700 a year or more. That is to say there were less than 300,000 families out of a total of 7,000,000

which reached the level necessary for comfortable middle-
class living. Not that there was a plateau at this level, or at any
level in British incomes over the century. Indeed, the variation above our chosen point was enormous, with gaps yawning
far more widely than the gap between those who had enough
to live adequately in the middle class and those who did not.

There were in Edwardian times 120,000 'capitalists' who
were reckoned to own two-thirds of the wealth and they
obviously constituted a large proportion of those with seven
hundred or a thousand a year and above. There were something like forty thousand landowners who owned twenty-
seven out of the thirty-four million acres in the country. Some
of these of course were aristocrats and perhaps a case might be
made out to show that there was a useful sense in which these
people were upper class, not middle class. We have already
seen that the very rich and powerful played a distinctive role
especially in politics even after the transformation. In this
arena, in the relationship between the country house and the
suburban dwelling, there was a cleavage between the bourgeoisie and the landed families.

But Bennett's typical hesitation between upper and middle
class shows how difficult the distinction was even in his day.
In fact in the twentieth century the upper class has been a
nullity, just as the second class was for so long on our railways.
The only sensible course for the historian is to put the people
at the very top in with the rest of the successful, and face the
fact that this makes the whole an extremely various group of
persons. We can now recognize the second misconception in
the historian's stereotype of the solid middle class, that of
homogeneity, in income, and in occupation. However vivid
the impression which these privileged people give in the
sameness of their attitudes and tastes, nevertheless their surroundings, their experience, their wealth, and its sources were
all very various indeed – these lawyers, clerics, imperial
officials, businessmen, doctors, professors and plain receivers
of dividends and rents.

The confusion over class distinctions and their relation to
political and other forms of power has led in the last decade to
the appearance in English of a new word, beginning its career
as such words often do as a piece of slang, a smart expression
for journalists and satirists. This word is the 'Establishment'.
Vague as its meaning is, if it yet has a settled meaning at all,

this term seems to express what Bennett was trying to say rather better than anything else we have to hand. What he had in mind turns out to be very much more like an Establishment than it is like that class community which we found amongst the workers and the poor. Instead of a solid middle class, with an upper class above it, we should rather think of a minority of some 300,000 families which several million families were busy imitating, and imitating rather unsuccessfully because they had not enough money to do it well. The figure of 300,000 belongs to the 1900's; it is a much bigger number of families now and it is growing rapidly. It is still a small minority, to some extent an isolated minority, but nevertheless the goal of social aspiration.

The resemblances between this situation and that we have tried to describe for the traditional world are coming into view, together again with the very important differences. Mimesis, social imitation, did not first appear in England in late Victorian times. The perennial complaint against citizens and citizens' wives from the middle ages onwards was that they imitated their betters, the aristocracy. This was resented for more reasons than one, although the most important was no doubt ordinary snobbery and the contempt of those who could afford to live well for those who could only pretend to. There was also the knowledge that some at least of the imitators could in fact afford more than those whom they imitated, and would be in their places before long. In a society where downward mobility was, as we have seen, probably greater than upward, and where status was regarded as a fixture, part of an unchanging universe, this led to legislation as well as to satire. In high industrial times such an attitude has become impossible and movement in every direction is undoubtedly much easier. The perpetual growth of the privileged section of society has become a possibility, even a reality, both because the whole population has been growing and because ever expanding wealth has made for an increase in the proportion of the rich to the whole.

There is a feature which the two systems manifestly shared, the presence of a large marginal area between upper and lower, a penumbra, as we have called it, to the privileged minority. This interesting region could only be very roughly sketched in the case of pre-industrial society, but by Arnold Bennett's time its outlines have become fairly clear. In 1909 income tax began at £3 a week, and the figures show that there were 800,000 incomes between this, the lowest level, and the level where we believe true 'solid middle class' living was possible, that is at £700 per year. This was the area of the imitators, the people in between the working-class community below them and the privileged above them. To make it manifestly clear who these people were, let it be repeated that they were placed below those who could objectively afford a 'middle-class' standard of living, and above those who were by universal agreement working class, manual workers, men and women living under the threat of poverty.

These in-between families with £150–£700 a year were the chief of the aspirers, the Mr Pooters of the Edwardian world. They were the people whom Arnold Bennett missed out when he walked round London looking for his readers, and from whom he himself had his own origin. There can be little doubt that *Clayhanger* might well have been found on the mantelpiece of Mr Pooter's sitting-room, if it had been written in 1895, rather than in 1909. It would have found a place along with the rest of the bric-à-brac, not quite as appropriate as the two stone lions which, as Mr Pooter tells us, graced the flight of steps leading up to his front door, but a likely book for his rebellious son Lupin to be reading. George and Weedon Grossmith who contributed their pieces on Mr Pooter to Punch in the 1890's were as shrewd in their observation of English life as Bennett, Wells or even Shaw.

There were nearly three times as many people of this type as there were with an adequate middle-class income. Some of them could justly be called more than aspirers, for even with four, three, or two hundred a year a man could do very well in 1909, especially if he belonged to a respected occupation like that of the clergy. He could often afford a servant, and sometimes had expectations of succeeding Mama and Papa in their genuine establishment. Or he might resolve to make his own way up to solidity; opportunities were not wanting to the really vigorous and enterprising, especially those willing to go abroad.

Even if all the families of the imitators are added together only about a million at the very most, a seventh of the whole number in the country, can be made out to be middle class. Considering how this seventh now appears to be composed it would seem to be extraordinary to think of this section of society as a 'solid' community or even a community at all. Moreover it cannot have been true that the whole remaining part of the population was embraced within the working-class community, over 85 per cent of the whole country. There is yet another intermediate area, an area considerably larger than the one we have classified as the area of aspiration, which has to be traversed before we reach the working class proper. In order to observe the people living there it is necessary to go below the £3 level, beyond the realm of a somewhat uncertain light given out by the income-tax figures. Only if large numbers of people from this region of society are admitted into the middle-class could it ever become a fifth, a quarter or a third of the population.

Some of these people certainly had a claim to middle-classness. At least they felt themselves to belong to the professions, the lettered and liberal occupations, rather than with the manual workers. From the little which is objectively known about their way of life it seems that, although aspiration was out of the question for them, they also were subject to mimesis. Deliberately rejecting the artisans outlook, what else could they do but model themselves upon their betters? But if for that reason we include them with the middle class, perhaps now dropping the adjective 'solid' as conceivably intended in some vague way to qualify one part of the middle class but not the whole, this is what we find in terms of income. 'Elementary schoolteachers' were a large element of this type, and three-quarters of them in 1909 were women, whose average income was £75 a year. The same sort of thing is true for office workers, in business and in government, especially local government, who made up most of the rest of the people in this category. White-collar workers they are called now, but it is worth mentioning that in the 1900's they did not contain many women. It seems quite out of the question to try to classify them on the conventional three-layer scale, especially if one layer is null. We need a wholly more realistic vocabulary.

This subject like all social description becomes tedious if it is pressed beyond a certain point. All that the reader is required to acknowledge is that the 'solid middle class' of the incautious historian and social commentator turns out on closer inspection about earlier twentieth-century society in Britain to be to a large extent bogus. Bogus is used here in its

original technical sense, meaning blank types put in to fill out
space. Perhaps it may be doubted, whether these claims have
ever been seriously made about the middle class in our
country over recent generations, and a reference or two is
required here.

The late Sir Arthur Bowley was a distinguished statistician
and social historian of the first half of this century. By
reckoning in the white-collar workers generally and insisting
that everyone who was not working class must belong to it,
Sir Arthur fixed the middle class at 23 per cent of occupied
men in 1901, 25 per cent in 1911 and 26 per cent in 1931,
growing steadily as we have already noticed but checked by
the blight of the Depression. Mr Bonham in his very interesting study of the *Middle Class Vote* decided that it comprised
30·1 per cent of the electorate in 1951 and was again growing
rapidly. No less an authority than the late G.D.H. Cole
willingly accepted this figure for the class as a whole in the
1950's, though he admitted the difficulties about defining the
middle class.

Perhaps all that it has been possible to do in this section is
to convict them of the rather cumbersome and misleading use
of an obsolete terminology. There are other ways of describing
the 'middle class', and Seebohm Rowntree suggested and consistently used the expression 'the servant keeping class' for his
purpose, which was to find a way of putting on one side all
those who were neither in poverty, nor ever likely to be so. It
has none of the political and other overtones of *the Establishment*. For that reason, because it lays the emphasis on the fact
of social superiority alone, this is the phrase we shall have in
mind as we turn to the issue about revolution in England since
1901.

iii   *The Social Revolution of our time*

When we discussed social change in England 300 years ago, at
a time of military violence over civil issues, it was concluded
that to talk of social revolution was inappropriate. Though
there were breaches in the political fabric and constitutional
changes which were so abrupt and sudden that the most
extreme descriptions have always been applied to them, the
notion that the social structure itself was radically changed
had to be rejected. The third and last of the issues which has

to be considered in this swift survey of English society in the earlier twentieth century is whether something which might be called social revolution has been happening in our time, although neither civil conflict nor, as yet, any sharp constitutional conflict has taken place.

The discussion has to go on in recognition that the general contrast between seventeenth- and twentieth-century English society is the one which seems to us now considerably more important than any other known to English history. If by the exercise of historical ingenuity it could be attached to a particular set of events, there can be no doubt that it would have been called revolution, *the* revolution in fact. This being so, any change confined to the period since 1901 could only appear as incidental. There is a further complication too. No one in the later twentieth century whatever his definitions could possibly decide whether a social revolution occurred earlier in the century, because everyone is still caught up in the process under description. Only the decision to defy convention and to choose deliberately to write history from the present backwards puts us in the uncomfortable situation of having to raise such a question at all. We must return to this crux in our final chapter.

Meanwhile we can address ourselves to the following possibility. Even in the light of the overall change which can be observed between the older, traditional social world and the industrial one which has succeeded it, a change of shape in the social structure of our country (which might turn out to be a critical one) does seem to have taken place since 1901. The argument will be that some sort of crystallization may have been taking place, with its apogee between the years 1940 and 1947. The result was a reduction in the social height, to pursue the spatial metaphor about social relationships: to go even further with the image, from a pyramid, lofty and slender, English society began at that date to look something more like a pear, tending to become an apple. Because it has an altered shape in fact, people have tended to change their image of English society, if only by very little. Englishmen, perhaps even more Englishwomen, have ceased to look upwards as much as they had always done; outward-looking has begun to compete with upward-looking.

These newer metaphors, directly they are written out on paper, begin to look even more gawky and inadequate than the older ones. Let it be clear before any attempt to justify them has been made, how modest is the claim being put forward. It is no cataclysm of the Eastern European type which is here at issue. The society described in the Jugoslavia of the 1950's by Djilas obviously differs from the Jugoslavia as it was in 1939 by a great deal more than our England differs from the England of Mr Neville Chamberlain, even of Mr Lloyd George.

The fact that productive capacity has stayed almost entirely in private hands clearly distinguishes the nature of the social change in the two countries. The change in Jugoslavia and in other countries has also been a change towards greater industrialization, a very rapid advance indeed towards a society dominated by the factory and the office. This has not been open to the English in the twentieth century to anything like the same extent because we have been highly industrialized all the time. Moreover the system of social status in our country is still officially much as it always has been, even if in fact it has been considerably less definite, whilst in the communist countries status has been completely transformed. If the height of the social ladder in England is now much less, the number of rungs is somewhat the same.

The inappropriateness of *revolution* to describe these changes is obvious when their nature is considered. It is a fact for example that in 1898 no less than 13,000 people in England and Wales died of the measles, and there are no doubt plenty of people still alive who can remember the terror which these infectious diseases caused, especially amongst families with children. By 1948 this number had dropped to about three hundred, and the other infectious diseases show the same amazing decrease in their incidence and in their power to kill. Deaths from diphtheria dropped from 7,500 to 150 over the same period, and deaths from scarlet fever show a hundredfold decrease.

Changes like these can only be counted as marking a deliberate transformation consciously contrived. It is tempting to call these things revolution, yet this merely makes us think of them in terms of a conflict, a turning point and final victory which is almost physical. And this is a nuisance.

There was, nevertheless, a critical point in these medical advances, when mortality really began to go down sharply. This point also came in the early 1940's, or somewhere near

that time, for it was in 1937 that the effect of the sulphona-
mide drugs first began to be felt, and in 1945 that penicillin
went into general action. But the experts count the new drugs
as only one amongst a whole list of other changes, much more
general and long-term, such as better sanitation, better housing, cleaner bodies and so on. All these tendencies combined
then to produce this triumphant result in our country, though
we must remember that they are features of contemporary
Western industrial society as a whole. We may notice that
this achievement marks the early twentieth century as a time
of progress far more rapid and intense than any process of this
kind which took place in the nineteenth century. Yet it was
the nineteenth century which called itself the century of
progress and which historians have always thought of under
this title.

Perhaps it may seem surprising that the point at which the
shape of English society can be seen to have changed came
during the last war. For this was when our country was in
greater military danger than it has ever been, and under a
government, the Churchill coalition, which certainly did not
take office to bring about reform, least of all of the social
structure.

But the sociologists have recognized for a long time that
national warfare, especially warfare which requires a high
proportion of citizens to participate, tends to produce changes
of social attitude and policy, in the 'reformist' direction.
There was such a tendency during and after the war of 1914–18
all over Europe. The programme of the Levellers in the late
1640's has already tentatively been brought under the same
heading. Universal military conscription is one of the characteristics which distinguishes twentieth-century societies
from their predecessors and in Britain in the early 1940's
participation in the national war effort was at a level rarely
equalled anywhere at any time. Not only were able-bodied
men conscripted to fight but all mature men were required to
work. Not only were women enrolled voluntarily to help in a
womanly way but all women were directed to some task useful
to the war effort. Factories, institutions, communities, everything British was made to play its part with an efficiency and a
success which is a high tribute to the British administrative
skill, whatever its record since that time.

The impression should not be that under these quite unique

circumstances the people of this country, or a particular number of them having support from many others, deliberately decided to introduce something like a new social order in the early 1940's, and that they succeeded. The overall changes we are discussing were not exclusively a matter of the social results of medical advances, of changes in mortality, of a rise in real wages and alterations in the distribution of income. Such advances might conceivably have come about without any governmental or political policy, being at play, as they did to a large extent in the U.S.A. over the same period. Deliberate shaping of social change did go on at the same time, however, in England. But before anything more is said about the causes of the transformation, a little more must be added about mortality and about the family.

We have talked at some length about the number of children born to peasant women 300 years ago, and made some reference to changes at age of marriage of women and numbers of children born to a marriage. These varied in ways which may turn out to be of great interest for the study of social and economic history and of social structure. The nobility and gentry showed similar fluctuations in these respects, but with them the process is clearer. It seems more obviously a question of deliberate policy in reaction to the changing situation. Over the last half-century and more there has been a very remarkable deliberate change in England of this kind, affecting now every level of society, almost every married couple.

In the later years of the nineteenth century over four children were still being born to every marriage. Though, as we have seen, average household size in England remained the same from the seventeenth to twentieth centuries, by the 1950's it had fallen by a quarter. This was due, among other things, to the fact that the figure of births per marriage had fallen to $2\frac{1}{2}$ per family, a decline of over one-third in less than two generations. Although the family means something very different in the industrial world from what it meant in the pre-industrial world, this phenomenal fall in the numbers of children has meant an enormous change in the position and outlook of women. Together with the lengthening of their expectation of life, this change, in Professor Titmuss's authoritative opinion, has brought about something like a total transformation.

'At the beginning of this century,' he wrote some years ago, 'the expectation of life of a woman aged twenty was forty-six years,' and we may notice that it had increased by nearly a quarter since Halley made up his life table in the 1690's. 'Approximately one-third of this forty-six years,' Titmuss continues, 'about fifteen years, that is to say, was to be devoted to child-bearing. Today the expectation of life of a woman aged twenty is fifty-five years and of this only four years, about a fifteenth, is spent in child-bearing.' He also tells us that about half of all working-class wives had borne between seven and fifteen children by the time they had reached the age of forty, in the early twentieth century, that is to say. All this is entirely different today.

One is tempted to say that a society which has changed so far and so fast in such a fundamental particular is quite simply a new society. The emancipation of women, beginning with the right to vote, has meant the addition of a new and a different half to public society. Though the direct political effects have not yet been as dramatic as such language as this might lead one to expect, the final outcome is not yet apparent. For it has all happened very recently, within the twentieth century. Once again, the rate of transformation in Victorian times begins to look modest in comparison.

The change in the size of the family was undoubtedly deliberate, as deliberate as that which came about amongst the bourgeoisie of the city of Geneva in the early years of the eighteenth century, for it was likewise due to the use of contraceptives. It cannot however, be dated to the 1940's, like so many of the other changes we have discussed. The lowest point reached by the biological family in England occurred during the Great Depression of the 1930's. Still freedom from the tyranny of repetitive child-bearing only means freedom to join in the world of work in times of full employment. And full employment only began in 1940. The proportion of English men and women out of work since 1940 has never reached for any full year the level at which it ordinarily stood over the whole from the 1890's to 1939, excepting only the years 1914–18. It is possible, in fact, that more people have been continuously occupied in paid labour during the last thirty years than ever before in our history.

If full employment has been the crucial matter in the emancipation of women, it has played almost as considerable

a part in the virtual disappearance of poverty from the lives
of whole families which has been so marked a feature of
twentieth-century English social development. Even full employment, however, has not prevented destitution among the
aged. One reason for this is the presence of so many older
people in relation to those in full vigour and earning power
which has come about with increased expectation of life.

Legislative action in support of full employment has occupied the Parliament of our country a great deal during the
twentieth century but it would be a bold man who claimed
that full employment has been brought about by deliberate
political action, or that unemployment will never return for
the same reason. Nevertheless, bursts of welfare legislation
have undoubtedly led to the intensification of the rate of
social change, in education, and in the social services generally
as well as in the maintenance of minimum standards of living.
It seems just to say that the series of measures passed in the
late 1940's has been so far the most conspicuous and the most
effective. Under Churchill's coalition government a series of
reports and of individual Acts began which continued almost
without interruption into the years of Labour rule from
1945–51. The Butler Act of 1944 was looked upon for nearly
twenty years as the charter of educational opportunity for our
generation, for it instituted the principle that a secondary
education, free of charge, was the right of every English
citizen who could pass the proper examination, the notorious
11 plus.

We may already have outgrown this very moderate educational ambition, just as the classic of the British Welfare
State, the Beveridge Report, published in that year now seems
more than a little antiquated. 'Full employment in a free
society' as Lord Beveridge's remarkable document was called,
was a world best-seller in its time, as much read in the Western
hemisphere as in Britain. Its great principle was that everyone
in Britain from the Queen to the pauper child should be
insured against financial misfortune, against the economic
effects of loss of work, health and youth. Most of its provisions
were enacted by the Attlee governments. The National Health
Service, like all the other enactments of those reformist years,
codified and made into a culmination, all the earlier legislation
of that kind. Then came the new towns, the nationalization of
industries, the final democratization of the parliamentary

system, and many other things – all of them having their
origins in plans which were laid down before even the war
was won in 1945. In the 1970's this whole structure is diminish-
ing and parts of it may be dismantled in England, though
other, richer, more expansive countries, which have built for
themselves more elaborate and efficient versions of the welfare
state, still sometimes look to Britain as the creator of the
original model. The downgrading of these institutions in our
country does not of itself imply that their foundation should
be denied the title of fundamental social change.

The actual shift of opinion in favour of radical reform seems
to have taken place about 1943. From that point on it might
be said that 'ideological politics' became at last the accepted
pattern in England. This seems to be the decisive argument
in favour of the later 1940's as a time of critical social change
and we must pursue it a little further.

The Labour Party began in 1901 as a practical political
proposition, and its success was rapid for the first twenty-five
years. This was not surprising since what we should quite
spontaneously call the natural support of the Labour Party,
that is to say the working people, constituted then and has
ever since at least two-thirds and probably more like three-
quarters of the whole population. With the great extensions of
the franchise in 1919 and in 1929, the complete disappearance
of the Liberal Party in favour of the Labour Party, and a
situation where Conservative and Labour governments alternated, were to be expected.

But though the Labour Party did head minority governments in 1924 and in 1930–31, which were both in their own
way political disasters, this did not occur. Nor did the Liberals
take a final quietus. If we take a great gulp at a huge pudding
of a historian's problem we might claim that what happened
was this. The society of England was unwilling to accept
ideological politics where there are two possible governments,
one of the economically privileged and the other of the economically dissatisfied. Not until 1943. In that year apparently
it did accept the prospect of Labour rule and of nationalization, the very distant possibility of socialism. In the last
decade it seems that even ideological politics has begun to
look a little out of date. The effect of the great change we
are describing has turned out to be a bringing together of
the two opposed attitudes, not an intensification of them.

But when every qualification is made, this shift still looks as if it was decisive, although Labour governments have not lasted long, and although fears of socialism as others understand it have turned out to be baseless in our country.

So much for an attempt to make the social history of England in high industrial times history of critical social change, in particular a reduction of the social height, if that patient metaphor will stand. If the exact meaning to give that phrase is still in doubt, we may pick out one last little strand from the bewildering tangle of social developments in twentieth-century England which may make it a little clearer. In 1901 personal domestic service was the major occupation of all the employed women of the country, a million and a half servants there were amongst the four million women at work. It was the largest occupational group for men or for women, larger than mining, engineering or agriculture. By the end of the First World War the numbers had fallen so far and so fast that there was an official inquiry. But even during the 1920's and 1930's when everyone, men or women, one might think, would have been glad of a job and when the demand was as great or greater, domestic servants continued to get fewer. By the 1930's they were down to half, though still a considerably sized occupation. By 1951 the female domestic servant had practically disappeared – all 'servants', men and women, in institutions and in houses numbered only about 175,000; in the same year the numbers of women in offices reached exactly the number of domestic servants in 1900. The price of domestic help has risen in the last twenty years more than almost any other item of household expenditure, but servants are still not to be had. Englishwomen simply will no longer do the personal work for other Englishwomen, whoever they are asked to serve. The social height is too low.

Understanding Ourselves
in Time
Chapter 10

It is very easy to show how important contrast is to understanding. The architect in his drawing and the painter in his
picture both casually introduce some human figure, to give the
onlooker a proper sense of scale and an opportunity to contrast
the scene with himself. When the astronomer sets out to show
us what our earth is like, he finds it important to talk about
other planets, other sunlike stars, other solar systems. When
he tells us that its diameter is 8,000 miles, he also tells us that
the diameter of Jupiter is 86,800 miles, and this adds to our
understanding. In fact we feel we can understand fully only
when we can confidently say 'It might have been otherwise',
and give the details – what it would be like if the earth were
hundreds of times as big, and five and a half times as far from
the sun; how heavy things would be, how long the day, how
cold the night.

The astronomer is genuinely interested in Jupiter for Jupiter's sake, quite apart from the comparison which that planet
and all the others offer to him with our earth. In the same way
the marine biologist is interested in the plankton of the sea
and the geneticist in the varying types of drosophila fly,
interested in them dispassionately and not simply for what they
can tell us about our own environment and about how to
devise ways in which we can control it. We call this attitude
scientific, and a scientist will often insist that he has no other
reason for his interest in what he works on.

We may look a little quizzically at a man who says this to us,
but we must freely admit that men do not find out about their
world exclusively with themselves in view. Or rather, for the
point raises philosophical questions, the sense in which all
human knowledge is knowledge for human purposes can be
very general indeed and can be virtually ignored in such
activities as pure mathematics and general scientific theory
at large.

But it is true nevertheless that all human knowledge gets
caught up into the overriding interest which we take in ourselves and in our doings. Even the pure mathematician, if

asked what he is doing with himself, will talk in this way. The sort of scientific endeavour which everyone is disposed to call really important brings the two elements clearly into view. The theory of continuous creation of matter, for example, very much of the mid-twentieth century, is extraordinarily satisfying to all of us simply in the scientific sense of adding to knowledge. But the other interest it arouses, its possible effects on ourselves and our own experience, is even greater than this. If the theory is true, then the world had no beginning and will have no end, just as the universe has no boundary. Neither the time sequence nor the space continuum in which men live have any sort of boundary or limit. This is knowledge about ourselves and it fascinates us. Even if for when the theory is abandoned as a part of 'scientific' explanation something in the change which it has made in our view of ourselves will remain for ever.

We may now turn with these very general considerations in our mind to the activity of the historians. Since we can only properly understand ourselves and our world, here and now, if we have something to contrast it with, the historians must provide that something. It is true that people and nations and cultures vary in the extent to which they wish to understand themselves in time in this way, but to claim that there has ever been a generation anywhere with no sense of history is to go too far. From this point of view therefore all historical knowledge is knowledge with a view to ourselves as we are here and now. But, and here is our second consideration, historical knowledge is also interesting in itself, objectively, 'scientifically' once more. It is in fact almost always of greater intrinsic interest than Jupiter's moons, or the wingspan of fly populations, because it is knowledge about people with whom we can identify ourselves.

Historical knowledge then, and the activity of the historian, need no apology. Without such knowledge we could not understand ourselves in contrast with our ancestors, and possessing it we also satisfy a spontaneous interest in the world around us and in the people who have been within it. Taken together, though with the emphasis on the first source of our interest, history often provides useful knowledge which we could not have in any other way. In order to know how to change and improve the National Health Service in our country, for example, it is necessary to know what it actually consists of and knowing that almost always means getting to know its history. So it is that the politician and administrator finds himself going through the story in chronological order; how before 1911 everyone in England had to pay for medical attention, although in New Zealand and in Germany health insurance was already in force; how in 1911 Mr Lloyd George got the first National Health Insurance act passed and how various acts succeeded it as the century went on, until in 1948 Mr Bevan and the Attlee government . . . and so on, and so on. The same sort of chronological explanation is necessary, along with some considerations about geography and economics of course, to understand why Jugoslavia will not fit into the Communist Bloc, or why it is that the Elgin marbles are in the British Museum and no longer on the site of the Parthenon.

Historical knowledge for use might perhaps be regarded as distinct from historical knowledge acquired to understand ourselves in time and to satisfy our curiosity about our past. But these distinctions need be pressed no further for our present purposes, and we must recognize that the functions of the historian which are implied by these elementary considerations scarcely make it likely that this subject will be a progressive one. If this is what the historian has to do, it is not to be expected that what he is doing in England today should be very different from what he has always been doing, here and elsewhere. There cannot be a 'new history' in quite the sense that Einstein founded a 'new physics' nor indeed a new branch of historical study of quite the type of radio astronomy, which is a new and very recent branch of physics as a whole in virtue of its subject matter. Nevertheless the shift of interest towards inquiries of the sort which are reported with such brevity and sketchiness in this book, ought perhaps to be called a new branch of history.

The phrase 'sociological history' has been occasionally used here as its title, but it might almost be better to use 'Social structural history' instead. This new title is required first and foremost to register a distinction in subject matter, for confessedly historical writing has not previously concerned itself with births, marriages and deaths as such, nor has it dwelt so exclusively on the shape and development of social structure. But the outlook is novel as well as the material, at least in its emphasis. Perhaps the distinctive feature of the attitude is the frank acceptance of the truth that all historical knowledge,

R

from one point of view, and that an important and legitimate one, is knowledge about ourselves, and the insistence on understanding by contrast.

From this flows an irreverent impatience with established conventions of the subject as it has been traditionally studied in our country. The search for contrasts in social arrangements leads one to demand that English society shall not be seen for itself alone, but alongside French, German, Spanish, Dutch, Italian, Scandinavian society, as one variation on the Western European pattern. But even this cannot be wide enough. Russian and Eastern European societies, Asian, African and Oceanic societies too, are relevant to the study of our own, if contrast is what we are in need of. The object of the English historian of his own country may remain to get to know his own society, but now as one amongst others.

The search for contrast does not end even here. It is not simply geographical. We all know (and an exasperatingly imprecise thing it is to know) that in England and in Western Europe we live in an 'advanced' industrial society, to be further described as a 'capitalist' as opposed to a 'socialist' industrial society. There are in the contemporary world societies which are not industrial at all in the sense given to the word here. These are the primitive societies, as we somewhat patronizingly call them, of Africa, Asia, Australia, South America and Oceania. But what is 'industrialization', what are 'socialist' and 'capitalist' economies, what indeed is 'society' and what is objectively known and knowable about the constitution of societies and the ways in which they cohere, change, evolve, solve their conflicts and fight them out?

These are questions which have had to concern us in this essay, but they cannot be called exclusively or even predominantly historical questions at all, even if the historian has his responsibilities in helping to answer them. They are to some extent economists' questions, and so fall within the province of the most exact and advanced of the social sciences. For this we should be grateful. But too great a reliance on exclusively economic analysis has led in the past to all the sterilities of the economic interpretation of history. The complete description of questions of this sort is sociological as well as economic, and one of the important discoveries of the contemporary historian has been that he has carried on as if this were not the case.

History, we now begin to recognize with some dismay, has been written as if questions about social structure and types of society, questions about causation too, were fairly straight-forward and answerable by common sense and a little econo-mics, the more the better, but always fairly elementary. Historians have in fact tended up till now to look upon that area of inquiry which we have called social structural as if they knew it all already. This unfortunate tendency might be called 'naïf sociologism'.

We must not, after all, exaggerate the importance of the differences between the new historical criticism and the old; no doubt the distinction between naïf and sophisticated socio-logism, if that is what should now replace it, will look very uncertain to those who come after us. But the somewhat sud-den recognition that historians have habitually attempted to solve complicated problems of social structure and social causation by guessing a little, with help of a few insignificant statistics, has undoubtedly had a disconcerting effect. We have glanced back over our history books and found them full of the crudest sociological generalization, of highly unconvinc-ing speculation on the nature of social development. This has led to scepticism, and it was inevitable that the new historical criticism should have begun by being negative. But we have chosen not to confine this essay merely to critical analysis, and to make an attempt at something more positive by the use of the method of overall contrast.

Some of the difficulties of deciding to compare rather than to recount, as historians ordinarily do, must have been evident throughout this essay, especially in the last chapter. So deeply embedded in the whole tradition of writing history is the feeling for development, process, evolution, for the necessity of knowing everything that happened in between, that the whole enterprise may seem wrong-headed, especially to those whose interests lie in the interval missed out here, the eighteenth and nineteenth centuries that is to say. To many it may seem unhistorical in the final sense, since it abandons the method of explanation by telling the story. Even the sym-pathetic critic may feel that it could only succeed at the very superficial and introductory level; directly there is time and available information to go at all deeply beneath the surface any impression that there could be two constants capable of entering into an intelligible contrast must soon disappear.

Perhaps this objection should be discussed a little further, for it is justified to a large extent. England in 1700 cannot be at all adequately described as wholly pre-industrial nor England in 1901 as wholly industrialized. A claim of this kind would have to assume in the first place that the expressions themselves have agreed and constant meanings, which they do not. Industrialization has been defined in almost as many ways as there have been historians and economists who have studied that elusive process. It assumes in the second place that the entity England was in fact without industry at the first chosen point and wholly industrialized at the second. There are many historians who could maintain that both these claims are quite without foundation, that the eighteenth century saw not the only but simply a particularly conspicuous 'industrial revolution', one of a series which goes far back beyond 1600 and still continues. Nothing can have been more obvious from the brief discussion of English society in recent times than that it has been in intensifying flux rather than in constant 'post-industrial' condition, and that many of the points of contrast with the world we have lost have made their appearance only very recently indeed.

It may be simple-minded or even rather worse than that, to respond by appealing again to the reader's ordinary familiarity with his own surroundings, especially in respect of the scale of life. Still it was not found necessary to insist that the working man since 1901 has ceased to do his daily work in the circle of his family and has become almost entirely subject to the discipline of the factory and the office, to the necessity of going there and back to work every day, to all the experience known as mass living. Surely we know all this in a much more straightforward way than the historian seems to think that he knows how society works at any time he chooses to study it. Of course if this leads people to suppose that because we all know that economic organization is no longer almost entirely a familial matter, that therefore the family no longer plays any part in economic life then it does become deceptive. Yet the self-evident importance of the overall comparison does justify its being drawn in heavy outline, and only a direct confrontation between our society before and after whatever it was that went on between 1700 and 1900 gives it sufficient emphasis. It does enable us to understand ourselves by saying with conviction: 'It might have been otherwise.'

The same point could be made for the other two heads which were chosen for twentieth-century England, though here the issues are more complex. When talking of the middle class in the twentieth century it was not necessary to compare directly the general similarities and differences between the ruling segment of the older world and the social and political establishment of the newer world, though some remarks had to be made about the pattern of social mobility. But surely it does not have to be elaborately reasoned that an *élite* minority cannot nowadays live the whole political, intellectual and social life of a whole country. We all know this already, in a way. We know that representative chambers, parties, elections in our system, the whole machinery of totalitarian politics elsewhere, have had to come into being because élitist politics cannot work in our world in the easy, spontaneous way described earlier on. When it comes to authority in contemporary politics and to the possibility of revolution, we may perhaps hesitate somewhat. But we recognize easily enough the profound difference in these crucial respects which has come with two very obvious and evident changes. These are the departure of a common religious belief shared by everyone, and the arrival of universal literacy and with it universal access to the public, political world. These must have much to do with the fact that revolutionism is now a credible political belief and actual social revolution a possible tactic. We all know also that the disappearance of servants means more than an inconvenience to the rich.

Historical contrast if too blankly presented may obliterate the subtler forms of change and survival. This was perhaps apparent in what was said about the country house in the politics of the old world and of the new, a topic which along with the many others urgently requires a defter and more informed analysis. Authoritarianism arising directly out of the patriarchal family in the manor house may have departed from the scene. But allegiance and submission to the father figure continue to play their parts in the psychology of politics, even if actual fathers now push prams and have thrown the rod away. The Pope, as was said elsewhere in trying to make old Sir Robert Filmer possible to believe in, is still Papa, and Stalin died Little Father to the Russian people.

Contrast over time, furthermore, might conceivably be allowed to divert attention from contrast over space, or rather cross-cultural comparison as the anthropologist might put it; understanding ourselves in time is after all understanding ourselves in one dimension only. It might be thought that it would be so much more illuminating to draw the comparison with the Trobriand Islanders, or the Nuer, or the Ainu of the Northern Island of Japan, vanishing survivals of societies wholly pre-industrial in everybody's sense and offering a much profounder depth of possible distinction. Only a glance or two has been made in this direction and the thorny problem of how to combine the different types of comparison, cultural and chronological, has been left on one side. Obviously there is much more to be said, and the beginnings of work on the feudal era in Europe as compared with contemporary African society may yet yield a great deal.

But it is an impressive fact that Louis Henry, when he made the first move towards a really scientific historical demography, the earliest element to appear in a properly sociological historical method, deliberately rejected contemporary under-developed societies in favour of the societies of our predecessors in Western Europe. He wanted to get to know what 'natural fertility' was and he decided that he would be more likely to find out from the village of Crulai in Normandy over the seventeenth and eighteenth centuries than from any twentieth-century primitive society, however benevolently administered and however carefully counted and registered. His reasons were entirely statistical nevertheless; no extra-European unindustrialized society yet keeps its *état civil*, as the French say, its births, marriages, deaths and so on, with the accuracy of the parish priests and parish clerks even of Stuart England. This being so, quantitative comparison may perhaps not turn out to be as efficient for cross-cultural as it already is for chronological contrast.

Figures are not everything, even in our present mood of preferring any set of facts which can be counted over all those which arise from impressions, literary, legal and otherwise. The justification of the method chosen for understanding ourselves in time may seem to need sharper illustration. We may take it from the size, structure and function of the family and household.

The evidence about the household as it was in England before the industrial process began has been referred to on various occasions throughout this essay, though not presented in a systematic way. It seems to make impossible any belief that the independent, nuclear family-household of man, wife and children is an exclusive characteristic of industrialized society. When all allowance has been made for the very different assumptions about the household which then obtained, and the very different kinship relationships too, it remains the case that there ordinarily slept together under each roof in 1600 only the nuclear family, with the addition of servants when necessary. Therefore in that vital respect our ancestors were not different from ourselves. They were the same.

The assumption seems to have been that the contrary was true, an assumption made not so much by historians, too preoccupied with traditional activities, but by the sociologists themselves. Much of the alienation discussion of our time seems to suppose that the horror of industrialization was in part the result of separating the nuclear family from the kin group and the kin group was usually conceived of in terms of joint or extended households.

There is more to this than a faulty account of how things have changed. Our whole view of ourselves is altered if we cease to believe that we have lost some more humane, much more *natural* pattern of relationships than industrial society can offer. When we inquire, for example, what we are trying to do for the lonely old people who are becoming so lamentably common as the twentieth-century decades go by, we find ourselves assuming that they must be restored to the family, where they belong. Perhaps none of those who write so urgently about these problems have a very clear notion of the situation which they are trying to restore. But few of them can have realized how inappropriate it is to think of restoration at all, in the sense of returning to the historical past. We have already talked of the identical error in relation to broken homes and the criminal tendency of our young people and shown that the problem of our ancestors in this regard may well have been worse, not better, than our own.

In fact, in tending to look backwards in this way, in diagnosing the difficulties as the outcome of something which has indeed been lost to our society, those concerned with social welfare are suffering from a false understanding of ourselves in time. Not completely false, of course; if that were so it would make nonsense of our general title. We have seen that in the traditional world the family did fulfil many functions which are left to very different institutions in our day, or which are not fulfilled at all.

But was it more 'natural' that this should have been so? Was *The World we have lost* a more appropriate one for human beings to dwell in? These are very vague and general questions, unlikely to be worth trying to answer in this book. But the point of importance to our argument is to have got into a position where such questions must arise. To recognize their urgency is also to begin to take a different view of our own place in time, and more than this. It may, perhaps ought, to change our view of what we should be trying to do. We can only begin to get into this position if we admit that historical knowledge is knowledge to do with ourselves, now.

Answering these questions does also yield objective knowledge about the past. The demonstration that the society of pre-industrial England maintained the principle that each marriage meant a new household, and that the whole social structure can be ranged round that one critical feature, could justifiably be claimed as an addition to 'scientific' knowledge, much of it very remote indeed from simply knowledge with a view to ourselves now. It may make a great deal of difference to the work of the anthropologist, the sociologist and the social sciences generally as well as to social history. The conviction that this piece of information belongs to a type of historical criticism previously little practised is suggested by the fact that the evidence on which it was based was not new, but always available in very obvious places.

This somewhat arrogant claim can perhaps be made most convincingly in respect of the liability of the peasants to starve, not exactly a part of the principle of the one-marriage household but closely connected with it. Hundreds of parish registers have been published in England, more than in any other country. This has meant that millions and millions of entries from obscurely written, badly preserved documents have been painfully transferred into print at considerable expense for the use of thousands of persons bent on tracing their ancestry. Apart from the biographers, no other users have ordinarily been found for them, and as we have seen it has occurred to no historian up to now to try to see if the registers could tell us whether our ancestors did in fact sometimes die of starvation. Only in the last year or two have they realized that they could be used for the purpose of family reconstitution, and then only as a consequence of the pioneering work done in France.

A romantic might say that this looks like a breach of faith with the Cowlmans and the Lancasters who, it will be remembered, were two of the tiny group of families so far known to have starved in England, in the year 1623 at Greystoke. Perhaps this infidelity is merely a part of the inevitable tendency to look on past individuals as important and worth investigating only if they show forth some political, economic, social or intellectual trend which the historian is concerning himself with. The indifference to questions such as these looks peculiarly inhumane, a failing which comes from too much concern with abstractions. Still it is not for any generation of historians to condemn its predecessors too easily, for who can tell what blindness our successors will detect in us? The additions to the historical record which the close study of the contents of the humble parish registers will bring, may conceivably turn out to have their biological importance.

In order to undertake genetic analysis, it is necessary to be able to study a community of specimens over a number of generations, the more the better. The great disadvantage of human beings for genetic study is that the generation is so long. With drosophila it is possible to observe the passage of ten generations in a matter of days. With humans ten generations would take some three hundred years to observe. Now three hundred years happens to be within the period during which the registration of births, marriages and deaths can be studied from this evidence, and in England we can go back two or three generations further.

It is difficult as yet to see how this opportunity might be used. If we refer to the example of the age at sexual maturity which has been discussed in the text, we can see how vague and confusing the evidence is likely to be, even on a point which in principle might be examined from the bare facts appearing in the parish registers and on the forms used for the reconstitution of families. No one would yet venture to suppose that the problem of distinguishing a possible genetic element in the fall of the age at menarche from the effect of improved diet and living conditions can be solved. Nevertheless the evidence exists to make some initial study of recent human biological history. It is necessary for biology even more than for sociology to understand its subject matter in time, over the generations.

The historian cannot hope to make his contribution to studies of this sort unless he is rather differently equipped than he has previously been. He must obviously be something of a statistician; at least he must have that statistical expectation and caution which so clearly distinguishes the inquirer after truth from the creator of impressions. He must have some economics, some sociology, even conceivably some genetics, as well as anthropology. But it would be wrong to think of the historian of the newer sort solemnly sitting down to acquire this extra-historical knowledge before he even begins to examine the evidence or to write about it. What must come into being is a working community where the historian is in the confidence of the economists, the statisticians and the others. Nevertheless the responsibility for enabling us all to understand ourselves in time must still rest where it has always rested, on the historian as an individual.

It is sometimes said that Clio the Muse is dead and that history is no longer written as literature. Perhaps the difficult situation we have been trying to explain is to some extent responsible. Once the historian brings himself to recognize anew that what he knows he knows with a view to himself as well as with a view to the past, this situation may change again. Herodotus had no doubt that what he wrote was for his contemporaries, relevant above all to his own generation. Neither had Lord Clarendon, nor Lord Macaulay. Macaulay indeed, and this is why he is now criticized, was perfectly aware that England under Victoria was the culmination of the story he was telling, and that the past had to be appreciated where it anticipated that splendid era, recounted as leading up to and evolving into it. Though we must be suspicious of the evolutionary, culminatory element in this attitude we must envy him the frankness with which he came out with the story as it looked to him. He might find it difficult to understand why we, his successors, are so much less attracted to the task of making literature out of how the past looks to us.

Certainly the imaginative reconstruction of a former society can only foster an interest in its people as people. The shortcomings we have mentioned have been called failures in sympathy as well as of method, and if the future is to see the historian in partnership with the other social scientists, it is important that he should never lose sight of his humanity. Naïf sociologism may indeed have come into existence because of an unwilling and largely unaware subservience of the historical imagination to the dogmatic social principles of an earlier generation. These principles dealt exclusively with those rise-of-a-class interpretations which have been criticized here, together with their wearisome insistence on cataclysm, crisis and revolution.

There has been a tendency in fact for English historians to give currency to certain features of Marxian historical sociology, which they have made no conspicuous effort to understand, perhaps because its political associations have been so inimical to them. Advantage was not taken in creating from it historical hypotheses at a time when it really was a novel and developing system. At the present time this half-recognized attachment stands in the way of a confessedly sociological historical criticism of the type we have tried to recommend. In such a new historical criticism the Marxian element in sociological thought because of its explanatory power will play a formidable part.

Perhaps too much fuss has been made here of what in the end will turn out to be just another swirl of opinion which is not simply historical. It could easily be shown that the interest historians are beginning to take in the contrast between English and European society before and after industrialization is also an interest recently acquired by politicians and economists, though their eyes are turned on 'underdeveloped countries' in the present world for the most part. Nevertheless I have no doubt myself that the sort of questions which arise out of an attempt to explore our own, contemporary, late twentieth-century relationship with what we have called the world we have lost could have arisen from no previously established form of historical inquiry. History, I believe, is about to claim a new and more important place in the sum total of human knowledge.

General Note

Files of the Cambridge Group for the History of Population and Social Structure

In the original edition the notes, collected together in this section, were intended to provide the academic reader both with the references to the data used in the text and with a little guidance to the relevant literature. In this edition this second function has been considerably extended, and an attempt has been made to present a summary of titles published since 1965 on the subjects concerned, as well as a guide to sources. For this reason a short description of the sources assembled by the Cambridge Group for the History of Population and Social Structure has been included, and a means provided whereby the files held there can be cited. A list of authorities has also been added, though not all titles cited are included. The notes for each chapter are preceded by a general note on sources and on recent research. All titles are published in London, unless otherwise stated. The publication date (used with the author's name as an abbreviated reference) is of the edition or of the impression consulted; a date in brackets indicates when the work first appeared.

Sources for Demographic and Social Structural History being assembled and analysed by the Cambridge Group for the History of Population and Social Structure

The specific source in unpublished documents for the first edition of *The World we have lost* was the embryo of the collection of listings of inhabitants of English communities before 1801, which has now become one of the files (File 3 in the succeeding notes) of the Cambridge Group for the History of Population and Social Structure. This file remains the most important for the development of the studies described in an introductory way in the present work, but all the other files of the Group are relevant to them, and have been used in this second edition. Its research objectives and procedures are described in the following publications:

Peter Laslett, 'The History of Population and Social
  Structure', *The International Social Science Journal*,
  1965 (in French and English).
E. A. Wrigley, R. S. Schofield, in the *Newsletter* of the
  Social Science Research Council (London), No. 2,
  February 1968.
Peter Laslett, 'Historical and Regional Variations in Great
  Britain' in *Quantitative Ecological Analysis in the Social
  Sciences* (ed. M. Dogan and S. Rokkan), Cambridge, Mass.,
  M.I.T. Press, 1969.

A current bibliography of the publications issued or in
preparation by the Group or by members of the Group is
issued at the beginning of each year, and may be obtained
from its Cambridge address, 20 Silver Street.

  The five files of the Cambridge Group relevant to the
present book are the following:

FILE 1 *Reconstitution*

Select English parishes only. At present Colyton, Devonshire; Hartland, Devonshire; Easingwold, Yorkshire (North
Riding); Banbury, Oxfordshire; Aldenham, Hertfordshire;
Sedgley, Staffordshire; a group of three Bedfordshire
parishes (Southill, Campton and Shefford). The process of
family reconstitution, has been or is being carried out on
these select parishes, and the operations themselves are
being computerized. Its methods are described by E. A.
Wrigley, in Wrigley (ed.), *An Introduction to English
Historical Demography*, 1966, and their computerization
by R. S. Schofield in Schofield, 1970 (i) and (ii). In his
article in the *Transactions of the Royal Historical Society*,
1971, Schofield gives the briefest and perhaps the most
useful description of the techniques with an indication of
its usefulness to historians, demographic, social, social
structural. From family reconstitution it is possible to
recover quite exact information on such matters as age-
specific birth rates and death rates together with age and
order within family at marriage, for the parishes concerned
alongside of less complete evidence on expectation of
life. The life cycle of individuals and their general
personal ecology, that is relationships with the community,

can be studied by this technique, though next to
nothing can be recovered about the actual structure
of family and household regarded as domestic groups.

FILE 2   *Aggregative Analyses*

Returns from about 500 English parish registers, being
monthly totals of baptisms, marriages and burials from
1538 (the beginning of ecclesiastical registration in England)
until 1837 (the final year before civil registration began).
These parishes are mostly fairly large (with a population of
1000 or above in 1801), are rural rather than urban, and
were selected with a view to the requirements of reconstitution rather than from the point of view of typicality.
The collection, then, which is still growing through the
activities of volunteers who do the extraction of figures
locally for the Group, is by no means a random sample of
all 10,000 English parishes, and the geographical spread is
uneven. Nevertheless, the collection represents a twentieth
of all the parishes and perhaps a tenth, an eighth or even
more of all such recordings that were ever made before
1838. The file already constitutes the largest body of such
data ever assembled for any country. It is of particular
historical value because all three series, baptisms, marriages
and burials, begin in 1538 in England whereas in France for
example the three are not present until late in the 1600's.
A number of the registers represented by returns in this
file do not begin before 1600, which is the limiting initial
date to qualify for inclusion. All these data are now in
machine-readable form for computer analysis and numerical
results should be available before long.

FILE 3   *Listings*

Photographs of lists of inhabitants dating from before the
English Census (1801) with some up to 1841, when the
Census began the satisfactory recording of relationships
within households. This file lies behind much of the text
of the present book, but it must be said that only a few
of the workings for individual settlements are cited and that
research has proceeded much further than the discussion
here implies. There are some 250 documents in this file,

which also represents the largest such collection yet made for any country, with the possible exception of Japan. Unfortunately the lists are concentrated in some areas (Kent, London, Westmorland, Staffordshire) and rare or absent in others (e.g. Lincolnshire, Oxfordshire, Cornwall, Cheshire), and common at some dates (the 1690's and the 1790's) and not at other times. The original techniques for hand analysis, still being used to some extent, are described in Laslett's contribution to Wrigley (ed.), *Introduction to English Historical Demography*, 1966, and its modification for computer treatment in Laslett, 1969 (i). This last article, the first of two on *Size and Structure of the Household over Three Centuries*, presents the results of the analysis of the hundred best documents in the file. Auxiliary files and cross-comparative techniques are being developed for areas outside England; see Laslett, 1970 (ii)

FILE 4   *Literacy*

Returns from a random sample of three hundred English parish registers recording ability to sign the marriage register, by sex and (where possible) by occupation, from the date 1754 when such signing was first required until the 1840's. For previous years, back to the early seventeenth century, these records are being supplemented wherever possible from other sources; applications for marriage licences, statements of witnesses in ecclesiastical court cases, the 'Protestation Returns' of 1642, are amongst them. Only limited use of this file has been made here.

FILE 5   *Parameters*

Details of select ecological characteristics for every community represented in Files 1–4, that is to say over 900 English settlements. The parameters include height above sea-level, population at various dates, dispersion of settlement, crop type, distance from London, distance from the nearest market town, whether a seat of gentry, etc. Little use has been made of this file for *The World we have lost*.

Notes to the Text

CHAPTER 1

The major source is in the discussion of domestic, economic and social relations by the men of the time, but crucial information can be gained (mostly by implication, but sometimes by direct statement of the man drawing up the list) from Cambridge Group File 3, Listings File. Literary evidence on the structure of the family and the functions and duties of its members is found in the considerable body of religious advice given by the clergy, generally the Puritan clergy, to their people and printed either as sermons or in the form of treatises on the family: for example, William Gouge, *Of Domesticall Duties*, 1622; William Perkins, *Christian Oeconomie*, 1609 (*Workes*, vol. 3, Cambridge, 1618); William Fleetwood, Bishop of Ely, *The Relative Duties of Parents and Children, Husbands and Wives, Masters and Servants* (1705) in his *Compleat Collection of Sermons*, 1737. Modern works are scanty, but three titles may be recorded here: C. L. Powell, *English Domestic Relations, 1487–1653*, New York, 1917; R. B. Schlatter, *The Social Ideas of Religious Leaders, 1660–1688*, 1940, and Edmund S. Morgan, *The Puritan Family: religion and domestic relations in 17th century New England*, paperback, ed., New York, 1966.

Morgan's book contains the clearest description of familial roles, duties and practices known to me for any European-type pre-industrial society. Although its subject is New England and the Puritans there, most of its contents would apply almost unaltered to English society as a whole at that time. The great difference between the two systems of course was in the existence of divorce in New England, and in the attitude towards marriage as an institution – see below, chapter 6.

1 See Sylvia Thrupp, *History of the Bakers' Company of London*, Croydon, 1933, p. 17, etc.

2 'No baker should sell bread in his own house or shop, but only in the open market, and only on Wednesday or

Saturday.' This was an immemorial rule of the London
bakers and was in full operation in Stuart times (see
Thrupp, 1933, p. 35), but it would be unjustifiable to assume
that it was the practice in all trades and in all towns.
Undoubtedly too some London tradesmen lived in houses
apart from their shops. See *The Inhabitants of London in
1638*, edited by T. C. Dale for the Society of Genealogists,
1931, and for shopping in the open air, without wrappings;
without even coins enough to pay, see Dorothy Davis,
A History of Shopping, 1966.

---

3   See Morgan, 1966, especially page 42 and references.
In New England, as in Old, wives often run the family
finances, but the most impressive evidence of the mana-
gerial functions of officially subordinate wives is found
when the husband was imprisoned or otherwise incapaci-
tated. See for example the letters written by the wives of
Royalist gentlemen taken captive during the English Civil
Wars, like those of Dame Ann Filmer to Sir Robert Filmer
in Laslett, *Sir Robert Filmer*, 1948.

---

4   Indenture between William Selman, Husbandman, his
son Richard and Thomas Stokes, broadweaver, of Wiltshire,
signed in 1705. We have found that the actual numbers of
apprentices, formally so called, seem to have been somewhat
exaggerated by historians, and indeed by contemporaries.
Of 1,739 males in the position of servants in the sample of
100 English parishes from Cambridge Group, File 3
(including 9 London parishes) (see Laslett, 1969(i)) only
229, less than 8 per cent were called apprentices. That
'servants' included the status of apprentice nevertheless is
clear from all the sources, and especially from the city of
Bristol in 1696. There up to 70 per cent of males called
'servant' in a taxation return were found to have been
apprenticed; see Ralph and Williams, 1968, pp. xxiii–iv.

---

5   Paper for the Board of Trade, 1697, printed in H. R.
Fox Bourne, *Life of John Locke*, 1876, vol. ii, p. 377 on.
The work, and the schooling and play, of English children
at this period are well described with a mass of detail from
literary sources for the most part, by Pinchbeck and

Hewitt, *Children in English Society*, 1969. The classic
treatment of pre-industrial childhood, however, is Ariès,
Centuries of Childhood, 1962 (1960). There is an interesting
contrast between these two books and the rather more
numerical approach followed here. Ariès' insistence that
there was an enormous change in the institution of childhood and in the attitudinal structure of the family, between
medieval and modern Europe, is very impressive and
magnificently illustrated from the writings of the time. But
it is not verifiable from the evidence of English community
listings (Cambridge Group, File 3), nor indeed from any of
our data.

---

6   See below, p. 97, for expectation of life.

---

7   Sir Thomas More's *Utopia* was published in 1516; Sir
Wm Petty's various works on *Political Arithmetick*
appeared at different dates in the 1680's. Good examples of
the intense curiosity of Stuart Englishmen about the social
system and sexual arrangements of 'savages' in America,
Africa and Asia are the reading habits and library lists of
John Locke and also of Isaac Newton: see John Harrison
and Peter Laslett, *The Library of John Locke*, Oxford, 1971
(1965).

---

8   Grimm's *Fairy Tales* were first issued in German in
1812–14, but were translated into English at once, to swell
the repertory of such literature already becoming popular.
It may be significant in view of the origin of Marxist social
protest in the same country at the same time that traditional
industrial life seems to have been romanticized on the
widest scale in Germany.

---

9   For the movement of persons between Settlement and
Settlement, see below, pages 156–8, and the references in
footnote 168.

---

10   See the remarkable listing of the inhabitants of this
community in the *Newdigate Papers* at the Warwick Record
Office, C.R. 136, vol. 12, p. 64 and on. It is to be noted
that in this paragraph and elsewhere in this essay the words

'household' and 'family' are used interchangeably, as the
men of the day used them: compare Laslett, 1967(i). A
full discussion of household and family in past time, with
suggested definitions and principles of analysis, will be
found in Chapter 1 of Peter Laslett, *Family and Household
in the Past*, in the press.

11   For the Herberts, see John Aubrey, *Natural History of
Wiltshire*, 1685, ed. J. Britton, Oxford, 1847. For the
Howards, see *Selections from the Household Books of the Lord
William Howard of Naworth Castle*, Surtees Society, 1878,
and Laslett, 1969(i), p. 207.

12   On the county musters see E. E. Rich, in the *Economic
History Review*, Second Series, II, 3, 1950, and for a very
revealing record of one of them, John Smith of Nibley,
Men and Armour for Gloucestershire, 1608, published 1902.

13   Cromwell commanded 26,000 or 27,000 men at Marston
Moor, and this must have been one of the largest organized
crowds ever to have assembled before Napoleonic times in
England. The greatest strength of the armed forces was
70,000 for a brief period under the Commonwealth, see
C. H. Firth, *Cromwell's Army*, 1902, p. 35.
    No doubt the crowds which assembled in London during
the parliamentary crisis of the 1640's were of considerable
size, but little has been done on English evidence of this
period to rival George Rudé's remarkable book on *The
Crowd in the French Revolution*, Oxford, 1959.

14   On markets, market days and market areas, see *General
Note* to Chapter 3. There is a list of schools in W. A. L.
Vincent, *The State and School Education, 1640–1660, in
England and Wales*, 1950; for the universities in Stuart
times, see M. H. Curtis, *Oxford and Cambridge in Transition,
1558–1642*, Oxford, 1959. The number of schools in England
in the mid-seventeenth century is now known to be greater
than Vincent realized, though he tended to exaggerate the
size and permanence of those he found. Mr David Cressy of
Clare College, Cambridge, and of Pitzer College, Claremont,
California, is investigating this question, and rightly insists

that the extent of educational activity is not to be judged
from the scale of institutional provision.

---

15   For the builders see D. Knoop and G. P. Jones, *The
Medieaval Mason*, Manchester, 1933, and various articles on
this theme. For large-scale industry and its organization,
various articles by J. U. Nef, especially that in the *Economic
History Review*, 1934. For the miners, G. R. Lewis, *The
Stannaries*, 1908, J. W. Gough, *The Mines of Mendip*,
Oxford, 1930, and J. U. Nef, *The Rise of the British Coal
Industry*, 2 vols., 1932.

---

16   *Institutional living and widowed persons*
The numbers, size and organization of almshouses instituted between 1480 and 1660 are amongst the subjects
dealt with for London and select counties by W. K. Jordan
in his three important volumes on philanthropy during that
period – *Philanthropy in England*, 1959; *The Charities of
London*, 1960; *The Charities of Rural England*, 1961. Few
seem to have contained more than a dozen or twenty
inmates, but in 1660 something like 1,400 people may have
been living in such institutions in London. This was out
of a population of something like 400,000, and the rarity of
institutional living in the old world can be judged from the
fact that in our sample of 100 pre-industrial villages, only
335 people of a total of some 70,000 were living in this way:
See Laslett, 1969(i), p. 207. As for the situation of widowed
persons not in institutions, 74 per cent of all widowers
headed their own households, 18 per cent were in the households of others, and 7 per cent were solitary. The figures for
widows are 58 per cent heading households, 24 per cent in
the households of others and 14 per cent solitary.

---

17   *Servants*
Servants made up 13·4 per cent of the total population
of our 100 villages (see Laslett, 1969(i), p.219): 28·5 per
cent of all households had servants, and the sex ratio was
107, that is to say there were 107 men and boys for 100
women and girls. The proportion of the younger age groups
in service naturally varied, but could be very high. This is
clear from the following figures for the then village of

Ealing in Middlesex in 1599 (pop. 427) and the village of
Chilvers Coton in Warwickshire in 1684 (pop. 780).

	Ealing	*Chilvers Coton*
Per cent of age group in service:		
Aged 15–19, Male, Female	72, 47	34, 24
Aged 20–24, Male Female	78, 58	23, 43
Total of servants: Male, Female	68, 41	40, 40
Per cent of servants in population	25	10
Per cent of households with servants	34	18

Though evidence is still fragmentary, it seems probable that
traditional English society was exceptional in the numbers
of its servants. They were plentiful in France, but not quite
on the English scale, but far less common in Eastern and
Southern Europe or in Japan. Nevertheless servants, and
the institution of service (living-in, to do the work of the
family (household), seem to have been universal in the
traditional societies we have so far examined.

18   *Working at Home*
For the cloth-makers of Beauvais, see the classic work of
sociological/historical description, Pierre Goubert, *Beauvais
et le Beauvaisis*, Paris, 1960, Part I, Ch. viii, and for the
actual size of undertakings see p. 284. The extent of
employment outside the home for persons other than the
father is difficult to discover, even at periods later than the
seventeenth century. It appears that by the nineteenth
century many sons and daughters, and in the industrializing areas like Lancashire, even many wives and mothers
went out to work each morning and returned in the evening.

19   *Life Cycle of Humble People: Servants*
Richard Steele, *The Husbandman's Calling*, 2nd ed., 1672,
pp. 76 and 86. The life experience of humble people in
earlier times is not easy to recover, and the first accounts
based on evidence supplied by the persons themselves seem
to be the examinations undertaken by the local magistrates
in connection with the law of settlement, starting in the
mid-eighteenth century. These documents (e.g. those for
the parish of Denton in Norfolk, dating between 1755 and

1831) show that the date of leaving home for service was very variable (between 9 and 18 or even later), though 12 may have been the most common. They confirm that servants rarely served more than a year or two in one place, though longest usually in their first place, and that they often remained only a few months. They bring out the importance of regular servant-hiring times, and confirm that marriage almost always ended the period of service both for males and females, and that servants virtually never lived in their own homes. Nevertheless the relationship of a married labourer to a particular master was also sometimes called 'service', if he worked for that master only, especially as a skilled or semi-skilled employee such as shepherd, cowman or thatcher. These exceptions, and the marginal vagueness of the terminology makes for complication and a study of servants from this and other evidence is in progress; compare Laslett, 1964.

---

20   *Farm Family Bye-Employments*

The great importance to the budgets of modest working families of activities pursued at home is clear from many sources. Some (for example a remarkable listing in Cambridge Group, File 3 for the village of Corfe Castle in Dorset in 1790) actually list the pittances gained by wives, teenage boys and girls, dependent widows, etc. 'Knits' is the commonest description of the method of getting pennies. The desperate poverty of the countryside of late Victorian times was due in part to the disappearance of these rural bye-employments; see the example of Ridgmont in 1903, cited on page 217 below.

It has now become possible to compare these activities in England with the remarkably similar situation which existed in Japan at the same period, profoundly different as the two economies were in other ways. In one 'county' in that country in 1840 55 per cent of all income came from activity of this kind, and in some villages the level was as high as 70 per cent. In comparing this record with that of European countries, Professor T. C. Smith who has analysed the remarkable recording which gives these details implies that the level of such activity must have been similar to that in contemporary Europe, but that England was more advanced and richer. Unfortunately we have as yet found no documentary opportunity to check these statements from English records. See T. C. Smith, '*Farm Family Bye-Employments in Pre-industrial Japan, Journal of Economic History,* 1969.

---

21   Karl Marx and Frederick Engels, Manifesto of the Communist Party, 1848, in *Selected Works*, Moscow, 1951, vol. 1, p. 35.

---

22   *Capitalism and Industrialization*
The tendency of recent economic historians, especially those with a Marxist bent, has been to distinguish *industrial* capitalism, the capitalism associated with large-scale enterprise which first appeared early in the nineteenth century, from capitalism generally. The authoritative source for this view is Maurice Dobb, *Studies in the Development of Capitalism,* 1946. The transformation of family life referred to in the present work must be taken to mean the drastic reduction and now the virtual disappearance of the productive, employment-providing functions of the household, the removal of the site of economic activity from the family dwelling. Though little is yet known about how the constitution and membership of the household changed during industrialization in England, the recent demonstration that its mean size (and the distribution of households by size) was virtually unaffected before the early years of the twentieth century (see Laslett, 1969(i) 1970(i), implies that the family group can hardly have been transformed in all directions by modernization. Its residential and consumption functions were not affected until quite recently, and this is true for countries whose industrial history has been entirely different, for example in Japan.

---

23   See Steele, 1672, p. 104.

CHAPTER 2
Weber's concepts of class, status and power in relation to pre-industrial European society have been much written about, especially with relation to England, but there is no work specifically addressed to the theory of the subject.

The position taken up in this chapter about class and status generally is roughly that of W. G. Runciman: see his contribution, 'Class, Status, Power?' in J. A. Jackson (ed.), *Social Stratification*, Cambridge, 1968, and his *Social Science and Political Theory*, 1963, ch. VII: compare also the reader compiled by R. Bendix and S. M. Lipset, *Class, Status and Power*, 1967 (1963). J. H. Hexter expresses contemporary scepticism about multi-class divisions in early modern England: see his *Reappraisals*, 1965 (1961), especially on 'The Myth of the Middle-class in Tudor England', and 'Storm over the Gentry'. This latter essay is a contribution to the vast literature on the rise of the gentry, and contains a list of works, which can be filled in from Lawrence Stone, *Social Change and Revolution, 1540–1640*, 1967 (1965). Social structural description, especially of the gentry themselves, has gone forward as an incidental to this controversy, but there have been some studies specifically directed to it. The yeomen are dealt with by Mildred Campbell, *The English Yeoman*, 1942, and the labourers are well described by Alan Everitt in J. Thirsk (ed.), *Agrarian History*, vol. IV, 1500–1640, 1967: see also G. Batho on the landlords. A recent critical description of the early Stuart social structure is found in Zagorin, *Court and Country*, 1969.

Original sources for this chapter, apart from Cambridge Group File 3, are the works published and in manuscript, of Gregory King and such descriptions of English society as Edward Chamberlayne, *Angliae Notitia*, 1669, 1670, 1671 . . . 20th Edition, 1702.

---

24   Some parsons and parish clerks, naturally, were more generous, and others less generous, in distributing titles to their entries and it would be foolish to expect any rigorous consistency. We have used the burial entries as the most revealing for the purpose, and results of such analysis (along with those for marriages, see below) will be published in due course. Here are three arbitrary examples: Manchester, 1653–5, 3·9 per cent of 2,380 death entries contained some title like 'gentleman' or higher, and the addition of those marked *Mr* or *Mrs* brought the total up to 11·3 per cent. Of those buried at Ludlow in Shropshire, between 1632 and 1641 5·2 per cent bore some such title, and between 1599

and 1633 the proportion was 6·6 per cent at Wem in the
same county. Studies have been sent to the Cambridge
Group of the registers of a group of Yorkshire parishes,
showing that persons actually named as gentry in birth or
death entries there in the eighteenth century varied from
less than 1 per cent (Addingham, 1767–1812) to over 3
per cent (Otley, 1721–40, Ilkley, 1718–1810) – work of Mrs
Mary Pickles.

---

25   The Statute of Artificers, (5 Eliz. c 4), para. IV,
quoted from R. H. Tawney and E. Power, *Tudor Economic
Documents*, 1924 (1951) vol. I, p. 342, modernized.

---

26   Serjeant Thorpe, Judge of Assize for the Northern
Circuit, his charge to the Grand Jury at York Assizes,
March 20th, 1648, printed in *Harleian Miscellany*, vol. II,
1744, p. 12.

---

27   King's table was printed by Charles Davenant in his
*Essay upon the Probable Methods of Making a People
Gainers in the Ballance of Trade*, in the year 1699. This
version is reproduced here on pages 36–7. It differs in detail
from that which forms part of a manuscript treatise
entitled *Natural and Politicall Conclusions Upon the State
and Conditions of England*, by Gregory King, Esqr, Lancaster Herald at Armes, A.D. 1696, along with other tables
of importance for the study of pre-industrial society.
In this work, which was never published in King's lifetime,
no explanation is advanced as to why the general distinction was made, and very little evidence to justify any of
the statistical work is offered. We have found, however,
that King's figures are surprisingly accurate wherever we
have been able to provide independent checks on them.
King's manuscript treatise was printed from an original in
the British Museum (Harleian MSS 1898: there are other
manuscripts) in 1802 by George Chalmers as an appendix
to an edition of his *Estimate of the Comparative Strength of
Great Britain*, and again from the same source in Baltimore,
U.S.A. in 1936 by George E. Barnett under King's title.

---

28   See the very important article of D. C. Coleman,

'Labour in the English economy of the 17th century', in the *Economic History Review*, new series, VIII, 3, 1956.

29   Sir Thomas Smith, *The Commonwealth of England* (1560's), published 1583, edition of 1635, p. 66. The parish records of the seventeenth century make it clear that labourers did hold office as churchwardens and constables, and often attempted administrative tasks beyond their capacities as readers and writers.

30   William Harrison, *Description of England*, 1968 (1577, 1587), pp. 113–14.

31   Act of 12 Car. II, Cap. IX.

32   See for example the books of Christopher Hill. The position taken up in his very stimulating and influential general history of England in Stuart times, *The Century of Revolution*, Edinburgh, 1961, is rather different from that which he took up in 1949, when he made the following statement about events in England from 1640 to 1660: 'Very briefly summarised, our subject here is the story of how one social class was driven from power by another.' (*The Good Old Cause*, edited by C. Hill and E. Dell, 1949, p. 19.) Professor Brough Macpherson is responsible for the general reformulation of the position about capitalism (or the 'market society') and seventeenth-century England. See his important book *The Political Theory of Possessive Individualism, Hobbes to Locke*, Oxford, 1962.

33   No more general claim is made for the definitions of class and status in the text than that they seem to correspond to the uses made of the concepts in the loose discussions of historians, particularly Marxian and post-Marxian historians. Only action groups are by definition of importance for them because only action groups can enter into historical events, such as rebellion, revolution or governmental action. Obviously if the common work-situation of individuals be taken as the critical characteristic of class, as for example by David Lockwood (see *The Blackcoated Worker*, 1958), or if 'the way a man is

treated by his fellows' is taken to be its essence, as it is by
T. H. Marshall (*Citizenship and Social Class*, Cambridge,
1950), it would be possible to identify many social classes
in Stuart England, but none of them, it is claimed, was
likely to ever come into relation with another, or others, of
them, in such a way that collective group conflict, such as
the Civil War of 1642–8 could possibly have been created.

---

34   About 200 seems to be the number of such families
referable to England and Wales in successive editions of
Chamberlayne. King allots 6,400 *persons* to his 160 noble
families, but all except 4 or 5 in each family must have
been servants.

---

35   See Hollingsworth, *Demography of the Peerage*, 1964.
Nearly 40 per cent of peers' sons born between 1550 and
1674 married daughters of peers; this proportion fell to 25
per cent for peers born 1700–1749. Mr D. N. Thomas, in his
M.Phil. thesis for the University of London, 1969 (*Marriage
Patterns in the British Peerage in the 18th and 19th Centuries*)
shows that peers marrying outside their order chose mostly
partners from the gentry, but married extensively into the
bourgeoisie and the professional classes, sometimes even
into the lower levels of society.

---

36   I owe much of this paragraph of the text to Mr
Andrew Sharp, late of Trinity College, Cambridge, now of
the University of Christchurch, New Zealand, who is
engaged in a dissertation on the peerage under the Commonwealth in relation to political thinking.

---

37   Sir Anthony Wagner, the present Garter King of Arms,
suggested these criticisms of the view that the emphasis on
the divide below the gentry was the distinguishing feature
of the traditional English social system. Studies of listings
of inhabitants (Cambridge Group, File 3) show that the
description gentleman was fairly consistently conferred
throughout the period from the sixteenth to the nineteenth
centuries, and this is confirmed on the whole by the parish
registers in spite of the vagaries noted above, note 24.
Examples can be found of the birth or death (scarcely ever

the marriage) of persons known to be gentle being recorded
without acknowledging the social distinction, and rather
more often of such titles being conferred on persons whose
claims look uncertain. Richard T. Vann discusses these
points with great acuteness in his *Development of Quakerism*,
1969 (see pp. 50–81; Vann has to abandon distinctions
between yeomen and husbandmen). Sources of other types
confirm the continued pre-occupation with gentle status,
even the distinction between a *Mr* and a *Gent.*; see for
example lists of subscribers to books (Laslett, 1969(ii)).

---

38   6 and 7 William and Mary, c.6. This act, and the
returns to which it gave rise up to the time of its repeal in
1705, are of great importance to English history both
demographic and sociological. The listings of inhabitants
in Cambridge Group, File 3 on which so much has to be
based, are commoner for the period 1695–1705 than for
any other in pre-census times, and there is a danger that
our view of pre-industrial social structure as a whole may
for this reason (and because of the connected work over
the same years of Gregory King, see note 27) be true of the
1690's only. The act, its origin, its importance, its research
possibilities, its workings, are authoritatively discussed by
Professor Glass: see Glass, 1965, 1966, 1968, 1969.

---

39   See note 31. In the twelve first companies (Goldsmiths,
Drapers, etc.) the assessment went like this: Master £10
(equivalent to that for an Esquire), Liveryman £5
(equivalent to that for a gentleman); the liverymen were
ex-masters or potential masters and of the same social
standing), yeoman £3 (above a clergyman £2, but below a
gentleman).

---

40   *The poverty line in seventeenth-century England*
The families which Gregory King names as making up
that half of the population which was 'decreasing the wealth
of the kingdom' seems a rather miscellaneous assemblage:
seamen, 'labouring people and outservants', cottagers and
paupers, common soldiers and vagrants (see page 32).
Evidently King was not anxious to be specific about the
poor, and the major interest in these descriptions is what

they did not include. Obviously King did not think that
'shopkeepers and tradesmen', 'artisans and handicrafts'
were in permanent poverty since he places them above the
'decreasing' line, but this does not mean that the carpenters, bricklayers, masons, thatchers, weavers, coopers
and so on were always out of poverty. It seems much more
likely that they were in poverty at certain times of their
lives, or in bad seasons, or for some weeks even in good
seasons, but not perpetually dependent in the way that
labourers, cottagers, paupers and the common soldiery
were. This was the pattern of the industrial proletariat in
the late nineteenth century and the early twentieth century
when they were studied by Rowntree and Booth, see below
Chapter 9.

The statement in the text is true if King's estimates are
reliable. In an economy of the type he was describing any
person in receipt of a transfer income from the wealthier
people must surely be in need of such an income in order to
subsist, and this is the sense in which it seems best to
understand King's concept of 'increasing or decreasing' the
national wealth. It is very difficult to believe that such
transfers were taking place in order to equalize wealth, or to
add to the incomes of those who already had enough to
keep them out of poverty. No doubt such transfers did
go on in favour of the craftsmen who were sometimes liable
to poverty, but on balance craftsmen appear to have been
self-sufficient, which was perhaps why King did not think
of them as permanently among the decreasers.

---

41   Harrison, 1968 (1577, 1587), p. 115.

---

42   William Lambarde, *Perambulation of Kent*, 1570,
published 1576, reprinted at Chatham, 1826, p. 6,
modernized.

---

43   Thomas Westcote, *A View of Devonshire in 1630*,
edited by G. Oliver and P. Jones, Exeter, 1845.

---

44   Thomas Wilson, *The State of England*, 1600, edited by
F. J. Fisher, *Camden Miscellany*, 1936, p. 20.

45   See for example Sir John Doddridge, *Honors Pedigree*, 1652. The argument seems to have gone on since Elizabethan times, and Sir Thomas Smith took the minority view that apprenticeship did derogate from gentry.

46   *Urban Gentry*
See *The Visitations of London, 1633, 1634 and 1635*, Harleian Society, 2 vols., 1880–83. On merchants who had country houses at an earlier time, see Sylvia Thrupp, *The Merchant Class of Medieval London* (1948), Ann Arbor, Mich., 1962, and on city/country dynasties, Sir Anthony Wagner, *English Genealogy*, Oxford, 1960, p. 141, etc. As for gentry resident in cities, 4 of the 67 families resident in the London parish of St Mary le Bow in 1695 of known status (74 families in all) were described as gentry, and 16 of 205 (255) in the similar parish of St Peter Mancroft, Norwich, in 1694. There were 91 gentlemen, 21 esquires, 8 knights and a baronet in Bristol in 1696 (see Ralph and Williams, 1968, p. xxii). All these proportions are higher than the estimate for the population at large.

47   Westcote, 1845, p. 52.

48   *Some Considerations of the Consequences of Lowering of Interest*, 1692, Works, 1801, vol. 5, p. 71.

CHAPTER 3

The source for this chapter is mainly File 3, the listings file, of the Cambridge Group. But much important information is contained in parish documents, of course, and in ecclesiastical court cases, such as those printed by Brinkworth, *Archdeacon's Court*, 1942. Although there are great numbers of studies of medieval English villages in pre-industrial times from the political, economic, social, genealogical and even the demographic points of view, some of which are cited in the following notes to this chapter, I am not aware of a general work on the English village as such after medieval times and before the nineteenth or twentieth centuries. Something of the marketing structure can be gathered from a valuable chapter by Alan

Everitt in J. (ed.) Thirsk, *Agrarian History*, 1967, but
nothing has been written of the order of G. William
Skinner's remarkable analysis of *Marketing and Social
Structure in China*, 1964–5. The location, interrelationship,
size and structure of English settlements just before
industrialization remain to be investigated. For London,
however, important discussion has been undertaken by
Glass, 1966–8 and 1969, and Wrigley, 1967.

49   *Decline of Rural Communities*
See A. M. Carr-Saunders, D. Caradog Jones and C. A.
Moser. *A Survey of Social Conditions in England and Wales
as Illustrated by Statistics*, Oxford, 1958 (using the 1951
census), pp. 50–5. In 1961 as in 1951, over two-fifths of all
the English people lived in the conurbations, another fifth
in other towns greater than 50,000 in size, and a fifth only
in rural districts: see the *Preliminary Report to the 1961
Census of England and Wales*, p. 9.

In 1961 rather fewer people, 36·6 per cent as against 38·7
per cent of the population, lived in the conurbations than
in 1951, and there was a very slight increase in the
proportion living in rural areas. But the inhabitants of
towns of 50,000 to 100,000 went up quite sharply, and if
the drift to the great cities can be said to have been
checked, it would be impossible to show that country life
of a traditional kind had ceased to decline. These changes
may in any case be an effect of the suburbs spreading out
into areas still officially beyond the boundaries of towns.
Ronald Blythe's attractive book, *Akenfield, Portrait of an
English Village*, 1969, presenting rural experience in the
words of the inhabitants of a Suffolk settlement, implies a
transformation of life in the countryside which has been
rapidly intensified in recent years. What had survived of
the old agricultural village society, and especially
institutions like the parish church, seems to be being
supported by dormitory dwellers and by retired persons
almost as a kind of middle-class hobby.

50   For the size of London on the eye of industrialization,
see Glass, *Papers on Gregory King*, 1965, where King's
estimate is closely analysed: see also Wrigley, *London's
Importance*, 1967, especially references in footnote 1.

Tokyo is reckoned to have numbered a million people in the Tokugawa (period 1615–1868), and Japan may well have been more urbanized in the great city sense than any other country, since Kyoto and Osaka are said to have numbered up to half a million. (Paper on *Town and City in Pre-Modern Japan*, c. 1967, communicated by Prof. R. J. Smith of the Department of Anthropology, Cornell University.)

51   *Size of villages*
The Wingham area documents are in the Kent County Record Office. The difficulty with them, as with all problems of size of settlement, is the extent to which each named place in fact represented an independent settlement and not just an arbitrary area which existed for some traditional or administrative reason. Certainly the sixteen communities with less than 100 people, nearly a half of the sample, look rather suspect as villages, and some of them may have been gentlemen's seats rather than settlements. Nevertheless the distribution of settlements by size is known to be usually pronouncedly skewed in a negative direction, and in the nineteenth-century English censuses, places of under 100 inhabitants were still common. In 1801, of 100 named places, 14 were smaller than 100, the mean size was 476 and the median 273. In 1871 the median was still as low as about 380, and 12 per cent were smaller than 100. In both census years 15 per cent of the whole population was living in settlements of less than median size and in 1801 only a quarter in settlements of the order of the English pre-industrial city centre, that is places of 3,000 inhabitants and more. By 1871 this proportion had more than doubled and was soon to treble.

52   See Glass, *Papers on Gregory King*, 1965, p. 186. The source excerpted there is a manuscript notebook of King's called by Glass the Kashnor Manuscript, and now in the National Library of Australia. The table analysing the towns and cities is on p. 2 of the manuscript and is reproduced by Glass along with a paragraph of King's acknowledging the help and collaboration of John Adams, Adams, so King declares, worked at the Hearth Tax returns and Spelman's Villare Anglicum to prepare his own *Index Villaris* – for

both these works see below. The table drawn up by King
is in the form of totals of *houses*, not individuals, for each
town and in the text the figures have been converted into
populations by the use of the multiple 4·45 persons to a
house, the figure which Glass shows was the one used by
King himself.

53   See Goubert, *Beauvais*, 1960. On p. 255 he prints a
list of the number of *feux* in the thirty-five towns coming
after the three greatest from lists dating from 1713 and
1726. They have been converted into the approximations
given in the text by multiplying by five. Rough as this
work is, nothing at all comparable is yet possible for
England. Professor Goubert tells me that in France the
urbanized population was nevertheless not so much greater
in proportion than it was in England.

54   See J. Carrière, *La Population d'Aix-en-Provence à la
Fin du XVIIe Siècle, étude de démographic historique d'après
le registre de capitation de 1695*. Faculté des Lettres,
Aix-en-Provence, *Travaux et Mémoires, XI*, 1958,
mimeographed, from *La Pensée Universitaire*, 12 bis Rue
Nazareth, Aix-en-Provence. No English record of anything
like this extent has survived for so early a period and all
the facts in this study are of great social structural interest.

55   The Lichfield listing is amongst King's papers in the
Harleian Collection in the British Museum, no. 7022, folios
1–42; for comment see Glass, *Papers on Gregory King*, 1965,
pp. 181–3. This listing still counts as the longest to contain
ages and other particulars for any English community in
Stuart times yet added to Cambridge Group, File 3.

56   The figures for Norfolk parishes and for parishes in the
other counties referred to, come from Sir Henry Spelman,
*Villare Anglicum, or a View of all the Cities, Towns and
Villages in England* (1656), 2nd edition 1678. Spelman is
wrong about Lancashire, however, for he gives it only 36
parishes, yet 64 was correct in the 1650's.

57   Social structural and demographic work has been done
on all these villages, of an elementary character except for

Colyton, which is the first English village to have had its families successfully reconstituted (Cambridge Group, File 1). The published registers are also the evidence used for Widecombe (The Devon and Cornwall Record Society, Exeter, 1938) and Greystoke (transcribed and edited by A. M. Maclean and published at Kendal in 1911), but more extensive sources have been used for Cogenhoe, see Laslett and Harrison, 1963.

58   For the influence of ethnic origin on the social system in various areas of England see the work of George Homans, *English Villagers of the 13th Century*, Harvard, 1942, and 'The Frisians in East Anglia', *Economic History Review*, 1957.

59   For an authoritative discussion of enclosure and the voluminous literature on that subject see G. E. Mingay, *English Landed Society in the 18th century*, 1963, especially see pp. 179–88 and references. Recent writers seem unwilling to comment on the actual amount enclosed by 1700, if only because the precise area in, or potentially in, cultivation is so problematic, but one-seventh is the traditional proportion for about that date.

60   *Colonial American Demography and Social Structure*
The facts about English settlements in Massachusetts cited here all come from a study by S. C. Powell of the townships of Watertown and Sudbury, Mass., and the connections of those who established them with Sudbury, Suffolk, and Weyhill, Hants, Shaftesbury, Dorset, etc. Much of this important material, with an interesting analysis, was published as *Puritan Village, the Formation of a New England Town*, Wesleyan University Press, Middletown, Conn., 1963. The suggestion that the model for the New England township is to be found in the co-operative society of peasants in an open-field village was made as early as 1910 by William Cunningham; see *Common Rights at Cottenham and Stretham*, Camden Miscellany XII and references.

Though the materials on the early history of the structure of colonial communities is as yet little explored, and may not turn out to be as fruitful for detailed analysis, especially accurate demographic analysis, as English materials, several very interesting studies have recently appeared. Kenneth Lockridge on Dedham, Mass., 1966; Waters on Hingham, Mass., 1968, and especially the two monographs, by Demos on Plymouth Colony, 1970, and Greven on Andover, Mass., 1970, are opening up research on New England in a very promising way. Greven's book contains a thorough bibliography.

Virginia and the Southern colonies generally are not yet so much worked on, but Edmund Morgan is preparing a study of Virginian social structure in relation to the origins of slavery, which should set things going.

---

61   See Laslett, 'Gentry of Kent', 1948, and the work of Morgan cited in footnote 60.

---

62   See W. G. Hoskins, Galby and Frisby, in *Essays in Leicestershire History*, Liverpool University Press, 1950. Dr Hoskins also presents the social history of the much bigger village of Wigston Magna nearby (*The Midland Peasant*, 1957) until late in the seventeenth century as one dominated by substantial peasants and not by gentry.

---

63   For John Adams, see Dictionary of National Biography and for his *Index Villaris* see Glass, *Papers on Gregory King*, 1965, pp. 186–7. Adams' book was published in a revised edition in 1690 and again in 1700. In his original preface Adams said that 'I have used all possible Care, Industry and Pains in comparing the Villare Anglicum of Sir Henry Spelman (see above note 56), and the printed Tables of Speed's Maps, with the Maps themselves . . . regulating the whole by an Abstract taken from the Books of the Hearth Office' and Gregory King in the Kashnor Ms. (Glass, 1965, p. 186) repeats that this was what Adams did.

---

64   The county histories give numerous examples, e.g. Hasted on Kent, 1782.

---

65   For gentry in urban areas, see note 46, and for their distribution in a midland county, and their presence in

the county town, Warwick, see P. Styles, 'The Social
Structure of Kineton Hundred in the reign of Charles II',
Transactions of the Birmingham Archaeological Society,
1962. This is one of the very few studies of an important
subject, though see W. G. Hoskins on the Caroline Gentry
in *Devonshire Studies* (with H. P. R. Finberg) 1952.

66   The enquiry is known as the Compton census and
gave rise to several documents now forming part of
Cambridge Group, File 3.

67   Compare standard of 13·4 per cent for pre-industrial
England: see note 17 and Laslett, 1969(i).

68   That is documents forming part of Cambridge Group,
File 3. Reference is made in note 37 above to the confusion
which is often found in that file between yeomen and
husbandmen, a confusion which worsens in the eighteenth
century when labourers seem to absorb both, the larger
cultivators becoming farmers. It is notable, however, that
the detailed statistical analysis of 100 of the documents
established consistent differences between yeomen,
husbandmen and labourers in such parameters as mean
size of household, proportions of resident kin etc., see table
on p. 72 and Laslett, 1969(i).

69   See Hasted, *Kent*, 1782, II, 815.

70   This is Cogenhoe, Northants: see Laslett and Harrison,
Clayworth and Cogenhoe, 1963. Between 1618 and 1628
mean household size there varied between 4·92 and 5·11
and the actual size of the village between 150 and 185
(standard error 6·3). Similar calculations can now be made
for two French villages in the Pas-de-Calais in the
eighteenth century. At Hallines from 1778 to 1790 total
population varied between 228 and 272 ($\bar{X}$ 3.1). At
Longuenesse from 1761–76 population varied between
333 and 386 ($\bar{X}$ 8.7). See Laslett, *Brassage de Population*,
1968.

71   The great difference made to the social structure of a
village community by a married parson is well illustrated

by the position of the family of Christopher Spicer at
Cogenhoe, whose establishment was the largest in the
village from 1618–28, in the years when the manor-house
was vacant; compare also the position at Clayworth, see
Laslett and Harrison, 1963.

72   See above note 68, and Laslett, 1969(i).

73   Listing published by K. J. Allison, *Bulletin of the
Institute of Historical Research*, 1963. This listing is one of
the earliest in European history to give complete familial
detail with ages.

74   See Laslett and Harrison, 1963.

75   On the social structure of late seventeenth-century
London, see note 50 and references. The 9 London parishes
in Cambridge Group, File 3 have a mean of 27 per cent
servants in the population, and of 66 per cent of households
with servants. These proportions varied between 20·2 per
cent and 48 per cent (St Andrew Wardrobe) to 35 per
cent and 80·5 per cent (St Mary le Bow). These high
percentages were not confined to the capital since almost
30 per cent of the population of the central, high status
parish of St Peter Mancroft, Norwich, were servants in
1694, and 58 per cent of households had servants.

76   See Best's *Farming Book*, 1857 (1641), p. 93,
modernized.

77   *The Towne Booke of Clayworth*, described in Laslett and
Harrison, 1963, is an example of this.

78   The document containing the listing for Goodnestone
(see above p. 56) goes on, very exceptionally, to provide
these details.

79   See the Rector's Book of Clayworth described in
Laslett and Harrison, p. 43, and the parish register still in
the parish, which records the christening of Elizabeth,
daughter of Ralph and Anne Meers on June 10th, 1679.
The couple had evidently married outside the village. Their

little girl died in the following September. It is interesting
that Anne should have had the courage or the conscientious-
ness to bring the child to the font after such a public
rebuke, for it shows the hold the church still had over the
people. Noteworthy too is that Ralph Meers should
have become a churchwarden at Clayworth, although a
labourer all his life.

For the practice of Easter communion, the duties of
parishioners to attend and of the priest to refuse the cup to
the sinful, and for the making out of lists of communicants
(which was required by the canons of the Oxford diocese)
see Peyton, *Churchwardens' Presentments*, 1928, pp. xxxvi
and xxxvii.

---

80 See K. S. Inglis, *Churches and the Working Classes in
Victorian England*, 1963. The contrast between the evidence
presented there for the working-class suburbs of Victorian
England and the situation at places like Goodnestone and
Clayworth two centuries before is truly astonishing. It has
been doubted, however, whether church going was so
faithfully maintained in Stuart times, amongst the servants,
labourers and paupers.

---

81 *Rector's Book* (see note 79), pp. 114 and 140; (135
Easter Communicants, 1696, 126 Easter Communicants,
1701) and other passages cited in the article by Laslett and
Harrison.

For compulsory attendance at church services, on holy
days as well as Sundays, see e.g. Shaw, *Parish Law*, 1733,
p. 97, or any collection of ecclesiastical court documents.
Peyton, in his edition of the Oxfordshire cases, discusses
compulsory attendance at the sacrament also, and the
difference it must have made to the village community
when everyone's presence in church ceased to be required
after the Toleration Act of 1689, pp. xxxvi–xlvii. This
may explain the fall in communicants at Clayworth:
compare quotation of 1692 (an archdeacon's letter about
church attendance) in Brinkworth, 1942, p. lxx.

---

82 Sources described in Laslett and Harrison. It might be
added that there are occasional records of such meetings in
schoolhouses where these existed.

83   See Powell, 1963.

84   The files of the meetings of the justices of the peace
of the counties at quarter-sessions are full of references to
the granting, abuse and withdrawal of licences to keep
ale-houses, but the numbers of inns mentioned are very
small. For a good example of this type of record, see
Lancashire Quarter Sessions Records, Sessions Rolls 1590–
1606, edited by James Tait, Chetham Society, Manchester,
1917. Inns were used for meetings of institutions of
considerable local importance, however, even for those of
the archdeacons' courts; Peyton, *Oxfordshire Peculiars*, 1928,
p. lxi.

85   Gregory King preserved a copy of this listing of the
inhabitants of Harefield in 1699, and it is to be seen
amongst his papers in the Public Record Office, ref.
T64/302.

86   It is recorded by John Aubrey, see his *Brief Lives*,
ed. O. L. Dick, 1949, p. 148.

87   For the Wawens, see Rector's Book of Clayworth.

88   The Clayworth documents do not include the Wawen
estate records and we know nothing of how they ran their
land. The best example known to me of a landowner who
recorded his decisions and reflections on how much land he
would let, how much day-labour he would use and how large
a household he would keep and how much he would get
done for him by piecework is Robert Loder of Harwell, who
had a small gentleman's estate on the site of what is now
the Atomic Energy Establishment, and whose account book
was published in 1936 by G. E. Fussell, *Robert Loder's Farm
Accounts, 1610–20* for the Camden Series, vol. 53. Loder
keeps calculating that he would be better off if he did no
housekeeping, but nevertheless in some years had eleven
people in his 'family'. The pressure on him to maintain his
establishment must have been very strong, for as all his
readers have noticed, he was hypersensitive to profit and
loss. His farming and household arrangements are far from

clear, unfortunately, and he would seem to have meant by
keeping servants 'at board wages', not only or even usually
having them with him for a whole year at a time, but
having them come and live for the ploughing, or the
threshing, or the harvest. Much work on the actual
disposition of labour on the land remains to be done.

---

89.   E. Corbett, *A History of Spelsbury*, Banbury, 1962,
p. 170.

---

90   In the Gloucestershire muster rolls of 1608 (see John
Smith, 1902 (1608)) several villages are given in which
every male inhabitant of military age is recorded as servant
to the lord of the manor, for example Postlipp, 'whereof
Giles Brodway gent, is lord' and where eleven 'servants to
Giles Brodway, gent' are the only names mustered. There
is no way of demonstrating that such villages consisted of
nothing but one great house, since some of these men may
well have been outservants and householders: there were
perhaps other male inhabitants unfit for service. But the
lord of the manor's establishment was obviously the
community for all practical purposes.

---

91   See Chapter 6, and Laslett and Harrison, 1963.

CHAPTER 4

The sources for this chapter are mainly File 1
(reconstitution), File 2 (aggregative returns) of the
Cambridge Group for the History of Population and Social
Structure, with important additions from File 3 (listings).
Research into historical demography and biological history
has grown considerably since this book was originally
written and it is good to say that there now exists in
English a compendium of technique, an authoritative
general statement of the position which research has now
reached and an up-to-date guide to sources. The first of
these books, *An Introduction to English Historical
Demography*, edited by E. A. Wrigley, 1966 (see note on
the Cambridge Group) remains indispensable to the student

of this developing subject, though even in the last 4 years
methods have been changing, especially in respect of
computerization. The second, E. A. Wrigley's *Population
and History*, 1969, is a masterly survey, not only for its
extraordinary feat of compression but also for the
hypotheses which it advances and the critical discussion it
contains. The third, T. H. Hollingsworth's *Historical
Demography*, 1969, is a compendium of titles, data and
results, accurate and extremely useful as a bibliography,
though ill-organized and wayward, even captious, in its
discussion of the demographic problems. A beginner should
be guarded against discouragement by this book. A further
and much shorter title, Schofield's article on 'Historical
Demography' of 1971, is particularly terse and
illuminating.

Two further general titles may be mentioned: a volume
called *Population in History* edited by D. V. Glass and
D. E. C. Eversley in 1965, which has a remarkably useful
selection of titles published over a number of recent years,
and the issue of *Daedalus*, the Journal of the American
Academy of Arts and Sciences, devoted to historical
population studies, and edited by Stephen Graubard in
1968. For those with an interest in the comparative nature
of historical demography, and cross national, cross cultural
and cross temporal comparisons are essential to the whole
pursuit, the obvious first step is to France. The literature in
French is daunting in its extent but there has been a recent
statement of its aims and progress in a special number of
the well-known journal of French social history, *Annales:
Economies, Sociétés, Civilisations*. It was published in 1969
under the general title *Histoire Biologiques et Sociétés* as
No. 6 of the 24th year of the journal.

No attempt has been made in the revision of this chapter
to extend its coverage over this enormous and growing field
beyond the necessary revision and extension of statements
published in 1965 which seem unsatisfactory and incomplete
in 1971.

---

92   The references here are to Romeo and Juliet, Act I,
scene ii, lines 8–11; scene iii, lines 69–73; The Tempest,
Act I, scene ii, lines 44 and 54. It has now been suggested
that Lady Capulet might in fact have been an old woman

(see above p. 84), if the reading 'a mother' be substituted
for 'your mother'. See Richard Hosley, in *Shakespeare
Quarterly*, Winter 1967.

---

93 *Age at Marriage*
Taken at random from vol. II of *Canterbury Marriage
Licences 1619–60*, edited by J. M. Cowper, Canterbury,
1894. Mrs Vivien Elliott, of Lucy Cavendish College,
Cambridge, provided these figures and statistics in revision
of those printed in 1965, which were however not very
different. The difference in age at marriage between gentle
and other grooms is significant at ·05, for gentle brides at
·02, and for the age gap between partners at ·01. Since the
social status of those married by licence shows an obvious
tendency to be higher (there is a noticeable excess of gentry
in the entries), and since those higher in the social scale on
the whole married younger than the rest, this bias is perhaps
compensated for. Some work has been done on the age at
marriage from these sources by other scholars (notably
by J. D. Chambers in his *Vale of Trent, 1670–1800*, [1957],
where marriage partners are classified by social origin) and
we ourselves have compared the results from Canterbury
with those obtained from Lincoln, Nottinghamshire,
Gloucestershire and elsewhere: the whole class of record is
usefully discussed by P. McGrath in his note published in
B. Frith's edition of *Gloucestershire Marriage Allegations*,
Bristol, 1954. Mrs Elliott is making a concerted attack on
these materials for demographic and social structural
purposes. Much more accurate and socially
representative data on age at marriage from family
reconstitution, though confined to individual settlements,
amply confirms these results. At Colyton, women had a
mean age at first marriage of $26\frac{1}{2}$ to $27\frac{1}{2}$ from 1560 to 1647,
when it rose to 30 and was actually three years higher than
the age of their husbands. It remained above 25 until 1800
whilst the age of men never fell to that level, see Wrigley,
1966(ii). The French results are similar, though never so
remarkable. At Crulai mean age at first marriage for men
in the seventeenth and eighteenth centuries was 27·2 and
for women 24·6 (Gautier and Henry, 1958, p. 84) and in
Brittany in the eighteenth century women at first marriage
were always older than 25, men 30–31 (Goubert, in

Daedalus, 1968, p. 594). In the Census Report for 1881, mean age at marriage for England and Wales is given as 25·9 for men and 24·4 for women. It had not varied by more than 0·3 years since 1867 and it was stated that the English marriage rate was the highest in Europe and we marry at an earlier age than all other European countries, except Russia. Schofield, 1971(i), contains some searching remarks on the importance of the age of marriage to general historical study, as well as to demographic history.

94   These figures are not published as such by Hollingsworth, *Demography of the Peerage*, 1964, and Wrigley (1969, p. 104) using data from Hollingsworth's Table 6 on p. 15, calculates mean age at first marriage of peers 1600–24 at 21·4 for women, 26·8 for men.

95 *Age at sexual maturity*
These figures are all from J. M. Tanner, *Growth at Adolescence*, 2nd ed., 1962. The known facts and the then state of research on this intricate subject are conveniently summarized, with references, in an editorial entitled 'Early Maturing and Larger Children' in the *British Medical Journal*, August 19th, 1961. The statistical basis of such work for periods earlier than the twentieth century has sometimes been called into question and it will be some time before reliable inferences can be made. Work in progress at Cambridge on a listing of the Serbian (orthodox Christian) inhabitants of Belgrade in 1733 which gives crude ages for nearly all inhabitants (see Laslett, 1970(ii)) shows that over 70 per cent of all women aged 15–19 were married. Though only a few of these very young women had children accompanying them, it must be presumed that all were past menarche, since it was a strict rule of the Christian church, Eastern as well as Western, that marriage was conditional on both parties being sexually mature. It is not therefore easy to suppose that mean age at menarche can have been as high as about 17 at Belgrade in 1733 (which from the Norwegian and English figures Tanner assumes to have been the general European level in the earlier nineteenth century), and the impression is that most women were marriageable at about 16 or earlier. There is evidence, moreover, that in fifteenth-century

Italy the situation was rather similar: see note 97. If in these countries at these times menarche was already at about the age characteristic of industrial society in the early twentieth century, then the inferences made in the text about late sexual maturity in Elizabethan society generally are perhaps too strong. Nevertheless the question of date of maturation is so important to the whole subject of this book that it has seemed best to retain the very speculative account of it given in the text.

---

96   *Child marriage*

For Porter's play see Malone Society, 1912, ed. Greg, vol. II, pp. 650–69, and for Lyly's *Mother Bombie* see *Old English Plays*, ed. C. W. Dilke, vol. I, 1814.

I am indebted to Professor Muriel Bradbrook, Mistress of Girton College, for the literary references to child marriage quoted in the text, and the discussion of them is mainly hers. A valuable treatment of marriage in Elizabethan dramatic literature will be found in an essay by A. Percival Moore published in 1909 for the Leicestershire Architectural and Archaeological Society, called *Marriage Contracts or Espousals in the Reign of Queen Elizabeth*. Several passages are quoted from the minor dramatists, though the interest is not in child brides. Moore cites however from T. D. Whitaker's *History of Craven*, the case of Margaret, Lady Rowcliffe, who was married in 1463 at the age of 4, and was a widow by the age of 12: she remarried then, but the bridegroom's father undertook that 'they should not ligg togeder til she came to the age XVI years'. This is the plainest indication I have seen of the time at which a woman of late medieval times could be expected to be sexually mature.

---

97   *Child marriage*

For Lady Rowcliffe, see Moore, 1909, quoting Whitaker's *History of Craven*. The diary of Robert Furse is printed in *Report and Transactions of the Devonshire Association for the Advancement of Science, Literature and Art*, Plymouth, 1894, vol. XXVI, p. 181. These two cases closely resemble the marriage customs of fifteenth-century Italy, and the rarity of such practices in England in the sixteenth century may point to a sharp difference due to culture as well as to period. In the town and surroundings of Arezzo in Tuscany

in 1427–30, for example, 'Girls *maritate ma non ite* that is
who expected to have tax deducted when the marriage
contract (in negotiation) was concluded, had an average
age of 15·4 years. If their daughters attained 17 years
without having found a husband, their fathers grew
desperate.' See Klapisch, *Fiscalité et Démographie*, 1969,
p. 1327.

98   See B. S. Rowntree, *Poverty* (of 1961) and the *British
Medical Journal*, Aug. 19, 1961, p. 502, editorial.

99   *Married brothers and sisters coresiding*
This law is borne out by all the listings of communities
which we have so far examined. In England, no instance of
married siblings making up one household has been found
as yet, for example, and the proportion of households
containing married children with their spouses is usually
negligible, see Laslett, 1970(ii). The collected papers of the
conferences reported upon there, show that the simultaneous
presence of two married couples was rare in seventeenth-
century France and eighteenth-century Holland or Corsica,
but seemingly rarest of all in England. At most 30 of 1,445
households in six English settlements contained more than
one married couple.

100   See P. Willmott and M. Young, *Family and Class in a
London Suburb*, 1960, Table III, p. 37 and compare the
same authors' *Family and Kinship in East London*, 1959
(1957). The figures and percentages are not, of course,
strictly comparable with those from pre-industrial England
quoted in the text.

101   See E. W. Hofstee and G. A. Kooy, 'Traditional
Household and Neighbourhood Group in Parts of the
Eastern Netherlands', *Transactions of the Third World
Congress of Sociology*, 1956, vol. IV, p. 75. In his paper to
the conference of 1969 (see Laslett, 1970(ii)), A. M. Van
der Woude analyses Hofstee's general theory of the
sociological history of the Dutch family, and shows that it is
quite inappropriate to eighteenth-century Holland, where
mean household size often fell below 4·0.

102   See e.g., Lancashire Quarter Sessions (Tait, 1917), pp. 56, 143, 247, 260 etc.

103   Gregory King estimated that 2–2½ per cent of the houses in the Hearth Tax returns were empty, but more than this in London; Glass, *Papers on Gregory King*, 1965, p. 185. Eight out of 117 houses in Harefield were vacant in 1699. There were times when housing does seem to have been short in the pre-industrial era, notably perhaps under Elizabeth, when population was increasing.

104   S. C. Ratcliff and H. C. Johnson, Warwick Quarter Sessions, Vol. 5 *Warwick County Records*, 1939, p. 65.

105   The Colyton figures are from Wrigley, 1968, p. 574: for a critical analysis, see Hollingsworth, 1969, pp. 186–9. Gregory King's figure is to be found amongst the calculations in his papers now in the Public Record Office, ref. T 64/302, pagination not given. Halley's table is reproduced here from M. Greenwood, *Medical Statistics from Graunt to Farr*, Cambridge, 1948, p. 44. Hollingsworth interpreting Ruwet, estimates expectation of life at birth in a Belgian village in 1635 to have been about 23 (Hollingsworth, 1969, p. 171).

Surprisingly high estimates for expectation of life in the New England colonies come from Demos, 1970 (who prints figures for both men and women after age 21 on p. 192: his figure of 45 at birth comes from an earlier article): Greven, 1970, pp. 107–10: Lockridge, 1966, see Section VI. But the quality of these data and the consequent reliability of these estimates has been doubted, and work in progress may well revise them downwards, at least for the eighteenth century.

106   Story slightly extended, using further documents, from Laslett and Harrison, 1963. In many of the listings in Cambridge Group, File 3, one or two members of a household are found on parish relief, or even in the poorhouse, when the head is not. It is often an 'inmate', or a widowed relative, or even a parent of a spouse.

107   At Clayworth in 1676, two-thirds of the solitaries were widowed persons; in 1688 all of them were. In 1599 at Ealing out of 7 solitaries 3 were widows; of the 26 solitary persons at Lichfield in 1696, 14 were widows and 4 were widowers; 8 of the widows were paupers.

---

108   See Best, 1857 (1641), pp. 116–17. On the next paragraph in the text, see notes 161 and 162 below.

---

109   *Orphaned Brides and Bridegrooms*
First results of reconstitution by computer (Cambridge Group, File 1) show that there is no significant difference in age at marriage by birth order, for males or females. This implies that marriage did not ordinarily depend on the death of either of parent. If it had done younger children would have been able to marry earlier than older children.

The proportion given in the text of about a quarter of all marriages being remarriages can be confirmed from any detailed register, but it varies, as might be expected. At Crulai it was 19·4 per cent (Gautier and Henry, p. 83). At Manchester, of 397 marriages in the 1650's 132 (33·3 per cent) were remarriages, where one partner or other had been previously married and 46 (11·5 per cent) remarriages where both the partners had been widowed. Of 305 brides marrying for the first time, 178 (58·3 per cent) had lost their fathers, and of 279 similar bridegrooms, 136 (49 per cent) had lost their fathers too. For the general importance of a child surviving its parents, see Schofield, 1971.

The Manchester registers for 1653–65/6 were published in 1949, edited by J. Flitcroft and E. B. Leech for the Lancashire Parish Register Society. They are particularly detailed during the period of civil registration under the Commonwealth, 1655–7.

---

110   See Laslett and Harrison, 1963. Clayworth is the only settlement in File 3 of the Cambridge Group which has this information, but registers sometimes note cases of repetitive marriage. Those for Adel were edited in 1895 by G. D. Lumb for the Thoresby Society.

111   *The Nubile unmarried* in England and in France in
in pre-industrial times as well as since, together with the
relatively late age at marriage, mark these countries as
European in the sense used by Hajnal in his famous article
European Marriage Patterns, 1965. These characteristics
distinguish Northern and Western Europe on the one hand
from Southern and Eastern Europe and much of the rest
of the world on the other: the contrast with Belgrade in
1733 (see note 95) is striking.

These important issues will be reported on in the volume
arising out of the Cambridge Conference of 1969, see
Laslett, 1970(ii). Though the information on age in File 3
of the Cambridge Group is so sparse, and marital
descriptions the least reliable of details which can be
recovered, unmarried individuals are found in English
settlements after the age of 50. Gautier and Henry state
quite forthrightly, however (1958, p. 76), that amongst
women 'the proportion of the unmarried amongst the old
was low, if not very low'.

112   For the effect of suckling in delaying fresh conception,
see Gautier and Henry, Crulai, 1958, especially Chapter
VII, and Wrigley, *Population and History*, 1969, p. 92 etc.

113   See Henry, *Families Genevoises*, 1956. The facts about
recognizing family limitation are given in Wrigley,
Population and History, 1969, see e.g. pp. 87–8. The family
reconstitution at Banbury, from which the figures in the
text are drawn, is being carried out by Mrs Susan Stewart,
and promises to be very interesting in many directions.

114   See Wrigley, *Family Limitation*, 1966, and for
contraception in France in the 1770's, see Chamoux and
Dauphin, *Châtillon*, 1966. The whole subject of contraception
in historical times is discussed at length in the special issue
of the French periodical *Annales*, 1969, no. 6: see especially
the article by Dupâquier and Lachiver.

115   The 24 English parishes whose collective quotient is
quoted here come from File 2, Aggregative Returns, of the
Cambridge Group, and have been specifically studied for
illegitimacy. See the table on p. 142 above and below note
157.

116   The places from which the figures on this page are taken all come from Cambridge Group, File 3, and represent most of our present (April 1970) information on age distribution in England before the Census. A newly discovered document for Grasmere, Wordsworth's village in Westmorland, in 1683, yields a mean age of 28·4.

---

117   The account of childhood in traditional England given in the text can be filled out from Philippe Ariès' remarkable book, *Centuries of Childhood*, 1962 (1960), though some of his inferences from his exclusively literary sources are rather different from my own from listings. It is not yet clear how far these differences are due to variation between England and France. Morgan, *Puritan Family*, 1966 (1944), Chapter V, is the best description of childhood in the English-speaking family, though it can be filled out for New England from Demos, 1970.

CHAPTER 5

Sources used for starvation are Cambridge Group, File 3, and the information contained in Goubert on *Beauvais*, 1960. Goubert's book remains the fullest discussion of the subject and even the analysis in Wrigley, *Population and History*, 1969, which is the only other consideration of the problem in English, draws heavily on Goubert's illustrations.

Plague is far better documented, though the one source of figures covering any number of communities is also Cambridge Group, File 3. The large recent book by J. F. D. Shrewsbury, *A History of Bubonic Plague*, 1970, contains a a great deal of information as well as extensive discussion. Important as it is, some of the historical judgements in this book are remarkably naïve, and the mortality statistics occasionally inconsistent with figures in Cambridge Group File 2. The medical problems are authoritatively treated in L. F. Hirst, *The Conquest of Plague*, 1953, and there is an acute and interesting recent analysis in Hollingsworth, *Historical Demography*, 1969 (see especially appendix II, with an exhaustive bibliography on this subject which has a voluminous literature).

118   See Goubert (*Beauvais*, 1960) Chapter III, *Structures Démographiques*, and especially section 3, *Analyse des Crises Démographiques*, for an impressive exposition of this tendency in the Beauvais area, and for references to previous work in France, also superficially surveyed in the article by Laslett and Harrison, 1963, p. 172. The evidence from a dozen or more villages is presented in the volume of graphs appended to Goubert's work. In conversation Professor Goubert has told me that the one-crop, one-harvest, textile-producing character of the Beauvais region may be the reason for its particular liability to periodical starvation, which is not so easy to demonstrate in all areas of France. Compare Wrigley, *Population and History*, 1969, Chapter III for the effect of mixed farming on the food situation of the English peasantry.

119   Evidence for starvation in Scotland can be found in many sources, and is particularly well marked in the Register of the Scottish Privy Council. It seems to be most conspicuous in the early 1620's when the English evidence is clearest, but Scotland, like France, was also stricken in the 1690's, see below.

120   The manuscript diary of John Locke is in the Bodleian Library and this volume is MS Locke f. 5, see pp. 19–22. His English has been modernized. I cannot confirm his check on Alice George's account of Queen Elizabeth's journey to Worcester. She did go there in 1575 but not in 1588, as far as I can see.

121   Best, *Farming Book*, 1857 (1641), pp. 42–3.

122, 190   *Residential Propinquity and Kinship Networks*
The facts about Bethnal Green are summarized and compared with those for Woodford in Willmott and Young, *Family and Kinship*, 1959 (1957), Chapter 4, showing that middle-class parents, especially elderly ones, are as apt to live close to their middle-class children as working-class parents are. This result has been confirmed since for other British cities. No detailed analysis has been made as yet for the evidence on propinquity of residence of kin in the

listings in Cambridge Group, File 3, apart from the one
quoted in the text for Lichfield, though the data have been
collected. They give the impression that the town dwellers
of pre-industrial England were no more liable to live in
propinquity with their kin than town dwellers are today,
and they may perhaps have been less liable to do so. Since
the peasantry lived in such small communities, they could
only have resided within easy reach of a large number of
their kin if each settlement had been composed of only very
few kinship networks. Though parishes varied in this
respect, the evidence is all against supposing that this last
circumstance was at all common. In traditional England
your relatives may have lived within a small area, but
difficulty of travel and inability to write must have made
everyday communication far more difficult than it is in a
contemporary working-class area or middle-class suburb.
For a further discussion in relation to literacy, see below
p. 203 and note 190.

---

123   John Graunt, *Natural and Political Observations upon
the Bills of Mortality, 1662*, etc., reprint edited by W. F.
Willcox, Baltimore, 1939, p. 33. For a definitive assessment
of the accuracy and value of Graunt's work, see D. V.
Glass, 'John Graunt and his Natural and Political
Observations', *Proceedings of the Royal Society*, B, vol.
159, 1964.

---

124   The account in the text is based on Goubert, see note
198. In a petition of the hard-pressed tax collectors of
Scotland to the Chancellor of the Scottish Exchequer in
February 1700, asking for remission of the excise because
of starvation, famine is defined by the following
characteristics. 'Many people dye starving': 'the generality
of the yeomanry cannot afford enough for their support':
imports of food are insufficient: famine and the fear of it
are publicly admitted: famine exists in other parts of
Europe. All these circumstances, the document declared,
were present in Scotland in 1698. Scottish Record Office
E 8/58. The Scottish Parish Registers, almost every one of
which is in the Edinburgh Record Office, apparently nowhere
go back as far enough as to make it possible to check the

effect of these circumstances on births, marriages and deaths.

---

125   Goubert 76–7. In the original text the price of bread is sometimes given in *deniers* and these have been converted to *sols* at 10 *deniers* a *sol*. For the Scottish quotation, see note 124. It has to be said that the original insists that the eating of such food was 'never before heard of in this nation'.

---

126   The parish registers of Ashton-under-Lyne, Lancashire, were published in 1927 and 1928 by H. Brierley. The parish was already heavily engaged in textiles. Though unfortunately marred by gaps, the registers contain extraordinarily full information, especially for the years 1590–1640, including abortions, suicides, etc. The Yorkshire area mentioned covers the parish of Leeds and the wapentakes of Morley and Agbrigg, whose vital statistics are surveyed in a useful article by Michael Drake, 'An Elementary Exercise in Parish Register Demography', *Economic History Review*, 1962, using calendar years not harvest years, and births, not conceptions.

---

127   For Greystoke, see note 57. My attention was drawn to these registers by Dr W. G. Howson of Lancaster, whose article on 'Plague, Poverty and Population in Parts of North-West England', 1960, is a most suggestive and interesting one for the question of levels of subsistence in England.

---

128.   Statement of the Westmorland Justices quoted by J. Thirsk, 'Industries in the Countryside', in *Essays in Honour of R. H. Tawney*, ed. F. J. Fisher, 1961, Cambridge, p. 82. Mrs Thirsk goes on to say of these northern counties: 'A crisis of famine and consequent plague could easily be precipitated by a harvest failure. The justices . . . of Westmorland . . . were explaining the gravity of a crisis caused by the scarcity of bread.' Howson talks of the culminating disaster of 1622–3 as affecting the whole North Western area, and indeed its consequences may well have been felt all over the country. In 24 parishes (see note 115) a surplus of baptisms over burials of 2,175 in the decade

1611–20 and of 2,015 in 1621, gave way to a surplus of 9 burials over baptisms in the decade 1621–9, and examination shows that, as at Ashton-under-Lyme, the bad years were 1622–5.

129   See Wrigley, 1966(ii), p. 85. By no means all the registers in Cambridge Group, File 2 show burial surpluses in the 1640's, nor is the effect in the early 1620's by any means universal.

130   For the mortality pattern of pellagra, see F. and V. W. Sargent, 'Season, Nutrition and Pellagra', *New England Journal of Medicine*, 1950.

131   I owe the extract from the Wednesbury register to Mr J. F. Ede, late of Wednesbury Boys' High School. The registers of St Margaret's, Westminster, were published in 1914 by A. M. Burke, and give causes of death from May 18th to November 28th, 1557. The fact that 16 of the 181 so accounted for were due to famine may call Graunt's confidence into question.

132   This type of activity of English governments and city fathers is well summarized in E. Lipson, *The Economic History of England*, 9th edition, 1947, vol. i, p. 302, etc., vol. ii, pp. 419–48.

133   The account in the text is based on Shrewsbury, *Bubonic Plague*, 1970, and on Hirst, *The Conquest of Plague*, 1953. Shrewsbury follows the bubonic plague all over the British Isles from its arrival in the fourteenth century to its departure late in the seventeenth century, using literary sources of all kinds, and after 1538 the parish registers, sometimes basing his diagnosis on the analysis of deaths by month and year.

134   *Disappearance of Bubonic Plague*
Hollingsworth, in his account of the plague (*Historical Demography*, 1969, appendix II, etc.) includes the Black Death itself amongst the outbreaks which caused their highest mortality much earlier in the year than the late

summer. He presents the results of mathematical analysis of plague, which lays down that the severer the plague, the shorter its duration, and this might well mean that very dangerous epidemics exhausted themselves rather earlier than the classic London plagues of 1625 and 1666. Hollingsworth is content to state it as proven that the bubonic plague disappeared from England because of the extinction of the black rat, but Shrewsbury will have it that it was due rather to a change of the trade route to Central Asia from overland to the ocean, neither of which assertion seems to me very satisfactory. The great French authority on the plague, J. N. Biraben (see his *Plague in France*, 1968), suggests that an immunizing disease, bacteriologically related to the plague, may have been spreading in the relevant period in Europe. It is Biraben also who insists that *pulex irritans* may have been capable of spreading bubonic plague from individual to individual, as well as body lice.

135   See J. C. Cox, *The Parish Registers of England*, 1910, p. 175.

136   By Biraben, see note 134.

137   See Goubert, 1960, pp. 59–67. But he reaches a very different provisional conclusion for Brittany (see note 118), which he now believes was worse off in the eighteenth than the seventeenth century.

138   For the Ashton-under-Lyne registers, see note 126, and for infantile mortality at demographic crises, Goubert, 1960, p. 54. The rise in this index at Greystoke, 1623–4, is naturally not very well documented.

139   See Graunt, 1939 (1662).

140   The burial practices of earlier times are described in the rewarding work by J. S. Burn on *The History of the Parish Registers in England* written by him in 1829 and revised in 1862. See pp. 127, 224 of the 1862 edition. See also Steel, *Parish Registers*, 1968, Vol. 1, p. 72.

141   The figures from Crulai must be regarded as the most
reliable for a rural French community, though that for the
Paris region is based on the largest sample (see Henry
and Levy in *Population*, 1962). Goubert gives the Auneuil
figure, and on p. 40 he prints the details of infant and child
mortality for the village of St Laurent-des-Eaux in
mid-France, to demonstrate that the high rates round
Beauvais were not exceptional. Paul Deprez presented the
figure from Vieuxbourg to the International Population
Conference in September, 1961.

142   See Wrigley, *Mortality*, 1968, p. 570, and for an
account of infant mortality, its relative levels and its
significance in industrial and pre-industrial urban and rural
society, his *Population and History*, 1969. Figures from the
reconstitution of Banbury (see note 113), seem to imply a
much higher infantile mortality rate than has been found
elsewhere in England, which is interesting since Banbury
is more town-like than the other places so far subjected to
the process.

143   For Graunt's exercises, see note 123. Unfortunately he
breaks down his totals of burials under headings for the
years 1629–36 and 1657–60 only. Since Graunt had a
heading 'Abortive and Stillborn' his abortion figures are
more straightforward. In our own day the estimated rate
of spontaneous abortion is $7\frac{1}{2}$–11 per cent.

144   Infantile mortality is reckoned at Clayworth from
persons recorded by Sampson in his parish register as dying
within 12 months of their registered births, together with
other burials of 'infants' so described. The cereal indices
have been reckoned from his own meticulous accounts,
entered into the *Rector's Book* every year, of crops which
he grew and sold. It takes no account of course of the
varying proportions of these grains in the food of the people
in his village, or of such things as the substitution of
cheaper for dearer grains when prices rose.

145   *Rector's Book*, pp. 46–9. Harvest in 1678 was
'very sickly for servants'. Unfortunately the names of

children born in 1678 and 1679 are missing, so we cannot recover infantile mortality. The late Professor J. D. Chambers of Nottingham, the authority on this area, believed that high mortality at Clayworth and elsewhere was 'more a reflection of epidemics than of harvest conditions. . . . The standard of life was such as to enable the Nottinghamshire peasantry to withstand the worst effects of bad harvests' (letter of May 1963).

CHAPTER 6

The sources used in this chapter are again Files 1 (reconstitution), and 3 (listings) of the Cambridge Group. Accurate and detailed information from File 1 on such subjects as illegitimacy and prenuptial conception can be quite extensively supplemented from File 2, aggregative returns. A special sub-file on bastardy is being developed. Records of the disciplinary courts of the church are a most important source of additional information, and the presentments from the Oxfordshire Peculiars, edited by Peyton in 1928, contain a valuable survey of data of this kind.

No historical study has yet been made of sexual behaviour and conformity to norms in and after the pre-industrial period, though much has been written from literary sources. Articles are beginning to appear however, such as those of Hair on *Bridal Pregnancy*, 1966, and 1970; Marchant, *The Church under the Law*, 1969, is a study of church discipline in which a lot of attention is given to sexual offences.

146   The intelligence quotient of the rural population has consistently fallen below that of the urban population as measured for schoolchildren, though very recently the correlation has been questioned. For a portrait of a contemporary village as a 'dying culture', see W. M. Williams, *The Sociology of an English Village: Gosforth*, 1956.

147   See J. Ruwet, in *Population*, 1954; for a criticism see Goubert, 1960, p. 51. The view now being taken up is slightly different from the one criticized in the text. The

rise in illegitimacy ratios in England in the middle of the eighteenth century is becoming known, and is being explained as a reaction to industrialization. Though this process does cause anomie, it also implies an increase in prosperity, and therefore this view modifies the very general assumption that irregular behaviour of the kind in question increases at a time of depression and deflation, and decreases in times of prosperity and inflation.

---

148   *Homosexuality, etc.*
For acts of sexual incontinence, excommunication, etc., and for the attitude of ordinary people towards such sexual offences, see the cases printed by Peyton in 1928, Brinkworth (1942), or any collection from the Archdeacons' Courts. The title buggery was given to all offences 'against the order of nature committed by mankind with mankind, or beasts, or by woman willingly with beasts'. It was always punishable by death, but the form of execution seems to have differed from time to time: being buried alive, being burnt or drowned are all mentioned. By the early eighteenth century it was a felony, which presumably meant death by hanging, and it was insisted that actual penetration must be proved. This information comes from an ordinary manual for local magistrates, *Nelson's Justice of Peace*, 2nd ed., 1707, pp. 115–16. The paucity of cases makes one hope that the life of the homosexual was not in fact lived in terror of death.

---

149   This statement could only be demonstrated from a considerable body of evidence, which would be difficult to collect because chasms are so common in registers at that time. It is based on the unsystematic examination of births of bastards in February and March 1660–61 which would betray irregular intercourse in May 1660.

---

150   See Foxon's articles in the *Book Collector*, vol. 12, 1963, 'Libertine literature in England, 1660–1745'.

---

151   Low fertility lasting until the early '20s is attested by the French demographers and is one of the facts which complicate the issue of the age at menarche: most evidence

points to very regular conception within marriage, even if fertility was lower than it would be today without contraception.

---

152 See for example the statement about a wife's duties of cohabitation in William Gouge (see note to chapter 1); unwillingness would lead her husband to the whorehouse. Bawdy houses are mentioned in ecclesiastical court cases, and parish constables were given directions about suppressing them – see Shaw, *Parish Law*, 1733.

---

153 *Illegitimacy totals and repetitive bastard bearing*
In his work on illegitimacy at Wem, Mr R. A. Laslett found a total of some 590 bastards baptized between 1581 and 1812, of which 177, or 30 per cent, came from mothers who brought more than one spurious child to the font. The proportion due to 'repeaters' was 20 per cent during the early high, from 1581 to 1640, when however the ratio of illegitimate baptisms barely reached 4 per cent. The repeater proportion fell to 10 per cent in the low period, 1641 to 1720, when the ratio fluctuated between 1 per cent and almost 4 per cent. This proportion rose to 40 per cent in the final high, when the bastardy ratio rose steadily to 14 per cent at the end of the series. In 1801–10, when the ratio was over 12 per cent, a good 50 per cent of all bastards baptized were born of 'repeaters'. As for mothers of these serial illegitimacies, Sarah Wilde had six between 1773 and 1785, Martha Evans four between 1779 and 1798, Sarah Thornhills four between 1805 and 1810. Similar phenomena have been found at Colyton by Karla Oosterveen and at Alcester by Mrs Peggy Ford in connection with family reconstitution. The added details thus available show that sporadic instances of bastardy running in families may be found, though only a little of the total can be due to these cases. Girls who had had illegitimates afterwards sometimes got married, bastards did the same, and the tendency could run through men as well as women. These results will be published in Laslett and Oosterveen.

---

154 The number of acts of sexual intercourse likely to take place for any given conception presents a complex problem, requiring information about the timing of acts in relation to the point in the menstrual cycle when the woman ovulates, see for example Lachenbruch, *Intercourse and Conception*, 1967. The relevant information is unlikely ever to be available for extramarital conception, especially in past time. In 1960 Tietze estimated that under our own conditions of physical well being and within marriage the probability of pregnancy from a single act of coitus was about 1 in 50, and it must inevitably have been considerably lower between casual partners under less favourable, perhaps often the least favourable, conditions for conception.

155   A study made by geneticists of 1,417 white children about 1960 in the Detroit area showed that 1·4 per cent were demonstrably not fathered by their mothers' husbands, although not admitted by those mothers to be illegitimate. The corresponding figure for 523 negro children was 8·9 per cent: see Schacht and Gershowitz, 1961.

156   See Tait, 1917, pp. 94, 107, 228, 238.

157   This study is under preparation by Peter Laslett and Karla Oosterveen of the Cambridge Group, and will present in detail the results from the 24 parishes now published here, together with a critical appreciation of their dependability as an indication of behaviour over the whole country. The general question of bastardy ratios in relation to fertility levels will also be discussed, and an attempt will be made to analyse the reasons why levels of illegitimacy in pre-industrial England seem on the whole to have been positively rather than negatively related to sexual deprivation. Documentation for the other figures presented in the text will also be given.

158   The Westminster Registers (see note 131) have an editorial note on bastardy: those of St Augustine's, Bristol, were edited by A. Sabin in 1956. In the parish of St Saviours, Southwark, in the period 1601–20, the registered illegitimacy ratio was less than 1 per cent.

159   Ashton Registers (see note 126), p. 448, modernized. On the burial of suicides, see Steel, 1968, p. 74.

160   These calculations will be found in an appendix to S. E. Sprott, *The English Debate on Suicide*, La Salle, Ill., 1961, though rates are there reckoned as proportions of total burials rather than as proportions of the population.

I owe this reference to Mr Keith Thomas of St John's College, Oxford.

---

161 *Pre-Nuptial Pregnancy*

For the registers concerned, see previous notes: for Gosforth, see note 146, and for the Wylye and Cartmel, see the registers edited by G. R. Hadow, etc., in 1913 and H. Brierley, etc. (Lancs. Parish Register Society) 1907, 1957. The Crulai rates have been calculated from Gautier and Henry, 1958, and those for the three villages from Ganiage, 1963. The study of pre-nuptial pregnancy (called by him bridal pregnancy), has been extended since this table was drawn up by P. E. H. Hair: see his articles of 1966 and 1970. Drawing on 77 parishes in 24 English countries, he found that roughly a fifth of all brides were pregnant at marriage before 1700, and two-fifths after that. Rates did not appear to rise between the sixteenth and seventeenth centuries, and were higher in the North, and apparently in the West, in the earlier period than they were elsewhere. This is interesting in view of our finding that illegitimacy was higher in the early seventeenth century in these areas, but though Hair's second article is much more detailed than his first, it is not possible to say whether the full pattern of pre-nuptial pregnancy over time was similar to that of illegitimacy levels. These regional details come from his second article, based on rather fewer cases, and he is able to trace the phenomenon into the nineteenth century, where in one parish no marked rise is shown. Hair on the whole confirms the view taken in the text that promiscuity cannot be assumed, but is somewhat less impressed by the possibility that the phenomenon can be explained by pre-marital contract: he is sceptical of the effectiveness of church discipline in the matter.

162, 163 *Marriage Contracts and Sexual Intercourse*

See A. P. Moore, *Marriage Contracts*, 1909, p. 291, modernized. No such overt admission of sexual intercourse being the normal thing after a contract had been finally settled has been found elsewhere in this authority from the Leicestershire area, or from anywhere else in England. Nevertheless the impression given by many of the marriage cases so far published, especially those from the earlier period (see e.g. the volume edited by James Raine for the

Surtees Society in 1845) is that cohabitation was assumed after conclusion of the contract. The contract itself is ordinarily in dispute in these proceedings: it is much less frequently a question of whether intercourse took place.

163   *A Mountain Chapelry*, being a guide to the parish of Ulpha, written in 1934 by H. L. Hickes, and revised and reprinted in 1950 and 1960 by B. S. Simpson. For Scottish proceedings, see for example the *Sessions Book of the Parish of Minnigaff* privately printed in 1939 for the Marquis of Bute, edited by Henry Paton. I owe the passage from the Ely depositions to Roger Schofield; it has been modernized and slightly contracted.

In 1888 it was categorically stated that persons who had contracted espousals publicly in the required form, when cited for cohabitation, could only be required to solemnize the marriage in church, could not be punished in any other way. See the *Churchwardens' Accounts of Pittington*, etc., edited by Barmby for the Surtees Society, vol. 84, p. 347.

164   For the quotation from Gouge, see *Domesticall Duties*, 1622, pp. 198–9, 202–3, and for that from Perkins, *Works*, 1618, vol. 3, p. 672.

165   *Marriage by the Morall Law of God Vindicated against all Ceremonial Laws of Popes and Bishops destructive to Filiation, Aliment and Succession and the Government of Families and Kingdoms*, 1680 (Wing L 690).

166   P. Girard and C. Piolé, *Aperçus de la Démographie de Sotteville-les-Rouen vers la Fin du XVIIIe siècle*, Population, 1959. It should be noted however that a very high rate of pre-nuptial pregnancy, well up to English standards, has since been established for the three villages studied in the work of Ganiage, see note 155.

167   Age specific (and also sex specific) birth rates, marriage rates, and death rates are of course much more informative for demographic purposes than crude rates of the kind given in the text: see the discussion in Wrigley, *Population and History*, 1969, especially Chapter 3, where figures are quoted from Colyton and elsewhere, including contemporary underdeveloped societies. In spite of the unreality of relating entries in the register for a population so subject

to change due to migration as pre-industrial village communities (see below), Hollingsworth in *Historical Demography*, 1969, recommends that rates of this kind should be worked out wherever possible for communities where listings are available, that is to say, for all the items in Cambridge Group, File 3. It may become possible to provide a number of figures of this kind, but it so happens that the village community concerned frequently lacks the parish register for the relevant years.

---

168 *Turnover of Population in England and France*
From Laslett and Harrison, *Clayworth and Cogenhoe*, 1963, pp. 180–2 slightly modified. It is not possible in 1970 to modify these statements further, since it remains the case that the documents from these two villages represent almost the only detailed and reliable evidence for turnover in England. One further source has come to light of a somewhat different character, in the remarkable listing for the parish of Cardington in Bedfordshire in 1782, which, though it does not contain every individual resident there, records very fine detail of the biological families of the heads of the households, and even specifies what had happened to the children born into them. Migration as servants to places within the district, or to London or elsewhere, is specified, together with places of residence after marriage. An analysis of this evidence is contained in an article by R. S. Schofield which will appear in French in *Annales de Démographie Historique*, 1970.

It has become possible since 1965, however, to examine in much greater depth turnover in two French parishes in the late eighteenth century, those discussed in note 70 above. The article cited there shows that turnover was of the same order in these eighteenth-century French villages, but if anything slightly lower than it had been in the seventeenth century in Clayworth and Cogenhoe. The more detailed study of Hallines and Longuenesse, promised in the note of 1968 is still under preparation by the Cambridge Group.

CHAPTERS 7 AND 8

The same sources are used for these chapters as for the previous ones, with the addition of some material from File 4 (literacy) of the Cambridge Group. Secondary sources

are largely those quoted for Chapter 2. No specific
monographs have been devoted to social change and
revolution as such in traditional English society, though
political institutions have been extensively discussed, and
political sociologists have yet to pay much attention to this
body of evidence.

169   Max Weber, *General Economic History*, translated by
F. H. Knight, Collier Books edition, 1961, chapter 12,
especially p. 132.

170   *The Pleasant History of Jack of Newbury*, in Deloney's
Works, ed. F. O. Mann, 1912.

171   E.g. by George Unwin, who recognized that the tale
was mainly mythological, but called it 'not unacceptable
as evidence', *Studies in Economic History*, 1927, p. 195. See
also S. T. Bindoff in his Pelican History, *Tudor England*,
p. 125, though he is very tentative in his statements about
Jack of Newbury.

172   *The Law Book of the Crowley Ironworks*, edited by
M. W. Flinn, in 1957, for the Surtees Society. The full
document is in the British Museum, Add. MS. 34,555, a
tedious but extremely important body of evidence.

173   See Lewis Coser, *The Functions of Social Conflict*,
1956, and especially the introductory chapter for the history
of conflict theory amongst the sociologists.

174   Peter Laslett, Foreword to J. H. Hexter, *Reappraisals
in History*, 1961.

175   Thomas Hobbes, *Behemoth, The History of the Causes of
the Civil Wars of England*, 2nd ed., 1682, opening sentence.

176   Max Gluckman has presented this phenomenon in a
succession of books and articles, of which perhaps the most
important to our subject is *Order and Rebellion in Tribal
Africa*, 1963, see e.g. the essay there on 'Succession and
Civil War among the Bemba'. The historians of what are

still called medieval and feudal institutions in Europe have
taken some interest in comparative studies of his kind, and
the anthropologists have reciprocated, but the historians of
the 'Early Modern' – 'Renaissance' period have not yet
responded to any extent.

---

177   See *Class and Class Conflict in Industrial Society*
(1957), English ed., 1959.

---

178   *Controversy over Theories of Crisis*
See context quoted in note 174. The very marked
opposition of opinion on the nature of political breakdown
in mid-seventeenth century England, and its relation
to social change or revolution, is made clear in an
extremely hostile review of the first edition of the present
work by Christopher Hill, in *History and Theory*, vol. 6,
1967. I do not feel disposed to modify the statements
attacked there, though an egregious error of fact about
dates of parliamentary meetings, etc., was corrected in
later impressions of the first edition. Hill restates his
convictions about revolutionism in *Reformation to Industrial
Revolution*, 1967, and an allied view and an interesting one,
is developed by Zagorin, *Court and Country*, 1969. The
structural-crisis interpretation of these generations and
events is presented in essays from *Past and Present*, collected
and edited by Trevor Aston and introduced by Christopher
Hill under the title *Crisis in Europe, 1560–1660*, 1965.
English happenings are there related to European ones: see
especially a particularly trenchant essay by Eric Hobsbawn,
'Crisis in the 17th Century'.

---

179   See Laslett, commentary on science in seventeenth-
century England, in A. C. Crombie, ed., *Scientific Change*,
1963, pp. 801–5.

---

180   The story of Abigail is told in Peter Laslett,
Masham of Otes, in *Diversions of History*, edited by Peter
Quennell, 1954. It will be seen from the table printed above
on p. 72 that gentry had markedly more resident kin in
their households in the 100 pre-industrial English
communities than any below them in the social scale.

181　The proposition about witchcraft comes from Keith Thomas in his comprehensive and remarkably suggestive work *Religion and the Decline of Magic*, 1971.

182　I owe almost all of what is said in the text about catechizing and political socialization to Gordon Schochet, late of Trinity College, Cambridge, now of Rutgers University. A preliminary statement of his conclusions can be found in his article 'Patriarchalism, Politics and Mass Attitudes in Stuart England', 1969: a full presentation is in the press as part of a book on patriarchalism in political thinking. Schochet makes no reference to the archdeacons' courts, the evidence of which so Peyton claims (1928, xxxv–) shows that catechizing was an irksome duty, extensively neglected by the clergy in the seventeenth and eighteenth centuries. The actual cases printed in the volume, however, and certainly those from other areas, do not entirely confirm this view. The churchwardens complained of failure to catechize repeatedly, up to the middle of the eighteenth century.

183　Bishop Fleetwood, *Sermons*, 1737 (1705), pp. 232–3.

184　John Lilburne, *The Free Man's Freedom Vindicated* (June 16th, 1646), pp. 11–12, slightly abbreviated and modernized. See T. C. Pease, *The Leveller Movement*, Washington, D.C., 1916, p. 128.

185, 186　*Servants and the Franchise*
James Tyrrell, *Patriarcha non Monarcha*, 1681, first pagination, p. 83. For this book and its relationship with Filmer and Locke, see the work cited in note 184, and for Filmer himself see Peter Laslett, *Patriarcha, and other Political Works of Sir Robert Filmer*, Oxford, 1949. The puritan colonists could not see their way to admitting women, children and servants to political rights. See Richard C. Simmons, 'Godliness, Property and the Franchise in Puritan Massachusetts', *Journal of American History*, Dec. 1968.

186　See the famous Putney debates, edited by A. S. P. Woodhouse as *Puritanism and Liberty*, 1951 ed., pp. 53, 60 (Ireton's appeal to the 5th Commandment) and 61. In *The*

x

Case of the Army soberly Discussed (Thomason Tracts E.396
10, July 3rd, 1647) it was argued that the law of nature
giving all authority to the head of the family prevented
'the servants and prentices not yet free and children
unmarried' then in the army from participating in such
political activities. It has recently been pointed out,
however, that the Levellers were, as might be expected,
occasionally inconsistent on these points. R. Howell and
D. E. Brewster quote a tract of 1653 where 'all the people
of England, as well masters, sons, as servants' choose
representatives in Parliament – though no woman is
mentioned (*Past and Present*, 46, 1970, p. 74). The view that
all Levellers always excluded a class called servants from
political participation, and that this class included all
employed persons, that is the great majority of all males
and a majority of all household heads, is put with great
persuasiveness by Macpherson, *Possessive Individualism*,
1962. The contrary view is argued by Laslett in 'Market
Society and Political Theory', *Historical Journal*, 1964,
pp. 150–4.

---

187   Laslett, *Gentry of Kent*, 1949. Professor Alan Everitt
has taken the study of the community of gentry in Kent
and Sussex much further than this article: see especially
his book *The Community of Kent and the Great Rebellion*,
1966, and compare the work of Professor T. G. Barnes on
Somerset.

---

188   Thomas Wilson, *The State of England*, 1600 (see note
44), p. 24, modernized and slightly abbreviated.

---

189   *Families Dying Out*
The reconstitution at Banbury (see above note 113) is the
first in England which is expected to yield fertility rates
by social and economic status. When these figures are
available, we shall have a more exact idea of whether
privileged people were in fact more fertile or lived longer
than the rest of society. The evidence on the baronetcies
comes from Kimber and Johnson, *Baronetage*, 3 vols., 1771.
The third volume lists 205 baronets as being created by
James I between 1611 and 1625, and marks 110 of these as

being extinct in 1769. This represents 53·7 per cent dying out after 144 years, if we reckon all James I's baronetcies as having survived till at least his death in 1625. The preliminary calculations about male lines excluding cousins, etc., comes from a first exercise in modelling lineages given English succession rules, now being undertaken by Dr E. A. Wrigley. The assumptions for the examples given in the text are that the sex ratio at birth is 100, and that a child has a 50 per cent chance of living till his or her father's death, which seems realistic enough – see note 109. Given an average number of children of 4, the probability of a line being broken by the fifth succession is ·85 and even if it is assumed that two-thirds of children survive to the death of the father, the probability is about ·5 at five children to a family.

190   Lancashire Quarter Sessions, 1591 (see ref. in note 84), p. 56. In his introduction to these records James Tait comments on the singular use of the word 'gentleman'. Servants are frequently found taking time off to visit their families and friends, as for example in the settlement examinations.

191   It is significant that Macfarlane concludes of Ralph Josselin, the Essex parson of the mid-seventeenth century, both that his kinship network was relatively restricted, and that he turned for assistance to neighbours and friends rather than relatives. One of the reasons for this was true even of someone so much a part of literate society as Josselin, it would look as if those below him would have been much more cut off from their kindred. It is very difficult to imagine that the kinship network of a traditional English village can have been much more elaborate than the 'attenuated' set of relationships described by Williams for his *West Country Village* in the 1950's (Williams, 1963, Chapters VI and VII) and in my view it was even less developed.

192   See W. P. Baker, *Parish Registers and Illiteracy in East Yorkshire*, East Yorkshire Local History Series, no. 13, 1961 (From the Society, 2 St Martin's Lane, Micklegate, York). Baker gives some information on the practice of signing at marriage in English registers after 1754, and the

subject is critically discussed by Schofield, *Measurement of Literacy*, 1968. The resemblances and difference between pre-industrial England and contemporary developing societies are well brought out in the volume for which Schofield's essay was written, *Literacy in Traditional Societies*, edited by Jack Goody, 1968.

193   For Crulai, see Gautier and Henry, 1958, and for the growth of literacy in the eighteenth century see M. Fleury and P. Valmary, 'Les progrès de l'instruction élémentaire de Louis XIV à Napoléon', *Population*, 1957.

194   See Lawrence Stone, 'The Educational Revolution in England 1560–1640', *Past and Present*, no. 28, 1964, p. 43. This pioneering article is revised and extended by the same author's further study, 'Literacy and Education in England, 1640–1900', *Past and Present*, no. 42, 1969. The sources used by Stone are some of those being studied as part of File 4, the literacy file, of the Cambridge Group, and the final analysis of the figures held at Cambridge when published will certainly modify the picture drawn in these articles.

195   The Leicestershire figures, which are the first to show the hoped for consistency in these particulars, were contributed by Miss Hetheriston to Cambridge Group File 4. For book-ownership see Laslett, 'Scottish Weavers, Cobblers and Miners who Bought Books in the 1750's', *Local Population Studies Magazine and Newsletter*, no. 3, Autumn 1969. Of 398 persons recorded as subscribing to a serious theological work published in 1757, no less than 120 were weavers, 8 were tailors, 6 were smiths and two were coal heavers. Of 606 persons subscribing to a similar book 2 years later no less than 242 were weavers and 34 were shoemakers. Further sources of this kind have been found for Wales, where surprisingly humble persons owned poetry books in the eighteenth century, and other work in progress on the subject shows that subscription lists to eighteenth-century books may have more to tell us about the distribution of booklearning down the social scale.

196   See previous reference. In 1962 Mark Curtis
contributed to *Past and Present,* no. 23, 1962, a study of
The Alienated Intellectuals of Early Stuart England analysing
the surplus of educated clergy, an important development
of his book on Oxford and Cambridge, see note 14.
Cressy's dissertation (see note 14) will analyse both
university development and the extent and growth of
literacy in Stuart times, together with the relationship
between them. In his first published note (*Past and Present,*
1970) he has shown that the impression of an inrush of
gentry into the universities has arisen to some extent
because of an elementary error in translating the Latin
names for English social grades. *Ingenuus,* meaning *yeoman,*
has been translated as equivalent to *generosus,* meaning
gentleman. See also Hugh Kearney, *Scholars and Gentlemen,*
1970.

197   E. P. Thompson, *The Making of the English Working
Class,* 1963, p. 526.

List of Authorities

ARIES, Philippe, 1962 (1960), *Centuries of Childhood*, translated by Robert Baldick. Original: *L'Enfant et la Vie Familiale sous l'Ancien Régime*, Paris, 1960.

ASTON, Trevor, ed., 1965, *Crisis in Europe, 1560–1660*, London.

BATHO, G., 1967, *Landlords in England*, in Thirsk, ed., *Agrarian History*, Cambridge, 1967.

BENDIX, R., and LIPSET, S. M., 1967 (1963), *Class, Status and Power*, Glencoe, Ill.

BEST, Henry, 1857 (1641), *Rural economy in Yorkshire in 1641, being the farming and account books of Henry Best, of Elmswell in the East Riding of the County of York*, edited by C. B. Robinson, for the Surtees Society Publications, vol. XXXIII.

BIRABEN, J.–N., 1968, 'Certain Demographic Characteristics of the Plague Epidemic in France, 1720–22', *Daedalus*, Spring, 1968.

BIRABEN, J.–N., with LE GOFF, J., 1969, 'La Peste du Haut Moyen Ac', *Annales*, 24ᵉg année 6.

BLYTHE, Ronald, 1969, *Akenfield, Portrait of an English Village*, London.

BRINKWORTH, E. R., 1942, 'The Archdeacons' Court: Liber Actorum, 1584', vols. I and II, *Oxfordshire Record Society Series*.

CAMPBELL, Mildred, 1942, *The English Yeoman under Elizabeth and the Early Stuarts*, New Haven, Conn.

CHAMBERLAYNE, Edward, 1702 (1669), *Angliae Notitia: or the Present State of England*.

CHAMBERS, J. D. (1957), *The Vale of Trent, 1670–1800*, Supplement to *The Economic History Review*.

CHAMOUX, Antoinette, and Dauphin, Cécile, 1969, 'La Contraception avant la Révolution Française: l'example de Châtillon-sur-Seine', *Annales: Economies, Sociétés, Civilisations*, no. 3.

CLAYWORTH, Rectors' Book, 1910, *The Rectors' Book of Clayworth, Notts.*, ed. Harry Gill and E. L. Guilford, Nottingham.

CURTIS, M. H., 1959, *Oxford and Cambridge in Transition, 1558–1642*, Oxford.

Daedalus, volume 97, no. 2, 1968, Historical population studies.

DEMOS, John, 1970, *A Little Commonwealth: Family Life in Plymouth Colony*, New York.

DOBB, Maurice, 1946, *Studies in the Development of Capitalism*, London.

DUPÂQUIER, Jacques, and LACHIVER, M., 1969, 'Sur les Débuts de la Contraception en France', *Annales: Economies, Sociétés, Civilisations*, no. 6.

EVERITT, Alan, 1967 (i), 'Farm Labourers', Chapter VII in Thirsk, *Agrarian History*, 1967.
  (ii), 'The Marketing of Agricultural Produce', Chapter VIII in Thirsk, 1967.

FLEETWOOD, William, 1737 (1705), 'The Relative Duties of Parents and Children, Husbands and Wives, Masters and Servants', in *Compleat Collection of Sermons*.

FURNIVALL, F., 1897, *Child Marriages, Divorces and Ratifications* etc., *The Early English Text Society*.

GANIAGE, Jean, 1963, *Trois Villages d'Ile-de-France*, Paris, INED.

GAUTIER, see Henry.

GLASS, D. V., 1965, Two papers on Gregory King, in *Population and History*, ed. Glass, D. V., and Eversley, D. E. C.
  1966, Introd. to *London Inhabitants Within the Walls, 1695*, *London Record Society*, Leicester.
  1968, 'Notes on the Demography of London at the End of the Seventeenth Century', *Daedalus*.
  1969, 'Socio-Economic Status and Occupations in the City of London at the End of the Seventeenth Century' in *Studies Presented to P. E. Jones*, London.

GOUBERT, Pierre, 1960, *Beauvais et le Beauvaisis*, Paris.
  1968, 'Legitimate Fecundity in 18th Century France', in *Daedalus*, 1968.

GOUGE, William, 1622, 'Of Domesticall Duties'.

GRAUNT, John, 1939 (1662), *Natural and Political Observations upon the Bills of Mortality*, Baltimore.

GREVEN, Philip J., 1970, *Four Generations: Population, Land and Family in Colonial Andover, Massachusetts*, Ithaca, N.Y.

HAIR, P. E. H., 1966, 'Bridal Pregnancy in Rural England in Earlier Centuries', *Population Studies*, 20.
  1970, 'Bridal Pregnancy in Earlier Rural England Further Examined', *Population Studies*, 24.

HAJNAL, J., 1965, 'European Marriage Patterns in Perspective', in Glass and Eversley, 1965.

HARRISON, William, 1968 (1577, 1587), *The Description of England*, ed., Georges Edelen, New York.

HASTED, Edward, 1782, *History of Kent*, Canterbury.

HENRY, Louis, 1956, *Anciennes Familles Genevoises*, Paris, INED.

1958, *La Population de Crulai*, (with E. Gautier), Paris, INED.

HEXTER, J. H., 1963 (1961), *Reappraisals in History*, London.

HILL, Christopher, 1961 etc., *The Century of Revolution*, Edinburgh.
1967, *Reformation to Industrial Revolution*, London.

HIRST, L. F., 1953, *The Conquest of Plague*, Oxford.

HOLLINGSWORTH, T. H., 1964, 'The Demography of the British Peerage', supplement to *Population Studies*, vol. XVIII, No. 2 (Nov. 1964).
1969, *Historical Demography*, in the series *The Sources of History: Studies in the Uses of Historical Evidence*.

HOWSON, W. G., 1960, 'Plague, Poverty and Population in Parts of North-West England', *Transactions of the Historic Society of Lancashire and Cheshire*.

JOSSELIN, Ralph – see Macfarlane.

KLAPISCH, C., 1969, 'Fiscalité et Démographie en Toscane, 1427–30', *Annales*, 24, vi.

LACHENBRUCH, P. A., 1967, 'Frequency and Timing of Intercourse: its Relation to Probability of Conception', *Population Studies*, vol. XXI, no. 1.

LASLETT, Peter, 1948, 'Sir Robert Filmer, the Man versus the Whig Myth', *William and Mary Quarterly*, 3rd. ser., vol. 5.
1948, 'The Gentry of Kent in 1640', *Cambridge Historical Journal* IX, 2.
1963, 'Clayworth and Cogenhoe' (with HARRISON, John) in *Historical Essays presented to David Ogg*, ed. Bell, H. W., and Ollard, R. L.
1964, 'Market Society and Political Theory' (a review of Macpherson, 1962), *Historical Journal*, VII, 1.
1966, 'The Study of Social Structure from Listings of Inhabitants', Chapter 5 of Wrigley (ed.), *English Historical Demography*.
1968, 'Le Brassage de la Population en France et en Angleterre aux XVIIe et XVIIIe Siècles: Comparaison de Villages Français et Anglais', in *Annales de Démographie Historique*, Paris, Société de Démographie Historique.
1969 (i) 'Size and Structure of Household in England over Three Centuries', *Population Studies*, XXIII, 2.
1969 (ii), 'Scottish Weavers, Cobblers and Miners who Bought Books in the 1750's', *Local Population Studies*, 3.
1970 (i), 'Change in the Size of the Household in England in the Early 20th Century', *Population Studies*, XXIV, 3.
1970 (ii), 'The Comparative History of Household and Family' (Size and structure of domestic group in Serbia (Jugoslavia), Japan, United States, France and England in historical times), *The Journal of Social History*, Fall 1970.

LOCKRIDGE, Kenneth A., 1966, 'The Population of Dedham, Mass., 1636–1736', *Economic History Review*, 2nd ser., vol. XIX, no. 2.

MACFARLANE, Alan, *The Family Life of Ralph Josselin*, Cambridge, 1970.

MACPHERSON, C. B., 1962, *The Political Theory of Possessive Individualism*, Oxford.

MARCHANT, R. A., 1969, *The Church under the Law: Justice, Administration and Discipline in the Diocese of York, 1500–1640*, Cambridge.

MATURITY, 1961, 'Early Maturing and Larger Children', *British Medical Journal*, August 19th, 1961.

Minigaff, Session book of, Privately printed for the Marquis of Bute, translated and edited by Henry Payton, 1939.

MOORE, A. Perceval, 1909, 'Marriage Contracts or Espousals in the Reign of Queen Elizabeth', *Reports and Papers of Associated Architectual Societies*, vol. XXX, pt. I, paper for the Leicestershire Architectural and Archaeological Society.

MORGAN, Edmund S., *The Puritan Family: Religion and Domestic Relations in 17th Century New England*, New York, 1966 (Revised and enlarged), Boston 1944.

PERKINS, William, 1618 (1609), 'Christian Oeconomie', in *Workes*, Cambridge, vol. 3.

PEYTON, S. A., 1928, 'The Churchwardens' Presentments in the Oxfordshire Peculiars of Dorchester, Thame and Banbury', *Oxfordshire Record Society*.

PINCHBECK, I., and HEWITT, M., 1969, *Childhood in English Society*, vol. I, *From Tudor Times to the 19th Century*.

PITTINGTON, Co. Durham, 1888, 'Churchwardens' Accounts', ed. Barmby, *Surtees Society*, vol. 84.

POWELL, C. L., 1917, *English Domestic Relations, 1487–1653*, New York.

POWELL, S. C., 1965 (1963), *Puritan Village: the Formation of a New England Town*, Middletown, Conn.

RALPH, E., and WILLIAMS, M. E., 1968, 'The Inhabitants of Bristol in 1696', *The Bristol Record Society, Publications*, vol. XXV.

ROWNTREE, B. S., 1922 (1901), *Poverty: a Study of Town Life*, London.

RUDÉ, George, 1959, *The Crowd in the French Revolution*, Oxford.

RUNCIMAN, W. G., 1963, *Social Science and Political Theory*, Cambridge.

1966, *Relative Deprivation and Social Justice*, London.

1968, 'Class, Status, Power?' in Jackson, J. A. (ed.), *Social Stratification*, Cambridge.

x*

SCHACHT, L. E., GERSHOWITZ, H., 1963 (1961), in *Proceedings of the 2nd International Congress of Human Genetics, 1961*, vol. II, pp. 994–7, Rome.

SCHLATTER, R. B., 1940, *The Social Ideas of Religious Leaders, 1660–1688*, Oxford.

SCHOCHET, G. J., 1969, 'Patriarchalism, Politics and Mass Attitudes in Stuart England', *The Historical Journal*. In Press: *Patriarchalism in Political Thinking*.

SCHOFIELD, R. S., 1968, 'The Measurement of Literacy in Pre-Industrial England' in Goody, Jack (ed.), *Literacy in Traditional Societies*, Cambridge.

1970 (i), 'Population in the Past: Computer Linking of Vital Records', *Bulletin of the Institute of Mathematics and its Applications*.

1970 (ii), *Family Reconstitution by Computer*, Communication to the 5th International Economic History Conference, Leningrad, August, vol. 6, no. 1.

1971 (i), 'Historical Demography: Some Possibilities and Some Limitations', *Transactions of the Royal Historical Society*, vol. 22.

SHAW, Joseph, 1733, *Parish Law*,

SHREWSBURY, J. F. D., 1970, *A History of Bubonic Plague in the British Isles*, Cambridge.

SKINNER, G. William, 1964 and 1965, 'Marketing and Social Structure in Rural China' (Part I, vol. 24, no. I; Part II, vol. 24, no. 2; Part III, vol. 24, no. 3), *The Journal of Asian Studies*.

SMITH, John of Nibley, 1902 (1608), *Men and Armour for Gloucestershire*, London.

SMITH, Sir Thomas, 1906 (1583), *The Commonwealth of England*, ed. L. Alston, Cambridge.

SMITH, T. C., 1969, 'Farm Family By-Employments in Pre-Industrial Japan', *The Journal of Economic History*.

STEEL, S. J. and A. E. F., and others, 1968, *National Index of Parish Registers: Volume I; Sources of Births, Marriages and Deaths before 1837, volume I*, The Society of Genealogists.

STEELE, Richard, 1672 (1668), *The Husbandman's Calling*.

STONE, Lawrence, 1967 (1965), *Social Change and Revolution in England*.

TAIT, James, ed., 1917, Lancashire Quarter Sessions Records, Sessions Rolls, 1590–1606, *Chetham Society*, Manchester.

TANNER, J. M., 1962 (1955), *Growth at Adolescence*, Oxford.

THIRSK, J., 1967, editor of *The Agrarian History of England and Wales, IV, 1500–1640*, General Editor, H. P. R. Finberg.

TIETZ, C., 1960, 'Probability of Pregnancy Arising from a Single Unprotected Coitus', *Fertility and Sterility*, II.

TITMUSS, R. M., 1962, *Income Distribution and Social Change*, London.

VANN, R. T., 1969, *The Social Development of English Quakerism*, Cambridge, Mass.

WATERS, John J., 1968, Hingham, Massachusetts, 1631–66: 'An East Anglian Oligarchy in the New World', *Journal of Social History*, I.

WESTCOTE, Thomas, 1845 (1630), *A View of Devonshire in 1630*, ed., Oliver, G., and Jones, P., Exeter.

WILLIAMS, W. M., 1963, *A West Country Village, Ashworthy: Family, Country, Land*, London.

WILLMOTT, Peter, *see* Young, Michael.

WILSON, Thomas, 1936 (1600), *The State of England, 1600*, ed. F. J. Fisher, London.

WRIGLEY, E. A., 1966 (i) (ed.), *An Introduction to English Historical Demography* (with contributions by E. A. Wrigley on 'Family Reconstitution', D. E. C. Eversley, Peter Laslett, etc., q.v.), London.

1966 (ii), 'Family Limitation in Pre-Industrial England', *Economic History Review*, 2nd series, vol XIX, no. 1.

1967, 'A Simple Model of London's Importance in Changing English Society and Economy, 1650–1750', *Past and Present, 37*.

1968, 'Mortality in Pre-Industrial England: the Example of Colyton, Devon, Over Three Centuries', *Daedalus*.

1969, *Population and History*, World University Library. (Published simultaneously in London, New York, in France, Italy, Germany, Spain and Holland in the appropriate languages.)

YOUNG, Michael, and WILLMOTT, Peter, 1959 (1957), *Family and Kinship in East London*, London.

1960, *Family and Class in a London Suburb*, London.

ZAGORIN, Perez, 1969, *The Court and the Country: the Beginning of the English Revolution*, London.

Index

mar: 1. John Smith of this parish labourer & Persis Cook of
the same weare married 29 mary...

2. John Warden of greate Bealing husband ma— & Elizabeth Olint of this parish weare married 6. Novemb:

Baptiz Thomsin the daughter of John & Dorothy
1 Hullett was baptized the 18. Aprill
2 Mary daught of Willm & Anne Bernard bap: 8. August
3 John the sone of John & Thomase Cliffe bap: 23. February...

Buried willm Gonio a poore blind ma was bur: 29. Novemb

1620   Marriages
1 Thomas Smith & Pricilla Gonnie both of this parish
weare married the 15 of May.
2 John C son of Brasfeild & Anne Dorothy of this parish
were married the 28. October

Baptismes.
1 Mary the daughter of Jonas & Persis Smith was
baptized the 23. July.
2 Anne daught of George & Elizab: Fisher bap: 30. July
3 Frances daught of Richard & Elizab: Smith bap: 22. octob:
4 Anne daught of George & mary Cliet bap: 2. February

Burialls.
1 Joice the wife of Thomas Bernard was buried 22. Aprill
2 John Dorell husband ma was buried 22. January.
3 Mary Mabbs a poore old widow was buried the 12. February

1621   Marriages.
1 Thomas Clarck & Elizab: Lark were married — mar:

Baptized willm the sonne of John Cliffe was baptized — fe..
2 Richard the sonne of Thomas Libby was bap: 24. June

Married Elizab: Tucker an olde widow was buried — dece
4 John Gardiner & Anne Thorpe mar: 20. mar..

1622: John the sonne of George Fisher baptized 27. Apr..
Baptism John the sonne of John Gardiner baptized 22. April
Anne daught of Nathan: Neale bap: 19. mar..
John Castle sonne of willm Castle bap at Kendall 24. Jan..
Mary daught of the same ma bapt... both but...
Martha daught of Jonas Smith baptized 24. September
Edward sonne of John Cliffe baptized 5. Novemb
Elizab: daughter of Thomas Cliffe bap: 6. octob
... of John & Smith bap: 16. Feb.
... John ... sonne of Henry ... so clerke
... Spicer ... ... Gillet